PRAISE FOR

SOMETHING

"A hauntingly affecting historical novel with a touch of magic."

—*Kirkus Reviews* (starred review)

"Rich in historical detail, this suspenseful coming-of-age fantasy grabs the reader with the facts of life in medieval England and the magic spells woven into its landscape."

—*Publishers Weekly* (starred review)

"This darkly atmospheric debut novel is well worth its measured plot-building for its horrific, unexpected ending."

—*Library Journal* (starred review)

"This first novel is a beauty."

—Cecelia Holland, *New York Times* bestselling author of *The King's Witch*

"Not for the faint of heart, this pulse-pounding page-turner grabs you from the start and never lets you go. A wickedly clever and evocative combination of history, horror, mystery, and magic."

—*Booklist*

"Nicholas goes for the throat with *Something Red*. Rich in history, ankle deep in blood, and packed with brilliant writing and whip-smart plotting."

—Jonathan Maberry, *New York Times* bestselling author of *Flesh & Bone*

"Douglas Nicholas can artfully narrate a story. I was engaged from beginning to end."

—*Agenda Magazine*

"I was so enthralled with the tale, it was like leaving reality and stepping into a wondrous and mysterious time with so much magic in it. . . . You will not be disappointed."

—*Great Minds Think Aloud*

"Ably conjuring the beauties and drawbacks of the past, and with an engaging and unusual cast list, *Something Red* is a thoroughbred novel of nightmare terror, ruled by a force of sheer evil that seems, and may well prove, unstoppable. A Book of Shadows with a genuinely beating heart."

—Tanith Lee, award-winning author of *The Silver Metal Lover*

"This is a beautifully written work, with evocative prose which captures the essence of traveling in winter in Middle Ages England."

—*The Snarky Writer*

"Written with great skill, this atmospheric, yet gritty story will remain with you, and it is a wonderful addition to the long line of stories devoted to the magic of fairy tales."

—*Book Hog*

"*Something Red* absolutely blew me away. This is one of the best debuts I've read in years, and the story itself still haunts my dreams. It has all the best elements of Irish folklore, historical fiction, and a very frightening mystery at its core."

—*Chaotic Compendiums*

"The poetic nature of the language, the increasing of the novel's atmospheric spook, and the members of the traveling family made *Something Red* a winner."

—*Minding Spot*

"Douglas Nicholas has written a gut-wrenching, harrowing novel; however, he's also written a touching, realistic story about what made a family, love, and life during a thirteenth-century English winter. . . . Nicholas's storytelling painted this novel with historic realism that made it pop right off the page. . . . If you like a non-stop thrilling roller-coaster ride, hop on board!"

—*Popcorn Reads*

"Nicholas's beautiful prose, his detailed portrayal of life in medieval England, interesting characters, and underlying supernatural themes make this book a real gem."

—*BookBrowse*

"The most stunning debut novel I have ever read. The language is beautiful and descriptive; the novel is an incredible sensory experience for the reader."

—Examiner.com

"Nicholas handles characterization, setting and atmosphere deftly and expertly. . . . *Something Red* is an excellent debut from a gifted author."

—*Shelf Awareness*

"Memorable. . . . Legendary."

—*Pate Books*

"The language is exquisite, the erudition profound. . . . A sublime, can't-put-it-down read."

—*Daily Freeman*

"One of the biggest and best reading surprises I've had in a long time. . . . Nicholas is a master storyteller. . . . This is a rather quiet story that relies not on big action scenes, but on an irresistible mix of wonderful characters and carefully constructed moments that add up to an amazing reading experience. . . . I had goosebumps as I read the final page."

—*Books, Bones & Buffy*

"A hauntingly beautiful masterpiece of historical fantasy fiction, which offers perfect escapism and entertainment."

—*Risingshadow*

"This is a stunning debut novel of lyrical power and suspenseful drama. The hair-raising finale will keep you reading far into the night."

—Carol Goodman, national bestselling author of
The Lake of Dead Languages

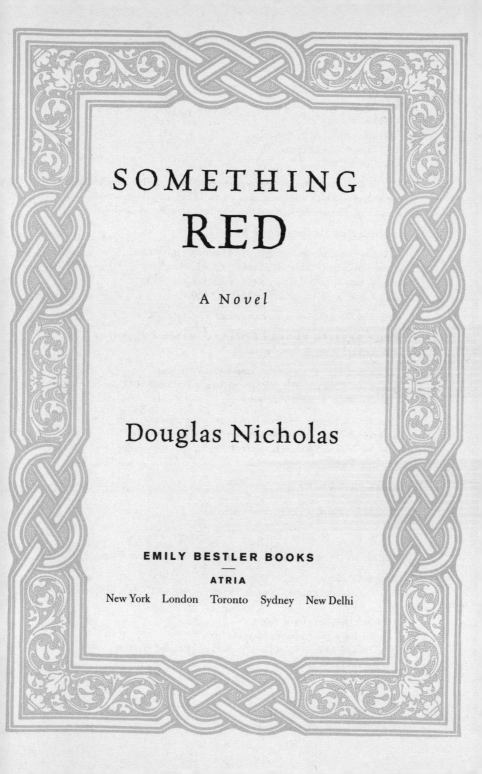

SOMETHING
RED

A Novel

Douglas Nicholas

EMILY BESTLER BOOKS
—
ATRIA
New York   London   Toronto   Sydney   New Delhi

ATRIA PAPERBACK

A Division of Simon & Schuster, Inc.
1230 Avenue of the Americas
New York, NY 10020

First Emily Bestler Books/Atria Paperback edition June 2013

EMILY BESTLER BOOKS / ATRIA PAPERBACK and colophon are trademarks of Simon & Schuster, Inc.

For information about special discounts for bulk purchases, please contact Simon & Schuster Special Sales at 1-866-506-1949 or business@simonandschuster.com.

The Simon & Schuster Speakers Bureau can bring authors to your live event. For more information or to book an event, contact the Simon & Schuster Speakers Bureau at 1-866-248-3049 or visit our website at www.simonspeakers.com.

Designed by Suet Yee Chong

Manufactured in the United States of America

10   9   8   7   6   5   4   3   2   1

The Library of Congress has cataloged the hardcover edition as follows:

Nicholas, Douglas.
    Something red : a novel / Douglas Nicholas.—1st Atria Books hardcover ed.
      p. cm.
    Includes glossary of Irish terms.
    In English with occasional phrases in Irish.
    1. Pennine Chain (England)—13th century—Fiction.   I. Title.
    PS3614.I3375S66 2012
    813'.6—dc23   2011044435

ISBN 978-1-4516-6007-4
ISBN 978-1-4516-6022-7 (pbk)
ISBN 978-1-4516-6023-4 (ebook)

For Theresa

Part I

THE MONASTERY

1

Part II

THE INN

61

Part III

THE CASTLE

157

Pronunciation of Irish names:

    Maeve = MAYV

    Nemain = NEV-an

Pronunciation of Lithuanian names:

    Lietuva = LYET-oova (Lithuania)

    Svajone = sva-YO-neh

    Azuolas = AZH-oowoh-las

    Gintaras = GIN-tar-as (hard *g*)

    Vytautas = VEE-tau-tas

Part I

THE MONASTERY

CHAPTER 1

HE WHEELS WERE SOLID
disks as high as Hob himself,
and the wood was warped a
little and wet with the snow now coming down hard
and clinging in patchy lumps to the rims. The main
wagon had the aft right wheel fast in a drift, and as
Hob added his slight frame to the stamping, cursing
struggle to free it, his foot plunged to the ankle in a de-
pression filled with a freezing gruel of snow and mud.

It felt like stepping into fire. Gasping with the
shock, he threw himself against the tailboard. A smell
of sweat and woodsmoke and rosemary came to him
from his left: Molly, her ample well-turned arms,
white as mare's milk, glimmering at the edge of his
sight. Before his face loomed the weathered plank he
forced his breast against. Nemain stood behind them
and skimmed handfuls of ashes beneath their feet. At
his right Jack Brown suddenly found purchase under-

foot, his toes in the green leather boots stuffed with straw digging in, scrabbling in ash and ice and pebbles, and Jack's grunting heave freed the wheel's lip just enough. The ox trod forward again, steaming like a dragon, and Hob staggered as the wagon sailed away from him.

Hob stumped ahead, limping with the pain in his foot. Molly threw her cloak again around her shoulders, over the *léine,* that shift-like garment from her native Ireland, that she favored on the road. The cloak, and then a shawl, and she was ready to take the reins again: did she never feel the cold? The half-grown boy went forward by the ox and walked with a hand to the draw bar; the heat coming from the vast body was perceptible. He wished he could ride in the wagon.

The snow diminished, but in its stead came a malicious little wind that drew claws across the back of his neck. It found its way up the sleeves of his woolen shirt and between the flaps of his sheepskin coat.

The road wound through winter woods, upslope and down, the land rumpled and complex, with frequent outcrops of naked rock. The view was open enough near at hand, but within a few yards the overlapping trunks foiled the eye. Yews, pale slim birch, massive oaks formed a close horizon; the wagons moved between wooden walls.

Hob began to feel an unease of spirit, an oppression. The sensation grew swiftly till his bodily woes shrank beside it. He looked left at the slowly passing forest, rightward across the rippling, smoking haunches to the trackside brush and more trees, climbing away to the west. He felt breathless and ill. He felt like a coney in a snare, and he could not tell why.

THE CARAVAN HAD COME from Ireby, away by the river Ellen. There had been little enough for them there, despite the town's sheep market, and Molly had planned to take them south and east through the mountain passes before the snows clamped down in earnest: this year, and the year before, had seen such cold and storm as not even the eldest village grandmam could remember. She hoped to make St. Germaine's, the hill monastery, before nightfall. It was where all travelers who used the Thonarberg Pass had to stay: one could not get over in a day, and night amid the eerie gorges and overleaning crags was unthinkable. There were stories of bandits who lived in cave and ravine, savage as stoats; there were stories of trolls who slept amid piles of bones and knew neither fire nor clothing.

"Gesu!" He made a frantic sideways leap to escape a great cloven hoof: the ox had performed a peculiar sidestep. It gave a flat dismayed bleat and stood trembling in place, rolling its large lovely eye. Behind him a sort of ripple passed down the tiny procession as first the ass and then the mare started and veered toward the trees to the east.

Through the volley of curses and the snap of reins coming from behind, Hob was aware of a thin, sour cry that drifted to him from ahead and to the west. His heart seemed to freeze. He was aware that he had seized the rope of the ox's bridle and was holding the big head, or perhaps just clinging to it. His eye was locked to the curtain of trees, and now he saw a flicker, a glint, of russet color: red as a fox, but tall, tall, high as a big man perhaps, but hard to judge, hard to tell from here, then gone as though it never was. A faint coughing snarl came down the wind, and the ox shoved hard against his chest, breathing moist heat through the folds of his sheepskin coat, its blunted horns to either side of his body. The huge beast was hiding its face against him.

He looked back along the road. Nemain, bent like a bow, labored to drag the ass back to the trail. Her thin wrists shone white as her grandmother's where they emerged from the too-big sleeves; her hands, lost in their woolen gloves, hauled desperately at the rope. Farther back he could see Jack Brown holding the mare's bridle and stroking her neck. But Molly, up on the main wagon's seat, sat leaning sideways with a taut searching scrutiny, her handsome head flung up, her nostrils flared.

Hob stared at her. He had never seen her so alarmed, not even that terrible night when the false pilgrims had rolled out from their cloaks by the fire, cudgels in their fists, robbery and worse in their hearts. The shawl had slipped back to her shoulders and her heavy mass of hair, water-gray with gleams of ice-silver in it, streamed back from her ruddy face, stiff in the slight breeze as though in the moments before a lightning storm.

The breeze spoke in the creaking trees, but nothing else. The snow was all but stopped. Molly turned forward. Her blue eyes, wide set and a little prominent, skimmed over Hob. She made a brushing motion with a gloved hand to set Hob moving, and turned back in the seat. "Away on, away on," she called over her shoulder in a low thrumming voice. It was one of her signals: that tone, and the twice-spoken command, meant everyone was to go quickly but make the least noise. Had she said it three times Hob would have left the ox and pelted off into the woods like a deer, snarl or no. Oh, she had them trained.

The wagons started up, the beasts weaving like drunkards from side to side as they tried to slew off into the woods where they sought concealment and safety, and the drivers pushed and pulled them back onto the middle of the track. There followed a lurching hustle through a gray-white nightmare.

Hob was later unsure of their passage through the forest valley. *Blur,* was what he thought, *Blur, cold, afraid, near to pissed my braies,* in after days, when he tried to remember. There was a sense of pressure on them all the time, like mice at the foot of the owl's tree, as they hurried along the road that sank to the ford, then through the shallow ice-rimmed stream, Hob splashing shin-deep in the bitter current but too frightened to curse, and up the farther slope.

After what seemed a very long time the road gained the low swells of the foothills, and here came one of the few moments Hob could recall clearly afterward. A spur of black basalt ran down to the road and forced it to curve around the base. The rock loomed beside the track, twice as high as the wagons. As the ox came up to the bend, Hob hauled back on the lead rope. The corner he must turn seemed to radiate a silent malevolence.

Molly set the brake, reached back into the wagon, and produced a sturdy hazel staff. She climbed swiftly down. She strode forward past the shivering ox, and Hob took a pace back, expecting to be chastised; but she passed him by and strode up to the very lip of the shadow cast by the outcrop, and now here came Jack Brown, the long hammer used on tent pegs in his knotty fist. He had seized in haste what was nearest the wagon door. The lump of iron at the tip of the three-foot shaft was half the size of Hob's head, and Jack's forearm was bunched with the effort. With his ungainly rolling walk, his back broad as a hall door, he seemed a kind of troll himself, but Hob was glad to see him between the wagons and that sinister rock.

Molly's palm showed pale in the gloom: she had flung her arm out sideways to halt Jack's approach. She stood as though breathing in the forest mist, her heavy body up on tiptoe, the hazel staff thrust in the ground before her. All at once she rocked back on her heels and shouldered the staff. She motioned Jack forward.

The dark man shambled forward past the rock, making Hob think *bear* for some reason. Molly called Jack *artan* sometimes; Nemain had told Hob it meant "little bear" in the tongue she and her grandmother spoke to each other. The hammer looked hungry or thirsty, weaving from side to side like a snake over a dish of milk. Just past the bend, just within sight, Jack stopped still.

Hob felt the hair on his neck prickling. He held to the bridle rope and stood in the middle of the road, waiting for his life to show him the shape it would take.

But Jack darted forward with the hammer, and came back raising on its tip only a bloody rag, coarse gray cloth torn away at one edge, clotted and caked a reddish black in the center and stained in streaks to the edges. He brought it back to Molly and they stood in the road and considered it like two farmers consulting over a stricken sheep. Molly put a finger to the clabbered mess, raised it to her tongue with a curious delicacy for such an act. Hob turned away and rubbed behind the ox's ear, a favorite spot with the beast.

FATHER ATHELSTAN had grown old; Father Athelstan could no longer keep a young orphan at the priest house. When Molly's caravan had come through a year and a half ago, the bent and shuffling priest had seen a chance to clear himself of his last obligation to the world. From Maeve, come traveling out of Ireland across the Irish Sea, Maeve whom everyone but Jack called Molly, from her he had felt, as the young and the old and the unclever often did, the blunt tide of animal goodness that moved along her bones. The wagons left a few days later with Hob looking back past the high wheels at the tiny chapel, the miserable rutted mud street that ran past the handful of cottages, until that day the whole of Hob's known universe.

Hob, who remembered no parents, who was too old to be mothered and too young for a lover, considered Molly with a confused awe that veered between love and fear. When he fell ill she wrapped him in skins and brought him heated mare's milk and herbs. When, as on this evening, she grew fey and terrible, he could not bring himself to look on her. He stroked the curve of the ox's coarse-haired neck and thought hard of warm stalls, clean straw, stout monastery walls, safety.

THE TWO CAME BACK, Molly plainly upset. With Jack it was hard to tell. Hob's eyes slid to them, then away. He determinedly observed the ox's wide neck; he kept his mind still and muttered *Ave*s. Behind him passed snow-crunching footsteps, Molly's bell-deep tones, Jack's harsh gargle. On the road to Jerusalem, far away in the Holy Land, Jack Brown had taken a terrible wound in the throat and another to his ankle: a confused oval of smooth silver scar at the side of his neck as big as a big man's palm, a ruined voice, a limp, were all the relics he brought back from that hot and haunted country.

". . . oh there's craft in it, it's as bad as I've seen, I want us on as quick as quick." Hob heard Molly's footsteps returning swiftly. He looked up. She stood over him with a curious strained expression. "*Stór mo chroí,* you must lead on as fast as you may, and mind the road ahead. I'll watch the forest, nor must you trouble yourself about it." He nodded stiffly, and she turned away quick and crisp and hurried back to her seat, waving to Nemain to mount the second wagon.

She had spoken to him with an elaborate gentleness and kindness, as one spoke to a spooked horse. It was this that frightened him more than anything so far.

He caught the ox's bridle rope; as soon as Molly was settled he pulled. Insignificant as Hob's strength was, the giant stepped forward, obedient but with an unconvincingly furtive air, as it skirted the rock and followed Hob down the track. It had a kind of trust of Hob, after a year and a half in which he had mostly been the one to feed and groom it, and it followed him as one might follow a parent, a sight at once comical and piteous.

They hurried on, slipping on the iron-hard ruts and steel-colored patches of ice, the wagons swaying dangerously; in their tearing eyes the chill nasty wind, in their ears the creak and groan of flexing wood, the thud and clop of hooves on the hard ground, the harsh whistle of breath in the bitter air.

Now, adding to their troubles, the road began to rise steeply. The beasts began to labor, the brakes were set and released constantly, and the muscles of Hob's calves and those along the front of his thighs began to burn and grow numb.

A pressure came to Hob. It rested behind his right shoulder blade. He could feel a hard cruel eye fixed on his thin boy's body, clear as clear, crisp as the clamping grip the shire-reeve used on poachers, just above the elbow: that old painful grip, all lawmen know it, they probably used it on Jesus at Gethsemane. A gaze like a bailiff's grasp had hold of Hob's innards. *Nor must you trouble yourself about it.* He looked fiercely at the wretched path ahead; he took another step, the tension on the bridle rope increasing and easing as the ox fell behind, caught up.

In forcing himself on, Hob felt the lock on his soul ease a bit, but his thoughts were all awhirl, too scattered even for a coherent *Ave.* He could manage but a mumbled *Holy Mary, Mother of God,* in time with his steps. Soon the difficulty of the grade and the lull of the chant snared him enough to let him forget the amber eye behind him. How did he know it was amber? His flesh knew it.

Up and up the road wound: oak and yew gave way to fir and claw-needled pine; long ribs of frost-broken stone stood forth here and there; the grade steepened. The land dropped away on the west. They were climbing the western flank of Monastery Mount, that the peasants still called Thonarberg, and the road was narrowing and hugging the rocky slope.

He walked bent forward against the grade. He walked this way for a long time, his right arm stretched out behind him, pulling on the lead rope. Suddenly he woke to his surroundings, as though he had been pacing in his sleep.

Ahead the road passed between two high outcrops of rock. On the east a spur of naked granite, veined with frost, ran to within a yard of the road. On Hob's right hand, where the slope plunged down into the rift between Monastery Mount and the broken crags and frozen rivers of

Old Catherine to the southwest and the Little Sisters to the northwest, now mostly behind them, a spine of rock climbed out of the gulf and bent toward the road. In the portal framed by these two bourne stones stood a small knot of hooded men.

There were three—no, four—and Hob had a moment when he felt bathed in ice water, before he recognized the rough gray mantles, the closed sandals stuffed with dried mountain grasses, that marked St. Germaine's Companions, the brothers of the Monastery of St. Germaine de la Roche, with their iron-shod staves, their reddened faces, their bodies hardened from plain fare and the highland winters. Their arms were scarred, their knuckles swollen, badges of their service to their oath: to maintain the safety of the road, from the crude gate the caravan now approached to the Thonarberg Bite, a point just over the crest of the pass that ran, threading through the mountains, along the western shoulder of Monastery Mount.

GERMAINE DE LA ROCHE, a gentle soul, born into wealth, in love with God and His works, had it in his mind to build a refuge high in the mountain passes, to gather some like-minded companions, away from distraction, where he could glorify God by prayer, by meditation, and by studying the precarious but tenacious existence of flower and moss in the desolate uplands. It took six years and a substantial part of his family's wealth to fashion a strong-walled compound off the Thonarberg Pass road, to establish a Rule and obtain the bishop's approval, and to gather his first set of comrades.

Wells were dug; a flock of mountain goats furnished milk, meat, cheese, and clothing; forays into the lower forests provided fuel and wood for carpentry. Four months of peace followed.

The monks' tranquillity was shattered in the dead heart of the night by a handful of pilgrims, bleeding and hysterical, battering at the gates. Close on their heels: banditti from the lower ravines, swinging their weighty saxes, knives that were as long as a tall man's arm from elbow to fingertip. The monks snatched whatever was to hand, and in the melee that followed, six of the wolf's-heads were stretched out lifeless in the freezing mud at the gate.

Next morning the pilgrims left generous offerings beneath the icon of St. Luke the Physician, Germaine's patron, and Germaine gathered his monks. His thin face, beneath the disordered wreath of brown hair tinged with gray, was suffused with a kind of rueful joy. "Comrades, God has held up a mirror to my vanities: He has shown me that in seeking retreat from this sorry world, I have been blind; I have scanted my calling. The apostle John said, 'Who says he loves unseen God, but who loves not his neighbor standing plain before him, is a liar.' Brethren, I have been indulgent with myself: love of God is not exercised without travail and danger." Some of the faces turned toward him were swathed in linen bandages. He beamed at them. "We will forgo our books; we will keep safe the pass."

THAT WAS eighty-five years ago, and the Monastery of St. Luke was now renamed the Monastery of St. Germaine de la Roche, long gone to his rest. Now as then the travelers were met at the double outcrop by a knot of vigorous monks, armed with their iron-tipped staves, many of them retired soldiers. They were, these days, largely illiterate, but skilled men of their hands, said to have developed a high degree of artistry in the use of their simple weapons.

Hob halted about a foot before the portal. The monk in charge came forward, an older man, perhaps forty-five. Below his robe were the knotty calves and thick ankles of a mountaineer who never takes a level step in a day, and clenched on his staff the knobby knuckles of one who has pounded sheaves of reeds to toughen his fists. Beneath the whitening brows, surprisingly mild brown eyes regarded Hob kindly; on the monk's left cheek was a complicated pattern of scar tissue.

"God save all here," said the monk.

"Amen," said Hob.

Molly had dismounted; now she came trudging up, the voluminous shawl cast about her shoulders, hooding the heap of silver hair, rendering her modest as a nun.

"Jesus and Mary with you, Wulfstan," she said cordially enough, although she wore a dire look.

An expression of genuine pleasure replaced the professional courteous suspicion of the warrior monk. "Mistress Molly," he said.

Whenever she stayed at the hostel the monks maintained, the first few days were employed in easing a host of small and great miseries with her herbs, her salves, the cunning grip of her big pale hands. Brother Wulfstan himself remembered lying on his pallet, a pain like Brother Cook's cleaver through his left eye, sick shivers, the rushlight in his cell assuming such haloes as the angels are said to wear.

Brother Abbot and the ancient Father Thomas, chaplain to the Order, had come in, and remained to guard against impropriety. To Brother Wulfstan they seemed, through his pain, ghosts or shadows. Next he remembered the wooden cup with a broth tasting like charcoal and thyme, with a vile bitter undertinge. Back, back a long way to the husk-filled burlap pillow; a hand, rough-skinned but not hard in the way that Brother Wulfstan's own hand was hard, was placed firmly on his forehead, preventing, it seemed, his head from bursting.

In ten or fifteen breaths he had sat up again, the tears of respite in his eyes, as the pain ran out from his body like whey through a sieve. He had peered into the lake-blue wide-set eyes, the round ruddy comely face, the queenly mane of steel hair peeping from beneath the shawl, and begun an earnest *Ave*. After some time old Father Thomas had managed, not without a certain mounting irritation, to convince Brother

Wulfstan that the Queen of Heaven had not left her Son's side merely to heal his dolors.

"A word with you, little brother," Molly now said; she herself was perhaps seven or eight years older than Wulfstan.

They paced off the road a bit, leaving Hob facing the little group of monks, their staves grounded in the ice-slick soil, their eyes flat as they studied him. Impossible to stare back at them: for something to do, Hob glanced behind. Jack stood at the side of the road, patient as one of the draft animals. Nemain looked past him at the gate, thin-limbed, her skin blotchy as her blood ignited with her new estate as a woman, her eyes green as spring grass; from beneath her shawl escaped a lock of hair red as apples. His only family, now, in all God's wide cold world.

Molly was speaking earnestly. Brother Wulfstan looked appalled. Presently they returned to the road. Brother Wulfstan signaled to the trio by the great stones, and each swung up his staff to his shoulder with a smooth practiced motion. They trotted forth from the gateway, spreading to this side and that to encircle the tiny caravan, sheepdogs taking station around a flock.

Molly clambered up to her seat and kicked loose the brake. Brother Wulfstan loped up to the head of the caravan; as he passed Hob, he gave him an encouraging double slap on the shoulder blades, as though to say, Let's go, let's go. It was like being struck lightly with a blackthorn root. Hob surged forward, dragging the lead rope. In a moment he had passed between the tall sentinel stones, and they were away on the climbing approach to the monastery.

He looked around as he stumbled upward: the harsh vigilant shapes at avant-garde, flank, and rearguard, Jack Brown's shambling strength, Molly turning her keen watchful face to either side of the trail, abruptly relieved him of a burden or constriction. His thin chest expanded, he drew a deep sweet breath, and his steps pattered almost blithely on the frost-hardened soil of the upward way.

From this point on, the road was flanked by a parapet of fitted stones, waist-high, on the downslope side. After a short time walking uphill, Hob's legs beginning to ache again, the caravan was passed by a squad of monks jogging down to the gate, the men leaning back against the decline. Hob realized that they must have these small groups going back and forth constantly, to monitor the roads between, and to relieve those who had left the portals at either end to escort parties of travelers.

At their left hand the flank of the mountain climbed sheer to Heaven. Presently the wall of rock receded somewhat from the trail, and soon afterward, they came to a cleft in the stone. The road ran on past this point, but a spur curved into the notch, and it was here that Brother Wulfstan turned in. They had come to sanctuary, near the end of the day, in the Monastery of St. Germaine de la Roche.

CHAPTER 2

HAT HE FIRST NOTICED: THE
dying off of the caustic wind.
Recessed into the mountain,
the cleft they had entered provided a natural shelter
for the monastery. The mountain's own meat rose to
either hand, while ahead, across the gap, St. Germaine
had had only to put a stout wall with a double-leaved
iron-studded doorway. When they reached the silent
unmoving panels of wood, Hob realized that they were
observed from a dozen or so slits, in the wooden doors,
in the stone wall.

A sudden rattle made him whirl. Behind the little
caravan, across the gap that looked out upon the gulf
between Monastery Mount and its nearest neighbor,
now moved a light portcullis, drawn from a niche cut
in one side of the rock. The monks of St. Germaine
were not easily taken at a disadvantage.

The travelers were now isolated between the

outer portcullis and the wall of the monastery proper. A postern opened in the main doors and a short but very burly monk stepped forth, in his hand a stubby truncheon of solid iron. In the opening behind him Hob caught dull glints of metal.

The monks' vows forbade them "to shed blood by the sword"; this they interpreted as a ban on the use of edged weapons. In consequence, avoiding conflict with the letter of their vows if not the spirit, they had become expert in the use of all manner of staff, mace, and bludgeon.

The stumpy monk faced Brother Wulfstan and held his free left hand before the expanse of his chest; the fingers writhed in a curious manner. Hob, standing by the patient steaming bulk of the ox, wondered at this mute ceremony. But Brother Wulfstan matter-of-factly held his own hand up and made twisting shapes in the freezing air. At once Brother Porter, for it was he, turned and stepped back through the postern and slammed it to. A moment later Hob heard the groaning of bolts, and the two leaves of the great solid gate swung back. Monks boiled out, darting past the wagons to face the portcullis in a roughly dressed line formation.

Brother Wulfstan walked forward, waving Hob to follow him. Hob obeyed, tugging on the bridle rope. There was a moment when he might have been anchored to the earth with a millstone, then the ox came to an understanding of what was required, and began to move. When the last wagon was through the double gates, the line of monks fell back through the opening, the doors were heaved closed, the iron bolts were slid into their brackets. Only then did the monks at the capstan that controlled the outer portcullis throw themselves at the capstan bars, their bodies bowed and their sandals scrabbling on the flinty ground, till the openwork gate had been retracted into the slot that St. Germaine's first monks had carved in the living stone.

In eighty-five years, the monastery had never exposed a clear opening between the walls to the outside world; the double-gate system, thought out by candlelight in the very small still cell that St. Germaine allowed himself, had never failed. Novices chafed at the constant turn-out drill when any conveyance must be brought in or out of the compound, but the older hands knew it to be a mighty pillar of their defense.

The wicked are often horridly inventive. Men with knives between their teeth had been known to lash themselves beneath wagons; men with crossbows had been known to secret themselves beneath a bale of hides, a quarrel aimed at Brother Escort's back: hence the passgate signs, changed constantly and known only to senior monks, that said, *No one now threatens me from hiding.* Only when Brother Porter had given the sign, Brother Wulfstan the countersign, would those ponderous valves open.

Hob now looked about him. He stood in a kind of bailey, with the outer wall spanning the cleft like a stone curtain, the blocks closely fitted, disdaining mortar. The cleft narrowed toward the back, and there, scorning to build in this natural hold, the monks had tunneled back into the naked rock, so that where a donjon might have been expected, there was a doorway and some windows, not overlarge, and then the faceless brow of the mountain.

The bailey itself was surprisingly extensive, for it ran some distance into the flank of the mountain, and its sides had been hollowed further by the industrious brethren. About the perimeter were stout-beamed wooden outbuildings: stables and byres; a smithy and armory; mews from which emanated harsh raucous cries and a faint jingling of bells; the buttery where ale and wine were stored in butts or casks; the laundry whence clouds of white steam from the tubs, dark gray smoke from the fires, issued forth from vents and from the open double doors; the dairy from which a novice now staggered, oppressed by an ash-wood yoke across his slight shoulders: swaying awkwardly from the yoke ends were two tubs of yellow-white cheese.

In the center of the bailey was a wide-mouthed stone well, with an ample roof like the cap on a mushroom, to keep out rain and bird-filth. Hob would later learn that there was another well deep within the keep; there was also a stream that emerged from the side of the mountain, and flowed in a thin flat sheet down the granite to one side of the compound, to cross the road in a channel graven by the monks for the purpose, and slide away down into the coomb. The water arose from the heart of the mountain and had never been known to freeze before it had crossed the road, howsoever bitterly the winter fell on the highlands.

The wagons were directed to a clear space between two stable buildings. Here monks assisted in unharnessing the animals and in directing them to stalls within the outbuildings. Hob, by Molly's order and by his own inclination, would not leave the ox till it was safely stalled for the night. The last rope was cast off, and he trudged forward hauling on the bridle, the ox with stretched neck following at some delay. The bailey was darkening into a blue-gray haze, and the yellow light from the open double doorway spilled out in a glowing rectangle onto the frozen pebble-shot dirt.

He stepped through the doorway into a paradise of warmth perfumed with hay and urine, where horses and oxen stood drowsing in a row of crude stalls along the back wall, which was the mountain itself. The heat from so many great animal bodies, from the oil lamps hanging from the crossbeams, fell about Hob's skin like a damp ecstatic blanket. He found that he was smiling foolishly; it was difficult not to.

The young monk who had led them within now indicated a stall. In a trough and two mangers at the back: clean water, hay, oats mixed with barley. Hob led the ox inside, and closed the stall door on its creaking wooden pintles. He looped the leather latch on the peg and leaned his face for a moment against the animal's huge side, still chilled from the outside air but with the indomitable warmth of breathing blood beginning to warm it from within. He put his palm flat against the hide.

He rested; with empty mind he paid attention to his body as it warmed by stages, happy as a snake on a sunlit stone.

After a time he roused. He spoke softly to the beast, removing its halter, offering it sweet hay; from a peg on the wooden wall he took a rough cloth, dried the creature's vast back. Molly called the ox *Milo;* Hob himself, when he was off some way alone with it, called it *Lambkin.* Hob had known and held lambs; he was aware of the incongruity of the term. Still, he felt it was an endearment one used to the very young or those beloved and protected; perhaps he had heard someone use it in this fashion. He could not quite remember who had been so called.

The stall door creaked against the latch; the leather stretched and held. The wooden drawlatch lifted, the loop came free, and Nemain slipped in.

An oblique person, Molly's granddaughter, lean and intense and silent. Her silence was that of one who carries gold in a secret purse, hoping not to be noticed. Hob's silence was that of a shy child, fearful of ridicule. In the last year and a half they had become somewhat comfortable with one another: the familiarity of two chicks beneath Molly's capacious wing, increasingly tinged with the cat-and-dog tension of sister and brother, for so Molly treated them, though Hob was a prentice and Nemain Molly's own flesh.

"Where is Herself?" asked Hob.

"She's away with Brother Wulfstan to pay her courtesy to Brother Abbot," said Nemain, her manner distracted, her voice low, almost faint. Hob could tell she was troubled. She had come to this country as a child, and her accent was never as strong as Molly's. When she was frightened, which was seldom enough, it grew more noticeable.

She went to the back of the stall and dipped up a handful of oats with barley for the ox. It lipped daintily at the mixture. The ox obeyed Nemain readily, although warily—she had somewhat of the way with beasts that her grandmother had. Hob had seen Jack Brown stop an animal by looking it in the eye, and what man or beast had ever resisted Molly's touch? But it was Hob that Milo, or Lambkin, loved and looked to for protection.

Nemain bent her head to watch the ox eat. "I could feel it," she said to the ox's forehead, or perhaps to the oats in her hand. "It watching me the while, and myself feeling it the while." A lock of her hair, a little greasy, stuck in two lank clumps, slipped forward, a startling red against her brow that was white as bone. Her hand began to shake.

Hob felt a surge of fellowship, or even kinship: he had thought himself alone with his fear. He came up and put an awkward arm about her thin shoulders, delicate bones beneath his hand.

He held her tensed body. For a moment she stood still; then she turned swiftly and buried her face against his breast: there was a muted sob, and then she just rested against the coarse cloth upon his chest. It was perhaps the last time in her life that he heard her crying at all.

Now Hob, who had last autumn completed his thirteenth year, his body still mostly hairless, his limbs thin, his waist slim, had an unexpected kind of awakening, a foreshadowing: what previously he had felt only for Lambkin, he felt for another like himself, with that sweet undercurrent, sensed but unnoticed, that underlies everything between brother and sister, father and daughter, son and mother, like a wide dark river whose path is belowground: nothing of itself can be seen, but the ground above is fertile and moist and ferns and grasses thrive along its course.

He looked down at her narrow skull, her hair a flaming red despite the grime of the long road, the white scalp gleaming here and there. Though she was a bit more than a year older than he, he realized he overtopped her by several inches; he had the entirely novel sense of himself as tall and protective, so that when the young monk opened the stall door Hob did not flinch nor did he spring back from Nemain, as he might have done but a few moments before. Instead he looked up beneath his brows, above his encircling arms.

The young monk, Brother Aelfwin of stalwart North Country Angle peasant stock, who in obedience to the dead hand of St. Germaine de la Roche had run guard duty alongside wagons carrying whores over the pass and endured the merciless teasing such women employ against handsome young forbidden men, hardly noticed either the embrace or Hob's defiant glare. Indeed, after four years in the rigorous life of the monastery, he knew a score of ways to dispatch a stripling like Hob, using only what might be found in the stall, or even his empty hand, but his attention this evening was fixed on his own hollow stomach and on dinner, nearly ready. His only concern was to collect the guests.

"Young man, young may," he said, "ye twa mun come the noo t'hae yer meal; gae ye left across bailey; yon double doors in t' angle o' wall. Dinna bide: ye've nobbut a moment till a' the porridge is gane." This last was said with a wink and a grin, and then he was gone, for he had to alert all the travelers and he himself was hungry with the robust eager happiness of early perfect health.

A LOW-CEILINGED HALL, wide but not too long, with thick pillars springing up to shallow groined vaults. Along the length ran trestle tables, a double row, scrubbed with coarse stones each day till they were a dull gold on top. Down the middle of the hall ran a trench in the old style, filled with blazing wood, the smoke drawn out through a slit in the central vault. Disks of the coarse black onion-studded bread, three days old and hard as wood, were set between every two places, and young monks whisked along the tables, scooping steaming ladles of boiled turnip and leek onto the dark rounds. Hot fresh loaves of the same bread were ranged here and there down the long table. Once each fortnight the monks served meat; once each month they themselves were allowed meat.

There were forty or fifty people seated there, without regard to place. St. Germaine spoke often of Christ's love of the rough plain people, and of St. James's respect for the poor. A spirit of wary provisional camaraderie prevailed among the travelers, varied of station in life, who broke bread there.

A passion for winter pilgrimages, thought to be more meritorious because more difficult, had begun to spread four or five years before, although the savagery of the last two years' weather had blunted its force. At the table against the far wall was a party of a score or more such cold-weather pilgrims heading southeast to the shrine of St. Cuthbert at Durham, men and women in ample robes of the rugged cloth called russet, belted with ropes. From some of these crude belts dangled the strings of prayer-beads known as paternosters; from others, the newer rosaries. Their staves were leaned against the rock; their broad-brimmed hats sat beside them on the benches; their leather scrips were slung behind them. They kept up a lively chatter, somewhat muted by self-consciousness, that filled the echoing stone chamber with a warm welcoming substrate of sound.

Molly was already there, seated near the front of the hall by the stand where Brother Lector would read from the lives of the saints at the monks' evening meal. She had donned a plain white woolen cotehardie and had pushed the snug sleeves up her arms a little way to keep them free of her food. She ate with her customary enthusiasm, her forearms square on the table, her cheeks full and the strong muscles bunching at the side of her jaw as she chewed briskly. Jack Brown sat beside her. The kirtle he wore over his shirt, the hose that cased his legs, were of dark red-brown wool; with his wide-backed body slouched before the table, he seemed an autumnal figure, rooted in the earth. But when

Nemain stepped over the bench to claim a place beside her grandmother the bull-shouldered man made room for her readily enough. Hob took his seat on the other side of Jack.

Jack Brown looked at Hob for a moment, a piercing regard followed by an unnervingly rapid loss of interest. It was a way Jack had; it was like an inspection by a dog who, having identified another member of the pack, finds no further reason for concern or interest.

Down the table were four men, stonemasons as Molly reported later, also on their way to Durham. There they would take service with the bishop as cathedral caretakers; the great cathedral erected in the new style by the Prince Bishops of Durham, with its ribbed vaulting and its flying buttresses up in the high shadows, was a post of honor for these craftsmen.

The one with snub nose and pouched weary eyes ate with concentration, but the other three were murmuring together and pointing here and there with professional interest to the groining of the refectory ceiling, for the hollowed-out halls of the monastery were also famed for their workmanship. The stone dust engrained in the masons' knuckles gave their muscular hands a gray and corpse-like appearance; the edges of their left hands bore scars from slipping on chisels slick with sweat.

A monk placed a leather bumper at Hob's elbow. Jack reached a thick arm to the center of the table; from a clay jar of honey beer he poured out a draft for Hob. Hob took a sip and felt the bite of the sweet-sharp drink against his tongue, with a faint aftertaste, a tang of tar from the pitch-jacked leather. A warmth spread through his empty stomach.

To his right sat three men-at-arms clad in travel-worn boiled-horse-hide gambesons, eating with hefty disk-guard dirks and their fingers, chewing impassively, muttering among themselves, a low comfortable profane grumble. Their hair was cut in the bowl-shaped Norman fashion. One was an older man with the pewter badges of a sergeant; the other two were young men, large-framed, features marked with past batterings.

"And where in Jesus's own sweet name would I be if I'd landed on those rocks? I hate 'em all, and she's the worst, the bitch, the sneak."

"Roger's no luck with horses or women."

"Shut up, Olivier."

"That hammerhead lassie's fooled you three times now." Hob glanced sideways. The rasping voice belonged to the sergeant. "Next time, do you knee her in the belly before you pull the cinch, make her dump her breath, pull it tight. Elsewise she'll have you in the muck of the road ten paces from the gate."

"Next time, do you ask for her hand in marriage before you tickle her belly."

"Shut up, Olivier. God take them all. I hate 'em. I had one step on my foot and half my toes were black for a fortnight. God rot them all. I'd rather march, if it weren't so fucking cold."

"Roger, Roger. The lassie's yours, you must settle her down. Just pull it tight next time. Knee her first, then pull."

Hob drew his knife and cut a slice of the rich dense bread from a loaf before him, and dipped it into the steaming heap of turnips and leeks on the trencher between his place and Jack's. Eddies of smoke from the fire trench made him cough a little. Beside him loomed Jack Brown's bulk, to anyone else a sinister figure. Eighteen months' familiarity, Molly's blessing, and the accepting nature of childhood: all had transformed Jack into an emblem of security rather than threat to Hob. As his stomach filled, as the hazed warmth settled about him, Hob grew sleepy and placid. He sagged against Jack's broad right arm. The dark man turned him an enigmatic glance, but made no move to dislodge him.

There followed a period of disjointed thought and dream. Suddenly Hob realized two things simultaneously: he had been at least partly asleep, and a late party was seating itself across the scrubbed board.

Two well-favored men, blank-faced, their blond hair confined by jeweled nets, their trim and muscular forms clad in a livery of gold and green and white, were settling a small, aged woman into her seat, just across the board from Molly. The woman had the slow, careful movements of the very frail. She sat down sideways and one of her esquires lifted her feet over the bench and in under the table; Hob had a glimpse of silken escaffignons, Heaven blue, on tiny feet, peeping from beneath her robe.

Hob had never seen such a handsomely attired person, and he sat up, yawning despite his kindled interest. He saw a delicate face, a long nose, and large light eyes, gray as the winter sea and slightly tilted, set amid a web of wrinkles; a lock of straight snowy hair escaped from beneath her wimple. Over a cotehardie of white linen she wore a quilted over-robe of green silk. About the cuffs, golden thread was worked into a repeating pattern of a great tree in which two birds perched, with sun and moon and stars above its canopy. Despite the robe she seemed cold, holding it tight at her neck and giving a little shiver from time to time.

The two esquires now took seats to the right of the old woman. To her left was a man in late middle years, with a beard of gray brindle, black brows, eyes the blue of May skies, kindly and humorous: he radiated benevolence. His crimson robe, its blue hood thrown back, suggested a doctor of medicine; certainly he was some kind of scholar. He noticed Hob straightening up and yawning, and he smiled gently at the boy. Hob had an immediate and unusual sense of his friendship and warmth, and further, a feeling that he knew that Hob had been asleep, and that further still, it was a secret between the two of them, and Hob grinned at him, hardly knowing why he did so.

Hob became aware that Molly, with her easy good humor, had introduced herself to the party and had managed to engage the scholar in conversation. ". . . Lady Svajone," he was saying. "We will . . . we will to going . . . we will to go our way homeward, to far Lietuva, across the . . . the seawater, far past Normandy, far past the Burgundians and the Rhinelanders." His speech was rapid, but oddly accented.

Lady Svajone leaned forward, her luminous eyes fixed on Molly. "Our home is being . . . many away. Is being much away. You also, you also from many away, from not, from not here?" Her voice was whispery but sweet, like a little girl with a sore throat.

Molly smiled at her and spoke slowly and simply. "My home is in Erin, what these folk call Ireland, across the inner sea," she said. Her strong accent became if anything more vivid, just from the mention of home.

"I am Doctor Vytautas," the scholar said. "We have find a . . . refuge? a refuge here for a while. Is been much of the not pleasant, the not peace, in our home countries." He took a sip of the honey beer. He smoothed his damp mustaches with a forefinger, a fussy gesture. "I am been secretary and physician to the family"—he indicated Lady Svajone with a kind of seated half-bow—"is now a score and a half of years. Much of the family holding is been . . . is losted, but now hope is coming that . . . well. We will return, now that the circumstances have, have more of the . . . of the favor."

"I wish you joy of it," said Molly. "Be said by me, exile has a bitter taste, and it's not from well-side gossip that I'm speaking at all."

One of the fair men leaned over and cut off a tiny bit of fresh bread for the old woman, placing it on her trencher of stale bread, beside her untouched portion of turnip stew. She put it in her mouth and ate it slowly. She said something in their language to Vytautas, a querulous note in the sweet faint voice. He stroked her hand, small and bony, the knuckles prominent and the skin near-translucent, spotted with age. He murmured in her ear. He looked up and said, "Gintaras . . ." He motioned to the young man, who cut another dainty piece. She toyed with the morsel and began a long mumbled complaint to Gintaras, who bent his head to hear.

Molly drained her jack of honey beer and reached for the jug. Her face had a flushed glow; she was beginning to sweat from the beer and the food and the fire. She leaned toward Vytautas. "Is it a poor appetite she has?" she asked in a low voice. "I have a remedy for a sickly nature."

He said, "Brother Abbot has speak of your . . . knowing? knowledge, your knowledge of the herbs. I have my own remedies, but my . . . stuffs, my materials are . . . thin? deplete? I would being grateful for some things of the summer woods, of the woods of this summer that has passed. Although . . ." He glanced sideways at his charge, then back at Molly, managing to convey, with the faintest of shrugs, the slightest lift of the eyebrows, how little he dared hope that anything might be of help.

Molly asked him a question in what Hob knew to be Latin. Vytautas's eyes widened with surprise, then crinkled with pleasure, and he relaxed into the comfort of a language in which he was fluent, the universal tongue of scholars. Molly leaned forward, searching his face, following along. In addition to her native Irish, she had a mastery of English, whether the near-German low speech used by the Angle and Saxon peasants or the near-French high speech of the Norman lords. Her Latin, though, was adequate but halting, and she had to concentrate not to be left behind.

The incomprehensible syllables washed over Hob. He found that when he blinked, his eyes would stay closed till he struggled to open them. The warm weight of food in his stomach, the honey beer, the heat from the fire trench, the hum of talk, left him in a happy trance, and he put his head slowly down on his crossed arms and listened to the sound of the conversation, and paid attention to the curious scenes that formed behind his eyelids, and slept.

* * *

HOB AWOKE A FEW HOURS LATER, on a blanket beneath which was the bunching rustle of straw, by the scent of it mixed with herbs: tansy to keep the vermin away, lavender to sweeten the tansy. The blanket on which he lay and the other with which he was covered were of clean undyed wool. Dimly he remembered stumbling up with Jack Brown to the men's dorter. Cots, frames of wood with leather straps webbed across and pallets of straw atop the straps, had stretched in a double row away down a long stone-walled room. The rushlight Jack had held had showed windows here and there, cut in the rock and closed with ironbound wooden shutters. Hob had sat on a cot and had let himself fall sideways. Jack Brown had pulled his straw-filled shoes off and lifted his feet into the bed, helped him out of the rest of his garments, and spread the blanket over him, the last thing Hob remembered.

Now he lay and looked into darkness, hearing, below the snores and grunts of his unseen roommates, a steadily growing discordant rumble outside the shuttered window. He swung his bare feet onto the icy wooden floor, and felt his way to the stone wall, and thence to the wood and iron of the shutter. He fumbled the peg from the loop, letting it hang on its thong. He pushed the big shutter open, to find himself on the second floor of the monastery, looking down at a torchlit scene in the bailey, a scant twelve feet below.

It had snowed again while he slept, and there was a fresh carpet of white. The torches held by several monks cast a ragged circle of yellow light that sparkled in the drifts. In the center was a rough litter, on which lay a scarlet ruin in tattered robes. It looked like a deer that had been inexpertly butchered. Molly squatted by one side of the litter, her skirts spreading on the snow, while Brother Abbot hovered anxiously beside her. On the other side Father Thomas knelt in the snow, administering the last rites to the broken corpse.

Fragments of speech drifted up to Hob as he hung on the windowsill, appalled and fascinated.

". . . blood be frozen on him, sithee . . ."

". . . found him i' valley, past t' ford . . ."

". . . what could, what could do . . ."

". . . traveling alane . . . alane, ye canna . . ."

The warrior monks did not easily lose their composure, nor did they now, but even Hob could hear the strong undertone of shock and disbelief in their gruff professional comments.

". . . wolves, or . . . a bear come out of winter sleep?"

". . . gutted like a . . ."

"But it were Brother Athanasius! And he fully armed!"

". . . been eaten at, the while he was fresh! Jesus, Mary, and Joseph!"

"Wolves?"

"Right hand is gone, sithee, and his eyes—"

"But it was Brother Athanasius!" Brother Abbot burst out. "Surely not wolves, surely not: Samson and Goliath together could not have stood against him. *What could kill Brother Athanasius?*"

Molly looked up from where she squatted, her forearms across her powerful thighs. "It was a piece of this robe that we found, and it lying by the trail." She bent her gaze again to the horrid thing on the litter. "There's a black shadowy art that's in this." Then, lower, "I can taste it." Everyone crossed himself at this, and Brother Abbot turned away, his hand over his eyes, but Father Thomas paused in his office to regard Molly thoughtfully.

Hob became aware of the spill of freezing air coming through the unglazed window. He felt his way back to his cot and returned with a blanket wrapped like a cloak about his shoulders. He noticed now, beyond the clump of murmuring monks, a closed traveling wagon, wide and long; it stood with chocked wheels against a blank stretch of monastery wall, just beside the doorway of the buttery. The wagon was paneled in rich auburn woods, glinting darkly in the torchlight. Ornate shutters, finely carved in a pattern of vines, with what seemed to be faces peering from among the leaves, were closed against the cold, save for one that was latched back, displaying a thin translucent pane of horn—to Hob a shocking extravagance—through which candlelight from within cast a wan glow. Lady Svajone and her close attendant physician had chosen to remain in the luxury of their traveling wagon, warmed by oil lamps and candles and body heat, rather than avail themselves of the monks' comfortable but austere dormitories.

There was a door at the back end, as in Molly's three wagons. The two blond esquires had risen from richly made sleeping furs, wolf and winter rabbit and pine marten by the look of them, laid out by the wagon's back wheels. They had been sleeping on guard before their mistress's door, like bandogs. Now they stood there warily eyeing the monks crowding around the litter, listening to the tone of dismay in a language incomprehensible to them. One unobtrusively held a drawn dagger down at his side, and the other stood with left hand on right elbow and right hand resting, as if by chance, on the hilt of his sword.

The door opened and Doctor Vytautas, swathed in a generous linen night-robe and a sable-lined pelice, came out onto the little back platform. He asked them a question. They shrugged; they pointed; after a moment Vytautas gathered the skirts of his robe in one hand and picked his way down the steps. The clack of his wooden soles on the steps came clearly to Hob; then Vytautas was on the snow, shuffling with short careful steps over to the little torchlit group.

He worked his way to the center of the monks, and the boy saw him start and cross himself as he came upon the litter and what remained of Brother Athanasius on earth. He knelt and examined the bloody wreckage. The torches fluttered a bit as random gusts came down off the mountainside. Shadows danced over the corpse, giving it at one point a semblance of movement that made Hob draw back involuntarily.

Vytautas conferred with Molly and Brother Abbot awhile, then hurried back to the wagon, his gait unsteady, his palm against his brow. He clattered up the steps and disappeared within, and now Hob could no longer ignore the pain seeping into his bare feet from the icy floor, the chill air fingering the blanket he wore cloakwise.

He leaned out and pulled the shutter to, fumbled the latch pin into place, and felt his way along the wall back to his cot. A moment later he was snuggled in, lifting his feet to trap a fold of blanket under them, ducking his face under the cover to warm himself with his own spent breath, slowly becoming comfortable.

He was too young and too tired to fret about what he had seen. Around him were the thick stone walls of the monastery, outside were the formidable monks of St. Germaine: he was safe enough at this moment, and warm as well. He slept; but he dreamed, and in his dream was a cruel amber eye.

CHAPTER 3

HE NEXT MORNING HOB took the opportunity to hear Mass in the monastery chapel. Brother Athanasius had not yet been laid out and it would be a day before a requiem Mass was said for him, but a grim mood seemed to permeate the roughly dressed walls: the calls and responses were muted, the echoes falling away into shadow and silence. The monks stood somberly on the bare stone floor and Hob lingered near the back of the little chapel.

Molly never set foot in a church of her own accord, although she would attend if it seemed unwise to refuse. Hob was unsure why this was. Molly would upon occasion say something that would utterly scandalize him, so uninterested did she seem in the question of her soul's salvation. She had little piety and less to say about it, although she would speak as a good Christian around such as the monks, and let herself be known by the Christian nickname Molly, rather than the pagan Maeve. The monks were glad enough of her healing to ignore their own misgivings about her.

Molly made no objection to Hob's hearing Mass when it was at hand, as now, but he never saw her at Christian prayer when the caravan was by itself. Nemain was much the same. The two had their own secrets. Jack Brown, now, would cross himself at roadside shrines, but had a soldier's rough indifference to church, except on the high feast days.

After Mass Hob came out into the bailey, glad to see the sun. He went back to the men's dorter and shook Jack awake, and together they made their way down to the kitchen to beg a little taste of something. They came away with a handful each of salt cod on stale rounds of bread and jacks of barley beer, which they took to the stables. They climbed atop a chest-high partition; this defined a half-room filled with heaped hay across the corridor from the stalled ox. There they sat, eating and drinking in a companionable silence. Hob watched with interest as the monks bustled about, mucking out the stalls and bringing in wooden buckets of icy water for the troughs.

Jack rubbed a hand over his face, trying to wake himself up. The luxuriant hair in curls over the tops of his ears and down his neck, the fine pelt that covered his hands and forearms, his bushy eyebrows, all were still of the darkest brown despite his forty-three years, and there was a dusky shadowy tone beneath his pale skin that turned him brown as bread in summer. Folk in the village where he'd been born and raised called him Jack Brown, Jack the Brown, or Brown Jack, to distinguish him from the village's other two Jacks: his friend Jack White, with his pale blond mop, and an older man, Jack the Fletcher, who made all the arrows for the archers up at the nearby castle.

When they had finished they took the leather mugs back to the kitchen and returned to the stables, Hob to tend to the ox and Jack to the mare and the ass. When Hob heard Molly's voice in the bailey, he put down the bucket of grain he held and went to see.

Grooms were backing brawny dappled-gray draft horses up to Lady Svajone's carriage, hitching them up in a manner Hob had not seen before, three horses abreast, with high-arched elmwood collars, carved and gaily painted with flowering vines, rising above their withers in a complex arrangement. The horses' droppings were steaming in the snow. Molly stood nearby, speaking with the foreign doctor, who seemed as agitated as he had been the night before. Nemain leaned against the wall by the kitchen door, wrapped in a warm cloak, biting delicately at a large chunk of toasted bread, still hot from the ovens. She was absorbed in watching the grooms buckle the horses into the harness.

"Be said by me, it's safer you'd be entirely did you wait till all parties were ready to take the road," Molly was saying urgently to Doctor Vytautas.

"Alas, she is insist, she is demand that we make the travel. She fears that she will never have the safe, the safety, till we come down from out these mountains. I am urging her to stay here and rest, but she refuse to make consideration of this. We have the guildsmen, the . . . the men who cut the stone?" Molly nodded. "They are to come with us. And we have Gintaras and Azuolas." He gestured at the esquires, engaged in readying their horses, a pair of fine matched blacks.

The Lietuvans worked with swift efficiency, deftly spreading saddle pads and heaving up saddles, clucking to soothe the restless mounts, tightening cinches. Their saddle pads were yearling bearskins, an accent of barbaric beauty beneath the ornately worked saddles. They threw tasseled reins back over the horses' heads and, almost in unison, vaulted lithely into the saddles.

The conversation resumed, but in Latin, Vytautas fluent and confident, Molly hesitant. Hob lost interest; he wandered over to Nemain.

She broke off a piece of the bread and gave it to him. "They're running from it," she said.

"Did you see that poor monk?" asked Hob.

"I heard somewhat of him," she said. "Herself is teaching me," she added obscurely. Hob knew that Molly instructed Nemain in the use of herbs and the cure of animals and people, instruction that Jack and he were not allowed to share. He supposed that Molly had found a lesson in the horrifying assault. The fear and misery of yesterday, held at bay by the new morning, began to seep back into his soul.

One of the grooms was pushing hard at the leftmost horse, one hand against the horse's breast and the other holding the reins close beneath the bridle. The rows of little bells along the cheekpieces tinkled brightly in the crisp clear air. The horse tossed its head and snorted, breath smoking, and backed awkwardly three or four paces. Another groom began to buckle it into the straps.

Two other wagons, plain and rugged, were already hitched to teams of workaday horses. These were for the handful of Lietuvan grooms and other retainers who traveled with Lady Svajone, evidently a person of some consequence. The masons had hitched an ass loaded with packs of their tools to the second wagon, and climbed up into the wagon bed, heavily robed against the cold.

"The masons are off as well?" said Hob.

"They are indeed."

"I had not thought they would leave the pilgrims. Herself says both are bound for Durham."

"I had not thought they would be so hen-hearted," said Nemain severely.

She seemed to have recovered from her own fears, even to have forgotten them. Hob found her bewildering these days; found her not quite the little girl he had played with last summer. In the last few months it had seemed to him that she was at times more easily troubled than he. She was more wary and alert. But then he would sense by her silences, her flushed keen glances, that something within her spirit was growing, bright as the ice rivers that ran down Old Catherine's gray sides. Sometimes he worried that it might also become as hard, or as cold. Hob, with his scanty experience, found her difficult to judge, as he found everyone difficult to judge. He had been the lost child, the boy in the priest house, playing with the village children yet not himself a child of the village, and then this: away on the endless road, with formidable Molly and her silent man and her fey grandchild.

There was a bustle. The two esquires trotted their mounts up and took station ahead of the gray team. Brother Abbot came forward to take his leave. Doctor Vytautas pressed a small leather bag into Brother's hand, enfolding it in both of his. Whistles sounded, a driver climbed to the seat of Lady Svajone's wagon, and Doctor Vytautas scurried to the rear of the wagon and skipped lightly up to the door. In a moment he had vanished within, and Brother Abbot gave sign to Brother Porter to open the great gates.

The procedure of the day before was reversed, the doors swinging open to reveal that the portcullis had already been drawn across the exterior gap. The monks of the day watch and the monks of Lady Svajone's escort over the crest of the Thonarberg—doubled since last night's discovery—trotted out together, to fill the exterior forecourt.

Hob and Nemain drew back a bit, for the grays were eager to go and dancing a bit in the traces. The driver braced a leather sole against the brake until the doors were open wide. Then he kicked it loose. The two esquires were already through the gate. Lady Svajone's wagon began to move slowly after them, toward the still-closed portcullis. The wagon's rowan-wood wheels had iron rims with little blunt spikes worked into the iron, so that they bit into snow and ice and mud. The gates swung closed behind the third wagon, the capstan monks gave a collective grunt as they strained against the bars, and a moment later Hob heard the squeal of the portcullis being retracted.

On the other side of the wall the drivers could be heard clicking their tongues and whistling to their animals; calls of farewell rang out crisply in the frosty air from the little train and from the monks who remained behind; the rumble of the wheels echoed from the mountainside. After a moment the portcullis squealed again. The postern opened and the monks of the day watch filed back in.

Molly came to Hob. "We'll be away ourselves on the morrow or surely the day next. See that you've stowed— Look at this face." She took him under the chin and began wiping his cheek with a fold of her skirt. "Must you be putting your whole face into the porridge? And what's this smutch up here?"

Hob screwed up his eyes as she scrubbed vigorously at his forehead, clucking and muttering. Finally she released him, with a little pat of approval.

"See that you've stowed and tied fast everything that's loose. There'll be a mort of haste upon us from the moment we're out the gate till we come off the mountain, and there'll be no stopping on the road to shift what's come undone. We'll not be playing for the good brothers, so you can leave the instruments in their wrappings. Then you're to help Jack look over the harness and the wheels and the like."

"Yes, Mistress."

"There's my lad."

In the event, they stayed two full days after that. Molly was kept busy tending to the monks and dispensing salves and ointments, and the others were glad of the rest. It was while Hob and Jack Brown were in the stables again, with Jack showing him how to mend a frayed leather trace, that they heard a string of Saxon oaths delivered with a strong Norman accent, a little way down the row of stalls. Jack and Hob wandered down to find one of the men-at-arms from the refectory, brush in hand, standing outside a stall and wishing hellfire upon the horse within. This was a tall mare with a large and ugly head, her ears laid flat and her lips drawn apart. As Hob came up, she darted at the soldier, lunging forward to the limit of her tether, her big yellow teeth snapping shut on the air with a loud click.

"She's half the devils from the Gadarene swine in her," the young soldier said to them as they came up. "I canna get in there for my soul's salvation and a sackful of silver groats." Twice he lifted the rondel dirk at his side a quarter-way from its wooden sheath, then slammed it back, not heeding what he did, seething in his frustration. "Jesus and Mary strike her dead!" Hob looked about to see if any of the monks were within earshot; he knew what Father Athelstan would have thought of this profane young man. The three were alone in this straw-strewn corridor built out from the monastery wall.

"Is she yours, sir?" asked Hob.

"No, lad, God be praised, no," said the other. "I'm a man likes to stay on his feet. We're bringing these horses from Bolton, up north, to the Sieur de Blanchefontaine. We're from the castle. You must have heard of Blanchefontaine."

"No, sir," said Hob. "But," he added, seeing the beginning of a frown, "we're from afar." A hoof thudded into the stall boards, and Hob and the young soldier jumped, but Jack just shambled over to the stall, limping as if his ankle hurt, and reached in. He caught the mare behind her jaw and stood there quietly with his hand in place while the mare looked at him, white all around the rim of her eye. After a moment her ears went up and her expression relaxed. She took a pace forward. Jack grabbed her ear with his other hand and bunched it up and released it, then stroked her neck. She began nickering and nuzzling against Jack a little; soon she settled into a deep quiet while he stroked her.

After a minute or two he looked back at the young man-at-arms.

"Oogh ai irrow," he gargled. The soldier gaped at him. "You try it now," said Hob. The young man stepped forward gingerly. The mare eyed him placidly. Jack motioned for him to enter the stall and use the brush. The soldier was not a timid man, and he stepped into the stall and began to brush down the mare. "My thanks, friend," he said.

Hob lounged against the stall and watched Jack pet the mare. The long corridor, sweet with hay and sharp with urine, echoed with the occasional lowing of oxen, the neighing of horses, the *slap, slap* of sandals as monks strode down the line of stalls, the hollow thump of a wooden bucket being set down. A few chickens were pecking hopefully amid the loose straw in an empty stall nearby, moving in random intersecting arcs, looking for spilled grain or for insects that had survived the winter indoors. Through doors farther down the corridor, open to the bailey, came the sound of chanting, drifting down faintly from some window set in the monastery's side.

Hob and the soldier, that same Roger who had sat beside him in the refectory, talked while Roger groomed the mare, Hob explaining how Molly's troupe entertained with singing, music, and story; how Herself was a skillful healer; how she could brew up the potent *uisce beatha,* the lifewater, from instruments stored in her wagons. All the while Jack stroked and patted the mare, who was by every indication now blissfully content.

"We wait here for three more of our comrades. They're to come with a string of horses from up near Holme Cultram," said Roger. "We will not remove till then. Do you persuade your mistress to wait for us, a few days, a sennight, a fortnight at most, and you can travel under our protection. You might winter at the castle. Sir Jehan is keen for any entertainment, and old Thierry, he's our smith and armorer, he's troubled fucking cruel with his joints. I'll swear and avow my lord could use a groom like your father, too."

"My father's dead," said Hob.

"Ah."

"This is Jack," Hob added, as if that explained everything. "But I'll ask Herself if we can wait for you. Though I don't think Jack would want to be a groom for Sir Jehan." He looked at Jack, who opened his mouth as though laughing, although what came out sounded more like a rhythmic wheeze.

The older sergeant came up the line of stall doors and looked in at Roger. "Doing a bit better with that she-snake, I see," he said.

"God's wounds, she nearly ate my fucking fingers before, the brute, the whore! But Master Jack here has a calming way about him," said Roger. He introduced the sergeant as Ranulf. Jack nodded amiably; he did as much as possible with gesture and expression, to avoid the pain of speech.

"And what's *your* name, my lad?" asked Ranulf.

"Robert, sir. Called Hob, sir."

"They're going on tomorrow. They're musicians and healers and such; I told them they should come with us to play before Sir Jehan. They'd find a welcome at the castle." Roger was eager to acquire some new musicians for the hall: the winter nights hung heavy on a young soldier's hands.

"You shouldn't be on the road alone, not with what I'm hearing this day past," said Ranulf. He hitched up his belt with a creaking of leather from his gambeson: he had a bit of a belly, and the belt, on which his dirk and purse were slung, had ridden under it. "Wait a sennight, you can ride with us."

"What I told them, wait for us." Roger's voice sounded somewhat breathless. Greatly emboldened by the mare's pacific state, he was bent over, picking up each hoof and holding it across his thighs, examining it for loose nails in the shoe, cracks in the hoof, pebbles. He was working on the last hoof when the mare swung her head around and looked at him, snorting. He put the hoof down at once and moved alertly to the side, ready to jump the stall door. Jack pulled the mare's head back to the front, and after a moment Roger picked up the hoof again, cursing softly.

"It's Mistress Molly who'll have to decide," said Hob. "But I'll tell her what you—"

"Do you know the fork in the forest road below Dickon's Ford, lad?" Ranulf had the habit of sergeants everywhere: he spoke and you listened, unless you outranked him.

Hob, who had traveled with Molly only for the span of a year and a half or so, looked uncertainly at Jack. Jack nodded.

"Yes, sir."

"The left or eastern road will take you to the castle. Mark you, it'll look like it's dwindling out a mile or so after the fork, deep in the forest, but never you mind, it'll recover, and it'll take you straight to Sir Jehan's gates. He's a stern and hard-handed man to his enemies, but open of palm to such as are skilled, like your mistress, and your father here."

"This is Jack," said Hob patiently.

"Your father, Jack, then," said the sergeant, and turned back to Roger. The two soldiers began arguing over the best way to teach the mare to behave like a proper steed for a Christian. Ranulf was insisting that Roger had drawn her as his mount and that he should be the one to ride her every day till they reached home. He didn't want to have to explain to the Sieur de Blanchefontaine's grim mareschal why they were bringing in a half-wild horse. Roger, on the other hand, wanted to lead her and ride one of the extra horses to come, and let one of the grooms at the castle teach her how to say her prayers like a little nun. Jack as usual contented himself with the occasional grunt or gesture.

Hob left the men there and made his way to the great wagon through the snow of the bailey. He put a foot in the rope loop and stepped up to the wagon's lip and pulled open the door. He entered the barrel-shaped cabin. He shut the door against the chill air and immediately opened two of the shutters a bit for light. He was aware that, with her three beasts and wagons, the musical instruments, the herbs, the portable still, Molly was a wealthy woman, but her wealth did not extend to Hob's wasting a candle in daytime.

He moved about the wagon for a while, tightening straps or cords holding blankets and chests in place, restowing Jack's tent-peg hammer. The even more formidable war hammer was in its brackets on the wall. Jack had bartered a fine dagger and two gold double-leopard florins for it during one of his earlier campaigns, dickering with a Switzer mercenary from a nearby camp. It was two and a half feet in length, with a ponderous head that had two faces: a flat hammer on the one side, a steel beak like a crow's on the other. A terrible weapon for crushing or piercing, and in Jack Brown's big hand it flicked up like a hollow reed stalk, and when he brought it down it fell like a boulder.

This wagon, the largest of the three, was where Molly slept, as did Nemain, except when Molly summoned Jack to her bed. On those nights Nemain slept in the smallest wagon, drawn by the ass, whom Nemain had named *Mavourneen*. The mare drew the middle-sized wagon where Jack and Hob slept most nights and, though well enough liked, had inspired no name, and was just "the mare."

He unwrapped the sheepskins about the musical instruments: the symphonia, on which Molly had made him a passable performer; the Irish harps that Molly and Nemain played; the goatskin drum that Jack had taken to so eagerly, again under Molly's tutelage. He inspected each for crack or chip or other damage. Finding nothing amiss, he carefully wrapped the sheepskins again about the flat circular drum with its bone tapper-stick, and about the harps. The symphonia he kept out awhile.

He sat upon the bench that ran along half the left side of the caravan and placed the symphonia on his lap. He tuned the three sets of double strings, and rubbed resin on the wooden wheel. His hands were stiff from the cold and he rubbed them briskly together till they warmed somewhat with the friction. He fingered the keys and turned the crank; the resined wheel scraped along the gut strings, making a doleful, resonant moan, the paired lead strings soaring above the two sets of drones. He retuned twice as the strings stretched. He practiced runs of notes for a time, and then "The False Knight Upon the Road," but he faltered after a few bars: a sinister meeting upon the road ran too near the fears that had come to lie across his soul.

After a bit he realized he was staring at the keys but seeing the forest path. He wrung his hands, forcing the tension from his fingers; he drew in a sharp breath. He began again, essaying "Lady Isabel and the Elf Knight," singing along a little as Molly had taught him, and the sound of the grimly triumphant old ballad drifted out the window: *If seven king's-daughters here ye hae slain,* the melody rising, falling, its sinuous curves echoing faintly from the monastery walls, filling the darkening bailey.

He thought of leaving this refuge for the ice-clad road, the drifting snow, the unknown thing that ranged the woods. He sang the old song of evil overthrown, and his fingers danced over the keys, though his hands were cold, and his heart was chilled.

> *If seven king's-daughters here ye hae slain,*
> *Lye ye here, a husband to them a'.*

CHAPTER 4

HE NEXT DAY, A REQUIEM Mass for Brother Athanasius was said, and then he was interred in the brotherhood's crypt. During Mass Hob stood again in the back of the chapel. Afterward the covered litter was borne from the chapel, the monks pacing behind, save for one who went before the bearers with an iron truncheon in each hand. He struck these together with a ringing clank, keeping a grave slow time, one stroke for each step. Hob followed them out, to stand watching them cross the frozen ground toward a small archway in the farther reaches of the bailey. All who were about other business paused to cross themselves and stand in prayer a moment. The archway, so Molly had told them, led to the crypt itself, far down a side tunnel, in a shadowy silent chamber hollowed from the mountain, where past members rested in niches in the rough-hewn gray rock. Here the still, cool air never grew warm, never grew cold, and the monks' footfalls were muted by rock dust from long-dead predecessors' picks. In accordance with the brotherhood's rules, no one save the officiating priest and the brothers themselves had been allowed to attend that interment.

Out in the cold, in the sun-bright bailey, all was commotion and hurry, the jingle of harness and clatter of hooves. Molly's troupe was preparing to resume their journey, and the party of pilgrims had elected to accompany them, for a little way at least. The pilgrims now stood waiting in a cluster near the open smithy door to take advantage of the heat from the forge. Their staves were leaned against the smithy wall. They drew woolen and sheepskin cloaks closer, they clapped mittened hands together. Their scrips were slung around their shoulders, and each of these satchels was bulging with fare from the monastery kitchens. The monks never asked for recompense for board or lodging, but any pilgrim of substance left a donation behind, and the largely self-sufficient monastery had never lacked.

There were a score or so of the peregrines, come from Carlisle, most of them burghers, guild-brothers in the tanners' guild. Their leader, Aylwin, a thickset man in middle age with a slab-cheeked cheery face, had come with his brother and one of his sons, and their three wives. A fairly prosperous free farmer from just outside Carlisle had also joined their party.

Now the wagons were ready to roll, and each pilgrim took staff in hand and trudged forward through the opened inner gate. Molly's troupe began in their usual order: Molly in the ox wagon with Hob at the ox's bridle to help guide the great beast, then Nemain, then Jack with the mare bringing up the rear. Molly brought the ox through the capacious doors to the outer ward. Hob had to keep hauling on the cheek strap of Milo's bridle, the ox repeatedly turning its head in wistful attempts to begin a turn back to the stable.

Molly halted the ox just short of the portcullis, and the pilgrims came crowding up to either side. The double escort of eight monks took their stations around the company.

Hob heard the gates close behind them, and a moment later the *clack, clack* of the pawls: just ahead, the portcullis slid sideways into the rock. Soon there was before him only the open cleft in the rock, the road that ran past the monastery, and the sheer drop beyond into the gorge. There was a moment's reluctance to step through those gates into the endless unprotected world, and then Molly clucked to the ox, and Hob grabbed the bridle rope and urged Milo forward.

They turned left, and immediately the road began to climb, winding up the side of Monastery Mount. The advance party of monks walked easily up the incline, springing on sturdy legs over rock and rut. They had brought tight-woven linen bags filled with ash from the fire trenches, and now with a motion as though sowing seed scattered ash and bits of burnt wood in handfuls on the trail ahead of the oncoming party, to assist foot and hoof and wheel in the struggle to secure purchase on the frozen ground.

The aches in Hob's legs, which had begun to fade in the last few days, now were reawakened. The ox toiled upward, planting its vast hooves stolidly in the mix of snow and dirt and ash. The pilgrims were digging into the trail with their staves, breathing heavily, and one woman, thin, black-haired, unremarkable in appearance but with bitter beautiful eyes, racked by a near-continuous cough, was supported on either side by her two sons.

Molly called to her, offering a place on the wagon seat, but she signed a refusal. One of her sons said, in shy courteous tones, "The mam's made a vow to walk the whole distance to the shrine, that mayhap the saint will grant a cure. She's afflicted sore with a theft of the breath."

The slope steepened. Molly got down from the wagon and walked by the ox, gripping the bridle by the cheek strap. She had a rope that went back to the wooden brake bar; if the wagon started to slip back down the slope she could pull it taut and set the brake. She sent Hob back to hold the ass's bridle, while Nemain drove; together the two youngsters would be sufficient to control the smallest of their beasts on this difficult track. Hob could see Jack, a few yards behind the small wagon, ambling along beside the mare, a hand against her neck. Jack with his powerful body seemed untroubled by the struggle against the increasing incline, though his limp grew more evident.

To their right the view opened up as the gorge widened. They were far above the tree line and the air was bitingly cold, the constant mountain wind whipping the hoods the travelers wore about their faces and making robes and cloaks stream sideways.

The snow that draped about Old Catherine's shoulders like a shawl began to glow as the sun climbed and Catherine came out from the shadow of Monastery Mount. The golden flush of the sun-bathed snowcap was shot through with glints of light from the rivers of ice winding down Old Catherine's eastern face; farther down a blanket of evergreens darkened the spreading flanks of the mountain. Hob had the new experience of watching two hawks from above rather than below. The birds, their broad flat wings spread like sails to catch the sun-warmed updrafts, moved in slow expansive circles through the gulf of air, peering down with grim intent at the rabbit-haunted forest glades.

The travelers toiled upward without major incident. At one point some rocks had evidently fallen from above onto the trail. Hob had to push the ass to the right to prevent the wheels' trundling over a rock the size of his head. He had steered too far, however, and a moment later the forward wheel screeched against the monk-built parapet bordering the trail, and despite Nemain's hauling on the reins to turn Mavourneen, the small wagon shuddered to a stop.

There was a general halt of the party. Jack and two of the monks heaved back on the wagon while Hob tried to get the ass to walk in reverse, straining backward with his arms thrown around its neck.

Mavourneen looked back in puzzlement, and an inquisitive velvet nose left a chill moist print on his cheek. He scrubbed at his face with his sleeve and tried again. This time he got the little beast to step back; the wheels were freed and they came forward again. Nemain, up on the wagon seat, looked once over the parapet and then at Hob, her eyebrows raised. Hob smiled sheepishly and turned upslope again, pulling at the bridle rope, his face hot.

Up and up, and soon there came in sight a rock formation with a jagged semicircular cavity in its side: the famed Thonarberg Bite. Fireside tales insisted the opening was ripped in the rock by a flying serpent, always well before the tale-teller's grandfather's time. This marked the highest reach of the pass. Part of the Bite overarched the trail, and as they trundled under this overhang, relief from toil was immediate as the slope reversed from steeply upward to gently downward.

Once past the rock jut, Hob saw the valley beyond sprawl out before him. This flank of Monastery Mount spread southward at a gentle grade, and the track could be followed with the eye, spacious and welcoming, down to the tree line, where it plunged into the forest. About two furlongs past the Thonarberg Bite was a boundary stone set up by the monks. The land here was clear to all sides; the caves and ravines that provided such excellent retreats for outlaws and bandits were all on the other side of the Thonarberg; escort was deemed unnecessary from here to the forest. In the forest lay other dangers, but the hand of St. Germaine did not stretch so far.

Farewells were said, and they moved past the eight monks, who stood quietly to watch them from sight. Molly remounted the wagon seat. Nemain plied the brake on the little wagon, and Hob, one hand to the ass's bridle, leaned back somewhat against the gentle slope, but the going was clearly easier and, were it not for the biting cold, would have been pleasant walking.

Molly, her hood pushed back, her cheeks glowing pink with the sting of the wind, leaned out from her seat on the ox wagon ahead and beckoned Hob forward. He trotted up to her.

"Lead on a bit, child. It's safe enough Nemain will be on this slope, so douce and gentle it is." Molly waited till he had hold of the bridle, and then disappeared into the wagon through the hatch behind the seat. He heard her open the rear door and swing down behind. He looked back and saw her climbing into Nemain's wagon, where she kept most of the herbs and powders she used for her remedies. In short order she returned, a clay jar in her hand, striding past him to the two young men and their dark-haired mother. Hob watched with interest as Molly walked along beside the little group, by the look of things explaining, cajoling, although he could not hear what was said.

Now the little group of four had stopped by the roadside, and as Hob and the ox came up to them, he saw Molly hold the jar to the woman's lips. Then he was past, too polite to look back but hearing a gagging cough, and the sound of someone spitting, and then spitting again. Milo decided at this moment to veer from the path, perhaps intending a subtle slow turn that surely would go unnoticed by Hob, and that would bring them around to a stableward direction. Hob whistled sharply between his teeth and gave a brisk tug on the bridle, and the ox slewed back to the center of the track, snorting in mild annoyance.

A moment later the woman and her two sons passed Hob, the woman now walking much more easily, the strain gone from her face and only one hand laid lightly on a son's arm. The three pilgrims drew ahead of Milo's slow plod. Soon thereafter Molly swung up into the driver's seat, moving with a surprising nimbleness for so queenly a woman.

Hob heard coming up behind him the *chunk, chunk* of a staff, thrust into the path to slow the bearer's descent. Aylwin, the jovial leader of the little pilgrim band, appeared at Hob's left hand, striding along, sniffing appreciatively at the keen air, his head turning from side to side as if eager to miss nothing of the barren snowfields and sterile rock ridges that lay to either hand. The long liripipe that adorned his hood twitched back and forth with his abrupt movements; Hob thought of a horse's tail lashing at flies.

"God save us, what a day tae be up and moving!" He grinned at Hob; he touched his forehead to Molly. He swung his staff forward with a flourish, striking it into the trail with a little skritching crunch; leaned on it as he walked forward; whisked it up and swung it forward again jauntily.

"We're doon fra Carlisle," he said, beaming at first one of them and then the other. Hob, struggling to hold the ox steady as it shied from the shadow of the palmer's darting staff, only managed to grunt politely. Aylwin, undaunted by this lack of encouragement, launched into an involved tale of the organization of the pilgrimage and the funding thereof; the selection by the guild of those to go and those to stay; the Carlisle Tanners' Guild, their current guild quarters and their hope for a new guild lodge; Aylwin's own enterprise as a whittawer; the distinction between tanning and tawing, the tawers or whittawers belonging nonetheless to the tanners' guild; his training of his sons and daughters and his son-in-law in the craft, and their various aptitudes, and the processes of tawing, all in a dense North Country speech that Hob found hard to follow.

They were coming down to the tree line, and Hob, looking at the advancing wall of trees, found himself sinking into apprehension: the fell thing that had driven them in haste up Monastery Mount had moved among the trees, and might it not have gone ahead? Might it not even now be waiting for them to enter the narrow track walled by tree trunks, shadowed by pine and fir branches? He felt his breath coming short as Aylwin chattered gaily about his art, having found in Molly, who always wanted to know everything, an attentive listener.

"First tha mun take t' hair fra yon hide, that's wi' lime, but leaves lime on, sithee, so theer's a bran drench, that'll take lime off again, and then tha's just begun, Queen of Heaven help us . . ."

Now they were moving in among the first trees of the wood. The snow was less here, but the sunlight was dimmed, cut into shafts and bars that lay across the path. Hob looked back. Jack was just entering the forest, and behind him the open slope of the mountain already looked beyond reach, as lost to him as last summer's bright afternoons.

". . . theer's t' scudding as takes off all t' rest o' t' hair and t' color as thy lime has left, then it's intae yon tubs, thy well-made tub being a thing of wondrous clever fashioning, Master Hunferth's oor cooper, a fine auld man, tha wilna find anither cooper t' like in t' North Country, auld Hunferth makks a tub looks like it's grown fra t' one tree . . ."

Hob heard Aylwin's voice, but faintly; the pounding of his own heart was hammering in his ears and he found it hard to catch his breath. He peered left and right down the forest corridors. The wood stretched away, silent; it seemed to harbor no living thing that was not rooted in the earth. Hob was not reassured.

". . . then tha mun mix t' alum, t' salt, t' flooer, t' yolk of eggs, but hoo much tha wonders, ah theer's mony would like tae ken, that's anither guild secret, and noo tha hast a mort of stirring and paddling wi' t' poles, great long wooden things and soon wearisome, and theer's days o' this, stirring like a cook . . ."

Down and down, the evergreens giving way to leafless oak and alder, beech and yew, but the path lightening only a little, for the forest was old and the limbs that closed from either side over the path were substantial enough to block most of the blue sky from view.

". . . then tha hast, after all is done, tae hang un up tae dry, hard as a board it comes, then ye put un aside and do nowt tae un for near a month, it lets t' alum set, sithee, then tae t' sawdust, t' which tha wets just a wee bit, and then tae t' stake, a sort of knife on a wooden horse it is, but not a sharp knife, sithee, more dull or blunt-like . . ."

Behind the cheery voice was the creak of the wheels, the clop of hooves. Hob listened for rustling behind the trees, for the click of claws, for that cry that had caused his heart to check in his breast. Yet there was nothing. He glanced back at Molly. She leaned a bit to hear Aylwin's instruction, and she seemed calm enough, but her eyes roved the corridors of the forest as did Hob's. Hob wondered at the sanguine nature of the pilgrim, as he strode along, carefree, absorbed in his topic. Surely all at the monastery had heard that there was some unknown danger abroad.

". . . and tha mun work thy hide this way and that ower t' knife, ower and ower, swinking and toiling a long weary time till t' stiffness come out and then yon hide, 'tis like butter, like summer butter, sithee, and then it's for my goodwife and her sister and their cousin, and they t' three finest glovers in Carlisle."

"And what is it ye dye it with—oak bark, say, or elderberry juice?" asked Molly. The reins were in her right hand and she braced herself with her left as she leaned toward him, swaying a bit with the bumping of the wagon over the rutted path, but every so often she would straighten and sweep her glance over the woods to the right of the path. She always watched everything and at times it had been what kept them all alive.

"Oak bark, t' juice of t' elderberry, logwood; then theer's thy sumac, fustic, or cochineal, and what we call Persian berries, but beforehand tha mun give yon hide a piss-wash, t' piss being stale, sithee, fresh is no good, and then tha'rt ready for thy dye-dip or brushing on, ower and ower . . ."

Hob found he was clinging so tightly to the ox's bridle rope that he was causing it to veer from the path. His breath came short and fast, and he looked from side to side faster and faster. When he looked left, his skin crawled with fear that when he turned back to the right he would see . . . he knew not what.

"Hob."

". . . and if tha dip it in t' dye tha mun egg t' hide again, and dry and stake it again . . ."

"Hob, *a chuisle,* come back here a moment."

He became aware that Molly was summoning him to her side. He paid out some slack on the rope and dropped back between Molly and Aylwin, who had paused from politeness while Molly spoke, or perhaps to regain some breath.

Molly put a firm hand on his shoulder and pulled him a little toward her. She leaned farther down to her left so she could speak quietly in his ear. "There is nothing," she said. "I'd be knowing by now and no mistake. Now be of good cheer and enjoy your walk."

He looked up at her; the relief from fear he felt was so immediate he almost stumbled: it was as though a wind he had been walking against had ceased. She patted him a few times and he moved to the ox's head, his spirits bounding up. Behind him he heard the pilgrim resume happily.

". . . and anyroad tha mun give it afterward a wash wi' copper salts, brings out t' blue, or iron salts for t' black, or tin salts as brings out t' red, sithee, and t' salts sets t' colors stronger as well."

They came upon a small knot of pilgrims who had paused beside a roadside shrine, the crudely made cross in a little roofed box fastened to a large oak just off the trail. There was a simple wooden bench on which to kneel, and two of the group were just rising, signing themselves with the cross. They had left some small items of devotion at the foot of the shrine, coins and ribbons, little crosses the pilgrims fashioned for the purpose from withes, done beforetime in the long evenings wherever they rested for the night.

Hob halted the ox and Molly set the brake as they came up to the little group of pilgrims pooled in the way. Hob looked up at Molly and she nodded. He went and knelt by the shrine and said three *Aves* and three *Paternoster*s. He prayed that they would finish the journey unmolested. After a moment Aylwin knelt beside him and bowed his head into his hands, silent for once. Molly remained up on the wagon seat. The other pilgrims were already beginning to stream away into the forest, and Hob got back to his post. They waited for Aylwin, and when he crossed himself at last and rose, leaving a coin at the shrine, Hob clucked to the ox and they moved off with a squealing of axles.

Hob looked back as he walked. Nemain did not even slow at the shrine, and Jack merely crossed himself as he drew abreast.

Hob set himself into the rhythm of march. The chatterings of the band of pilgrims ahead, and the scarce-heeded drone of Aylwin's expositions, became a pleasant background as he swung along through the trees. Now that the fear had gone he was able to enjoy the chill freshness of the air, the play of sunlight through the branches.

Tomorrow, late in the day, they should come to the inn that was their next destination; it was to be the last protracted stop before they drove south through extensive forestland. There was a faint unease in his heart only because this night they were to camp among the trees. Still, Molly had said there was nothing.

The day was clear; the threat of snow had abated, though the wind was now picking up and causing the bare branches to rub against one another, a doleful sound.

Aylwin passed him, flourishing his staff jauntily as he hurried on ahead to find a suitable campsite. The wagons toiled noisily on; every so often they would have to slow to squeeze between twisting ancient tree roots or moss-grown boulders that had narrowed the path. Hob could just see the last few pilgrims ahead, and just hear their chatter, trailing to a murmur.

THAT NIGHT THEY CAMPED in a clearing. Five fires, arranged in a loose ring, spat and crackled. Hob lay fully dressed even to his shoes, a wool throw over his sheepskin coat, between one of the fires and the wagons drawn up outside the ring of flame. The women were all within the wagons, at Molly's invitation, and Jack Brown and some of the younger men were taking turns on watch, walking around at the edge of darkness, where the trees and the black aisles between them began.

The woodland to the immediate north was royal forest; six knights served it as king's regarders, and the measuring of the regard or preserve, undertaken each three years, had been done this autumn past. The movement of the knights and their retainers through the woodland had driven the two or three resident outlaw bands to the south, and this stretch between Monastery Mount and Osbert's Inn was, according to all current reckoning, fairly safe. Nonetheless, Jack's instinct and experience had led him to organize sentry duty, showing the pilgrims what he wanted, mostly by gesture and example, but occasionally with a translation by Hob or Nemain of his thick rusty speech.

Now Hob watched Jack move about the rim of the camp, occasionally stepping out of sight behind a tree that his eyes might adjust to the shadows, the better to see any who approached. Hob's belly was full and he was tired from the day's march. He listened idly to the pilgrims' chatter, but much of it was gossip from the tanners' community at Carlisle, difficult to follow if one did not know those involved: the conversation ranged over advancements and declines of fortune, squabbles and maneuvering for position within the guild, modifications of technique planned or accomplished.

Suddenly he was aware that the fires were lower, and that Jack sat nearby—how had that happened? Jack Brown's ungloved hands were folded on the butt of the war hammer, beak-down in the dirt, and his forehead rested on his hands. He seemed asleep, but lightly, and the weapon was under his hand. Hob rolled onto his side and watched Jack through eyes that would not open fully. Something was different. . . . Hob realized that Jack was silent. He was used to the bone-rattling snores of the soldier, echoing through their tiny camps. Even as he looked, Jack lifted his head and scanned the clearing.

Across the nearest fire, two young men—Hob recognized the sickly woman's sons—paced quietly about the periphery, hefty staves in hand. Jack let his head drop once more, and Hob closed his eyes.

After what seemed a moment Hob opened his eyes and Jack was again on his feet and stalking the edge of the clearing. The fires were gray ash, with here and there a golden ember; down all the aisles of the trees to the east stole a thin gray-blue light. A chill breeze rose up. Morning was at hand.

THE PARTY BROKE CAMP quickly and were soon on their way. Near the end of the next afternoon the road dipped into a dell, through pools of shadow cast by the ridges around; the trees above were still lit by the declining sun, but here in this hollow there fell an early twilight. Hob found himself leaning back against the slope as the monks had done on Monastery Mount.

Clumps of gorse rose to either hand; as the travelers descended into the damp little valley, birch and hazel gave way to alder and willow. Ahead the track curved out of sight around a stand of snow-sodden pines, but Hob could hear the leading pilgrims exclaiming; an excited hubbub arose.

As the ox plodded around the turn, the way widened somewhat; the high banks to either side fell away; the declining sun fell brightly on open land. A broad trail swung in from the north and ended at Hob's left hand. On his right, set back a bit from the road, nestled into a forest clearing, now appeared the massive log-built sides of Osbert's Inn.

Part II

THE INN

CHAPTER 5

SBERT'S INN WAS COMPOSED
of three buildings that nestled
against one another and a stal-
wart high wall across the north front, forming a square
with a large courtyard in the center. Midway in the
north wall were wide double doors; these doors now
stood open, and within Hob could glimpse the first
pilgrims looking about eagerly at the night's accommodation.

Osbert's grandfather, Forwin atte Well, had
been a prosperous householder—Osbert still had his
tunic, dyed a forest green and trimmed with squirrel—
farming his three virgates of land, on which was the
excellent well that gave the family its name. Forwin
had supplemented his family's substantial wealth, as
many villagers did in those times, by providing hospitality to travelers and pilgrims in his own house.
Osbert's father, Ernald, had made the inn the focus of

the family's efforts, although the seventy-two-acre farm still supplied much of the inn's produce.

Ernald had built the inn of great logs to make a secure dwelling for the night; the more usual wattle and daub walls were in danger of being tunneled through. In Bywood Old End, the tiny village that lay perhaps a quarter mile from the inn, some of the outlying cottages had suffered the depredations of roving bands of thieves called housebreakers, who would break through a dried-mud cottage wall with a plowshare used as a ram, take what they might, sometimes injuring or killing those within, and disappear southward into the forest.

The inn doors were closed these days at sundown and opened only for departing villagers, and with caution, in the hours of darkness. Osbert had a fair amount of custom from these villagers; whole families would spend the evenings there, especially in winter with its long nights and idle days. Folk arrived in small groups at dusk, but left in one large band, with drunken quarrels and snatches of song echoing through the trees, whoops and whistles floating back to the inn, fading with distance, the noise falling off as each family turned in at its own dooryard.

Now Hob hastened toward the inn, his arm stretched behind him: the ox, usually so eager to reach the comforts of a stable, had decided to assert some small degree of independence, or perhaps just cross-grainedness, by refusing to be hurried. Hob noticed that the ground had been cleared of trees and high bushes for a score of yards around the walls. Someone had taken care not to leave cover for bandits approaching with stealth. And now, as he came near, Hob realized that what he had taken for the side of the house was a log wall about six feet high, and that it ran all the way around the compound, with gates set in it and another set of gates in the true wall behind. Between the two sets of walls was a narrow alley about ten feet wide. Hob had never seen a similar arrangement.

He led the ox through the outer gate and then the wide inner gate beside the main building, gates that led into a capacious courtyard. And now, pushing through the pilgrims who were milling about the courtyard and straggling into the inn itself through the inside door, here came the host to greet Molly, his face alight with much the same expression as Brother Wulfstan's had had.

"God and Mary with ye, Mistress Molly," said the innkeeper, coming up to the wagon and taking Molly's outstretched hand in both of his. "Welcome to my house. Which it's a merry night we see, whensoever ye come to us; we will have music!" And dropping his voice: "And the fill of the house of these fat-purse pilgrims ye've brought us, God be praised, else yon Jack would beggar me at table, him and his hunger, pack o' wolves 'ud be kinder to my larder. Left us barren he did, Egypt after t' locust ye might say, t'year before last." But he was beaming at her, and even Hob could tell his words were meant to have no sting, and he still clung to her hand, and gazed on her. Molly was a friend to him, but beyond that, Molly, stout and well-proportioned Molly, grandmother or no, was good to look upon, and Osbert was no child himself.

A few months' faring with Molly's troupe had taught Hob that she was never asked for payment for their lodging. If anything, she would come away with some fee or reward, in coin or in kind, for the music they made or the healing she performed. Sometimes gifts were pressed upon her just for her advice, or her mediation in some village quarrel, for everyone trusted her. She was wealthy not only in their equipage and the little purses of silver and gold stored here and there within the wagons, but in the web of friends and patrons she retained, scattered along the roads of England, and one of these was Osbert of Osbert's Inn.

"A blessing on your house and all within," said Molly. "It is my delight entirely to enter here."

Osbert atte Well was a large bald man inclined, as is the way with innkeepers, to portliness. A sand-colored beard worn in the old style framed an expression that managed to be both calm and wary, as if he expected some type of misbehavior from his guests, but knew himself equal to quelling it when it arose. From the outsize leather belt about his waist dangled a mostly clean linen cloth, somewhat stained at the bottom where he wiped his hands.

In keeping the peace in his house he was aided by three stalwart and jovial sons and a few housecarls. Forwin and Ernald resembled their father somewhat: fair-haired and great of body. But the third son, Matthew, favored Osbert's late wife, as did Osbert's handsome twin daughters, Parnell and Margery: all three were short, dark, lean.

FORWIN AND MATTHEW came up with a couple of housecarls to help the little caravan settle in. The two brothers were polite and even deferential to Molly and Nemain; Jack was greeted boisterously, with raucous jests about "oor Hercules, sithee," and much slapping of his back—the young men were plainly admirers. Hob was introduced, and Molly and Osbert wandered off toward the inn proper, deep in conversation.

Although Molly's little clan had not passed this way in the eighteen months that Hob had traveled with them, Nemain had told him of Osbert's Inn and its infamous mastiffs, who gave tongue only in the daylight hours. Now, over the noise of the pilgrims' chatter and the rumble of the wagons, Hob could hear a hubbub of barking and howling from the kennels at the southwest corner of the courtyard; soon came shouted rebukes, and a gradual cessation of the clamor.

Forwin showed them where to place the wagons, drawn up against the logs of the blank north wall, just inside the gate. With Osbert's sons and the two retainers helping, the wheels were soon chocked and the animals unhitched. Forwin led the way to the stables, and Hob and Nemain and Jack trudged behind, leading the three beasts. Osbert had good accommodation for man and mount, clean and well built.

After they had the three animals settled down and fed, Nemain and Jack and the brothers made their way back across the hard-packed ground of the inner compound to the inn. Hob wandered about by himself, all eyes; this was one of the most interesting places they had come to and he was eager to see it.

The size of the courtyard surprised him. Along the south side was the storehouse, divided into the pantry and the buttery and the well house; the inn proper, with its satellite dorters inside the courtyard, formed the eastern wall of the compound; the west wall included the kennels, stables, and pigeon cotes—the inn's pigeon pie had a kind of fame all its own—and along the front or north wall were various sheds and booths and a privy. To his disappointment the kennels presented blank walls to the courtyard, and the housecarls shooed him away: it was too dangerous to allow guests within.

He entered a door in the southeast corner, between the inn and the storehouse, and found himself in a short enclosed walkway where brooms were leaned in a corner; from wooden pegs hung coiled rope and a tattered cloak. Three wide doorways led from this passage. To his left must be the inn: a din of voices sounded just beyond, and now and again he could hear Molly above the talk and laughter.

Two doorways led to the right. He poked his head into one and found himself in the pantry, an Eden of tempting fragrance. A spacious counter ran thwartwise immediately inside the door, barring entrance to the rest of the long room. The pantry took up a good part of the storehouse. One of Osbert's elder retainers served as pantler, with two of the younger housecarls as prentices. The pantler nodded pleasantly enough to Hob, but after a bit, Hob realized that one or the other of Osbert's pantry crew was keeping an unobtrusive watch on him.

Hob stood just inside the doorway and looked down the room at the bunches of dried herbs and bags of spices, some grown locally and some that Osbert traded for. Smoked hams and mutton legs and cheeses swung from the roof beams. The walls, of roughly dressed logs chinked with clay, were lined with barrels and bins stretching away into the shadows.

He had to step in and move to the side as cook's mates came hurrying in, one after the other, from the inn's main room, where cooking was done in the great fireplace. A flurry of urgent requests, and the younger pantrymen began bringing meats and grains and spices to the counter to be taken away, while the pantler kept account with tally sticks.

After a hectic few minutes, the cook's prentices were gone; the pantler came up to the counter and leaned on his elbows. Hob said, looking about, "Is all this Master Osbert's, then?"

"It is indeed, cock. Tha's just come wi' yon pilgrims, hast tha? But surely tha's young to be away on pilgrimage?"

"Away on— No, sir, I'm with Mistress Molly's people."

"Is Mistress Molly come in again, then!" He spoke over his shoulder. "Perkin, Daniel! Here's Mistress Molly's lad, her what eased my little Hildelith of her fever."

After that, nothing would do but that Hob would be shown about the pantry and given a glimpse of some of Osbert's riches, with Tilred the pantler as proud as though they were his own.

He waved a hand at sacks and wooden bins. "Theer's thy anise, ginger, an' t' small cask is pepper; yon quarter-bushel cask is salt. Look tha aboon: theer hangs thyme, rosemary, and t' wee sacks are of mustard seed. Thae bins are turnips an' onions an' garlic, sithee, an' theer by t' wall be casks o' salt meat, an' we put up t' dried peas an' beans an' oats an' such in yon butts."

These last were barrels almost as big as Hob himself, stacked in two-tiered rows. His eye followed them as the pair marched deep into the pantry's recesses. In the back wall he could just make out a doorway into a large room, where even greater barrels loomed in the shadows: the buttery, where the butts of ale and wine were stored. "Yon's t'buttery, which young Master Forwin has in charge, sithee." To one side of the buttery entrance was a staunch well-made door, its bar secured with a cumbersome cylindrical lock. Osbert was reputed to have a store of silver coin; some said golden coin as well.

". . . and remember Tilred to thy mistress, lad," the pantler was saying. He plunged a broad hand into an open sack and poured a fistful of almonds into Hob's cupped palms.

Hob thanked him and wandered back into the passageway. He put most of the almonds in his pouch, then knelt and cracked a few with the hilt of his knife. Water splashed nearby; voices echoed hollowly from wooden walls. Hob, his mouth full, went to the third doorway, off to the courtyard side of the passage.

Here he discovered a small octagonal outbuilding, attached to the storehouse; this housed the deep handsome well, sturdily built of fitted stone, that had given the family its name. It had originally been outdoors, but then Osbert's enterprising father had seen fit to enclose it, and now water drawn up by winch and bucket could be poured into stone troughs that ran through the walls, in this direction into the adjacent inn, in that direction into the adjacent stables. Now none need haul large buckets of water across a courtyard slippery with slush, or break a skim of ice on troughs that watered the livestock.

"Killed? How could this be Tibby, then?"

"This were Tibby's grandmam, also called Tibby. Tha were nobbut a wee lad, an' young Tibby hersel' were never born yet."

Two men were toiling here. A strong old man, gray-stubbled, hauled at a winch handle, and up came a groaning oaken bucket, so full that the water spilled in sheets down its sides as it swayed on the rope. He lifted it easily from the hook and passed it to a younger man, who carried it, staggering a little, a few paces and poured it into one of the troughs, while his elder attached another bucket and began lowering it.

"An' Wimund threw the ax at her?"

"Nay, she were wi' Old Martin and Otho—both gone now—and

they all just set oot from here at inn, and t' moon bright, and they was all deep in drink. And Wimund, that had come that close tae knives wi' Otho over Tibby in courtyard—Master Osbert's faither, Old Master Ernald, near threw 'em tae mastiffs, he was that put oot at sich ruction—Wimund come ten, eleven paces behind, and his wood-ax in his hand, and callin' tae Tibby to come away and leave Otho. All of 'em staggerin', we could see it from yon gateway. Nay, lad, put that in t'other trough."

Hob leaned in the doorway, happily chewing his almonds and listening to the tale. The elder housecarl had to conserve his breath till the next heavy bucket was up on the lip of the well. He was panting a little, but only a little.

"And Otho comes roond wi' his knife already oot and starts back at Wimund, and Tibby throws hersel' on Otho tae keep him back, but Wimund's cast his ax at Otho already, sithee, and didn't it catch poor Tibby in t' back of her neck, and she drops in road, dead as a stane."

"Jesus save us!" said the younger man, and passed back the empty bucket. "Two more and she's done, Uncle."

"And Otho give a great cry, and he and Old Martin stand lookin' at her, and Wimund turns and walks into t' forest, and we seen nowt of him syne. Nor hide nor hair of him. He were outlawed; they read it oot at Mass, but none seen him syne." He paused a moment and regarded the winch handle absently. "She were a fine-lookin' woman, too. I fancied her mysel'."

The old man began to lower the bucket again, and now Hob, his mouth full of almonds and his ears full of the housecarl's tale, suddenly felt as though a cold shadow had swept over the inn. The creaking of the ropes and the squeal of the winch, the plash of the water as it lurched back and forth in the bucket, made it difficult to hear sounds from outside the walls, yet he almost felt that he had heard that cry, *that* cry, that he had first heard in the wooded valley below the Thonarberg.

He turned at once and went through the passageway to the common room of the inn, seeking Molly. After a moment he saw her across the room crowded with pilgrims, talking earnestly to Osbert. Nemain came up to him.

"Did you hear it?" he asked, his eyes wide and staring.

"I did not," she said. "There is a mort of noise here within; but it troubled me naetheless, and Herself says she felt it in the floor, through the soles of her feet. We are to do the round of the walls, with Jack and Ernald and others, and some dogs."

They stood together and watched as Osbert bent his head to listen to Molly, nodded, pursed his mouth, put his hand around and absently fondled the hilt of a knife sheathed behind his back. Hob fidgeted; he felt that he would jump from inside his skin if they did not do something, anything. He turned to Nemain.

"I got these from the pantler," he said distractedly. He opened his pouch and showed her the almonds. "His name is Tilred, he's a friend to Herself." He hardly knew what he said. "I'll come with you, about the walls."

She put her hand in and took a rough half of the nuts, transferring them to her own pouch. She squeezed his wrist affectionately. She smiled at him; but then her eyes shifted past him, at the door to the courtyard, and thence to the world outside, and her face closed down.

A SHORT WHILE LATER, Jack went out in the gathering dusk to the courtyard and came back with the war hammer at rest on his shoulder. Ernald and Matthew, each carrying an ax, were waiting in the little passage from the pantry to the hall, trailed by a pair of tall rough-coated hounds of brindled gray. Part deerhound, their ancestor had traveled with a party down from Scotland on embassy to the English court. The Scots had paused at the inn in the elder Ernald's time long enough for their deerhound to give a distinctive cast to later generations of Osbert's house dogs. Yet these were mixed enough that they did not violate the prohibition against keeping Scottish deerhounds: this fell on any person of lesser estate than an earl. These hounds were kept apart from the grim mastiffs who made up Osbert's night watch. The lean dogs, five in all, had the free run of the inn; they were whistled up when the men of the household went hunting.

The women had shed their veils as though preparing for exertion, and went bareheaded, an unusual sight when the troupe was among others, although grandmother and granddaughter were, on the road, more casual in their dress than was common. Molly had plaited her hair into a single braid, and it hung far down her back, and so had Nemain. With the hair pulled back so severely from their faces, they seemed to Hob to be stern and powerful, even young Nemain, and somehow remote.

The two women, Jack, and Osbert's sons went out the postern door in the side of the gate, with Hob trailing after the party. The little group crossed the narrow run between inner and outer walls and went through the outer gate. Slowly they walked the perimeter of the inn. The early evening was crisp and still. They stayed close to the weather-silvered logs of the outer wall that ran around the sides of the inn buildings and the front wall of the courtyard. Dry dead vines crunched underfoot and caught at their ankles; the nimble Matthew went ahead, pulling the occasional tangle of low brush and vine roots aside with his ax till the women passed.

At each corner of the compound Molly and Nemain paused, and stood side by side, eyes wide, faces strained, listening, listening. They sniffed the air, they turned about, they scanned the forest. Hob watched in fascination. An erratic wind blew this way and that; it moved the brindled fur along the hounds' shoulders. Down the women's backs the two braids, one red, one silver-shot gray, swayed and twitched in the currents of air, like two panther tails. The dogs looked where the two Irishwomen faced, but soon, after the way of dogs, became bored: one sat down and bit with explosive savagery at a spot on his left hind leg, chasing an itch along toward his foot; the other began investigating the base of the wall, to see if anyone of interest had left urine there recently.

Ernald hawked and spat. "Is there nowt, then, Mistress?" he asked Molly. His tone was polite, but he seemed as bored as the hounds.

"There is nothing," she said, and then, still looking away into the woods, reached sideways and took Ernald's arm firmly, "but be said by me, there was something hunting along our trail not a sennight since, and should it come here, see you and yours are within the gates." She shook him gently. "Do not be slighting it, Ernald, great strong lad that you are and brave as a bear: it is something terrible, that no one should run to meet."

THE COMMON ROOM was awash in noise when they returned. Most of the pilgrims had been shown their sleeping quarters, had left their bundles, not without some trepidation, and were now returned, hungry and thirsty and voluble. A log fire roared in the great hearth. The fireplace was tall enough for a man to walk into and stand upright, with two cauldrons swung on iron dogs out into the flames and a small pig on a spit turned slowly by a young boy.

The wayward smoke and grease of generations, whatever had not escaped up the chimney, had blackened the deep beams of the ceiling. Osbert's two daughters threaded their way among the tables with jacks of ale, and by the evidence of laughter and talk and empty bumpers before them, the pilgrims were no pack of sickly drinkwaters. Some villagers and carters and a pair of the shire-reeve's men were mingling with the pilgrims. Across the room Hob could make out Aylwin's jovial booming tones, and even the phrase "three finest glovers in Carlisle."

More of the local countryfolk were drifting in. A rangy farmer brought a sack of wool halfway into the great room before Osbert sent him back into the courtyard. With so little to do on the farm during these long winter nights, there was a deal of heavy drinking, and many folk from the farms and the village met for the evening at Osbert's Inn. Osbert kept a score of alewives from the farms and homes around busy supplying his buttery.

Out in the courtyard, a housecarl took delivery of the sack, and the lanky villager went back into the inn and up to Osbert, who had retrieved his tally stick from a few score of similar sticks that hung by threads against the wall behind a counter. Osbert reached behind his back and, from a sheath thrust through his belt, drew forth his knife: a surprisingly big knife, a real sax, fully a cubit long and useful in diverse ways, some more pleasant than others. With this he made several nicks on one edge of the flat tally stick: that was for the villager's credit for the wool. The other side showed deductions for the spirits Osbert served him. Hob wondered how the innkeeper knew which person each stick represented. As he studied the cluster of sticks hanging up, it came to him that each stick had different knots in the thread that held them to the little projections whittled in the log wall, but he could not see how Osbert remembered which sequence of knots identified this or that person.

A large group of villagers arrived, and then another, and now the room was nearly full. Hob was making his way toward Molly to ask her what he should do next, when Nemain's hand closed on his sleeve. Her eyes were bright; she was excited; she had gone from the stern distant priestess of an hour ago, pacing the inn's boundaries and scanning the woods for questing evil, to the mischievous young girl of last summer.

"Quick, they're taking the dogs to the walls, you should see them, I saw them last time, a whole pack black as Crow Babd and any one of them bigger nor Culann's hound, him that Sétanta killed."

"Who?" asked Hob. "Who?"

But she was pulling him toward the door that opened onto the courtyard.

FIVE BURLY HOUSECARLS issued forth from the kennels with ten of the half-wild dogs on braided leather leads, the biggest dogs Hob had ever seen. The mastiffs' necks were encircled by broad leather collars with small square iron plates sewn into them. These protected the dogs' necks from injury by beast or burglar—or by one another, in the occasional disputes over precedence that arose among them. The dogs pulled strongly toward the gates and one of the housecarls slipped a bit on an icy patch, lurching upright and yanking back on the leather to chasten the dogs he held.

Another of Osbert's men swung the gates partly open to allow them through, and now Hob understood the double wall and the narrow alley that ran around Osbert's Inn. They streamed through the gate into the narrow run between the inner and outer wall and the handlers slipped the leashes off, and retreated into the courtyard, closing and locking the big gates.

Later Hob would see, as groups of villagers set off for home, how the two leaves of the inner gates just filled the width of the run when opened fully. This enabled Osbert's housecarls to seal the dogs off from the gateway when guests left or, more rarely, to admit a late traveler who pulled the bellrope by the outer gates.

The dogs pelted off into the darkness, running the complete circuit about the inn one or two times in sheer exuberance. Hob went close to the grille in one of the gates, where he could see them racing past in a long file. Nemain came up beside him. He was struck by the way they never gave tongue.

"Why are they so silent?" he asked her.

"Master Osbert and his men train them to check their voices

entirely, the while that they're in the run, and to circle the ring all the night, some running, some resting. And any that come over the wall from without, won't they be rending him to bits, and then *eating the bits*." She said this with such ferocious enthusiasm that he had to turn away from the loping stream of night-black dogs and regard her for a moment. The color was high beneath her translucent skin; her mouth was set in a hard grin; she peered eagerly through the grille. Sometimes it was as though another person showed for a moment beneath her skin: someone older; someone used to command; someone harsh-handed and unforgiving.

After a time the mastiffs settled down, some throwing themselves to the ground and panting, some lifting a leg to mark the inner or outer wall. Yet all night long, at any hour, at least two of them were moving about in a restless circling of the inn. The ticking of their claws on the frozen earth echoed from the walls of the run, faint and sinister sounds in the darkness.

Tales of the inn's eerie guardians had spread through the shire, and over the years there had been only a few thieves hardy enough to attempt to steal from Osbert atte Well's storehouse, and these now were dead.

THE FIRE GRUMBLED and crackled in its stone cave. The common room was full, and Osbert's daughters, now abetted by several of Osbert's men and maids, were weaving in and out between the tables, laden with platters and trenchers and leather jacks of barley beer. The air was a rich mixture of delicious aromas, and Hob found his mouth watering.

Hob and Nemain and Jack sat at one end of a table near the fire. Molly was down by the door talking to Osbert again.

Margery atte Well whisked past their table, a short graceful woman bearing a wooden tray. On the tray a big bowl of frumenty steamed: wheat porridge in chicken broth, with egg yolks. She vanished behind a knot of pilgrims on the far side of the room. Hob's thoughts ran on how pretty she was, and how like her sister, and how Osbert told one from the other. He was wondering vaguely if, should he come to know them both, he would be able to distinguish them, when she appeared at his side. She bent to place a wooden platter on the table, a joint of mutton smoking in the middle amid trenchers of bread with heaps of pottage: in this case peas and beans boiled with garlic and a bit of fat bacon. As she straightened she caught sight of Hob.

"Well, here's a handsome lad," she said, leaning a hip against the table and looking sideways at him with a kick-the-devil grin. Her leg pressed against the side of his thigh. He had an impression of heavy-lidded dark eyes, a mane of brown ringlets beneath her thin linen veil, and, where the neckline of her shift hung away from her body, the shading of a faint winter tan into paler mystery within. He caught a bit of her scent, delicate sweat mixed with the woodsmoke that permeated everyone's garments, and for a moment he could not have spoken to save his soul. A confusion of feelings for which he lacked a name washed over him, and he sat and stared as though simple. The next moment she was gone, with a little laugh trailing after her.

"Would you ever cease a moment from your fierce courting and cut us a bit of that meat?" Nemain said in a voice dripping with honey. She wore a bland expression, but there was lemon mixed with the honey. The corners of her mouth quirked down for an instant, and then she forced herself back into a picture of blank sisterly innocence.

Hob drew his belt knife and cut her a slice of mutton, concentrating furiously on the task. He put a round of bread before her and on that the mutton.

She drew her own knife and cut a bite from the mutton, but before she ate it she regarded him for a long moment, and then to his utter surprise said kindly, "Well, you *are* a handsome lad entirely." She looked away and spoke toward the fire. "It's not that I care a traneen, mind." She turned back and addressed herself quietly to the mutton, and gave not one more glance in his direction.

AT FIRST THE PILGRIMS were clustered in one group, and the villagers drifted in and coalesced on the other side of the room, but soon the two groups began mingling. Questions were asked of the pilgrims about Carlisle—to the villagers this might as well be on the moon. The terrible tale of Brother Athanasius was recounted again and again, and the villagers crossed themselves, bright-eyed with mixed terror and fascination.

The most devout pilgrims ate and retired to the sleeping booths that Osbert had allotted them, but more of the pilgrims, to whom this was as much holiday as devotion, ate and drank and sought new acquaintance about the common room. The black-haired woman that Molly had helped went early to bed, but one of her sons was over at a villagers' table, matching ale for ale and having much to say to one of the village maids.

The noise soon became so great that when Molly returned to their table and began to speak to Jack, Hob was quite unable to hear her. Osbert's cook was an honest workman, though, and for a time Hob devoted himself to his meal, and had little attention to spare for his tablemates.

AFTER THE MEAL Molly sent Nemain and Hob out to the wagons to bring in the symphonia, the goatskin drum, and a *cláirseach,* one of the Irish harps. Jack moved a few smaller benches for them to sit on, by the side of the fireplace.

Jack took the drum; Hob seated himself with the symphonia on his lap. Molly raised a jack of barley beer and drank half of it off without stopping. She picked up her harp, and nodded to Jack. He placed the drum upright, braced on his left thigh; he whirled the short bone stick, with its knob at each end, in the fingers of his right hand; he struck up a sprightly rhythm. With that they began a series of lively country dances, Molly's strong fingers flickering over the harp strings. Nemain sat down by Jack and began clapping in a complicated pattern, sometimes with Jack, sometimes in between the booming beats of the goatskin.

The trestle tables were moved back a couple of feet on all sides; this cleared a comfortable space in the center of the long room. Some of the farm lads began a circle dance around Parnell, who twirled prettily in the center, her arms held in a sweet curve above her head, her curls flying, until her father rapped on the counter for her to take another tray.

Hob was accomplished enough by now to play the symphonia without looking at his hands. Molly had drilled them well, and Hob knew his place in each piece they played. He watched Molly for her signals, as did the other two, but he was able to look around now and then, to watch the dancing, the tables with their talking, gesticulating people. Hob was unused to so many people in one place, and here there were at least two score.

More and more he followed the progress of Margery among the tables. She seemed to give off a kind of dark glow as she passed back and forth among the generally more fair and ruddy villagers.

The dance they were playing ended. Nemain, in the moment of relative quiet, leaned toward him.

"I've heard some of the folk of the place say that 'twas their mother they took their looks from, the lasses and Matthew, and she having dark-fairy blood."

Hob blushed to be caught out so easily. But as they began once more to play, he found himself looking for Margery again. She seemed more enchanting the longer he watched her. He found it hard not to stare.

A young village wife, her face flushed and her gait unsteady, sat down near the players. She held a baby on her hip, and now drew a fold of her garments aside and began to nurse.

The room grew louder as the drink flowed. Several times one or two of Osbert's sons broke up quarrels; the two shire-reeve's men did not even trouble themselves to notice, for everyone knew that Osbert's Inn kept its own peace.

At one point Osbert himself came to a table that had gone from angry voices to tense silence, where two men were braced to rise, knuckles white on their knife-hilts. He leaned over and placed his two hands upon the table as though resting while he admonished the two hotheads. He spoke so quietly that Hob could not hear what he said, though the table was the next over. Osbert's forearms were almost as big as Jack's, and he let the would-be antagonists contemplate his arms, his heavy-bellied mass, and the sax sheathed at his back, and all the while speaking, first to one and then to the other, with the blandest of expressions. The men eased back on their benches, and Osbert straightened and signaled to Parnell to bring more ale. He nodded pleasantly to the villagers and went off to his other duties. Hob kept an eye on the table. The mood there was sullen for a bit, but as the strong drink asserted itself again, good humor gradually returned.

Close by Hob a housecarl appeared with a great wooden bowl and ladle and, wrapping his hand in a rag, swung a simmering cauldron on its iron dog away from the fire and into the room. Now he could the more easily fill the bowl from the cauldron. When he'd finished he took the bowl in both hands and hurried away; he left the cauldron projecting somewhat into the room, between Hob and the nursing mother. It simmered quietly, shedding a perfume of pea and lentil and mutton fat. Hob, cranking the symphonia vigorously, began to eye the cauldron, and despite his recent meal began to wonder if he might induce Osbert's scrvers to give him a small bowl.

The young mother's eyelids were drooping. The baby's mouth slipped off the nipple and the little creature began sliding off her lap, across her thigh, toward the cauldron. Hob had just time enough to realize the danger, and to begin to rise to his feet, when here came Margery from behind Hob's bench. She deftly snatched up the baby. The mother roused with a start. Margery put the baby on its mother's shoulder, took the woman's shawl and wrapped it as a sling about the baby, tied a careful knot, kissed the woman on the cheek, and was away down the room.

Scarcely four breaths had elapsed. Hob resettled himself. A kind of exalted admiration filled him. Nemain, clapping, swiveled toward him, so that the reports loudened in his ear and returned him to himself. He set his fingers to the keys and tried to find his place in the gallop of the dance again, but he no longer cared whether Nemain teased him or not. He played, but he looked out over the room, watching to see Margery pass by.

AFTER THEY HAD PLAYED several dances, everyone sprawled at ease on the benches, breathing hard and calling for Parnell or Margery to hasten before they perished of thirst. Osbert beamed at the procession of bumpers that streamed from the pantry to the great room, and made sure Molly's party never went dry. Molly quaffed off another pint of barley beer, and sent Hob out to the big wagon to fetch in the ring-and-stick.

Hob returned with a short ashwood pole and a weight. This was a crude ring of iron that had been weighed at ten pounds, and Molly handed it around to be hefted, announcing that she would match whatever they cared to wager that they could lift it as Jack did. Some of the young men from the village tossed it from hand to hand, teasing and daring one another, boasting. Molly had not been here in three years, and some of these young men had been striplings at that time. The older men warned that it was less simple than it appeared, but in their new strength all the farm lads wanted to try. Forwin and Matthew were placing bets on their hero Jack and grinning behind callused hands.

As with innkeepers all along the pilgrimage routes, Osbert was beginning to take on some of the functions of a banker: translating foreign coin into local produce, holding objects against a traveler's return, and the like. Here he marked the value of small coins the villagers wished to wager against their tally sticks, and when they lost, as was usual, he paid Molly in coin and collected in produce or labor from the local folk through the year, with a small increase for his service.

There was a short length of thong tied to the iron ring, the free end of the thong ending in a loop. Jack now laid the ash pole, an inch in diameter and three and a half feet in length, across the table. About a half inch from one end was a shallow notch cut in the wood, and about a half foot from the other end was a scorch mark.

When all had examined the iron ring to their satisfaction, Jack put his hand on the pole, on the six inches between the end and the burn mark, and Molly slipped the loop of the thong about the pole's other end, so that it settled into the notch. The iron ring now hung down on one side of the table and Jack stood at the other side, the end of the pole in his right hand.

There was a pause, then Jack's forearm muscles rippled up in a low swell, his breath hissed through his teeth, and the pole lifted slowly and smoothly, parallel with the tabletop, six inches. Jack held it there while one might count slowly to six, then lowered it steadily.

Molly held the end of the pole at the ring end while Jack turned his back on the table and took the pole again, this time in his left hand with reversed grip. He gave a little grunt and lifted the pole once more, the pole stretched out behind him. This time he bent slightly from the waist to help with the awkward angle, and the pole rose again, still straight and level with the table. Again he held it for a short while, then lowered it easily to the table.

Now Molly challenged the company: let him who could lift the stick level with the tabletop, and hold it for three breaths, and lower it smoothly, step forward and try; and double the bet for the reverse lift immediately after. A clamor arose among the local stalwarts, farm boys mostly, and one of the shire-reeve's men and even Ernald, who had failed at the attempt the last two times Molly's caravan had come by. His brothers cheered him on with good-natured malice, and then raised their bets on Jack.

Two carters, strong of body from the constant loading and unloading of cargo, placed their bets with Osbert and stepped into the line that formed by the table. Carters were often at the inn: Osbert traded his hospitality—lodging for cartmen and their beasts, security for their wains and cargo—in exchange for free transport of goods needed to supply the inn.

One by one the young men stepped up to the table. Now they discovered that ten pounds held close to the body is not at all like ten pounds a good English yard away. They grasped; they strained; usually the bar rose not at all, but sometimes it began to rise, faster at the end nearer the lifter, and wobbled, and the head sank quickly back to rest. Ernald managed to clear the table for a moment, only to have the weighted end dip and dive back downward, to hit the table edge with a sharp crack, while his faithless brothers hooted and slapped one another on the shoulders. One of the carters lost his hold entirely, and the weight and stick thumped to the rush-strewn floor on the far side, narrowly missing one of the deerhounds that lay beneath the tables. The hound bounded to its feet and scuttled aside, then turned a look of reproach on Nemain, who stood nearest the fallen weight: plainly it thought she had thrown it.

As the first contestants tried and failed, the men toward the end of the line jeered, and the first two lads looked surprised and ashamed at the difficulty. But as more and more of them struggled and huffed and cursed and failed, and laid down their copper piece before Molly or went to Osbert to borrow a coin against a mark on his tally stick, the first to lose began to recover their good cheer. That so many had not succeeded in even clearing the table demonstrated the difficulty of the feat, which had appeared so easy just a short while ago. The last few grasped the handle with a kind of grim resignation, and grunted, and joined the rest in defeat.

So the evening passed. The villagers left in two groups, one shortly after the other, and Hob wandered out after them into the cold night air to see the gates swung back by the dog handlers. They swung the gates outward, forcing the dogs back into the run, until the edge of each gate touched the outer wall, making a safe passage through the run. The outer gates were then opened, and the crowd of folk from the farms and from Bywood Old End set forth, several men bearing torches. They walked to the road and turned to the right, and were out of sight behind the trees, although for a brief time Hob could hear their calls to one another, some ragged attempts at song, and once a general burst of laughter.

The outer gates were swung shut and locked, and then the inner, which once again allowed the dogs to circle freely around the ring. Hob scurried back to the inn, glad to return to the fire's warmth. But Molly sent him right out again, along with Nemain, to return the musical instruments and the weight and stick to the wagons.

When they returned, Hob managed to wheedle a bowl of peas and lentils from the cauldron—an easy enough task, for Osbert was in a mood to coddle any of Molly's people. Molly and Jack sat drinking; the pilgrims, by twos and threes, retired for the night; after a while Molly sent Nemain and Hob off to their beds in one of the dorters.

THE DORTER, one of three sleeping rooms in the compound radiating out from the inn proper, was laid out in the old Saxon style: a fire pit ran down the center of the room, and along each of the long sides of the room was a raised platform of earth floored with wooden tiles. This platform was divided into sleeping booths, each booth closed off from its neighbors by a partition, with wool hangings across the front for privacy and warmth. Each booth was furnished with a straw pallet bed.

Osbert furnished bedclothes for an additional fee, and took no great notice of what transactions went on there between guests and the women of the village—some said even between guests and his own daughters—so long as there was no blood spilled. To scandal he turned a blind eye, and his custom increased. His wealth and influence in the region were such that no reeve molested him, and though the village priest was known to grumble bitterly, nothing more than that came of it.

With three such rooms, there were booths to spare even with the pilgrim band to accommodate. Molly and her people Osbert put at one end of a half-empty dorter, with linen bedclothes, all at house expense.

Hob had the very last booth all to himself; next to it was Molly's booth, then Nemain's, then Jack's. Despite the low fire in the pit, the air inside was chilly. He crawled into the booth and drew the curtain. He undressed and got under a blanket and threw his sheepskin coat over that. He raced through a *Paternoster,* yawning twice in the course of the prayer. After a while the air inside the booth grew warmer, if a bit stale. He was deeply tired; soon he drifted away into incoherent thought, then into dream.

He had slept only a moment, it seemed, when he was awakened by the thrashing of heavy bodies in the next booth. Molly had brought Jack into her bed. The boy lay in the booth and looked into darkness relieved only by two thin lines of faint orange light from the dying fire, creeping in at either edge of the curtain. The disorganized bumps and sighs, punctuated by Molly's murmurs, settled into a rhythmic thumping that rose slowly to a powerful galloping finish, wringing plangent half-hushed cries from Molly; her deep splendid voice echoed hollowly in the wooden booth. Jack, that silent man, was hardly heard from, save for a terminal grunt or two.

Hob, quite used to this nighttime music after so many months, found it if anything comforting, and as the nearby couple began to subside into quiet shiftings of weight, the rustle of blankets, whisperings, he grew drowsy again. But now he became increasingly aware of a pressure in his bladder. He burrowed down determinedly, but to no avail. At last he threw off the blanket and drew the curtain partway. In the half-light of the fire pit he dressed hastily, only partly awake and thereby clumsy. The knots that fastened his woolen hose to the front of his braies kept perversely coming loose. He threw his legs over the side of the sleeping platform and sat for a moment to pull on his shoes.

Hob stood up and struggled into his coat. He made his way down the long room, through the errant shoals of gray-blue smoke, to the door at the far end. This led to the courtyard. If the air within had been chilly, this was cold to snatch at the breath, especially to one warm from the bed. Hob scurried across the iron-hard dirt to the privy.

When he emerged, he realized that he was alone in the wide clear yard, visible only in the untrustworthy light of the rising gibbous moon and what small illumination, glowing through the scraped oiled hide that covered an interior window, came from fire and candle in the inn's main hall. Osbert must put his faith in the dogs, and feel no need for human sentries. This thought led Hob, cold as he was, to veer on his way back to bed, so that he might peek through the grilles in the yard doors at Osbert's gang of wolf-fierce guards on their night patrol.

The boy came up to the big doors. Already he was shivering a little as the cold slipped under his clothes. He looked through the grille, but the moon at this angle did not reach into the narrow gap between the walls; he could see nothing in the blackness beyond, unless it were a faint gleam.

Even as he bent closer, the gleam resolved itself into a dark and glinting eye, almost on a level with his own; an unseen lip lifted, revealing long curved fangs that caught the moon's rays through the grille, and a low rumbling growl of inexpressible menace came from just beyond the bars. He scrambled backward, shocked. He spun on his heel and half walked, half trotted back to the dorter, turning in a circle twice as he walked to make sure that the gate held against that terrible, just-glimpsed threat.

Back again in the comparative warmth of his bed, as his breathing slowed, he began to grin ruefully at himself. What a buffoon he must have looked! It was well for him that someone bound for the privy—what if it had been Margery?—had not crossed the courtyard at that moment. He had jumped backward like a puppy who, brashly digging at a promising hole, surprises an angry badger in its sett. What a white-liver he had seemed! He snickered a bit at his own expense; he sighed; he wriggled into a more comfortable position.

Then he sprang up, his back pressed to the rear of the booth, the hairs on his neck prickling. That brutal snarl, echoing with savage hatred, tore the darkness. By the sound of it the wolfish dog must be right outside the curtain—the gate *had been* open, then, and it had followed him into the sleeping hall, and in a moment would leap through the curtain. To think of those gleaming dagger-bones at his throat!

Did he dare to rap on the partition to wake Jack?

Jack! The next moment he had buried his face in his hands,

unsure whether to weep or laugh, or perhaps both, as he recognized Jack Brown's thunderous snarling snore. He threw himself back down on the pallet, and lay on his back staring up into nothingness. Now he was completely awake. He lay and listened to the snores; the scent of the smoky fire pit drifted in. He thought of this and that; he thought of the evening just past, of the wonder that was Margery, of the dogs circling in the frozen night.

Perhaps it was the snoring; perhaps it was the scent of the smoke. Eventually his thoughts came round to last summer, and the camp in the clearing, and the copper still, and the *uisce beatha,* and Molly's tale.

CHAPTER 6

AST YEAR, AT THE BEGIN-
ning of June, Molly had gotten a load of barley beer from
a nearby farmer, another of her admirers, and set up
her still in a woodland glade near a lake fed by two
brooks. There they had spent a few weeks, swimming and fishing and working at the task of making the *uisce beatha,* the lifewater that Molly drank
and sold and used in her medicines. Molly had them
feeding the fires, and watching the great copper pots
that traveled slung from the third wagon, and putting the thrice-distilled fierce clear liquid up in small
casks. Then more fishing and swimming, foraging
for firewood, distilling and redistilling: so the weeks
passed.

The animals grew fat, lazing about on long teth-
ers with little work to do. Jack and Hob turned brown

and Nemain turned red, her nose peeling, and Molly stayed out of the sun when she could, with incomplete success.

Now on this day, with June three-quarters gone, they were well established in the forest glade: cloth awnings stretched from the roofs of the wagons to tent pegs and a permanent campfire was ringed with stones from the brooks and the lake shore. Hob had been fishing by himself at lakeside, using what Jack had given him: iron-forged hooks, a couple of lengths of nettle-hemp line, and a stone weight for a sinker. He had caught a fine string of fish, which he swung now on a line threaded through their gills. As he passed through the bars of sunlight slanting into the clearing, the fish scales twinkled: a metallic glistening, then dark again. Nemain sat sewing a little cloth bag. She looked up, startled at the flash of fish scale; when she realized what he had caught, she dropped her sewing and clapped her hands, grinning.

Hob squatted by the small fire and began to clean the fish; Nemain finished her sewing and put the little cloth bag into her pouch. A muffled gasp made Hob look around; across the clearing he saw Molly's big wagon begin to sway from side to side. Molly's graceful forearm, all silky white, lay along the window bottom beneath the edge of the leather shade; her hand, strong and comely, gripped the sill hard. The whole wagon was soon rocking, and Molly's throaty cries were only slightly muffled by the wagon walls. Hob handed Nemain a few of the cleaned fish, and she put them beside her on a tray of leaves.

"They're at bulls and cows again," said Nemain, stripping a long twig of its leaves and threading it through one of the fish. She sounded pleased enough. "They've been at it the while you were fishing."

Hob took a small branch from beside the fire and bent to poke at the burning wood to give it more air. Nemain leaned forward swiftly and dropped a fish down the back of his shirt. Hob yelped and leaped up, then performed a rapid series of contortions, holding his shirttails clear of his body, until the fish slapped onto the dirt at the ashy border of the fire. He seized the fish tail and stood up, holding the fish like a weapon, and circled the fire with slow menace, but as Nemain scrambled up and ran giggling into the woods, he began to sprint.

He cornered her against a tree almost immediately: she could not run for laughing. He intended to drop the fish down the front of her shift. He advanced upon her with mock ferocity; she prepared to spring to either side. She feinted to his left, but he took a long step leftward, and she returned to the tree. She looked ready to bolt in one direction or another, but when he lunged at her, she remained in place.

His free hand darted toward the neckline of her smock, but by accident or design she moved slightly just at that moment, and this brought his curled hand down on the patch of bare skin by her neck. Beneath his fingers was the thin girl's sharp collarbone, and his fingertips rested in the hollow beside her throat, the flesh hot and smooth and wet with the sweat of her exertions.

Suddenly his revenge lost its appeal. He stood there an instant without moving. A stray beam of sun found its way through the forest roof; it lay across her features and her eyes glittered, green as the leaves above. Even at this time he had begun to overtop her, and now she looked up a little at him, with a most extraordinary expression on her face: mischief and mockery and a kind of burning intentness, a question. Hob could not tell what was happening between them.

The long moment passed. Then she snatched the fish and in two bounds was out of sight, running lithely through the bushes back to the camp. He did not run after her; he walked slowly back. He was acutely aware of his fingers: they felt as though they had been in very hot water, or very cold water.

When he got back to the clearing she was squatting by the fire, already beginning to grill two fish on long twigs. She grinned at him. He sat down and watched her for a moment, then began to clean the rest of the catch.

When he'd given her the last of the cleaned fish to grill, he picked up a small wooden water bucket and went down a sloping path beside the clearing. Here tree roots and the earth between them served as a crude staircase down to one of the brooks. At this point the brook widened into a rock-bottomed pool, shaded by copious fern; on the opposite bank wild roses spilled down toward the water's edge. Where the brook ran onward from the pool it tripped over rocks on its way to the lake, and the sound filled the cool dim space with a cheerful burble. Hob sank the bucket beneath the surface and hauled it up splashing and dripping. With an effort he made his way back to the clearing, pulling himself up by branches with his left hand, some of the water in the swaying bucket escaping over the rim, to wet his leg from knee to ankle.

They ate grilled fish from twigs and drank clear brook water from wooden cups. When they had done, he fumbled at the drawstring of his pouch. "I forgot," he said. "I found these for you."

Nemain gathered all sorts of small objects, as did Molly; certain stones, feathers, bone: they disappeared within Molly's wagon and sometimes Hob saw them again, woven into clothing or part of an amulet or charm that one or the other of them crafted. Hob had a feeling that old Father Athelstan would not approve; certainly they were never in the form of a cross, nor did the women ever take them to a priest for blessing. But he had come to know the sort of thing that would interest them.

Now he held them out on his hand, seven small stones from the bed of the brook he followed to the lake where he fished, blue-gray disks smoothed by the action of the stream. Wavering lines of smoky yellow circled the center of each stone. Nemain put out her hand and he poured them into her palm. She examined them minutely, holding them up to catch the sun's last rays, tracing the yellow pattern with a fingertip.

"Hob *a rún,* it's a rare eye you have," she said. She was clearly delighted, and he found himself to be absurdly proud, just because he had picked up a few brook-bed stones. Still, he was aware of a lingering sense of awkwardness. The moment against the tree lay between them: that hot wet skin, that green glance.

She said nothing more for a while, turning the stones this way and that as dusk fell and the firelight grew stronger. Then she looked up suddenly. "You're after giving me a present, and I'll be giving you one as well," she said. She drew the small cloth bag from her pouch and passed it across to him.

"What is this?"

"It's to put beneath your pillow. Smell it."

Hob put the packet to his nose. A fragrance, a complicated pleasant mixture of flowers and greenery with a strong tone of pungent yarrow, came to him. Nemain watched him slantwise.

"Put it by your head, and you'll sleep the sweeter."

He looked at it, puzzled, and then thanked her and put it in his pouch. After a while, when it looked as though the adults would not be rising at all that evening, they banked the fire and retired to their respective wagons.

Hob took off his clothes and spread blankets on the chest that served as his bed. He put the packet by his head and put his head on a rolled shirt. The perfume from the packet came to him, a pleasant soothing scent.

Across the clearing Molly cried out once, twice.

HOB AWOKE ALONE in the middle-sized wagon, with an unsettled, incomplete feeling: a dream ruptured midway, a significant revelation interrupted. He rolled over on his back and looked out the wagon window. The wooden shutter was latched back against the wagon side and the leather shade was rolled high and tied in place, despite the unseasonably cool night. He craned his neck, trying to see the stars, but the overarching branches in full leaf hid much of the sky. Fresh air played over his face, and the scent of yarrow came and went in the interior of the wagon. The lost dream nagged at him, a task left undone.

A strong golden glow moved and danced on the wagon's ceiling. He hitched himself up on one elbow to see. The fire had been built up again, and there on the other side of the clearing sat Molly, gazing into the flames, her back against a thick-bodied grandfather of an oak and a fired-clay jug by her side. Her hair was unbound, and fell forward over one shoulder in a rich gray tumble, down past her hip.

Hob took down a long linen shirt from its peg and pulled it over his head. He rolled off the chest and stumbled barefoot to the door. He was still half asleep. He swung down awkwardly from the wagon and made his way over to Molly.

He thought she might shoo him back to bed, but she said nothing. She wiped a film of perspiration from her round sun-reddened face with a wing of her shawl, though a cool night wind was moving through the broad leaves.

He stood next to her and she looked up and wordlessly patted the space beside her, on a cloth spread between the bases of two large roots. He joined her, leaning back, the bark rough against his shoulder blades. Molly put her stout arm around his shoulders and drew him to her side, smoothing the fine black hair back from his forehead.

"Is it that you can't sleep, *mo chroí*?" she said dreamily.

"I was asleep, and then I was looking out, and . . ."

Thunderous snores from Jack began to rattle through the clearing.

"Sure and there's not a creature sleeping within a league of that," she said. "Well, that's all that's left of him this night, that snore." She laughed a little to herself.

"I was dreaming, and it was, it was . . . I wanted to know what it was."

She turned a little and looked at him with more interest, although her eyes, blue as summer lake water, were low-lidded and focused on him with some difficulty.

"And what can ye bring to mind of it, at all, Hob?"

"It was . . . I forget." The fire, the wind, the trees, crowded in on the memory of the dream; it flew apart like the steam from Molly's kettles. He squinted across the clearing. "It was something that was, that was white, that gleamed, it was a gleam of white, and something else, something red. I wanted to know what, what—it was something important and I wanted to know, but I, I can't . . ."

"You men," said Molly, to Hob's delight. "You men never remember your dreams." She took a sip from the jug. "Jack, now, says that there's never a dream he remembers on waking, it's like a black sea he jumps into each night. You can learn from dreams: what was, or what's to come. But what's forgotten is no help at all."

Beyond the fire's yellow circle the moon threw patches of pale light where it made its way through the net of heavy branches. Close by, an owl gave voice to a startling series of barking screeches. The snores paused an instant, then resumed, a snarling undercurrent to the crackling of the fire, the pop of sap in a too-new twig thrown in with last winter's dead logs. Wisplets of smoke played in amid the flames, as though reluctant to join the main upwelling cloud.

Something about the snoring reminded Hob of Jack's harsh difficult speech. The encircling arm, the stroking hand, Molly's warm bulk, relaxed him, and made him bold. "Mistress," he asked, "what happened to Jack's neck?"

Now, he thought, *I'll be sent off for being the curious mouse at the larder.*

But Molly tilted the jug up again. From the side of his eye, Hob watched the thick shapely throat quiver as she swallowed, swallowed again.

"Well, I'll tell you some of it, *mo chroí*." Beads of moisture stood out on her forehead. A few damp silver locks had tumbled over her eye, and she pulled them back and tucked them behind her ear.

"Jack Brown was in the Holy Land. He was carrying a pike for Sir Baldwin, he being the castellan of Aiglemont, when that knight went on pilgrimage. Our Jack was one of sixteen in Sir Baldwin's company, and they traveling along with a whole train of others, pilgrims and men-at-arms on their way down to Jerusalem, and baggage wagons, and the Templars their shepherds on that stretch of road. It was some road of the old Roman folk they were on, dust and dry hills all around, and the heat terrible late in the day as it was, and didn't the Moors come at them in a rush, one minute nowhere and the next down upon them."

"The Moors are the Devil's followers, Mistress?"

"Something like," she said, and drank again. "Cruel dark men, on horses fast as thaw-water. With curvy swords like sickles, only with the edge outwards, if you see what I mean."

With Molly's lilt in his ears and the shifting firelight in his eyes, Hob seemed to see the clouds of dust, the column of wayfarers, the sun's beams stuttering along the polished lance heads. Pictures came to him as though he were watching, from a mountain ledge, the dwellers in a valley far below: clearly seen but very small, and not quite real.

THE FIRST ATTACK swept along the column like a Syrian sparrow hawk stooping at a snake. White cloaks billowed out behind the lean dark horsemen; the burning desert sun flashed and sparkled on the storm of scimitars; the riders in their quilted tunics were shouting what Jack had come to learn was "God! God is great!" in their rapid rattling speech. An uproar began at the rear by the baggage wagons, swelling toward Jack's position in the center of the march, in which was mixed the wails of pilgrims and the clank of colliding metal and the skeeking of wooden whistles as the sergeants tried to rally a defense.

Jack and his comrades had a scant moment to snatch at swords and war hammers, and to swing their short kite-shields around from behind their backs. All was confusion on the instant, the pikes out of reach in one of the wagons, no time for forming up. Jack got his sword out and swung his shield up just in time to parry a whistling slash at his head, stabbed ineffectually at the horse, then braced for the next rider, who passed him by but cut Leofric next to him crosswise, left shoulder to right waist, smooth as silk, and then was gone.

Another blur of striped tunic and white turban, a glimpse of narrowed black eyes, a prominent nose, and Jack hacked at the rider's thigh and felt the bite of the sword blade into meat, but the horse carried the brown man on away and then the greater part of the fighting was on up the line.

Jack looked around. Leofric was plainly beyond all help; Jack turned away and set himself, braced for the next assault.

Three more times the Saracens circled and raced up the column on their swift beautiful horses, the delicate hooves kicking up clouds of dust. The wind was picking up, too, and raising more dust and loose sand from the dry burnt land. The riders came a fourth time, out of the wind, and Jack had to squint against the grit that stung his eyes and half blinded him.

The day steadily darkened and the wind began to sing. The moving air ripped the top layer from the land and threw it against the stalled caravan and still the bronze men came, wave upon wave. Jack's throat was so dry that it burned. He set his back against an open-top wagon and hunched behind his shield, lunging whenever a rider loomed up out of the murk. He could not see a yard to either side, and the cries of his comrades came dimly above the blare of the gale. He was alone in a tan blankness.

The sand flung by the storm against his unprotected face and hands was beginning to wear away bits of skin, and his hands were oozing blood from dozens of tiny cuts. There was shouting toward the distant front of the procession, and the hissing ring of steel upon steel, the thud of mace upon flesh, a horse screaming, but nearby was only the moan and shriek of the wind, the gritty patter of sand upon his boiled-leather gambeson. He peered through the dun haze. There was nothing.

There was nothing, and then there was the Beast. It came bounding out of the brown clouds on all fours, and Jack's stomach turned to ice as he saw the big dark broad-backed shape hurtling toward him: massive black-furred limbs, a naked leathery breast, hands folded into fists the size of Jack's head, the knuckles pounding along the ground, a bestial mask of anger, fangs like a demon, and yet it was like a man and yet, yet, it was *not* a man.

The next instant it had slammed him against the wagon, his left arm pinned beneath the great body pressing against the shield, his sword somewhere in the dirt. From the shadow beneath a heavy shelf of bone, little red eyes bored horribly into his; black lips drew back from yellow canines, two inches long. A scorching breath was on his face, a salty animal reek in his nostrils. Giant hands gripped his arms and shook him like an infant; his chin rattled against his collarbone and he felt himself sinking into a dazed lassitude. His head lolled back and he felt the rim of the wagon's side at the back of his neck and he looked up into the roil of brown cloud in a stupor, a vast weight on his chest crushing the air from his body.

A searing pain at the side of his throat broke the dreamy paralysis of his limbs. He tried to scream but had no breath. He managed to draw up his right leg, and his right hand scrabbled at his calf, groping for the dagger strapped there. He drew the foot-long blade, struck blindly at the demon's side. It was like striking a young oak, but the thing sprang back. Jack fell groaning to the ground and scrambled beneath the wagon, chest heaving and throat a bloody mess.

He felt a hand close on him, just above his foot. Jack was a powerful man himself, and had wrestled Jack White and other burly men on feast days on the grassy field to the west of his village, but he had never felt anything like this grip crushing down on his ankle. The Beast began to drag him from beneath the wagon bed as though he were a child. Somewhere the wind howled and the shouts and clang of battle echoed, but beneath the wagon Jack was sunk in a soundless sobbing nightmare, his fingers digging into the sandy soil as an arm, thick as his own thigh, drew him slowly toward those drooling tushes.

He kicked back ineffectually with his free leg. He saw the wagon bed moving backward above him and then he was drawn inexorably from beneath its shelter. He heard a trumpet sounding, faint with distance. He could hardly hear it above the wind and the pounding of the blood in his head. The pounding grew louder and then louder and he realized that it was outside him, and a knot of Templars came barreling up the line, pitiless men on huge horses, appearing out of the whirling sands, the red cross stark against the dull gleam of battle-stained white surcoats. The horses' broad breasts smashed into the Beast, tumbling it under the heavy iron-shod hooves as they thundered past. The chargers, big as twenty-hundredweight draft horses, barely missed a stride. Jack was free.

Jack saw the demon for a moment, collapsed in a tangle of massy limbs, before the dust obscured it. Blood from his throat soaked the shoulder of his shirt beneath the gambeson. He pulled off his helmet. He ripped the kerchief he wore beneath the helmet from his head and jammed it against his neck.

He managed to roll over on his belly and crawl under the wagon again before lying still. He was unable to move further, and he lay there gasping and spitting with the sand blowing into his mouth, until the roaring in his ears grew louder than the roaring of the wind, and he fainted.

When the attack had been driven off, Jack was found beneath the wagon, barely alive. When he was well enough to ask cautiously, much later, concerning the Beast, no one could remember seeing anything like such a creature. There was only the blood-blackened sand; the battered wagons, some burnt; the bodies of two or three of the fine-boned Arab horses; and scores of Christian and Saracen corpses, some of the latter so badly trampled by the Templar destriers with their spike-studded horseshoes that they were naked and unrecognizable.

MOLLY PAUSED, and drank again from the jug.

"And they never saw the Beast again?" Hob prompted.

"They did not, surely."

"And did he ever go on to the Holy City, Mistress?"

"He went to the lip of his own grave and that's no mistake. The Knights of St. John got him well enough to come home, but he was sore sick for a long weary time. There was little enough left of Jack when he found me at St. Audrey's Fair at Ely. You've seen the wee bag about his neck?"

"Yes. He let me see inside it once, Mistress," Hob said.

Jack wore a thong about his neck, from which depended a little leather bag, and he took it off only when they went swimming in the hot part of summer. Hob had asked Jack about it one day, and the silent man had opened it to show him. Within were several small bunches of dried herbs, each tied with a lock of Molly's silver hair, and a little wooden figurine of a seated man, legs folded, with antlers growing from his head; in his hands he held out two serpents, whose heads were those of curl-horned rams.

"By the herbs in that bag, by potions I brew him up, by the power of the Horn-Man, Lord of the Beasts and a powerful god he is, Jack's relieved of the fevers he had from the bite of that Beast. Sure and had he not found me that feast day, there'd be no more Jack." She gave a little laugh deep in that soft white throat. "He's man enough now, though, and a bit to spare."

But Hob had seized on something she'd said. "Another God? Besides Jesus and the Father and the Spirit, Mistress?" Hob had a sudden vision of the old priest who had raised him, hands thrown up in horror.

"There are gods older nor the Christ," Molly said. "And before the first god was the first woman." She patted herself complacently between her legs.

Seeing him staring in amazement, she grinned and added, "Well, someone had to give birth to the world." She drank again and belched softly, the sweat standing out on her upper lip.

"And no, he never came into Jerusalem, the poor man, and him as decent a kern as ever shouldered a pikestaff."

After a while the breeze picked up a bit, making the flames flap, making sparks spit from the tops of the yellow tongues, and setting the leaves rustling, a drowsy sound. Soon thereafter Molly sent Hob off to his bed in the wagon.

He watched her from his window for a while as she sat against the tree, now and again sipping from the jug. The fire crumbled into ruddy embers; the moon's rays filtered through the trees, reasserting themselves with the waning of the firelight, and picking out the streaks of silver in Molly's gray mane. He lay back down. He thought of Jack, and the Holy Land, and the Beast.

Hob had heard tales of other monsters around other campfires, but he had never seen the very wound made by one. It was hard to imagine something beside which Jack would be as a child; so far Hob had never encountered anyone who was even Jack's equal in strength. It was unsettling. The sweet summer scents of green life, tinged with woodsmoke, drifted in at the window, to mingle with the fragrance from Nemain's packet; the wind murmured in the trees; but he lay wide-eyed, and it was long before he could sleep.

He did sleep at last, but he dreamed, and in his dream were two green eyes, a forest glade, an enigmatic challenge.

CHAPTER 7

OLLY SHADED HER EYES WITH her hand and looked west over the stable roof. She and Osbert stood together in the inn yard.

"You have the right of it, it *is* a fair day, and myself the more impatient to be away; for all things are inconstant, and of all inconstant things, it's only the weather that's more faithless nor a man with a maid," she said. Osbert had been urging her to stay, at least for a fortnight or two. Hob loitered nearby; he was silently praying that Osbert might succeed. He had no wish to part from the enchanting Margery, though he had done nothing but worship her from across the room.

"Snow is coming: the smell of it is on the wind. A few days to let that terrible thing pass off, that's surely well done, but another sennight and we'll be caught by the snows, and ourselves deep in the woods, and then it's wolves and who knows what else that we'll be surrounded by."

Osbert shook his head sadly and scuffed at the unyielding frozen dirt and ice of the yard. "Ye can stay the year, Molly, and longer if ye've a mind to, ye know that. There's Jack, sithee, but still—"

Molly put a hand on his chest and he fell silent. She looked in his face, and she left her hand on his heart and said, "It's a good-hearted man you are, Osbert *a rún,* and a strong-backed man as well; it's rare that a woman finds both, and here's a welcome offer that you're making me. But my business is drawing me on, and someday it will be drawing me back across the sea; and you are Osbert of Osbert's Inn. Would you be leaving it?"

After a moment he shook his head slowly.

"Nor can I see you happy away from it." She took her hand away. "And you yourself have said it: there is Jack."

IT TOOK THEM ANOTHER DAY to get everyone ready to take the road again; Osbert's Inn was a place that folk were reluctant to leave. At last Molly's beasts, well fed and rested, were hitched to the wagons. It was already past noon. Farewells had been said, and now Aylwin strode here and there with a sort of cheerful officiousness, chivying the pilgrims into a semblance of marching order. Hob noticed the black-haired woman, Haunild, with her sons, standing easily with a staff in her hand: under Molly's ministrations her condition seemed to have improved markedly. Three of the lean rough-coated hounds were threading their way back and forth through the group, caught up in the general excitement. One began to bark, and a moment later was answered by a horrifying eruption from the mastiffs' kennel, a deep bellowing chorus that froze all the travelers in place for a moment. Almost immediately there came the raised voices of the grooms, a crack or two of a dog whip, and gradual subsidence into quiet.

Aylwin straightened slowly: he had dropped into an instinctive crouch when the roar of the night-watch dogs had burst upon the air. He signaled to Molly that they were ready to go.

She began to climb to her place on the first wagon, then quickly backed down again and went to the center wagon where Nemain sat, reins in hand. Molly went straight to the rear door and clambered inside.

In a moment she reemerged from the little wagon with a small clay pot, bound in straw and sealed with beeswax. Hob was at his post by Milo's head, lead rope in hand. Molly took the rope from him and gave him the little pot. "Quick now, child, run in and give this to Tilred in the pantry. Tell him this is for his daughter; 'tis that of which we spoke the other night."

"Yes, Mistress."

She turned away. She slipped the lead rope into a notch on the wagon's footboard and prepared again to mount to the wagon seat, and Hob set off across the courtyard. One of the hounds decided to escort him and then, with canine perversity, sat down abruptly to scratch, right in Hob's path, almost tripping him. Hob gave an awkward hop over the oblivious dog, holding grimly to his fragile burden, and tottered a few steps till he regained his balance.

He found Tilred in the fragrant pantry—smoked hams, the sweetish scent of spilled beer, spices!—and gave him the clay pot. He then had to listen to Tilred's insistence, at great length, that Hob remember to convey thanks, effusive thanks, to Molly. Hob fidgeted, feeling a mounting impatience, knowing that she awaited his return. Finally he was free, another double handful of almonds in his pouch. He hurried through the enclosed walkway—the brooms were gone, but not the rope coils nor the tattered cloak, which looked as if it would hang there till Gabriel called all to rise again.

As he reached the door to the courtyard Margery was bustling in. He stepped aside, his back to the wall, to allow her past, but she strode right up to him, put her palms flat on either side of his face, and kissed him full on the lips. He stared, astonished, into her eyes, warm and merry, the rich deep brown of fine-grained wood.

"Haste tha back to me, ma bonny wanderer," she said with a laugh, perhaps teasing, perhaps not. She whirled away and was off into the common room before he could think what to do or say. He stood there: his mind was blank, but a great chime of happiness rang through his body.

From without came the sound of farewells, the rumbling of wagon wheels. He pushed himself away from the wall and walked out into the pale winter sunlight, the bite of the crisp winter air. His heart was singing within him. He caught up with Molly's wagon and she handed him down the end of Milo's lead rope. The gates had been flung wide and the pilgrims were streaming out, and he marched after them toward the opening.

Just before they sallied out, Hob turned around, walking backward a few steps, and scanned the courtyard. There stood Osbert and his sons, and some of the housecarls, waving, but neither of Osbert's daughters. He thought, as he had not for a long while, of Father Athelstan, standing in the middle of the village street and signing a blessing after Molly's retreating wagons, looking small and old, and somehow a little forlorn. Osbert atte Well, great strapping Osbert, master of the inn, yet had something of that lost look, as he bade Molly farewell. Hob swung about; he struck a brisk pace; in a moment he passed through the gates and so led Milo forth from the double walls of Osbert's Inn.

THEIR PATH AT FIRST took them eastward, toward Bywood Old End, but before they reached that little village they turned onto a broad track that led southward. Along this early stretch they passed some small stands of uncleared timber, and then the three great fields cultivated by the villagers of Bywood Old End: one left fallow; one planted to winter wheat and other fall plantings; one awaiting the spring planting of oats and barley, peas and beans.

The fields were divided among the villagers, so that they looked like the blankets sewed from scraps by the grandmams in Hob's old village: square furlongs and long narrow selions, all set this way and that to follow the runoff of rainwater, with triangular gores where the land was too irregular to fit into the larger pattern. Different villagers owned each piece, and those who owned more than one had their bits of property scattered here and there among their neighbors' patches. The borders of each patch, narrow strips of unplowed land, formed a pattern like the stitching of a quilt.

Hob swung along after the pilgrims, amusing himself by counting the furrows in each selion or furlong. He thought that the fields made a brave sight, and that the cold wind was refreshing, and that everyone he met was his friend. Margery's kiss still tingled on his lips, and the world was beautiful to him.

The fields were on each side of the road, and wooden fences ran along on either hand. They came upon a party of villagers engaged in winter work: refashioning a stretch of the fence that had fallen into disrepair. Most of them had been at the inn the night before, and some of the pilgrims lingered to say farewells. As Hob drew abreast there was a burst of laughter; the pilgrims, becoming aware of the oncoming wagons, moved off; the villagers, leaning on the rail with their mallets grounded, glad to stop work for a bit, touched their foreheads to Molly. They hailed Jack with a torrent of good-natured teasing about his feats of strength. There was much wordplay on his prowess with a weighty stick or shaft. Jack just waved and grinned: his throat would allow no more.

Gradually even Milo's pace, plodding but exceedingly steady, was enough to leave behind the last strip of farmland, the last stretch of fencing, and the trees closed in again. The day was bright but cold; the wind alternately strengthened and faltered. The trees on both sides of the track would stand straight as the wind died away. Then the treetops would again begin to bow and sway, and a moment later Hob would hear the skritching of the topmost branches and their tiny twigs, uncountable as stars, rubbing against one another. Finally the moving air would reach the boy, stinging his cheeks and whipping his fine black hair about, till he drew up his hood and held it close around his face.

Off a little way into the woods to the east, a movement caught his eye: two tiny roe deer in their winter coats of pale gray-brown. The pair had been foraging along the forest floor, picking through the sparse winter fare. Now they looked back at him as though fearless, or else fear-dazed. An instant later they turned and fled, barking their alarm. For a moment he could see their rumps flashing white here and there through the brush; then they were deep in the forest, hidden by the intervening trees.

AFTER A BIT the road widened and the trees fell back, giving way to a border of brush along the roadside. A few paces later they came to a clearing, an irregular oval from which three paths led generally southward. Molly had instructed Aylwin to take the leftmost path, which ran southeast down to Dickon's Ford; the last pilgrims to turn onto this path were just leaving the clearing as Hob came into it. The right-hand path led southwest, terminating at one of the little deep-woods villages; the middle path also went to Dickon's Ford, but by a somewhat more toilsome route.

Hob led the way into the leftmost path and the forest closed in again. The cold was piercing, but the boy's spirits remained high, and he strode along briskly, although with a wary eye on the treacherous surface of the road, a mixture of frozen dirt, frozen snow, and gray ice, rutted and trampled by previous passersby. His breath was smoking in the crystal air. His free hand in its wool glove held his hood close about his face. The moisture from his breath began to soak into the glove, and soon the world smelled like wet wool, and he was forced to switch hands.

The pilgrims could be heard ahead, but they remained out of sight. Hob looped the lead rope around his elbow and banged his gloved hands together to knock off the ice crystals forming from his breath. A little hedge betty or dunnock, pecking about the ground for stray seeds now that the summer's insects were nowhere to be found, darted up to a low-drooping branch, startled by the dull report of Hob's clap. It gave a series of staccato peeps, an alarm. After a moment it calmed to the point where it could venture its usual sweet warble, although Hob fancied he could still hear a note of reproach.

The road bent sharply around an upjut of rock; here the left side of the road rose somewhat while the right sank, and from behind Hob came a *screek* as the wagon slid sideways a bit on the icy surface. But the path's ruts, made when the dirt was wet in the autumn rains and now frozen into permanence, prevented any skid from progressing too far. In a moment the irregular bangs and thuds of the wheels grinding over the ice ridges resumed, but the squealing stopped. One of Hob's tasks in the morning was to work lard into the axles of all the wagons. The axles might protest a bit when first they set off, but soon the heat of friction softened the lard and worked it in, and for the most part Molly's wagons ran smoothly.

Hob settled into a kind of half-awake march, whereby he ignored his discomfort, and watched the walls of forest slowly move past. For a while he observed his surroundings—red squirrels chasing one another down and around the trunk of a pine; the little dragbelly tracks or half-collapsed tunnels left by voles in the snow; the flutter of two tree sparrows about a recessed pocket in the stone, halfway up a crumbling outcrop of rock. Soon, though, he slid gently into dreamy reveries, in one way or another revolving around Margery.

The road began to rise gently, and the wagon wheels slipped and caught, slipped and caught, on an unusually smooth length of purchase-less ice. "Hob, a bit of ash," said Molly, and he shook himself loose from the memory of Margery's mouth on his, a change of attention that jarred like cold water on the skin. He dropped back to lift the tight-woven bag of cold fireplace ashes from its peg on the side of the wagon. He moved up forward again and began to strew ashes here and there on the ice, providing a bit of grit for the wheels to bite.

A flock of chaffinches sported in the skeletal winter branches of the roadside bushes, chasing one another, their white wing bars flash-ing as they dove in and out of the labyrinth of twigs, a great deal of loud descending song, and often the cry: *spink! spink!* A handful of sparrows were in amid the flock, and a lone brambling with its white rump. Hob threw another handful of ashes and the birds exploded upward from the bushes to the lower branches of the trees; as the wagons moved past, they began to drift back down, the bolder first, then the more timid. By the time Jack passed them they were as raucous as before.

The air had become calm again, although very cold. Hob heard the wind beginning to murmur in the treetops, and reached a hand to pull his hood tighter about him, but after a moment realized that the trees were motionless above him, and that the murmur was unvarying. The southeast-trending path now curved to the left, running due east for a short stretch, which ended where the pilgrims awaited them, clus-tered by the bank of the Dawlish, whose mumble Hob had mistaken for the wind.

*   *   *

DICKON'S FORD was the only convenient crossing of the chilly little Dawlish, which, although more a large stream than a river, ran too deep elsewhere to cross safely.

The stream ran fast and shallow here over a bed of slate. The water sped in silver sheets over the wide plates of gray-blue stone, bunching up into low ripples where it traversed irregularities in the rock. When it ran through the little chutes between the edges of the slabs or dropped a few inches from one level to the next, the water foamed into white, but generally the rock bed lent it a dark, almost black color.

The Dawlish, as folk hereabout called it, was one of many brooks and rivers so named throughout England. Molly said it meant "black stream" in the old British tongue that was cousin to her own. She was drawn to such bright bits of knowledge as a crow is drawn to bright bits of metal or mica, and like a crow she hoarded them up.

Once Hob had remarked to Jack Brown, "At whiles it seems that Herself knows some morsel about everything," and after a moment Jack had just nodded.

Now most of the pilgrims dashed across on the rocks; the men carrying the few women followed more slowly. The Dawlish here ran only six inches deep; still, shoes and hose were wet to the ankle.

Hob trudged out into the icy water, and found himself checked after a few paces. Milo had stopped at the water's edge, snorting in alarm; the ox looked at Hob as though the boy had surely made an error. Hob clucked and yanked on the lead rope, and Molly snapped the reins on Milo's back. The ox began to move onto the slate streambed, managing to convey, by the tossing of its head and something of the set of its shoulders, a palpable sense of grievance. Jack tied the mare off to a tree and helped Nemain across with the little wagon, then crossed back to bring the third wagon over.

By the time they were all up safely on the farther bank, Hob's feet had gone quite numb. The day was declining rapidly toward evening, and in any event it was necessary to build a fire to dry off their shoes and warm their feet. Molly consulted with Aylwin and decreed that they should camp for the night by the Dawlish, which would at least provide running water.

They pulled the wagons into a semicircle, the outer curve facing the wind, and Molly sent Hob and Nemain to gather armloads of dry brush, mostly dead gorse and heather. The greater part of the men went foraging for branches, and Jack and Aylwin and another of the bigger pilgrims went deeper into the woods and came back dragging a section of fallen tree, two feet in diameter and the length of a tall man.

Three fires were soon laid. Molly produced flint and steel from the last wagon, and soon little tonguelets of flame were peeping up through the twigs and brush at the bottom of the mounds of interlaced wood. The travelers stood about, huddled and stamping, as the smaller branches caught, then the larger. The wood was not entirely dry, because of all the recent snow, and there was a billowing of smoke. Soon the big log in the center blaze began to ignite, and Hob stretched his hands happily toward the heat.

Here and there a pilgrim would lean on his staff and stand on one foot; the other foot was extended toward the fire. The redolence of steaming wool and leather was now added to the aromatic scent of woodsmoke, the crisp clear air of the woods with its touch of pine, the cold-water breath of the Dawlish.

Some of the provisions packed at Osbert's Inn were brought forth; a simple meal of dark bread and onions was prepared, washed down with water from the stream. Molly carried a small barrel of grain in the last wagon, and Jack fed the animals from this: an amount insufficient to satisfy, but enough to stave off weakness for a day. Molly arranged her journeys in one- and two-day stages in winter, when there was no forage to be had. In this way she moved from station to station, friend to friend, patron to patron, for it was impossible to carry enough in the wagons to feed the three beasts.

Once again the women retired to the wagons. Jack set watches about the clearing. Hob, too young for guard duty, joined those men off watch by the fire. The boy lay down as near as he dared to the dancing yellow glare. He left his sheepskin coat on but took off his shoes and rolled himself up in a blanket, and lay staring into the flames. Behind the crackling of the fire was the mumbling Dawlish, and once the hooting of an owl, and soon a chorus of snoring from the men ranged round the fire. Hob slept, half-aware of the changing of the watch, and soon the night passed into morning.

CHAPTER 8

AWN REVEALED A HIGH ROOF of thin pearl-gray cloud, in furrows like the peasants' fields, moving slowly against the still-black treetops. The fire, now ash and ember, was built up again. Molly provided a cauldron, and the company sat to a breakfast of porridge and water and bits of the hard cheese they had taken from the inn.

They were away early, eager to compensate for yesterday's late start. Two tracks led from the ford on this side: one that went eastward, the one that Ranulf had recommended, and one that plunged south, running along the Dawlish for a while, and then swerved to the southeast, following forested clefts in the mountains, heading generally toward Durham and York. It was this latter track that they were to follow, and Molly cautioned Aylwin not to let his company of pilgrims stretch out ahead of the wagons as they had done yesterday, for the woods to the south were reported to be infested with the bandits that the king's regarders had swept from the forest north and west of Osbert's Inn.

Jack Brown then, with Nemain and Hob as interpreters and a great deal of gesticulation on Jack's part, attempted to impart a rudimentary plan of defense from attack to the unmilitary Carlisle men: a circular formation, men on the outside, staves at the ready, striking at any who came near, and women grouped within the circle of their men. The whole group was to begin a slow shuffle back to the wagons, where the women were to climb inside, the men to put their backs against the wagon sides. They were told to concentrate on defending themselves from any attack that came nigh them, and to stay where the wagons would protect their backs, and to let Jack do the main work of repelling the bandits. At this last many looked skeptical, yet none was rude enough to contradict.

FOR A TIME, as camp was broken, the travelers looked thoughtful, even glum, as they considered Jack's instruction. Soon, though, the brisk walk in the crisp winter air, the subtle winter sunlight striking down through the naked trees, the chatter of birds seen and unseen in the branches, lifted their hearts. They were in deep forest now. Imperceptibly their pace increased, increased; soon they were strung out through the woods, the earliest of the party out of sight of the wagons whenever the road curved to avoid an ancient tree or rocky outcrop.

They had been traveling only a short while, during which Hob had had to scatter ash only once, when Molly began to grow uneasy. She turned and twisted on the seat, peering in both directions into the forest.

"Hob," she said at last.

The boy came back to her and reached for the bag of ashes, thinking that she wanted more traction on the hard-packed snow.

"Nay, lad, give me the lead rope, and run forward and tell Master Aylwin to halt. His people to wait in the road, and we coming up to them. Tell him it's a bad thought I have about this road and no mistake, and it's safer we'll be together."

"Yes, Mistress." He handed up Milo's lead rope, and began to trot forward. He just had time to become aware that all the birdsong had stilled, when there was a shout from forward, where Aylwin walked with the lead pilgrims.

At that same moment Hob heard a hiss and thump behind him. He slid to a halt, and turning about saw a speckle-fletched arrow sprouting from the wagon's forward left wheel, the shaft still blurred and humming with the vibration of its spent force.

Half a heartbeat was lost to frozen surprise, and then Molly kicked the brake shut and tossed the lead rope in Hob's general direction and stood on the seat to open the forward hatch. She drew forth a bow and quiver, slung them on her shoulder, drew her skirts up a foot or two through her belt to give her legs free play, and seized the rope ladder that hung from roof to seat. She swarmed up the swaying rungs with remarkable alacrity.

The half-barrel–shaped roof of Molly's big wagon had a two-foot-wide flat strip down the center. There were rope loops fastened to the roof on either side of the walkway strip, and Molly grasped these and hauled herself to the rooftop, grunting a little. She stood up and, balancing on the walkway, began to bend a linen bowstring to her bow: an Irish bow, slightly recurved at the ends, shorter than the Welsh longbow.

The pilgrims were in disarray, but each member of Molly's troupe knew exactly where to go and what to do in such an attack. Hob's guidance with the lead rope was a help to the sweet but unintelligent Milo, but the ox would also obey the reins held by Molly, up on the wagon seat. When not in use, the lead rope was trailed back and slipped into a notch on the wagon board; the knot on the rope's end held it in the notch. Now, as Molly was gaining the roof, Hob ran back and snatched up the rope, dropped it into the notch on the fly, and continued on to the back of the wagon. Here was Nemain with a similar rope that led from the axle of her little wagon. She dropped it into a notch in the tailboard of the big lead wagon, and Hob closed a wooden clamp on it and jammed a stout oaken pin through a hole in the clamp, locking the rope in. Jack had already fastened the rear wagon to the middle one in similar fashion.

Now no bandit could seize a bridle and turn a wagon off the track, into the forest, for with all brakes set each wagon acted as an anchor to the others. The ropes were too thick to cut easily. A few moments' study of a clamp would show anyone how to free the rope, but in a battle, with Jack ranging at a fast limp around the wagons, carrying his skullsplitter war hammer, three heartbeats' distraction meant death or maiming to an attacker.

Nemain sprang through the back door into the main wagon, closely followed by Hob. Nemain went right to the war hammer in its wooden clips on the wall and lifted it free with some effort. Hob threw open a chest and gathered up eight or nine arrows. He took a coiled spare bowstring and thrust it into his pouch. The coated linen bowstring left a slight residue of beeswax on his hand and through the tumult of excitement this foolish detail bothered him: he wiped his fingers on his shirt. He slammed the chest lid shut. The two squeezed past one another, Nemain to the back door to hand the hammer to Jack, and Hob to the front hatch, to bring Molly the clutch of arrows. On his way through the wagon he stopped before a group of three shields on the walls: round targes, two feet in diameter, the center boss bearing a spike. He snatched one from the wall and skimmed it toward the back of the wagon for Nemain to pass to Jack. He pulled down the other two and tossed these through the hatch onto the wagon seat and crawled through himself, the arrows in one hand.

The noise of the attack had been muted in the wagon and now the shouts and clangs burst about his head. He heard the *snap, snap* of Molly's bow, the hum of Molly's arrows, screams from the roadside brush. One targe had a strap in addition to the arm brackets: he slung this shield over his back, to protect himself; the other he skimmed up onto the roof. He began to climb one-handed, the clutch of arrows in his right hand. The rope rungs flexed and wobbled beneath his feet, but Hob was agile and blessed with an excellent sense of balance. In a moment he was head and shoulders above the roofline.

What came into view at that moment burned itself into his heart: many years later he could still bring it before his eyes, vivid as life. Past the targe he had just thrown onto the roof, past the swell and bunch of Molly's muscular calf, white as baptismal-font marble, decorated with a little blue river and tributaries formed from broken veins, he could see a bandit, a ragged golden-bearded grim-faced man, nimbly climbing to the wagon roof, and she all unaware. One knee in its tattered green hose was braced on the roof edge, one grimy hand gripped the rope loop, and the other stretched toward Molly's ankle to topple her from her perch.

With a shout Hob summoned all his force and stabbed downward with the bunch of arrows. One arrowhead penetrated the man just behind the wrist, between the long bones of the forearm, nailing the arm against the roof; another cut the web of skin between thumb and forefinger; the rest went wide, the sharp points stuck fast into the wood.

The brigand gave a bellow of pain, and then a moment later a shriek as he wrenched his arm free, the arrow still transfixing his forearm. Molly spun about and matter-of-factly swung a kick to his jaw with her heavy wooden-soled shoe—even above the din of fighting Hob could hear the thud—and the outlaw vanished over the side.

Hob looked up at Molly. Her expression was calm, distant, emotionless as a mask, or one of the carved saints in St. Germaine's chapel. But she bent and gave Hob a slap of approval on the shoulder, seized the cluster of arrows fast in the roof, and ripped them free. She thrust them into her quiver as she straightened; her head whipped from side to side, her narrowed eyes scanning the roadside trees and brush for sign of a crouching archer, for a new mark at which to shoot.

Hob scrambled the rest of the way onto the roof. The boy caught a glimpse of Gold-Beard as he reappeared, hunched over his wounded arm, scuttling for the cover of the roadside gorse bushes. Hob picked up the second shield and took station to Molly's left and a little in front of her. He held with his hands to the brackets on the shield back that a grown man would slip his left arm through. He held the targe in such a way that Molly was at least partially covered, as he was himself. He had to be active and supple to maintain his position, for she turned about quickly every few moments, so to shoot to either side of the wagon.

From up here Hob could snatch glimpses of the fracas from all sides as he leaped about, ducking and bobbing, trying desperately to keep the shield before Molly, who swung this way and that, placing her shots with brisk efficiency, as calm and careful as though feathered death were not whistling past her at every moment.

Up forward he could see that the pilgrims had at last remembered Jack's instruction, and bunched themselves in a loose ring with their staves held high and the women in the center. The whole group was shuffling back down the trail toward the protection of the wagons, moving in unison as Jack had showed them, a clumsy but effective way of preserving their formation while retreating.

The Carlisle tanners were no warriors, but they were well fed, and sturdy from their demanding work, while the wolf's-heads were poorly armed and half-starved. The pilgrims rained blows on their nearest attackers with their staves and succeeded in keeping them at bay, at least for now; besides, most of the outlaw band was engaged in attempts to gain possession of the wagons, where the most wealth was to be found.

The mass of broad-brimmed hats, seen from the wagon roof,

reminded Hob of a patch of mushrooms, and he began to giggle a bit and forced himself to stop. He was too excited to be very afraid, but he felt a bit as he did when he drank too much barley beer: a little dizzy, a little light-headed.

Molly spun about, and Hob, following, was once more facing aft. Nemain was crouched inside the rear door, with a smaller version of Molly's bow. She was not in his sight, but he could see black-tailed arrows, arrows that Molly had fletched with crow feathers, spit at an angle from the rear of the big wagon they stood upon. The shafts whirred away, first to this side of the road, then to the other. Nemain was watching the second and third wagons, and at the same time peppering the bushes, shooting to whichever side Jack was not guarding. There was less power in her bow than in Molly's, but it was an effective harassment of the attackers, and she was there to raise the alarm if a bandit made for the rear wagons.

"Last and left!" Nemain's high clear voice sang through the rumble of men shouting, and Jack, below, hitched the shield farther up his forearm so that his left hand was empty. He tossed the hammer from right hand to left and put his freed right hand on Mavourneen's rump. He vaulted over the little beast and the drawshafts to land on the left side of the wagons, a prodigious leap, and made for the rear of the second wagon, moving swiftly, his limp barely noticeable. As he went he switched the hammer back to his right hand and shook the shield down his left arm; his left hand once more took a grip on one of the brackets.

Two men huddled at the back of the little wagon, fumbling with the clamp that held the mare's lead rope in the notch. With a curse the shorter one drew a knife and began to saw at the thick rope, but by then Jack was upon them.

The war hammer swung up and over and down with a *whum,* ending in a dull thumping crack: the short bandit's collarbone had snapped beneath the blunt face of the weapon. He yelped; his arm dropped limp and the knife fell at his feet. The second man abandoned the rope clamp and whipped out a dagger. Hob, peering past the shield he held before Molly, saw the blade flash high, and drew a quick breath: he meant to shout warning to Jack. But an eyeblink later the hammer, sweeping in the wide lateral arc of its backstroke, singing in its passage through the air, irresistible, sank its crow-beak thirstily into the brigand's throat. He collapsed without a groan; he thrashed upon the ground, choking on his own blood.

The first man stood hunched, his left hand holding his useless arm immobile against his side: the grating pain of a broken collarbone is not to be ignored, and he had lost all interest in the world outside his body. He began to shamble toward the woods, and Jack, with the practicality of the experienced soldier, did not waste another moment with him; he knew he would do no more mischief that day.

ARROWS WERE SLEETING PAST THEM, high on the roof, yet Hob was conscious of no fear, but only that his mouth was very dry, and he would have given anything to stop for a moment and drink water. He caught another glimpse of the pilgrims' struggle, just as an outlaw scuttled in, stabbing with his heavy knife; the pilgrim he had attacked collapsed inward into the group. Cudgels rained blows about the bandit's head and he ran backward a few steps to rejoin the ring of desperate men who encircled the pilgrim group. A couple of the Carlisle men took their fallen friend under the arms and dragged him along with them in their slow progress back to the shelter of the wagons.

The mare and the little donkey shifted and danced in their traces, their eyes showing white and their ears flicking backward and forward in an attempt to keep track of each menacing sound, but the dead weight of the braked wagons kept them from bolting. Milo, whatever his other shortcomings, was wonderfully stolid in the face of noise and confusion; his eyes rolled here and there as shapes sprang from the forest, his ears turned to every scream and bang of combat, but he stood like a carved ox in his tracks, and waited for his Hob to return.

MOLLY'S ARROWS had taken effect: Hob could see forms slumped in the bare bushes and partially hidden by tree trunks, black-feathered arrows protruding from chest or throat, and the hail of arrows from the forest had all but stopped.

Hob looked over the side. Jack circled the wagons tirelessly. His limp was more pronounced, but still he moved with speed, rushing to meet any who dashed from the brush toward the wagons. The bandits ran by twos or threes toward the wagons as one or the other summoned the courage for an attack, but were so disorganized that they seemed unable to mount a concerted rush.

Jack was a franklin's third son who had taken service first with this knight and then with that, learning his trade from his comrades as he marched and fought. Natural strength and agility had made him a seasoned and relentless combatant. Now he was a match for any but a belted knight. A member of a hereditary military aristocracy, trained ruthlessly from childhood in the care of equipment and horse, the use of weapons, riding, a thousand tricks of combat: a Norman knight could leap into the saddle with a half-hundredweight of chain mail on his body. One of these would surely make short work of Jack. But anyone else, anyone less formidable than one of those professional killers, stood little chance against Jack's strength, Jack's skill, Jack's murderous hammer.

So it proved now. Three bandits came at him, backing him against the side of the wagon, ranging themselves in a rough semicircle. Jack launched himself at the one to his right, the shield on his left arm giving some protection against the two banditti on his left. He ran at the outlaw, who bore a short heavy falchion and a targe much like Jack's own, but without a spike. Jack came up to him and swung the hammer high.

The bandit kept his eye on the hammerhead; he set his feet and shifted his targe to take the expected blow.

Jack stopped short, still holding the hammer aloft, and kicked savagely at the inside of the wolf's-head's knee. The bandit went down like a poleaxed steer, bellowing in pain from the torn joint, dropping his short curved sword and letting his shield sag. Now the hammer fell, and the bandit was defenseless before it, and was battered flat, and lay lifeless upon the ground.

In the instant after his hammer-blow landed, Jack sprang backward; he came to rest facing the remaining pair, his targe before his face. One of the men had a woodsman's ax and from somewhere had procured a stolen shield, not the old-fashioned, body-sheltering, long teardrop shield, but the newer kite-shaped half-shield. He had scraped the paint from it, no doubt to conceal whose device had originally been on it, and it was down to the bare wood and the steel rim. The other had fastened a dagger to a two-foot length of ashwood, to make a crude kind of part-sword, and had a square shield of wicker, roughly constructed.

They were gathering themselves for a rush when Jack stepped in quickly, swinging the blunt end of the hammer down on the upraised kite shield. The shield held well enough, but the tremendous blow, delivered with all the power of Jack Brown's body, damaged the bandit's arm: it drooped, leaving his head and neck exposed. Jack leaped rightward, batting away the second man's dagger-sword with his targe, and swung the hammer again at the wolf's-head with the ax, but from the side. The crow-beak skimmed over the top of the drooping shield and caught the bandit in the temple, and he was dead before he dropped.

The last bandit backed against the little wagon with a thud, and Mavourneen looked around to see what had shaken the draw shafts. Jack closed in. The outlaw had passed that invisible interior boundary where all hope of prevailing has fled, and the combatant can see only the pain that advances upon him from his future. He pressed back against the little wagon, his wicker shield up under his chin, covering his throat; he was making little grunting thrusts with the awkward makeshift sword. His lips pulled back suddenly in an awful unwitting grin, a doglike baring of teeth against his oncoming doom.

Jack danced a little to set his feet properly, advancing with his targe held toward his quarry, then whirled the hammer in a roundabout swing that dipped at the last moment; the blunt head smashed into the bandit's ankles and swept his feet from under him. The outlaw screeched something Hob could not make out, his voice high and strangled with his fear, and as he lay on his back threw first the wicker shield and then the dagger-sword at his implacable foe. Jack Brown banged them away with the targe, one after the other, but the bandit had by then rolled under the wagon to the opposite side and scrambled on hands and knees for the cover of the trees, happy to escape.

JACK RANGED UP AND DOWN beside the wagons, methodically killing or crippling one outlaw and then another, and then seeking a third, till Hob thought of Father Athelstan's favorite quote from St. Peter, how Satan went about as a raging lion, seeking whom he might devour. The next instant he was ashamed for the comparison, and the instant after that, as a last cluster of arrows rattled against the wagon's side, the roof, and the shield he held, he was too busy for thought at all.

BUT THAT WAS THE END of the attack; the arrows rapidly dwindled to nothing, there was no bandit to be seen, and the pilgrims had reached the safety of the wagons at last, clustering about Milo, who looked about at them curiously.

"Mistress Molly!" Aylwin called up in a voice taut as a strung bow, "Jesus's sake, sithee tae puir Sawal; och, I prithee hasten!"

Molly was down from roof to wagon seat, and thence to the ground, in a moment. She hurried to the knot of men and women surrounding the supine form of Sawal, the pilgrim who had been knifed. The front of his clothing was soaked in red, and he had a little pink froth at the side of his mouth. She moved his garments aside, and spoke in rapid lilting Irish to Nemain, who darted into and out of the little wagon, returning with three of Molly's sealed jars in her arms and some clean linen thrown over her shoulder. Molly set to work: she stanched the bleeding with some of the cloth, smeared salves from two of the jars on the deep wounds Sawal had taken midbody, bound his torso round with the rest of the cloth, and held the third jar to the wounded man's lips. Sawal drank, then lay back, looking up aimlessly into the upper branches of the trees with frightened eyes. In a very short time his eyelids fluttered, then dropped, and he slept.

Molly directed his removal to the main wagon, where she secured him in her own bed, then left two women to watch him while she summoned Aylwin outside.

Hob had trailed along behind Molly since she had dismounted from the wagon, so to be ready should she need him. Now he heard her say to Aylwin, "We will not come to shelter before tomorrow, we going forward. But late though we were in taking the road yesterday, yet we reached the ford. Today is young. If we hasten back, it's at the inn we'll be before evening comes on, and Sawal may lie this night in a comfortable bed."

"How lang mun he lie at inn, Mistress?" asked Aylwin.

She spoke low. "Friend Aylwin, be said by me: you must not be in hope of him. His bread is baked. I will ease his pain, but he will die at the inn."

CHAPTER 9

OB SET A RAPID PACE ON THE way back. They splashed across the ford and retraced their steps on the track they had taken before—they built no fire, but pressed on with feet aching from the cold water. Now they were heading northwest through the woodland, back toward the inn.

Despite the shock of the attack and Sawal's sad fate, Hob felt the exhilaration of survival: sweet to be alive and young amid so much death. They were also on the path to the wondrous Margery. Hob was happy with Molly's praise of him to Jack and Nemain, calling him "quick and bold" in his attack on Gold-Beard, and he had hope that she might repeat it where Margery might hear.

Abruptly Hob slowed. Ahead of him was an unusual sight: a badger abroad in the daytime, and in the coldest part of the year, when they slept a good part of the time in their snug setts. It scrambled from the brush at his left and crossed the road with its deliberate, rolling gait. It disappeared behind some brush for a moment but then Hob caught sight of it once more, crossing an open patch of snow, heading determinedly into the woods to his right.

He increased his pace, pulling at the rope a bit to encourage Milo to greater efforts. They had been walking for less time than it took to draw a hundred breaths when a flock of starlings burst from the trees, again on his left hand. They swarmed into an oak on the other side of the road, for a moment clothing it in false leaves, jostling for position on the branches and emitting a storm of clicks and whistles, and then took off again, soaring over the trees, heading east.

Hob moved steadily along; but he looked after the starlings for a while. Then he scanned the forest on his left hand, but little could be seen beneath the ancient trees.

The wind picked up a bit, and for a space Hob trudged along with his eyes on the trail just ahead and his hood held closed by his free hand. After a little time he looked up, and was surprised to see how closely the dark woods crowded the trail to east and to west. To his left, deep in tree-shadow, he caught a glimpse of movement—pale bulks sliding between black-barked trees.

A moment later they came into sight, perhaps twenty of them: a small herd of the wild white cattle of the North Country. These fierce giants could neither be herded nor tamed, only hunted. They wandered vast tracts of woodland in search of winter food, far up into Scotland, and never sought shelter from the most inclement weather, except perhaps to stand on the lee side of a wood in the worst of a storm.

A great shape trod boldly out into the path and turned to face them: the king bull, the only bull to mate with the cows, who held its position by force of body and ferocity of temperament. Hob found himself perhaps twenty paces from the long square-jawed face, the heavy dewlaps of the monarch. Its horns, thick and powerful, swept outward at a sharp angle and then curved in again. Each tip was poignant as an awl: Hob could think of nothing but what bitter wounds the hooking of those horn-ends would make, should the bull choose to attack. The boy stopped short; behind him he could hear the crunch of Molly setting the brake.

"Hob," came Molly's voice from behind him, "do you but stand easy a moment; there's no harm in him for you."

Hob breathed a little easier to hear this, but Milo was more of a skeptic. The ox swung its head away from the king bull's glower and took an interest in the side of the road; stealthily it lowered its head, till its eyes dipped below the level of Hob's shoulder: now the boy's slight body occluded the sight of horned death. Milo was of a different tribe than the wild white cattle, and in any case had been robbed of all interest in the struggle to acquire a retinue of cows and hold it against lust-driven challengers, but plainly he wanted no misunderstanding to arise.

The patriarch stood in the road and glared arrogantly at Hob and Milo, while behind it its heavy-bodied brides, as well as the bachelor bulls it had vanquished, surged across the road, from one wing of the forest to another, left to right. When all had crossed it turned and trotted lightly into the forest gloom. The great beast was surprisingly agile, its tremendous musculature carrying it easily over the terrain with a springing step, almost a dancing gait.

Hob could hear that the pilgrims were beginning to catch up with the stopped wagons. Though they were downhearted and mostly silent, Hob could just hear their subdued muttering as they wondered about the reason for the halt, the sound swelling somewhat as more and more of them tramped up behind Jack's wagon.

When the forest shadow had engulfed the last hint of the herd,

Hob let out a sigh and set off once more. He set a quick pace, and for once Milo seemed uninclined to linger or stray. Soon the pilgrim voices trailed off again into silence.

"Hob, cease awhile," said Molly, after they had gone along for a bit, and simultaneously she set the brake again. Behind her the other two wagons came to a halt. Molly swung down and went back to Nemain. Hob looked around at them, puzzled: he knew they wanted to get the wounded man to Osbert's Inn as soon as they might. But Nemain set her brake, got down, and tied Mavourneen to the lead wagon. The two women walked to the western edge of the road and peered into the trees, heads cocked. They seemed to be more listening, or tasting the air, than actually looking.

Jack looked on patiently from the seat of the last wagon; the pilgrims began to come up and cluster beside him, asking why they had stopped. Jack spread his broad hands to indicate his ignorance. The mare took a pace to the side and began to paw in a desultory fashion at a small clump of desiccated grass, dead and frozen, poking up through the roadside snow; through the rumble of the pilgrims' muttering, the rattling of the grasses beneath the mare's hoof came clearly to Hob through the crisp air.

Finally Molly came forward again, and Nemain untied the little ass and threw the reins up to the seat; she put her hand into a loop and mounted the wagon in one agile bound. Her slim body seemed to Hob to fly from road to wagon, skirts flaring, effortless as a cat springing up to settle on a fireside bench.

"Is there danger, Mistress?" Hob asked, still gazing back along the little procession.

She looked off to the west and sighed. "It's a strange feeling and no mistake, lad. I sense that there is something, yet I cannot grasp it. You have at whiles looked at the sun, and then away?"

"I— Yes, Mistress."

"And what did you see when you looked away, and you just after looking at the sun?"

"It was like the sun, Mistress, but dark."

"And it moving with you, and coming between yourself and the world for a while, and then fading."

"Yes, Mistress, just so."

"It's a feeling like that that I have, and Nemain as well; something is to the west, or something *should be* to the west, and yet for all we can tell, there is nothing."

"All the beasts and birds we have seen since we left the ford have been moving from west to east, Mistress, as though they cared not to be in the west."

She looked at him in surprise. "It's an eye you have in your head, Hob." She gazed at him a long moment, then slipped her hand within his hood and patted his cheek. Her palm was warm against his skin, though she went ungloved on this cold day. "An eye you have in your head," she said again. Then she turned and remounted the wagon seat. "Away on," she called back along the convoy.

THE TRACK THEY WERE ON ran back through the peasants' fields—today no one was to be seen—and ended at that road that, to the east, led to Bywood Old End; to the west it went past Osbert's Inn and back toward Monastery Mount. It was late in the day when they turned leftward onto this road. Hob thought, *I am hastening back to her,* and despite the grim nature of their errand, an eagerness arose in his heart. He strained to see the inn that was so near, but a small patch of forest was between them and the inn's clearing, and all he could see was the trees, and above and behind the grove, two or three red kites circling slowly, their cruel hooked beaks just visible at this distance.

The wagons creaked along, far too slowly for Hob; the pilgrims came trudging in the rear, their chatter silenced. He could hear behind him the tramp of their shoes, the thud of their staves on the hard dirt of the road, but nothing else for a while. Then the cold wind came sighing again through the tops of the trees; a rushing moan masked the sounds of the subdued travelers.

In a very short while they rounded a small curve and came again in sight of the inn. To Hob's right came in the broad northern way; ahead lay the track back to Monastery Mount; on his left, the clearing and the inn. But something was amiss: the gates were ajar, and in the clearing before the walls was a group of villagers, the men all bearing flails, axes, billhooks, or scythes. The tools of the farm, but also the weapons of the peasantry.

There was a flurry of consultation in the group, and then a villager, not young but not old either, detached himself from the group and came with lagging step to meet Molly's little convoy. He was well-known to Molly; doubtless this was why he had been delegated to meet her.

He came up to the wagon, a sturdy balding man, an ax trailing unheeded from his right hand.

"God save thee, Mistress Molly."

"And you also, Luke," she said warily. "What is amiss?"

"Inn's been attacked, sithee, Mistress."

"Att— Speak you, friend Luke: what has happened?"

Luke looked down at the ground. He spoke without raising his head.

"They'm all been killed, Mistress, all on 'em."

Molly stood up on the seat and peered toward the inn. "All of them . . . *All of them?* But who . . . ?"

"Wild beasts or summat like: they be all tore up like."

Hob put his hand out blindly and held to Milo's harness.

"Was there no one that saw . . . ?"

"Nay, Mistress; some on us as come up this morning found gate open, sithee, and dogs dead. And 'twas only young Eadmund alive, what was t' groom's prentice, and he dyin', and oot of all sense wi' t' pain."

Over on the outer wall of the inn a crow alighted, then another. High above, the remorseless red kites made wide circles in the bright cold air.

"Did he speak at all? Did he say aught of what happened?"

"He were in terrible dolor, Mistress, and part of his face tore at, sithee. He were just chunterin', verra low. 'Twere hard to hear 'im, an' harder tae ken what he were on aboot: summat aboot a fox, he talked of nowt else for a time, but then he were just breathin' heavy and sayin' nowt, and then breathin' light wi' now and then a sigh, and then he died, right afore oor eyes."

"A fox? And what did he say of a fox, at all?"

"That were t' only word we could ken, Mistress; the rest was more grietin' and moanin', like, an' once a fearsome scream."

"And poor Osbert, so strong, and his sons, and his daughters, all gone?"

"Aye, Mistress, an' a' Master Osbert's men as well, an' a' t' guests. Two on 'em—t' guests, sithee—two on 'em was belted knights, that might ha' been grandmams for a' good thae gowden spurs done 'em. And one were armed cappypie, Mistress, wi' mail and a', and t'other as had his sword in hand, but t' hand nigh off above t' wrist."

The villager had a soft blurry voice, and he murmured his frightful news to Molly in hushed tones. Hob, holding to a strap against the ox's warm hide and gazing at the gates to Osbert's Inn, reflected on how pleasant the man's voice was, and how the sun sparkled in the snow that covered the inn's ridgepole. He felt like himself and not like himself. His thoughts seemed unable to settle, like the bright butterflies of last summer on a warm but windy day.

He began to walk toward the gates. He felt that he walked, and that he watched himself walk, all at once. Hob and his watcher came up to the wide-open outer gates, and now the devastation within the dog run came in view. The ten great black bodies lay this way and that. One had its chest torn out, but most had terrible long slashes along their sides and bellies. Something faster and stronger and more agile than they had opened them up, one after the other; and speedily, too, for they had fallen near one another. The whole pack working in concert had been unable to defend itself. Hob-the-watcher thought vaguely of one of God's swift angels, flashing past a bit above the ground, his arm out to the side and a dagger in his flawless hand. The mastiffs' entrails had spilled out onto the hard cold ground. Pools of dark ice spread out from the bodies: frozen blood.

The inner gates were open a foot or two. Hob and Hob-the-watcher slipped through the opening and stepped into Osbert's spacious courtyard, and stopped as though bowshot. The dead had been temporarily laid out on the ground by the villagers, each wrapped in a shroud of coarse white cloth. Hob came back entirely to himself with a rush, his heart pounding; his limbs were chilled, but the blood was hot in his face.

The shapes, some forty of them, lay like so many bundles on the icy ground, swaddled and anonymous, the white cloth stained in large part with red. They lay stiff and frozen with that utter lack of movement that proclaims the dead, save for one bundle, slighter than most. There the shroud had pulled away, just a bit, just at the very top, and there from a fold of the cloth escaped a lock of curly brown hair, tossing erratically in the bitter breeze. So: either Parnell or Margery. The merest mocking semblance of life. And by its side lay another muffled form, of sisterly size and delicacy. Hob stood and stared, in one wise utterly numb, and yet with a terrible feeling that his chest would soon burst open with the swelling of his pity and his horror.

Nemain came up behind him. She took his left hand in hers and slipped her right arm about his waist. "Hob," she said, "come away."

In a faint voice he said, "I have hastened back to her. So she bade me."

"Come away, *a chuisle*." With the gentlest of pressures she turned him from the terrible array, and led him back to the wagons.

THAT NIGHT HE LAY dry-eyed in the darkened wagon, alone, while Jack prowled about the camp, hammer in hand. The wagons were drawn up about a fire, at a short distance from the inn: none wanted to pass the night within those sad walls except those pilgrims tending to the dying Sawal, and the villagers left on guard, armed with axes and billhooks.

Hob's thoughts moved slowly, dismally. He was a traveler tramping down cold and muddy roads, groping through a clammy fog. Everyone at Osbert's Inn was dead: Margery! Osbert, his sons, his other daughter, what was her— Parnell. The housecarls, the cook, the guests, as well as the mastiffs outside and the deerhounds inside. Tilred the pantler. And that winch-tender and his nephew in the well house.

Hob sat up suddenly on the blanket-covered chest that was his bed. He was propped on one hand, staring into the darkness. That old winch-tender. Hob had listened as though it were a story, an entertainment around a campfire, and so had the winch-tender's nephew.

Father Athelstan had often praised Hob's ability to remember a phrase, a verse, a passage, in English or in Latin—Father Athelstan had no Greek—and to repeat it almost verbatim. Hob would try to explain: when he called what he had heard to mind, it was much as though he listened to it afresh.

Now suddenly Hob could hear the old man's voice again, and the underlying somber music that he had not marked at the time.

Jesus and Mary with us, Hob thought. *Will I one day tell this to some young man and he with his mouth full of almonds, listening just for the tale? "She were a fine-lookin' woman, too. I fancied her mysel'."*

Suddenly he burst into a flood of hot tears. He sat up all the way, choking and sobbing, rocking back and forth on the chest in the darkness. The water ran from his eyes and his nose and he reached down his shirt from its peg and buried his face in the cloth.

The weeping subsided at last, in a series of little gasping breaths. Something came to him, something not clearly defined. He felt it rather than thought it. He felt perhaps he understood something, that puzzle of children: the mysterious elusive grief glimpsed now and then in their elders. The smile that is tinged with melancholy, the glance away in mid-speech to the horizon-line, the remark behind which is an untold tale. Someone dead too soon, or traveled away for aye; an old man haunted by the flicker of a memory, some ghost of his young days. *She were a fine-lookin' woman, too. I fancied her mysel'.*

CHAPTER 10

T SUNRISE JACK LED THE beasts into the inn, one by one, and fed them from Osbert's mangers, and watered them from Osbert's troughs. Now they were hitched again to the wagons, and the little troupe was prepared to leave again, for as Molly had said, there was little they could do to help, and she had no desire to be embroiled in an inquiry by the shire-reeve or, worse, by the knights who had been sent for from the nearest stronghold of the Sieur de Meschines, in whose demesne the inn lay.

Molly had thrown a hooded cloak of the Scottish blue-gray wool about her shoulders, fastened it with her best ring-and-pin brooch, and gone in to pay her respects to what remained of Osbert and his family. She had come out with a grim and stony face and dry eyes. She went into the large wagon.

Hob's own eyes were red with last night's tears.

"She is more angry than doleful," he remarked to Nemain, who had stayed close by his side all day.

"A queen does not weep," said Nemain, who had not wept either. Hob was unsure of what she meant, but, gripped by a weary sorrow, did not care enough to ask.

In a moment Molly swung back down from the wagon. The overcast sun struck a wan gleam from the green enamel and the gold of her brooch; it seemed the only spot of color in that gray day.

She looked about the little circle, and seemed about to speak, but here came Aylwin, crunching up over the patches of ice and snow with slow tread, staff in hand. Hob was startled at the change in Aylwin's appearance. His shoulders slumped and he seemed slack within his clothes. His face seemed gaunt; his mouth drooped and his cheeks, so full and ruddy before, seemed wan and hollow.

"Mistress Molly." He stood still for a moment, as if this greeting had made off with the last of his strength; then he gave a great sigh. "Sawal ha' died, as tha kent, in t' bed, within Master Osbert's inn. Father Benedict will pray him intae ground, sithee, in t' wee churchyard here, and we mun stay for that—t' kind folk hereabout hae offered us lodging ower tae Bywood Old End. But then we mun return tae Carlisle—och, what am I tae tell puir Sawal's mam?" He leaned close; his voice sank. "I fear Satan be ranging yon woods, seeking wham tae devoor, as t'apostle says. Here is no ordinary pilgrimage t' noo, and I wi' my people tae consider, sithee."

Hob started, hearing his thoughts about Jack echoed so closely: he thought to find some sign in St. Peter's verse coming to his attention again, and he turned and looked about at the unreadable trees. Between the closely set trunks narrow aisles led away, quickly coming to darkness and shadow, and there was nothing to be learned.

"Wilt tha return wi' us, Mistress Molly? Tisna safe for thee and thine, an' ye'd all be welcome in Carlisle, sithee. I'm no small man i' t' guild."

"Let me speak to my granddaughter a short while, friend Aylwin, and then I'll come tell you what way we will take."

"We'll be within: t' womenfolk are washing puir Sawal, sithee." Nodding heavily to the company, he swung about and trudged off.

The four of them stood near the large wagon and watched him go. The cold made their ears sting, and the wind blew their cloaks about; Molly's hair streamed sideways, billowing like a silver flag, till she gathered it with both hands and drew her hood up over it.

Molly said, looking at Aylwin's retreating back, "Nemain. Is it on or back you would bid me go?"

Hob was startled by this. The two often consulted, but Molly taught, Nemain learned. Even when they lilted along in Irish you could tell who was guiding whom. Here for a wonder was Molly at a loss, and appealing to her granddaughter, that newest of women.

"Nay, seanmháthair, I cannot tell. I thought that thing gone ahead, or away, and it here behind us the while."

A great crowd of crows and ravens had been gathering since yesterday; they clustered in the nearby trees, on the walls of the dog run and the ridgepoles of the inn buildings. More red kites were arriving now, making wide loops in the air as they descended, looking to find a feeding crow and startle it into flight. There it might be robbed of its portion by the piratical hawks. A particularly bold kite, skimming too low, had to veer suddenly upward to escape the snapping beaks of angry crows. The mass of birds was in constant motion, lifting, circling, resettling. The cawing of the crows and the deep *cronk* of the ravens filled the air. The smell of spilled blood drew them, but the villagers would not let them at the dead, not even at Osbert's mastiffs, and the crows had nothing for the kites to steal.

Molly turned and peered intently across the short distance to the inn, her lips moving silently.

From the roofs of the inn a bunch of crows lifted suddenly and flew a slow circuit before alighting once more. One detached itself from the flock and flew straight toward them. It dropped down toward the large wagon, spread broad black pinions as it braked, and fluttered daintily to a perch on the nearest wagon wheel. It snapped its glossy wings shut. It was a very large crow, almost as big as a raven, and it regarded Molly with head cocked and an eye like a bead of onyx.

Molly pushed the hood back off her mane, gray as rainwater, thick as a river in flood. She reached beneath the cloak and from her belt drew a slim ring-pommel dagger. She stepped close to the big wooden wheel. She looked once up to the sky, her expression baleful, and then she spoke to the bird, something in Irish, and the crow shifted its position a bit, wings flickering open a moment for balance, a flash of shadow; yet it remained, awaiting her.

Molly held the dagger point to the thumb on her left hand and pricked deep. A fat drop of blood welled up. She held her hand out to the crow.

It moved its side-tilted head down and up several times, lizard-quick, eyeing the outstretched thumb, looking back up to her face. Then it leaned forward and captured the bead of blood, an action like biting a berry from a twig. The crow tilted its head upward, its horn-yellow beak scissoring rapidly as it sent the blood down its throat.

Hob, a scant three paces away, watched in fascination. He had never observed a crow so closely; at this distance he could see the bluish-purple cast to the black feathers on its upstretched throat as it drank, and when it lowered its head, the greenish sheen to the black feathers on its nape.

Molly sheathed the dagger and then pressed her thumb with her right hand, and offered another drop of blood to the crow; and then a third.

After the last drop the crow stood still a moment, looking for all the world like Father Athelstan pondering what penance to give a sinner; then it shook its lustrous feathers, gave a loud creaking caw, and leaped into the air. It wheeled around them once and flew toward the southeast. They watched as it dwindled to a small black fluttering rag, to a dot, and vanished over the trees.

"That is settled, then," said Molly. "It's back to the ford for us, and on, perhaps even to Durham."

"But how—" Hob began, but then he felt Jack's hand on his upper arm. The big hand covered most of it. He looked back at Jack. Jack just shook his head ever so slightly. The dark man slowly pulled him away and pointed toward the ox, and then went back toward his own place with the last wagon. Hob went and lifted Milo's lead rope from its notch in the footboard. Molly disappeared into the little wagon, then came out with one of her endless clay jars, full of a breath-easing potion for Haunild; off she went to find the black-haired mother, and to tell Aylwin her decision. She was back almost immediately. A few moments later Molly and Nemain took their places on the wagon seats and gathered up the reins.

But Molly gave no signal to start. A man was approaching from the inn with a long loping stride, a wiry ginger-haired man, lean, energetic: Hodard Squint, one of the shire-reeve's men and another of Molly's partisans.

"God and Mary wi' thee, Mistress."

"And you, Hodard."

He looked up at her, his eyes screwed up into slits against the cold, as was his habit. His expression was keen and intelligent. Hob saw a long-chinned face, framed in a hood of green wool; about his shoulders a scalloped half-cape of the same color flapped in the wind.

"Mistress . . ." He seemed uncertain how to proceed. His clever narrowed eyes searched her face a moment. "Mistress, tha mun hear summat. Master Osbert's storehouse has been brast open, and the gowd an' siller taken, sithee. An' Father Benedict gaes aboot, askin' what is a beast but needs gowd and siller as well; an' askin' about yon woman an' her wagons an' her strange ways, sithee, and they'm sent for knights fra the castle. If tha'rt t' gae hence, gae the noo nor tarry at all, an' gae far, lest Father Benedict wi' his waggin' tongue do thee a mischief. Sithee, 'twill be three days before yon knights come, Mistress, but when they come 'twill all be oot o' my hands."

Molly sat a moment. "My thanks for this, Hodard." She sighed, wrapped the reins twice about the brake, and swung down from the wagon seat, agile as a young maiden. "Come with me and look through my wagons."

"Nay, Mistress, tha needna show me . . ."

But she took him by the hand—it was as though the shire-reeve's deputy were a boy, Hob thought; but it was affectionate as well. She led Hodard Squint back to the door of the first wagon, and unlatched it, and climbed in, beckoning him to follow. She did the same with the remaining wagons, and when they emerged she said, "Now you can tell all that I was not weighed down with poor Osbert's gold and silver when I left here, and you the reeve's man; and before that I was with yon pilgrims, and Aylwin a respected man in the tanners' guild up to Carlisle."

"Naetheless, Mistress, tha'd best not tarry."

"Naetheless, friend Hodard, I will not be tarrying."

She embraced him warmly; then she turned and clambered swiftly up to the seat. Hob thought that the long lean face was somewhat reddened, but it may have been an effect of the same biting wind that toyed with Hodard's half-cape.

Molly nodded to Hob and he turned and led Milo around in a semicircle till the ox was once again pointed toward the road that led toward Bywood Old End, and to the juncture with the track that led down to Dickon's Ford on the Dawlish.

CHAPTER *11*

ACK AGAIN TO THE TURNING before Bywood Old End, back past the peasants' furrows, through the forest to Dickon's Ford, a dash across. Once again they did not stop to build a fire as they had the first time they crossed, but turned into the southward path and hurried on into the forest.

When they came to the place where they had been ambushed, they found stiffened bodies by the road. The bandits had not even stayed to claim their dead, and the birds, mostly crows, were already busy at them, a grim sight. Hob's heart had felt hollow in his chest since the inn, and neither the slain men nor the fear of attack could lower his spirits any further. Still, he was resilient as only someone of thirteen summers is resilient, and he had known Margery but a few days, and he did not want to walk into a sleet of arrows in another ambush. He dropped back to walk beside Molly.

"Will they come at us again, Mistress?"

She waved him on briskly. "There's nothing here now, and no mistake. They dare not linger, even to bury their dead, for fear the reeve's men will come along and take them. Away on."

He moved ahead of Milo once more—the ox had begun to turn its head, wondering why Hob was behind it—and quickly led the way past the rigid corpses, with their rustling, croaking, shifting blanket of attendant birds.

Soon they were past the signs of the battle—the trampled bushes, the bodies, the splash of blood here and there on a tree trunk, patches of flattened and crimsoned snow. The track they were on grew broader and a bit more comfortable to travel: the forest stepped back a few paces from the roadside, and the roots of the ancient trees no longer crept onto the snow-packed road, and the wheels need not bump over them, or snag upon them.

The wagons were actually moving into a broad wooded valley, and though their sight was hindered by the thick wooden palisades about them, the surrounding crags of the mountains were farther away. The little troupe traveled quickly down this valley, and met with no hindrance.

Soon the mountain walls began to converge again, and the road rose slowly toward a notch in the hills: Odo's Pass, sometimes called the Fellsgate. Once past this notch the road wound down toward the high fells eastward, and eventually toward the coast towns. There was a very slight grade, and some slipping of the wheels, and some strewing of ash by Hob, but generally the faring here was not onerous, and soon they dipped into a hollow and then began to rise again toward the brink of the pass.

As he topped the rim of the hollow and once again had a clear view of the road ahead, Hob slowed his pace, and slowed it more, at the sight of the pass; his lips parted; finally he came to a dead halt, and behind him the rumble of wheels ran down into silence, and brakes were set all along the tiny caravan.

*   *   *

A PORTION OF THE MOUNTAINSIDE had given way, and huge blocks and slabs of stone, looking as if they had been hurled by giants, had carried down with them earth and snow and whole trees. Odo's Pass was completely blocked, and there was no way ahead.

Jack and Nemain tied off their animals and came forward. Everyone looked at the tremendous mass of material blocking the notch; there was an air of general bemusement. No one moved or spoke for a moment.

Then Molly released the brake. "Turn the wagon, Hob *a rún*," she said. "It's back to the ford, and onto the eastern road. There's nothing for us here, and the day darkening as we sit." Jack and Nemain returned to their wagons, and Hob tore his gaze from the destruction before him.

They had had eyes only for the rock slide, perhaps a quarter of a mile ahead: the tangle of boulder and pine trunk and tumbled-down earth. But as Hob turned, heaving at the lead rope to get Milo to swing around and go back, his eye struck some way into the gloom beneath the trees. *"Uh!"* he said, the sound jolted out of him by surprise. He pointed to a spot about ten paces into the forest. This was well clear of the rock slide, and the ground here was unscarred by any upheaval.

There, embedded in the side of a snowbank, gray with rock dust, scarred by chisels, lay a hand, spread as in warning: *Go back*. It ended in a torn ragged stump of wrist, as though bitten through by monstrous jaws. The snow below the stump bore a stain like a sash trailing earthward, widening as it fell, fading as it widened, diluted with snow-water, red to pink.

"The masons," said Hob, in so quiet a voice that one might mistake it for calm.

"Turn about, Hob, and lead on, quick but steady," said Molly coolly. Once they had the wagons hauled around and facing back, they moved as quickly as prudence dictated, and as silently as thudding hoof and rumbling axle permitted.

It was as if the act of retracing their steps had released the snow. They had scarce gone ten of Hob's paces back toward Dickon's Ford, when movement at the boy's right hand caught his eye: a snowflake, swooping in irregular arcs, slid down the air. A moment later another followed, then two together; then the air was sprinkled with flakes, dark against the sky, white against the somber mass of trees. This continued for the space of twenty or thirty breaths, while Hob plodded as fast as he might back along the trail, encouraging Milo with clucks and little tugs on the lead rope. The wagons rumbled up the forest road, over root and stone and hard-packed old snow increasingly covered with slick new snow. After a while they bartered silence for speed. Molly called encouragement to the little troupe, and Hob could hear Jack's sharp whistle, as the dark man sought to spur the mare to greater effort.

Then a squalling wind filled the air with whirling whiteness, and vision was effectively foiled. Hob came to a stop, adjusted his hood, and began to walk again. He walked bent over a little, looking at the ground to his left. He had the lead rope in his right hand and his right arm straight out, so Milo would walk in the center of the track, but he walked on the left margin of the road, so that he could see the boundary between road and the brush-filled verge of the forest.

He trudged along for some little time like this, and then the wind dropped sharply and the snow all but ceased. There was a layer of new snow through which he tramped, but he could see about him once more. They were passing the ambush site again. The bodies now were covered with a light blanket of snow, and the trees about were dark with crows and the occasional raven, all of them fluffed into balls for warmth. They had taken refuge from the snow squall amid the tangle of branches, where at least some of the wind's force was broken.

The bodies covered in white brought Hob back again to the memory of the courtyard at Osbert's Inn and the two sisters' bodies, side by side in their shrouds. Because the walking was difficult and uncomfortable and above all monotonous, he gradually sank again into a dull gray sorrow, in which the constant need for movement was not enough to distract him from his grief.

When the bandit slain had receded out of sight, but well before they had come to the ford again, Molly called out to the boy, breaking him free of his ceaseless gnawing at the past: her voice was welcome to him for that relief.

"Hob, cease a moment."

She set the brake and dismounted the wagon. She gestured to the others. Jack and Nemain once more fastened their respective beasts to the wagons ahead and came up to the lead wagon. Hob came trailing back, the lead rope slack in his hand.

Molly slumped back against the wagon, leaning against the front wheel. There was a little splintery gouge in the wheel's wood, right by her elbow, where, after the battle, Jack had dug out the first arrow of the ambush with the point of his knife. Molly looked around the little group. Hob thought she had never seemed so weary.

"A fear there is to me," she said, beginning to lose her English as she thought hard in Irish, "that it's being herded we are." She made a visible effort to grip the foreign idiom once more. "I cannot tell at all. Those masons, surely they are all dead, if the inn is any guide to us; and they being dead, Lady Svajone with whom they traveled is dead, and her doctor is dead, and her esquires, and her grooms and drivers. This thing kills before us and behind us, and we not knowing what happens beyond the next bush. I have a sense of being toyed with."

She straightened, and looked at Nemain. She spoke formally. "Nemain, are we being herded?"

Nemain considered, and then said slowly and carefully, "Nor can

I tell, *seanmháthair*, but I can tell that there is some misdirection makes it difficult to know."

Molly said, very low, "Yet the Crow-Mother led me in this direction, from the inn, and I asking Her the road to safety."

"I was watching you the while, *seanmháthair*, and your face, and by the look of your eyes I did not think it was of safety you spoke. It was revenge entirely that I saw there."

Molly thought for a moment. "You have the right of it. There was a hunger for safety in my thoughts; but in my mouth, in my mouth, there was a bitter thirst for revenge. I know not which it is that Crow Babd has sent us." She looked away into the west, where a pearl-bright gleam in the roof of cloud showed where the sun had begun to sink toward the tree line, making for Ireland and making for its nest beyond Ireland, down in the Western Ocean. "It is a bitter, bitter thirst, and not my first taste either," she said, so low that Hob could barely make out her words.

After a moment she brushed her hands together in a dusting-off motion, and said, "Enough. We cannot return to the inn. We can take the eastern path and see what comes of it. Herded or not, it is back toward the ford we must go in any case. Away on."

As he took his place at Milo's head, Hob wondered why Molly and her granddaughter had been so careful to deliberate in English, rather than in their native speech. They had done it also outside the walls of Osbert's Inn, when Molly asked the younger woman whether to go forward or to return. It was as though Molly and Nemain felt that he and Jack ought to be included, perhaps because the course of the future now ran so quickly into shadow and uncertainty. He felt proud for a minute or two, but then, as he turned it this way and that in his mind, pride fell off and apprehension rose to take its place.

* * *

THE RESPITE FROM THE SNOW did not last, as all had known it would not. Snowfall began again gently, and again progressed to thick veils of white that fell straight down like river water falling over a cliff; then the wind awoke once more, and the snow came at them, stinging their cheeks, clustering on their eyelashes. With equal suddenness the wind changed, veering across their path, and eyes could again open wider than slits.

The snow's accumulation was startling in its rapidity. Hob was now trudging through ankle-deep snow and it was increasing with every twenty steps he took. Walking grew difficult, and driving the animals as well. Even Milo began to labor and snort, and the wheels of the wagon sometimes slid rather than rolled.

The wind was piling the snow into drifts when Molly called another halt, had the wagons all roped together, and sent Hob up to take her place while she took the lead rope herself. She tightened her cloak a bit and hoisted her skirt somewhat, tucking it into her belt. She had Hob reach back through the hatch and hand her down a staff. Then she set off once more. Now Hob in the first and Nemain in the second wagon had little to do but be ready with the brakes; Jack was needed back by the mare, who became difficult when she was frightened, as she was now by the increasing storm, and he walked beside her with a rope run back to the brake lever.

They moved off again through the forest, and for a time made better progress, although Milo, obediently following Molly as she led the way into whistling white emptiness, looked around every few minutes to see that Hob was still there; then, reassured, the ox turned back to the path.

Hob was hunkered down in his sheepskin coat on the wagon seat. The reins were held loosely in his gloved hands, more as a precaution against the unexpected than as a guide to the ox; Hob's foot was braced against the footboard near the brake, ready to stamp it shut. So they proceeded for a time, moving through a largely featureless world of tumbling snow and the barely glimpsed backdrop of the forest.

Hob became aware that Molly had stopped, and Milo as well. He kicked at the brake to prevent the wagon from running up into the ox's rump. He shielded his eyes with a glove, peering forward past Milo's blunted horns. Through the curtains of snow, blowing now nearly sideways, Hob glimpsed a group of riders, sitting motionless, blocking the trail.

There seemed to be perhaps a score of horses, although many behind the front ranks seemed riderless. Four riders in front ranged across the nearly obscured path. He could not make out the faces of the riders, muffled as they were in cloak and cowl against the weather, but the ominous stillness with which they sat exuded menace.

Suddenly the rider on Hob's right charged off the trail at an angle, the horse floundering through the drifts, in a headlong flight toward a nearby broad-trunked oak. They skidded to a halt just before a disastrous collision, the flung snow from the braking hooves leaping ahead in a little wave.

The mysterious rider sawed at the reins, hauling the horse's head around and kneeing it back toward the trail. From deep within the shadows of the cowl came a familiar voice: "Jesus wither you like that fucking fig tree in Bethany, you whore, you traitress! You near killed us both, you smoking pile of goat dung, she-devil, she-fiend!"

"Roger!" shouted Hob.

The unmoving rider in the center now lifted a hand, shaded his eyes from the whipping snow. "Who's that, then?" he called.

"Ranulf, sir, it's Mistress Molly's folk! It's Hob!"

Ranulf spurred up close to Molly; he touched his forehead.

"God and His saints protect you, Mistress," said Ranulf, almost shouting to make himself heard above the gale.

Molly had not met Ranulf at the monastery, but she had listened to

Hob's account, and had considered the soldiers' invitation before deciding otherwise. Now the world had changed around her, and any haven was welcome; she greeted the man-at-arms cordially.

"And you, sergeant," she said in a voice that by some means carried bell-clear above the wind. "Well met at this stormy crossroads."

When he heard this last Hob looked about in some surprise. At first there was nothing to see but the shifting veils of snow, behind which he could dimly perceive the black walls of the woods, the white folds and hollows of the ground beneath its steadily increasing blanket. Then he became aware of three irregular patches near the road, somewhat darker than the surrounding land. From the central patch protruded the charred end of a log: this was their campsite when first they crossed the Dawlish. At this spot crossed the southern road they had just returned on, the eastern road to Blanchefontaine Castle, and the short western spur that ended at Dickon's Ford. The Dawlish was very near, then—hidden from the eye by the blowing snow, hidden from the ear by the moaning wind.

There followed a period of some confusion, as the riders advanced and clustered about the lead wagon, the horses restless and frightened in the storm. The riderless horses now proved to be those mounts sold to the castle that Ranulf had awaited at the monastery.

Nemain and Jack Brown once more set brakes and trudged forward, to see what was toward. Nemain was hunched inside an enormous sheepskin cloak of her grandmother's, the fleece inward, yet she shivered somewhat; Jack's coat was crusted white across his broad shoulders, yet he seemed not to notice, and had only drawn up his hood as a concession to the weather.

"We make our way to Blanchefontaine, Sir Jehan's hold. We passed by Osbert's Inn at midday, and hope to come nigh the castle before dark, or mayhap soon after."

"And what was it you saw at Osbert's Inn, sergeant, and you passing by?"

"Slaughter, Mistress—we had hoped to stay a day there, but . . . I spoke with the reeve's man there, and he said you had left that morning, and he commended you to me. Come you with us to the castle, Mistress. This storm will only wax the stronger. You will be well received, and you are not safe out here: if the cold does not kill you, this terrible creature will."

"Indeed I had some such thought myself, the southern way being blocked, and the animals tired and hungry, and we looking to take refuge somewhere."

After some consultation about the order of march, Molly sent Hob back to help Nemain with the little wagon, while she mounted to the lead wagon's seat. Ranulf assigned one of his horsemen—Goscelin or Joscelin, Hob was never sure of the man's name—to ride beside Mavourneen, with a line to her bridle, as an aid to the two young ones in controlling the donkey, whose sweet temperament was somewhat offset by the fear and disorientation that the weather engendered.

Ranulf and the body of his men went forward, that the trampling of so many hooves might ease the passage of the wagons. Roger and another man rode immediately in front of Molly's wagon, each with two unsaddled horses trailing behind, lead ropes tied to the soldiers' saddles, and Olivier was off to the side.

Olivier slowed his horse till he fetched up level with Molly's seat on the big wagon. He rode alongside for a bit, a rangy, strongly made man. His rough tenor came clear through the moaning of the wind. He spoke loudly enough for Roger riding in front, and even Hob in the wagon behind, to hear.

"Mistress, I'll wager Roger would trade you his mare for that sweet little donkey."

Roger did not turn his head. His voice drifted back to them.

"Shut up, Olivier," he said.

* * *

Ranulf was clearly a leader of some experience. He set a pace that was brisk but not sufficient to stretch out the column, and every so often would walk his horse to the side and let the column proceed past him, counting his men and his horses: he wanted no one wandering off into the snowstorm. When Jack came past with the last wagon, Ranulf would turn his horse's head and nudge it into a trot up the line to resume his place at the head of his troop.

But after a while the brisk pace slowed to a plod, and then became a gritted-teeth struggle against the weight of the cold, the snow, the increasingly obscure path through the forest. Twice Ranulf halted the column to send out scouts to either side. He had them secure long lines to their saddles, the other ends held by their comrades, as they walked their mounts at right angles to the path to find landmarks that could not be seen through the whipping veils of white; after a bit they would come back and confirm the party's position, having ridden up close to this rock or that broken tree that normally could be spotted from the trail.

A dimming of the light behind the ceiling of cloud had signaled the close of day when the riders ahead of the wagons slowed and began to bunch up, and finally halted altogether. Molly set the brake and went forward through the snow to see what was amiss. When Nemain, leaning sideways to peer ahead, saw her grandmother dismount, she did so as well. Hob, cramped and uncomfortable on the chilly wagon seat, climbed down and followed her, thinking to bring some blood and hence warmth to his legs.

The two made their way up the column, past Roger and the riders ahead—Nemain had to skip aside as one of the riderless horses, restless, danced about on the trail, pulling at its lead—till they came to where Molly stood with Ranulf and a couple of his men, dismounted. They were staring down at a body at the side of the road. The experienced warhorses stood quietly, but some of the riderless horses, not yet trained, had backed to the ends of their lead ropes, nostrils flared at the scent of blood.

The corpse, plainly visible, lay on a patch of ground bare of snow, sheltered as it was under the thick lower branches of a mountain pine. It was a man in ragged green hose, grimy-handed, with a golden beard and a gash that ripped him from crutch to ribs. Parts of him, too big to be the work of birds, had been eaten. Hob gaped at him. Gold-Beard.

Behind the pine was a tiny clear space before the next rank of trees began, and there were snow-covered mounds there; beside one was a small dead animal of some sort. Hob squinted at it. It was a brown leather shoe, and part of an ankle clad in brown hose, that protruded from the snowdrift. Gold-Beard was not the only bandit to have been caught here by the nameless terror.

Molly stood from her examination. She turned in a circle, looking into the white whirl of the storm that was uncommunicative as the grave.

"Does it range these forests everywhere, and it scouring the woodland for meat the while?"

"The castle is not far, Mistress. Let us get behind its walls," said Ranulf. Then he turned to his men. "Mount!"

The column re-formed as Molly and the two young folk tramped back to the wagons.

BUT, AS THOUGH TO MOCK Ranulf's eagerness for refuge, the storm redoubled in intensity. Drifts lay across the trail, ice spicules stung the face, and the wind through the harp of the trees rose from moans and wails to a shrieking roar.

The light began to fail, and Ranulf had tallow-coated torches of pinewood broken out from one of the packhorses. He ducked inside Molly's big wagon and plied flint and steel. After some difficulty, a torch was ignited and he came out and lit the others from it. The resin and tallow warred with the snow and it was uncertain whether they would stay lit. Some went out; others held a spitting, wavering flame.

Halts to send scouts to the side, secured by lines, became more frequent. Finally they stopped. Ranulf could no longer tell where they were, save that the castle must be very near. Snow began to accumulate on the roofs and the left side of the wagons, on the horses' rumps and the riders' shoulders. Heads were bowed and hoods held close to foil the worst of the biting winds. Ranulf sent a man back to Goscelin where he rode at Mavourneen's head; after a moment's consultation, Goscelin undid leather lashings and handed over a curving shape swathed in goatskin: a hunting horn. The first rider took it and rode back up the line.

A moment later they heard the braying call of the horn from the head of the column. Nemain, on the seat at Hob's right, cocked her head to hear a reply. The horn wound again. She pulled her hood back; beneath her hood she wore a coif, a helmet-close cap of linen that covered her ears. She undid the laces under her chin and pulled up the flaps over her ears, the better to hear. She leaned across Hob, bracing an elbow on his thigh, and gazed into the darkening forest.

Suddenly the wind fell off sharply; the warm salt scent of her body rose to Hob from beneath the sheepskin cloak. She leaned, listening for an answer from the night. The ruddy fluttering light from Goscelin's torch played over her as she cocked her head to hear, and Hob found himself marveling, despite the aching cold tormenting him, at the translucent perfection of her ear, red-tipped in the frosty air, set close to the skull and delicately back-slanted—he wondered dreamily how he had never noticed this before. To Hob they two seemed sheltered in a circle of wavering red-gold torchlight, and the whole world left outside in the darkness, and before him flitted a brief, incoherent memory of last summer: warm sunlight filtering through the treetops, green leaves, green eyes.

"There!" she said, pointing forward but to the left, and just then the wind returned and slapped snow into his face, and he awoke to the night, and his fear of the unknown slayer, and his dull grief for the lost Margery; and Nemain was just a skinny girl again and halfway to being his sister. He wondered if he had slept for a moment.

Hob peered up the line of the stalled caravan. He could just discern, through the snowfall, Molly climbing down from her wagon seat, swathed in one of her shawls, and making her way forward. Presumably if Nemain could hear the horn's answer, Molly could as well.

Up at the front of the column Ranulf sounded the horn again and this time even Hob could hear the reply from the castle, not the raucous bawling of the cow horn Ranulf blew but a deeper bronze moan, just perceptible above the gale, but very different in tone from the voice of the storm.

Soon thereafter Molly returned to her wagon and the little column resumed its progress, moving ahead and veering slightly to the left. There was another stop to wind the horn, and this time the reply was close. The weather made one more prodigious effort to defeat them, the snow seeming a solid barrier, the wind shrieking. The company stumbled ahead—they were half-blind, but hope had set their hearts alight and strengthened their limbs, and they moved quickly.

And again the wind dropped off sharply, and Hob became aware of a looming darkness directly before them. The column of horsemen ahead halted, Molly's wagon halted, and Nemain set the brake as the little ass halted as well.

Goscelin looked back at Hob and Nemain from his place by Mavourneen's head. He was grinning broadly within his hood.

"The castle," he said.

Part III

THE CASTLE

CHAPTER 12

OSCELIN DISMOUNTED. HE wrapped his mount's reins and Mavourneen's lead rope about his free hand and held the torch high, peering through the snowfall to see what they were doing ahead. After a bit Molly's wagon rumbled on, and Goscelin began to trudge forward, leading the two animals toward a short movable wooden bridge.

The bridge spanned a dry moat, two fathoms deep and as wide across; on the far side a tall hedge of English thorn ran along the inner bank of the moat, an impenetrable wall of intertwined branches thick with three-inch flesh-tearing spears. Ranulf had placed men on both sides of the bridge, with the sputtering tallow-and-pinewood torches casting a fidgeting light over the snow-covered planks. To either hand the snow-flakes dropped into the golden torchlight, glittered an instant, and fell from sight into the dark ditch. The boards mumbled and banged beneath the hooves and wheels, and the wagon slid a little sideways, making Hob snatch for a handhold as his balance wavered. He sent a swift wordless prayer that the side rails of the bridge might be stout enough to hold the wagon if they struck. An instant later the skid stopped.

Then they were over the gap, still on the extended tail of the bridge. This tail rested on log rollers; the bridge could thus be drawn back toward the castle if necessary, leaving no way across the moat. The wagon rolled off the bridge tail and bumped down onto the clear stretch of snow-clad earth between the hedge and the castle gatehouse.

The gatehouse was formed from two round towers, midway in the western curtain wall. The towers were conjoined by a rectangular three-story structure that housed the entrance to the castle courtyard. The valves of the outer doors stood open, and Ranulf and the advance guard had already ridden in, trailing their share of the new horses. Their hooves rang on the stone, a hollow din, booming in the enclosed space. Molly's wagon followed them, and there was still room within the gatehouse passage for the small middle wagon. Goscelin walked them in under the ceiling, a low-arched affair of stone, pierced with round holes; each hole was perhaps a cubit in diameter. The walls on left and right had narrow vertical openings in the stone: arrow slits.

They were now in a sort of short tunnel within the gatehouse. Behind them were the front doors, already being swung shut by men-at-arms from the porter's gatehouse guard. The heavy valves swung closed with a ponderous grace; there was a muffled thud as they met. Other men grappled with handles set into the walls. The handles were set into squared-off logs shot back into holes in the side walls; these were now drawn out, gleaming with the animal fat worked into them as a lubricant. The beams were dragged across the width of the entranceway, sliding into brackets on the doors, strengthening the seal.

Ahead of the travelers was the portcullis, a heavy latticework of oak beams clad in beaten iron. The vertical beams ended at the bottom in sharpened steel points resting on the stone of the gatehouse floor. The portcullis could only be raised with much effort by guards in the chamber above this entryway; chains clanked upward onto a cogged wheel; pawls prevented it from slipping back down. But the lattice could be dropped immediately by one person: a kick to the braking lever released it, and the whole weight thundered down in an instant, and it was a sorry wretch who stood beneath those heavy pointed ends when it fell.

Immediately beyond the portcullis was another pair of solid doors, prohibiting a glimpse into the inner courtyard. Hob became acutely aware that they were in a trap, with Jack left outside. He told himself that they were among friends, that Ranulf and his men were in here with them, but the events of the last few days had tightened his vigilance till it thrummed like a plucked bowstring at any least threat.

To distract himself he looked around: at the doors with their huge bars; at the massive stone walls to either hand, curving inward with the shape of the two gatehouse towers; at the ceiling with its spaced holes; at the floor of fitted stone, littered with wisps of straw and bits of dried horse dung. The horses were fidgeting in the enclosed space and two watered the stones where they stood. The passageway began to smell of horse and, to a lesser extent, of leather, and men's sweat, and the smoke from Ranulf's torches with its resinous undertone. The close air, despite the many living bodies and the flaring torches, could not be said to be warm, but it was at least out of the wind and snow.

Hob nudged Nemain, and pointed out the holes in the ceiling; he could hear the sound of several men's voices up there.

"Those are murderesses," she said. She was only a year or so older than Hob, but she had traveled with Molly for many years, and knew much that he did not.

"Murderesses?" Hob said, confused: there was no mistaking the deep, harsh male tones above.

"That's what they call them, *murderesses,* those holes you're just after pointing at. If there's someone they don't like coming in, they trap them in here, and the next moment aren't they raining arrows or hot oil down through those holes. Murderesses."

"Oh," said Hob, looking up again. One was just above their heads.

There were more voices and grunts from above, a clank of iron pawls, and the portcullis began to rise, disappearing inch by inch through a slot in the ceiling stones, up into the guardroom above. Soon they heard it bang home. They waited; still the inner doors remained closed.

The horses danced in place, the clop of horseshoe on stone echoing and reechoing in the vaulted chamber. One horse was much larger than the others: a destrier, trained to a knight's service, worth many times the value of any of the other mounts. It stood still, tall enough that Hob could see it above the intervening horses, and looked about placidly at its lesser kin; it had the calm of a very large animal that had had fear trained out of it.

Roger's mare began to bite at the horse next to her, and he bent forward and punched at her neck; her ears went flat, and she curled her head around and snapped at his knee, just out of reach.

The sergeant stood in his stirrups, peering upward through the nearest murderess. He subsided, but a moment later was standing again, trying to see what the porter's crew was doing in the upper room. "God's wounds," bellowed Ranulf, losing patience at last, "are all you fucking lackwits asleep up there?"

A face appeared in one of the roof-holes. "There's snow what's drifted up against the inner doors, sarge; Waleran's away to the back shed for shovels."

"Bennet! Bennet, you whoreson fuck, we're perishing of cold down here!" Roger yelled up toward the speaker. He started to stand in his stirrups as Ranulf had done, but the mare moved in an intricate shuffle under him and he thought better of it and dropped back into the saddle with a thump. "Shake it off, Jesus's sake, and put it back in your braies!" And then, muttering, "Sweet Mother of God, get us in where it's warm!" He bunched the reins up in his fists as he tried to check the mare's antics; she was trying to scrape his leg against the wall.

"And God and Mary with *you* as well, Roger, you prick," the porter called, laughing. "Say an *Ave* while you're waiting that you may not burst of choler." He withdrew from the hole; they heard him say something and there came a gust of laughter from several men in the upper room. But very soon thereafter they heard the scrape of wooden-bladed shovels in the snow outside; there were several clanking thumps as heavy bolts were shot, and then the inner doors swung open.

Hob looked past Molly's wagon and the mounted men ahead, out over the snowfield that was the bailey, with thick flakes falling straight down onto an expanse of drifts. Here and there the track of someone tramping across the bailey from one building to another could be seen, but mostly it was a field of white. Spitting torches set in recessed sconces showed the entrances to smaller outbuildings that backed up against the curtain walls, and hinted at those high dark curtain walls themselves and at the loom of the great keep.

The horses clattered out into the night; their hooves fell silent as they stepped out into two or more feet of snow, with higher drifts. Ranulf led the way ahead, bearing to the right as he tracked toward the stables. The wagons trundled out, one after the other. Behind him Hob heard a rumble and a bang as the portcullis was dropped, and then the groan of the inner doors being swung shut. He was uneasily aware that Jack was still outside the castle with the remainder of the men-at-arms. In a few moments they had crossed the snowy courtyard, churning the smooth expanse into jumbled drifts, drawing near two connected stone buildings, low but wide—the castle stables, set against the eastern curtain wall at the opposite side of the bailey from the gatehouse.

Broad doors were thrown back, and Ranulf's men swung down from their saddles and walked their mounts and the new horses into the golden warmth. The near-silent shuffle of hooves through the bailey snowdrifts became a muffled drumming as the horses walked onto the hard-packed earth floor of the stables. Grooms appeared and quickly relieved the men-at-arms of the spare horses. The group began to disperse to left and right down the central corridor of the stables, heading for their individual stalls, passing from Hob's sight.

Ranulf rattled off orders and stumped back out into the bailey, heading for the keep to make his report. He was pressing with one hand at his lower back, walking stiffly after the long cold hours in the saddle.

He had assigned Goscelin and two other men to Molly's party. One went up to Milo's head; Goscelin surrendered his mount to the third man and pulled Mavourneen toward the wall beside the stable. After a bit of maneuvering the two wagons were backed up to the wall, side by side, and Hob and the first man-at-arms began unhitching the ox, while Goscelin helped Nemain get the little donkey out of the traces.

They worked with numb fingers to release the various buckles and ease the slipknots. Soon the clacking of the portcullis gears floated across the bailey to Hob's ears, as the porter and his crew went about admitting Jack Brown and the others, and then the second part of the group came floundering across the open courtyard. Hob felt better as Jack joined them. The dark man led the mare up and circled her about, then smoothly backed the third wagon against the curtain wall.

Jack had the wagon braked and the mare out of harness so swiftly that he finished a moment or two after everyone else. Molly and Nemain disappeared into the large wagon while Hob and the men walked the animals into the welcoming stable.

Grooms descended on them and led them to various stalls. The stable crew displayed a variety of clothing, but all wore the insignia of

Blanchefontaine Castle: a cloth badge sewn to their outer garments, bearing a stylized white fountain. Four lines representing water leaped from the fountain's top and curled to right and left, seeking the ground.

Hob tried to get Milo settled and fed, but he was bone-weary, and quite willing to let a pair of grooms push him good-naturedly from the stall. He and Jack joined Goscelin and one of the men-at-arms—the other had vanished somewhere—and went back outside to the big wagon to find Molly.

Molly and Nemain awaited them by the back of the large wagon; the door stood open, and a dim gold glow poured out into the steadily falling snow. Just inside the doorjamb was a stout chest, of cedar banded with iron, that Molly used for the finer elements of her wardrobe. Molly came up to Jack; she put a hand on his arm, and pointed out the chest. He went up and reached in for the rope handle on one end and dragged it screeching out onto the wagon lip. He caught hold of the other handle and slid the chest off the wagon and stepped back with it. Nemain climbed into the wagon and extinguished the candle, then closed the back door. From a thong looped about her narrow waist she took a small disk-handled key and secured the back door latch with its iron barrel lock, another sign of Molly's wealth.

Goscelin turned and led the way toward the keep. As they trudged toward the dark indistinct loom of the castle's main building, a thinning of the downpouring snow allowed Hob to see, a few yards away from Molly's caravan, two wagons backed against the curtain wall. Each had a layer of snow several feet thick on its roof. One wagon was a workaday transport, but the other was of fine dark wood, with shutters adorned with graven vines, leaves, faces: Lady Svajone's two wagons. The caking of snow on the upper surfaces of the carving brought the vine-and-leaf pattern into bright relief against the dark wood.

"Mistress! Look!"

Molly turned to follow Hob's pointing finger, and her handsome face broke into a grin. She stood beaming, her strong legs planted in a drift, snowflakes beginning to catch on her shawl.

"Well, and there's one thing that's come right. They must surely have parted from those poor masons, and denied that thing another feast," she said with pleasure.

"Unless," said Nemain darkly, shivering, lost inside her grandmother's cloak, "some of the men from the castle have found but the wagons, and all dead within, as at the inn."

"Nay," said Molly confidently, "I do not feel it so. We will meet them within."

Roger came up to them from the stables, tramping his way through the snow. "Come, Mistress," he said to Molly. "There's warmth and every good thing within; surely you have had enough of snow this day?"

"I have that," said Molly, and the party moved on toward the keep's looming darkness.

The keep had no entrance at ground level. Instead, an enclosed stairway ran up the south side. Entry was into a fortified forebuilding: a sort of miniature of the castle entrance, a cottage-sized stone building with a stout oak door in its eastern face, farthest from the gatehouse. The door was hinged with iron straps and pierced at eye level by an iron grille. Roger stepped up to it and knocked backhand; the iron lozenges sewn into the leather of his glove clanked against the grille. The inner grille covering shot aside, a guard examined Roger briefly, and withdrew; an instant later Hob heard the snick of drawn bolts, and the door swung open.

Roger and Goscelin and the third man-at-arms entered to a volley of greetings and the insults with which men express pleasure at the sight of friends. Molly's party crowded in behind. The room was warmed only by body heat and rushlight, but it was out of the snow and the wind, and just being within a real room after the snowstorm was a delight to Hob.

He looked around. The guardroom was bare except for a bench and table, a weapons chest, cloaks hung on pegs, a water bucket, and two hard-eyed guards: one quite large, one small and wiry. Hob, trying to return their gaze, at first thought the mismatch somewhat comical. Almost at once he changed his mind, deciding that he understood the reason some sergeant had paired them: one would be very strong, and the other very quick.

An arch at the back of the guardroom led to one side of a small unlit vestibule divided into two halves. The wall that divided the vestibule ran only partway to the back. It was necessary to walk to the rear of the vestibule, turn rightward around the end of the divider, and double back again to gain the bottom of the stairs. In this way no light from the guardroom reached the bottom half of the stairs; it was lit entirely from the torches in brackets along the upper part of the stairwell.

The party bunched up for a moment in the dim-lit second part of the vestibule. The entrance to the enclosed stairway was faced with ashlar, and peeking from behind the lintel stone were the iron teeth of another portcullis. Unlike the great portcullis that closed the keep, this smaller gate was kept raised, unless there was an attack under way. Now, drawn up as it was so that its iron fangs lined the top of the opening, the portcullis gave the stairway entrance the suggestion of a mouth, yawning wide to devour all who would enter.

But Goscelin and his comrade trudged prosaically through the arch and led the climb up the stairway: broad stone treads and modest risers in a rectangular corridor also lined with ashlar. Molly and Nemain followed next, the girl trailing her hand along the smooth stone. The stairs were completely enclosed, with neither window nor arrow slit. Roger held back and offered to help Jack with the chest. Jack just shook his head; he carried the chest easily. He managed to convey his thanks with a smile, a dip of the head. They went up together, the young man-at-arms pointing out this and that aspect of the castle's defenses to

Jack, the older veteran, who listened and nodded but did not speak. Hob tailed along behind.

Halfway up, the stairway leveled out for about seven or eight feet. The floor beneath their shoes here was dark scarred wood, with chains running from the near corners of the wood up at an angle to wind around small capstans set in the walls, perhaps eight or nine steps above.

Roger stamped on the wood as they traversed the landing, producing a sepulchral *boom*.

"If anyone comes so far with ill intent—not, mind you, that anyone has, yet—we'll pull this up. There's a pit beneath our feet, and this little bridge closes off the stairway above, and stops any arrows they're shooting up at us. But best of all, it shuts off the light from above when it's up, and anyone coming up those lower stairs in a rush, without torches"—he pointed backward with his thumb, not looking—"well, they're in the dark, aren't they, and their friends crowding up behind them, and a big fucking drop before them. The drop's twice as high as I am." Roger gave a hard and merciless grin; suddenly he looked ten years older, and much grimmer. "There are spikes."

They trooped on up the stairway. Hob could hear a murmur as of many people, a bustle of activity, drifting down from above. The air grew perceptibly warmer as they neared the top landing. Here they found heavy doors, with the inevitable pair of guards lounging near. The Sieur de Blanchefontaine did not follow military ceremony out here in the northern forest, but the Scottish border was not distant, with its clansmen under uneasy Norman rule, and a Norman lord had many enemies: there was a careful roster of rotated guards, men who remained armed when others had hung sword-belts and mail and boiled-leather gambesons on pegs, men leaning against the walls or sprawled on the outer benches in the hall or at the main entrances, eating and drinking very little. New guests were unobtrusively watched; so discourtesy was avoided and safety preserved.

As they came up the men pulled the doors open, with the inevitable barrage of greetings for Roger. There was speculation that a certain Lucinda might be easier to live with now that Roger had returned to comfort her; although it seemed that Olivier, who had just preceded them, had reported that Roger's mare had replaced Lucinda in his affections, and that he had paid the mare the sort of attention formerly reserved for Lucinda, and so on, without mercy but without malice either; all this Roger accepted with a grin, and there was a great deal of slapping of backs and shoulders.

Hob and Jack followed Roger through the arch that led from the stair landing into the great hall. Before them was a carved wooden screen that stood across the entranceway, four feet in, blocking their view: it was several feet wider than the doorway, so that they had to walk a few paces sideways and turn around the end of the screen to enter the hall. The screen was another device to slow down attackers, and to prevent arrows from being shot from the landing into the hall.

Once around the screen, Hob found himself at one end of a long high hall, with perhaps forty men and women bustling here and there, setting up rows of trestle tables and benches, positioned lengthwise up the room. There was a low hubbub of conversation; the occasional burst of laughter; the odd bang or screech of wood as tables and benches were dragged from the walls to the center of the room. As the tables were assembled in long lines down along the room, rough aisles took shape between them.

The broad planks of the floor were covered with rushes. A faint rattling could be heard beneath the growing din: a handful of boys were strewing a fresh layer of rushes atop the old, working from baskets of the tubular stems. The baskets stood here and there in the aisles. At least one lad was sprinkling some mixture of dried herbs between and beneath the tables. Hob thought to detect the scent of lavender and lady-of-the-meadow, and the warm sweet smell of winter savory; perhaps there was germander as well.

Across the width of the hall, Hob spied Ranulf, a little girl on one hip and a broad grin on his face, talking with a heavyset woman, a bit younger than he, with a plain pleasant face. Roger clapped Jack on the shoulder, pointed up the hall toward Molly, and ambled off to report to Ranulf.

Hob's face began to tingle. He became aware that there were two fireplaces against the far wall. The smaller was down at this end of the hall; an enormous hearth dominated the upper part of the big chamber, and for the first time in what seemed a year, Hob felt real heat beating against his skin.

Molly and Nemain stood talking amid a small knot of splendidly dressed people. The sudden heat after the brutal cold of the storm had brought a ruddy glow to Molly's cheek, and Nemain's throat and face showed a rose blush overspreading her pale skin.

Jack carried the chest up near them; he stopped a respectful five paces short. Molly looked about, still talking, and nodded. She pointed to the floor, and Jack set the chest down in the rushes with a soft thump, and sat down on it, waiting. Hob came up beside him and loitered, trying to see and hear without seeming to do so.

He sauntered forward a step or two toward Molly and the two people with whom she was closely engaged: a tall richly dressed woman with a bunch of keys at her girdle, clearly the chatelaine, and beside her, a grim knight whom Hob at first took to be her husband.

Hob's English tended to be more low speech, with its roots in the thick Anglian and Saxon dialects, but Father Athelstan, though from a Saxon family, had been chaplain to two Norman lords before the changing tides of fortune had beached him, elderly and lame, in his position as pastor of Hob's little village and, later, Hob's protector. He had intended Hob for the Church, and he had taught Hob some rudiments of writing, although they had not gotten far past the alphabet when the old priest's eyes began to fail, and instruction began to falter.

Still, Father Athelstan spoke of a cousin in the bishop's service, and of sending Hob thence when he should be more grown. To that end he had insisted that Hob learn to serve at table as a page, and to speak passable, if somewhat accented, Norman English, and many summer afternoons Hob spent learning to assist at Mass and to spell out letters with all instruction conducted in crisp nasal Norman English, studded with French terms like currants in a bun, while through the windows the warm drowsy air brought the guttural Germanic accents of the village lads shouting at their play.

Molly had swept like a salt breeze from the Western Ocean through the little hamlet, and convinced the ailing old man to apprentice Hob to her service, and swept out along the road again two weeks later. Father Athelstan she left, with bottles of her potions in a goatskin bag, standing in the roadstead, one hand raised in farewell, next to a priest house that suddenly seemed curiously empty to him, and which he felt reluctant to re-enter.

Now Hob watched Molly, and Nemain as well, in travel-stained garb, speaking to this mighty lady, both boldly confronting their hostess and the grim figure beside her, and gradually his ear became attuned to the Norman speech of the highborn, more sophisticated than Ranulf's, and certainly more well-mannered than Roger's.

He was still a little distance away and so, even as his grasp of the idiom returned to him, he could hear only disjointed phrases. He heard "Ireland" and "gone into exile"; he thought he heard the word "queen" or "queens," and—to his surprise—Molly's real name, "Maeve"; and then, as Molly's expression darkened, "stalked us through the woods." The Norman knight and lady looked at each other with concern at that point, and Hob guessed he knew their topic at that moment.

A boy perhaps a year his senior passed by, the white fountain badge on the breast of his tunic, a large bundle of dried rushes held in the crook of his left arm; with his right hand he was throwing handfuls down along the aisles. Where the planks of the floor met the wall was a small pile of dog droppings, dried almost white, and he swerved to bury it deftly beneath a layer of rushes. Every sennight or so, or before major festivals, the hall was broomed clean, down to the boards, and new rushes laid, but tonight the serving lads went ahead with the everyday practice of covering the old rushes with a new layer.

As the boy came back, Hob stepped out of his way, contriving to come a bit closer to the central group, to learn how Molly fared with her introductions. It did seem to him as though Molly was as comfortable as she was at Osbert's Inn, and as sure of a reception, and gradually the atmosphere thawed, and he had a chance to examine the woman whom Molly addressed as "Lady Isabeau."

Lady Isabeau was tall for a woman, nearly as tall as Molly, but slender where Molly was stout, with a smooth immobile face that looked as if it had been carved from ivory, pale and serene. Hob stared at her: glossy black hair bound about the brows with a broad white linen fillet and partially concealed by a veil that draped down her neck; dark eyes beneath dark brows plucked thin; unsmiling lips, full and well shaped. There was so little expression on her face, and its beauty was so unworldly, that Hob had a moment when he thought her an apparition, or a graven figure. *"Blanche comme la neige,"* came to his mind, a song Molly had taught him, *"belle comme le jour."* The thinnest of scars ran from her hairline down her forehead, divided her left eyebrow, and curved along her cheek to the corner of her mouth, and seemed at once to augment her beauty and to reinforce its carven stillness, as if some wright's chisel had slipped in the course of fashioning her visage. A linen band of the sort known as a barbette ran down from the fillet at her temples and passed under her chin, framing her face, and rendering her features all the more austere.

Her gown was a muted purple; heavy embroidery of red and blue circled its neckline, and it was gathered by a zone of gray silk, sewn with pearls, that circled her hips. From this belt depended a silver ring, as wide around as a big man's fist. On the ring was a bunch of black iron keys, of varying sizes: the symbol and reality of her standing as administrator of the household. As she spoke, she fiddled with the keys as though they were prayer beads; they gave off a continual muted clink, just barely audible to Hob above the rumble of voices, the thuds and thumps of plank tabletops settling onto their trestles.

If Lady Isabeau suggested a figure rendered from cool ivory, Sir Balthasar was her antithesis: one in whom the sanguine strove with the choleric. Hob's first impression was of long, flat, darkly ruddy cheeks, clean-shaven in the Norman style; a clenched jaw; a grim unforgiving mouth. The knight seemed to radiate a black heat. Sir Balthasar was a man tall and brawny, with thick strong limbs and a hard-fleshed barrel-shaped body. His shoulders, which strained against the linen of his tunic, were not so much wide as heavy; his calves swelled the cross-braces of his hose. He was still in his prime, but at the far end of it, his black eyebrows beginning to show the luxuriant tangle of the aging male. From beneath these thickets two stony black eyes peered out at the world with the suspicion, the arrogant belligerence, of the wild white king bull.

He was dressed with almost clerical severity: over his long gray tunic was a surcoat of darker gray; his hose were green; his belt and shoes of dark green leather. Even the coif he wore, the linen helmet fastened beneath his chin, was a pale gray. Fastened to his surcoat was a brooch worn as a badge: a silver disk inlaid with murrey-colored enamel, against which the white fountain of Blanchefontaine stood out, rendered in raised silver. At the right side of his belt, a heavy dagger nestled in its green leather sheath: its hilt was plain, wrapped in leather strips; its pommel was a sphere of gray pitted iron, darkened with age. The impression that he made on Hob was one of implacable force.

It was not until Lady Isabeau said, with a nod to the knight,

"Sir Balthasar has heard from certain of our people that you are of good repute among the countryfolk about atte Well's inn," that Hob realized that this was the formidable Sir Balthasar, the mareschal whose wrath Ranulf had cautioned Roger against arousing, and not the lord of Blanchefontaine himself.

As forbidding as the knight was, Hob noticed that Nemain, who stood quietly by as Molly spoke for all of them, held herself erect, gazing coolly at Sir Balthasar as though he were the supplicant seeking hospitality and not she, and he of lesser station at that.

Hob, though, was thinking that he had never seen such grandly dressed persons, save only Lady Svajone and her entourage. As though the thought had conjured them up, here, making their way down the hall with difficulty, was the Lietuvan party: Lady Svajone, and Doctor Vytautas, and the noblewoman's two-peas-in-a-pod esquires.

CHAPTER 13

HE OLD WOMAN WAS SUP-
ported on one side by Azuolas,
the stockier of her guards, and
on the other by Vytautas. The doctor walked with
prim steps, keeping pace with the tiny noblewoman's
slow progress, but his eyes were on Molly's face, and he
gave her a delighted smile.

Behind them paced Gintaras, lithe as a panther,
looking about him, expressionless, alert for any disturbance that might come too near his frail charge. Even
a boisterous serving-maid might do harm to those delicate old limbs. He had divested himself of his sword,
as a guest in this hall—only the guards went fully
armed indoors—but, perhaps from habit, his hand
did not stray far from the dagger slung down beside
his right hip. Its hilt was carved from some rich pale
wood, the pommel representing a fanciful bird's head,
with its neck ruff rendered as pointed scales rather

than natural-seeming feathers; the bird's eyes were balls of what looked to Hob like lead, perhaps to add weight for balance.

Lady Svajone tottered up to the group and saluted Lady Isabeau and Sir Balthasar. Then she turned to Molly and took both the Irishwoman's hands in hers. Azuolas unobtrusively steadied her with a hand beneath her elbow and the other across her back. "I am happy, we are well meeting again, and also, also though you, you, you is coming through the white, the white, the coldness . . ." Here she gave up all attempt at language, and just grinned at Molly with the pure unaffected pleasure of a child meeting a playmate. Vytautas stood beaming at them from the side.

Lady Svajone had established herself by some means as a person of influence in the castle. With her affectionate greeting of Molly, all reserve on the part of Lady Isabeau seemed to vanish. She ceased to jingle her ring of keys; she turned to a page who stood attentively just behind her, a boy perhaps eleven years of age, clad in livery of murrey. Against the deep claret of his blouse the ubiquitous fountain badge was worked in white thread. Lady Isabeau introduced him as Hubert, and gave him instructions for the settling in of Molly's party. She kissed Molly on both cheeks, and then Lady Svajone as well; the grim knight gave a small bow; and the two moved off, trailed by Lady Isabeau's attendant women. The lady and castellan of Blanchefontaine were immediately surrounded by a small cloud of pages: some who came to report, others who were dispatched again on errands—a castle does not run itself.

Vytautas caught sight of Hob, and nodded to him, a nod that somehow seemed to Hob to recall their meeting at the monastery, and to suggest that this in some manner made them old friends. Hob smiled, and bowed politely as Father Athelstan had taught him.

". . . glad we are to be seeing you," Molly was saying. "We're after having no word of you at Osbert's Inn"—Hob thought to himself that if he had not known what grief lay behind those two words, he might have missed the slight hitch in Molly's voice—"and weren't we set upon by a band of wolf's-heads, an ambush in the forest, and then we're thinking you must be meeting an evil end on the road—"

The little noblewoman broke in. "Nay, nay, we are not at this, this inn, we are travel the road to here, coming here, we are going with the, the steps of quickness. This inn, we passened them by, at this inn, I am being so fearend—"

"Frightened," murmured Vytautas.

"Frighten, yes," said Lady Svajone, not quite mastering it, "and wishened to pass it by, the inn, and we are running till we are run to this . . . stonehouse, this"—here she looked at Doctor Vytautas—"*pilis?*"

"Castle," said Vytautas.

"Casta, yes, this casta," she said. "When we cross the water, the, the flat place in the water, the not deep place, we are crossing that little river, is remind me of my homeland, so many rivers, and then we are saying fare them well to the masons, they are with us till then, and we come here, through the forest, and to here, to this place."

"We came to the inn after yourselves had passed, and stayed but a few nights. And then we went back there, after the attack it was, and . . ." Nothing in Molly's face or voice changed this time, but she fell silent for a few moments. ". . . and found everyone within killed, and many of them friends of mine, and they all despatched by some murthering thing, some huge beast, what we call in Erin an *ollphéist,* a monster, and it haunting our trail all this time."

Lady Svajone's hand flew to her throat, and she leaned more heavily on Azuolas. Her mouth opened in surprise; her white eyebrows lifted high in shock. This latter action further revealed her eyes, clear eyes hitherto half-concealed in their drooping wrinkled lids, eyes of a true gray, large and slightly tilted. Hob found them surprisingly lovely amid those aged features.

"Makes terrible! Terrible! All those peoples who, who, they are to be, being, your friends!" She wrung her hands; she gave a little shudder. The two esquires looked on, enigmatic as cats. They watched the group carefully: they knew that something was wrong, but had no knowledge of the language. Gintaras looked pointedly at the doctor. Vytautas pursed his lips, shook his head very slightly, and the younger men relaxed somewhat.

Lady Svajone leaned forward, looking up into Molly's face. "But we are hearen that this Osba's, Osbra's, is strong place, yes? And we are see, as we pass, those so strong walls. . . . Is like little wooden casta, yes?"

Molly nodded. "Like a little castle, yes, and protected by ten great dogs as well, and weren't even those dogs slain along with the people."

The old woman began to tremble violently. "Makes terrible! The monks are tell us of this dogs, these dogs, when we are at the, the monk casta."

"Monas—" began Vytautas fussily, but she waved a hand at him.

"Yes, yes, with the monks, they tell us stay at Osbra's, the dogs to protect us. How can people not be so fearend, frighten, if even these big dogs is, are—to dead, to death? Killet, are killet, and their bellies slashet open like fishes! I am frighten to ever leave this casta!" The tiny frame was shaking perceptibly, and she seemed near tears in her terror.

Vytautas seemed alarmed by such extreme emotion, and he stepped close to her and said something in a soothing tone in their own language, and with an arm about her shoulder, took her wrist with his other hand and surreptitiously felt there for the echo of her heartbeat, while darting a look at Molly that was both a warning and an appeal.

But Lady Svajone broke free and tottered forward; she embraced Molly and, as she looked up into Molly's face, she sighed and visibly relaxed. A smile overspread her face and she said, breathless, "I am happiness that you have come to me, my dear, for happiness that you are safe and also because I am to be safe, to be feel safe, with you near."

Molly, as was her instinct, put her arms around the little woman and made comforting noises, and indeed the Lietuvan was so small that she seemed a child in Molly's embrace. At last she stepped back with another sigh. At once Azuolas was beside her again, ready to bear her up if she began to fall.

"It's happy I am to see yourselves as well," said Molly, "and it is well that you parted with the masons at the ford. We ourselves went south, and we found . . . some indication that the masons, the same that set out with you, that they were after being killed as well, and by the jaws of this beast, and others as well, nearer to this castle. We were after thinking that you, also—well, that your bread was baked; that yourselves were after perishing with the rest."

The old woman put her hand out and Azuolas smoothly slipped an arm under it for support. But now that her first panic had passed, she maintained her composure to a great degree.

"Makes terrible," she said quietly. "They are going them, they are walking them to the house of God, to builden in the house of God. Terrible, terrible." Again she put a hand to her throat. "I am frighten that it follows you here to this casta. We will be killet, killened, like those at the inn."

A shadow passed over Molly's face as the specter of the inn arose again, and Hob himself thought: *Margery*.

"It's safe enough that you are here," said Molly.

"But the people are killet at the inn, what was so safe."

Molly gestured toward the hall. "Consider how much higher are these walls than the inn's, and they being thicker as well."

And with pats and murmured assurances, Molly and Vytautas between them managed to calm the old woman down. Behind them, Gintaras kept a stern and wary eye on the little page Hubert, who stood fidgeting nearby, a bit too close to Lady Svajone for the esquire's liking.

Presently they took their leave, and continued their slow progress down the hall, and Molly's party was free to continue.

* * *

WITH A BOW TO MOLLY, Hubert turned and led them up the hall; at the rear came Jack, walking easily with the chest. Toward the front of the hall a curtained alcove led to a turret stairwell. They wound their way up and up. The shallow wedge-shaped treads of stone were worn a bit where others had gone before; all noises were amplified by the stone cylinder the stairway was set in; midway, an arrow slit admitted a fitful stream of cold air.

They came out into a corridor. One side was stone, with windows to the outside; the shutters in these windows shifted and groaned as the bitter wind sought entrance. The hallway was noticeably cooler than the great hall below, with its two fireplaces. Hubert led the way past a sturdy oaken door, stopping before another such. He opened this and stood aside for Molly and Nemain to enter.

This was a solar, a private apartment within the castle. An outer room, and a smaller inner room with a curtained bed-closet. This was of oak, with a feather mattress, sheets, pillows, quilts: Hob marveled at such luxury. Two could sleep in it, secure from drafts and warm by reason of shared body heat. Molly pointed and Jack brought the chest into this room, depositing it with a thump.

Hob was looking about at the rooms: walls covered with rough white plaster, a small fireplace in the outer room and a somewhat larger one in the inner room, and here came two men in the ubiquitous Blanchefontaine white-on-murrey livery, bearing wood-and-leather-strap cots and simple bedding, for Jack and Hob to use in the outer room. Behind them came two men struggling with a heavy wooden tub lined with cloth and filled with steaming water, which they placed at Molly's direction in the inner chamber. When they had gone, Nemain closed the door to the inner room, and Hubert was left with Hob and Jack, who threw himself down on one of the cots without any bedding and let out a gusty sigh.

Hubert turned to Hob. "Let me show you where the garderobe may be found, and I pray you tell your mistress, for I will soon be needed elsewhere."

He led Hob out into the corridor and along to the garderobe, away at the corridor's end. This privy was down a short hall that led into the east wall of the keep, ending in a turret room that overhung a sheer drop: behind and below the castle ran a small river valley. The page showed Hob the box where straw was kept, to clean himself with.

As they returned along the hall, Hubert halted before a stone basin in a recess. He showed Hob how to work a valve at the end of a pipe that sprang from the back of the recess, like a branch growing through a wall. A gout of water sprang forth into the basin, swirled away into a hole at the bottom; Hob stepped back in astonishment. Hubert laughed. "There's a tank above and water brought up from the well and down from the roof cisterns to feed it. You may draw water to wash yourself, or to drink." There was an air of proprietary delight in showing this unsophisticated visitor a feature of castle life, but the young page's open and friendly manner drew on the unforced camaraderie of boys, and Hob could take no offense.

Drawing Hob by the sleeve away from the recess, Hubert asked, "Do you not have such, in your castles away in Ireland?" and not waiting for an answer, rattled on: "How does it come that two queens travel with so tiny a party? Are they outlawed? Have you come with them from Ireland? What is it like to sail on the water?"

Hob looked desperately along the passage toward the door of Molly's solar. "I, we . . ." he stammered. Just then another page, perhaps fifteen years of age, appeared at the end of the corridor.

"Hubert!" he called; he made urgent gestures and turned to go back.

"I pray you will excuse me," said Hubert, and bowed prettily, and hastened off after his older fellow, leaving Hob to make his way back to the solar.

* * *

Soon after Hob had returned, the inner door opened and Molly called Jack in to carry the tub out to the outer room, which he did handily, carrying the full tub that two men had wrestled with, puffing only a little, and spilling only a cup or so. Molly shut the door again after him.

Jack bathed first, washing himself with a soldier's practical efficiency. He rose, dripping like a dog, and accepted a dry cloth from Hob; he toweled his thick locks with one hand while pointing to the now-cooling water. Hob threw off his clothes and bathed hastily while Jack dressed in livery that Molly had given him. It had been a while since they had had the luxury of bathing, and Hob was surprised to find a faint suggestion of down at his groin. The water began to take on a chill, though, and in any case Jack was now dressed and gesturing for him to hurry.

There was a set of livery for Hob as well, a little large, but serviceable. Over hose of green went an overshirt of watchet-colored wool; to Hob's delight there was a leather belt dyed a rich blue, with a gilt buckle. Hob had never seen these garments, which presumably Molly had produced from the trunk that Jack carried in; the occasion for them had not arisen in his time of traveling with Molly and her troupe.

The door to the inner room creaked open, and Molly came out, and Nemain behind her. Hob stared at them in wonder. Molly had her mass of gray hair coiled up against her neck, and a white veil floated down over it, not really concealing the silvery gleams beneath. One end of the veil ran under her chin and back up, knotted at her temple so that it hung down again as a tassel. Her gown, rather longer and more flowing than currently fashionable, was of a night-blue silk, worked in silver-gray thread that formed a border of the Irish endless-knot design, the coils writhing and crossing all the way around the neckline. Molly's hips, robust and shapely, were girt about with a white leather zone;

from this were slung her ring-pommel dagger in its sheath, her keys, her pouch.

And here behind her was Nemain, gowned in woodland green, boyish hips cinched with a cloth-of-gold zone; her fiery hair, new-washed, had been left uncovered, but bound about with a cloth-of-gold fillet. Hob hardly recognized the mischievous playmate of last summer.

Molly took Hob by the arm. "Hob, *a chuisle,* do you mind that you told me that your old priest was after teaching you your manners at table?"

"He showed me, Father Athelstan, he showed me somewhat, Mistress, but—"

"You must act my page, lad; do you cut and serve for Nemain and myself, for I have told them that we are two queens, and we in exile, and you and Jack all our retinue, and one must look these Normans in the eye, bold as a badger, else they'll try to trample you into the earth." She gave his arm a little squeeze and turned away.

Nemain was eyeing him critically. She reached out, tugged at his overshirt where it was bunched beneath the leather belt, plucked a thread from the shoulder.

"Are we ready, then?" asked Molly.

"A moment, *seanmháthair,* till I find the garderobe," said Nemain.

"I can show you," said Hob.

They walked along the corridor to the garderobe. Hob waited outside, suddenly embarrassed, and surprised at his embarrassment. In the greenwood Nemain would go behind the nearest bush, and talk with him the while, but here things seemed different. *Nemain* seemed different, and when she emerged he felt strangely awkward with her; quickly he turned and started back.

They came to the fountain, and he showed her where the water came out of the wall. He was a bit disappointed when she was not as impressed as he had been: she had been in castles before, and he had not.

The two walked slowly back along the corridor toward the solar, and Hob asked in a low voice, "Why did Herself tell them she is a queen?"

"It's a queen that she is in truth, away in Ireland, though her people are scattered, and so am I a queen."

Hob began to laugh, but his laughter faltered when he saw her face, and trailed away.

"But she is just Mistress Molly!"

"She is Queen Maeve, away in the west of Erin." Nemain paused a moment. "She's never the great Queen Maeve, of course, who's after dying a long time since, but she's a queen of her own people, and in her own right, and so will I be, my mother being dead as she is, and my father."

For a moment Hob was too surprised at all this to speak. Life with Molly's troupe was a constant procession of revelations, and Nemain in particular often left him confused, but this was like suddenly stumbling upon an old Roman road in the midst of thick forest. Questions rose to his lips, so many that his thoughts became too tangled to choose one. Finally: "Who—who was the great Queen Maeve?" he asked plaintively.

"I'm just after telling you, she's dying a long time since, and there's many a night we'd hear the storytellers tell of her and her great war, and the boy that's killing the great hound and taking its place, and didn't he learn his warcraft from the woman called Shadows, and then he's grow-ing up and holding off Queen Maeve's armies—you should ask Herself to tell you of it, I have no gift for it, and here we are and they waiting for us."

And sure enough here was Molly just coming out of the solar with a page sent up to show them back to the hall, and Jack trailing behind in his new livery. Nemain went to walk with Molly, while Hob, his head whirling a little, fell in beside Jack. The page led them to the turret stair-way down to the hall.

The party trooped after the page, down the winding staircase once more, and into the hall, already filled with sound and scent and light: Hob had never seen so many candles and torches in one place. The tables ran lengthwise down the hall, but at the hall's head, near the great fireplace, was a low dais, one step up, with a large table set crosswise upon it, draped in cloth: here sat Lady Isabeau, the mareschal and castellan Sir Balthasar and his wife, Dame Aline, a handful of lesser Blanchefontaine knights, the castle chaplain, and the castle's guests.

Dame Aline, somewhat younger than her husband, was a short, sturdily built woman with fair hair beneath a white lace coif, small square hands, a merry giggle. She had a mask of light freckles across her face that on feast days she hid beneath a powder of rice mixed with dried white rose petal: a faint scent of rose hung about her even tonight, when she wore no powder. Her cheeks were full, making Hob think at first of a squirrel with acorns in its cheeks. He thought her plain, especially next to the ivory perfection of Lady Isabeau. As the evening wore on, though, she seemed more appealing to him, by reason of her blithe chatter, her delight in each jest, and above all the contrast she made with the dire ominous bulk of her husband. He sat beside her and cut her meat, as was polite: men cut for women, the younger for the elder, the lesser for the greater. When he had done, she placed her hand on his arm affectionately; she smiled in his face. Her rounded cheek, her easy laugh, lent her a childlike prettiness, and Hob wondered that she had no fear of the sinister castellan, who made even the tough-as-gristle sergeant Ranulf uneasy.

Beside Lady Isabeau was a seat left vacant for Sir Jehan, Sieur de Blanchefontaine. Sir Jehan was still somewhere out in the howling blizzard with a small hunting party, and from the distracted air with which Lady Isabeau continually looked away down the hall toward the entrance, Hob guessed there was some concern for his safety.

Molly and Nemain were shown to seats at this table, and Hob to a bench behind it, set along the eastern wall, where the pages serving at table waited in a row, watching carefully to see if they might be wanted to fill a cup, cut meat, bring towel and water that their patrons might clean their hands between courses. One was the fifteen-year-old, whose name proved to be Giles. The little page Hubert was there as well, and attached himself to Hob, for which Hob was grateful, for his memory of procedure was quite sketchy. He confided as much to Hubert, explaining that they had been long on the road, and he feared that he might shame himself and his ladies by a misstep in his serving.

"Would you like me to guide you in attending your ladies?" asked Hubert, the thought of himself as a guide to his new and somewhat older friend plainly appealing to him.

"But yes, if it please you," said Hob, dredging up some Norman courtesies from Father Athelstan's lessons.

Hubert indicated that Hob should follow his example. From a sideboard the page took a little ewer of water and a small shallow basin. He took a cloth from a pile of them and spread it on his shoulder. Then he went up to Lady Isabeau, gave a little bow, and held the basin out before her. She put her hands over the basin and Hubert poured water sparingly over them, catching the overflow in the basin. Deftly placing the ewer in the partially filled basin, he whisked the cloth from his shoulder and held it out for Lady Isabeau to dry her hands. With another little bow, he retreated a few paces before turning round.

"Now you—quickly, your ladies are waiting," said Hubert, turning Hob toward the sideboard where a pile of towels, a set of ewers and basins, stood waiting. Hob took up ewer, basin, cloth, and went to Molly first. It was more awkward than it seemed, pouring just so much, contriving not to let the cloth droop into the basin, struggling with the feeling that Nemain was laughing at him in her thoughts, and perhaps the rest of the company was as well. When he came to serve her he dared not look her in the face for fear of being mocked, or made to laugh; instead he kept his eyes cast down, concentrating on the task.

For a while thereafter Hob was caught up in the whirl of attending Molly and Nemain: a white broth of coneys demanded the setting out of silver spoons and the cutting of sops, small pieces of bread for dipping; fresh trenchers were needed as bowls and tureens of turnips, salted olives, frumenty, fritters, and forcemeat in a galantine made their way from the kitchen, with great joints of boar and venison that must be transferred, portion by portion, to Molly's plate or Nemain's. Hob would arrive at the table right after the server had placed a platter smoking with big cuts of meat on it, draw his belt knife with his right hand, grasp a chunk of the boar or venison with his left hand, and hack it free. Then quickly onto one of the plates with the portion, and there cut it further into pieces small enough for Molly or Nemain to eat with her fingers, or from the point of a knife.

Some of these table duties he knew from Father Athelstan's instruction, some he guessed from the circumstances, but much of what he did was prompted by hissed instructions and nudges from Hubert. By the end of the dinner Hob felt a real affection for the little page, who seemed only concerned with helping him.

From the pages' bench Hob had a view past the high table, to the long hall beyond; at the central table, a few yards down the hall, he could see Jack, sitting with Ranulf and the crew that had escorted them to the castle: Roger, Olivier, the soldier called Goscelin or Joscelin, and the others. Hob could hear everything that was said at the high table, but the noise from the long tables down the hall came to him only as a confused rumble.

Beyond Ranulf's squad was a section of table occupied by a group of perhaps a dozen men: dour, fair men with light eyes, bearded, two with long drooping mustachios. Hob had seen them before, at the monastery: Lady Svajone's Lietuvan grooms and wagoners and servants. Like the two esquires, they kept to themselves: taciturn men, isolated in any case by their inability to understand the language spoken around them.

A nudge from Hubert sent Hob hurrying to the pitcher of wine nearest Molly, to refill the goblet that sat before her. Then he filled Nemain's; his former playmate turned a blank look upon him, which somehow—a slight crinkling at the corners of her eyes, a quirk at the side of her mouth?—managed to convey a cool amusement at the situation.

A short while later Lady Svajone entered the hall from a turret stairwell, supported between Gintaras and Azuolas. Slowly she made her way to the high table. Doctor Vytautas, trailing behind, paused by the grooms' table. The Lietuvans all stood out of respect for him. There was one who seemed to function as a sort of foreman; Vytautas put his hand on his shoulder and motioned the others to sit. Vytautas spoke to the foreman, leaning close to speak in his ear, the man nodding, tugging at his mustache. The doctor clapped him on the shoulder; the foreman bowed; Vytautas resumed his progress toward the high table.

The high table was furnished with chairs, unlike the benches that lined the lower tables, and the esquires settled their tiny charge in a chair. Azuolas took the one to her left. Soon Vytautas sat down close at her right hand, while Gintaras stood behind her chair. The three men thus encircled her and kept her from being jostled, while Azuolas served as her page, cutting her food and filling her goblet with wine.

Doctor Vytautas told her something in their own language, gesturing toward the Lietuvan wagoners' table. Hob could just hear them through the din. To his ears their language sounded like water in a brook: stones clicking against one another, then the rushing of water. The old woman began to toy with her food with no enthusiasm. She sipped at the wine, while first Vytautas, and then Azuolas, offered her a morsel of this or that designed to tempt her. Occasionally she would nibble at one of these dainties.

Beside the four Lietuvans sat the chevalier Estienne de Tancarville, a knight from Normandy, traveling to Scotland and partaking of Sir Jehan's hospitality rather longer than he had expected, as the drifts piled up on the roads. On either side of the table were arranged the elderly Sir Archibald and his wife, Dame Florymonde; four junior castle knights, Sir Tancred and his brother Sir Alain, a second Sir Alain, very short and broad, and the laconic Sir Walter: these carried themselves with the unconscious arrogance of the Norman. Across from Sir Walter sat Father Baudoin: young, sour, dry-lipped.

From time to time a page was able to divert one of the dishes being removed from the table; the boys shared from these generous leavings. As busy as Hob was, he found time at intervals to nibble at the pastries and trenchersful of odds and ends that Giles or Hubert had secured for the pages' use. As the meal went on, and dishes multiplied and the general confusion of serving increased, more and more treasures found their way to the pages' bench. After a while Hob felt as though he had eaten a full meal.

The hall occupied a central position in the keep. Corridors wrapped around it, and it occupied this level and ran up through the next floor, so that the ceilings were doubly high. Hob, his eye running around the walls, past the embroidered hangings, the sconces for the torches, the shields of the household knights with their colorful blazons, noticed a balcony, perhaps twelve feet across, and shielded from view by a carved wooden screen.

"What might that be?" he asked.

"Oh, that—that's where the musicians play, visiting musicians; it's when my lord holds feast on the holy days, they're grand to hear," said Hubert.

"Can you see them?"

"Not very well," said Hubert. "But they can see through the screen, and play when my lord signals to them."

At this point two of the other pages, Drogo and Bernard, appeared with a new prize just cleared from the high table, a half-full bowl of blankmanger, a kind of thick custard: chicken and rice pounded to a paste, boiled in almond milk, sweetened with sugar. The boys dipped sops into the mixture, and Hob found himself so absorbed in the swirl of taste that Hubert again had to nudge him to attend Molly and Nemain.

He was hastily cleaning some unknown sauce from his fingers with a napkin, dabbing at his lips, and when he looked up from his task here came Hubert again, grinning, having smoothly intercepted a barely tasted dish of hare in civey and a small loaf of some bread, lighter and softer than Hob had ever seen. He broke it open; steam escaped from the gap, and the interior was white and smooth. It was the first time Hob had ever seen white bread, though he had heard of it from Father Athelstan. He had just taken a bite, charmed by the texture and taste, when he became aware of a commotion, and he paused, his mouth full.

There was a disturbance at the end of the hall, by the screen that hid the entrance. Lady Isabeau's head came up sharply and she craned to see. The men scattered here and there as guards, who still wore their weapons though they sat at various tables, some eating, now rose smoothly and moved toward the screen, converging on the doorway, reinforcing those who were formally on watch at the entrance. Sir Balthasar had paused, a piece of thick crust halfway to his lips, unheeded, the crust dripping a sauce golden with saffron onto the layered cloths that covered the table. But a moment later bursts of laughter and cries of greeting dispelled the tension, and around the end of the screen strode Sir Jehan, tall and rangy, grinning toothily, and soaked in blood from shoulder to shin.

CHAPTER 14

HE SIEUR DE BLANCHEFON-
taine stalked up the hall, trailed
by five huge dogs, their coarse
fur oatmeal-colored where it was not spattered and
stained with red. As he advanced the knight shed his
cloak; it must once have been a deep blue, but now
was mostly crimson. A page scurrying behind gathered it up, soiling his own livery as he did so. Sir Jehan
reached the dais with a light leaping step, pulled off
gauntlets stiff with gore and a fur hat soaked with melting snow, and tossed them toward the pages behind the
high table. The page beside Hubert caught them. Sir
Jehan kissed his wife's hand and then her cheek, murmured something to her, and turned to the company.

Hob saw a tensely muscular man, broad-shouldered
but lean-waisted, with an impression of enormous energy
pent tightly within. A triangular face sloped from wide
cheekbones to a chin like a boat's keel; the deep-set eyes

were blue, or perhaps gray—something light, at any rate. Red hair, more orange than Nemain's fiery scarlet, grew in a peak a quarter of the way down his broad forehead. The effect, with his taut and toothy grin, was that of a distinctly lupine ferocity, overlaid with a perhaps insincere good humor.

Molly was introduced to him as "Queen Maeve from Ireland." He made no comment but bowed deeply, in such a way that it stopped just shy of mockery. He welcomed her under his roof; he exchanged pleasantries with Lady Svajone; he greeted his knights and dames Aline and Florymonde.

His speech came in short bursts of eloquence; his eyes, restless, sought the corners of the room, the guards, the firelight, the dogs. Hob, with part of his attention on the table in case he should be needed, nevertheless had time to puzzle over the lord's strange effect on him. Under the Sieur de Blanchefontaine's elaborate courtesy seemed to lie some kind of restless humor: fevered merriment, an unhealthy excitement.

Hob had a sense of great wariness. He did not like the way Sir Jehan smiled and smiled, while his eyes glittered in a way that suggested cruelty. Sir Jehan had spoken nothing that lacked kindness—and yet, and yet: the boy thought to himself that being near the knight made him feel as though he were in the narrow monastery stall with Roger's powerful, eye-rolling mare; as if Sir Jehan might at any moment, at a signal heard only by himself, take a turn toward menace.

"I pray you excuse me," Sir Jehan said with a bow to the assembled company at the high table, "while I . . . repair my appearance. I have been scouring—" He peered down the hall at the screened entrance through which he had entered. Hob followed his gaze, but could not see what had captured Sir Jehan's interest. "Scouring these snow-drowned forests—" He swung about, and caught sight of Hob. He looked startled and angry to see a strange face among the pages, an expression that lasted for half a heartbeat, and then smiling, smiling again. "Scouring these forests for my meat; the results are as you see."

Hob felt the skin at the back of his neck prickle as it strove to erect the hairs there. The boy, with his excellent recall of things once heard, now could hear Molly, rising from Gold-Beard's corpse and asking if the Terror ranged the woods everywhere, saying "and it scouring the woodland for meat the while."

And then Sir Jehan was gone, striding through the archway beneath the musicians' gallery. The dogs who had come in with him were clustered about the fireplace, where two grooms with pewter basins were washing the blood from their fur. Even sitting on its haunches, the dog nearest Hob was up past the groom's waist. A third groom appeared with several cloths; the dogs were toweled dry. They bore the treatment docilely enough, although there were a few muttered protests, rumbles in the deep chests that could be heard even amid the noise of the hall.

THERE WAS A PAUSE in the serving; the company rested, and sipped at wine. Hob took this opportunity to lean back on the bench, his shoulders propped against the wall, and gaze about him. Never had he seen such activity, amid so much light, after sundown, not even at Osbert's Inn.

The stone of the walls was covered with white plaster, as was the custom, and that was covered to a great extent by hangings depicting battle or the hunt, or allegories of love. Above the great hearth near the dais, of necessity bare of cloth covering, the occasional backdraft of smoke had over the months coated the plaster above the fireplace with varying amounts of carbon soot, as though veils of black and of dark and light gray hung from the ceiling. When Hubert saw him looking up to where they reached the ceiling, he told Hob that when the warm weather returned, Lady Isabeau would decree a whitewash, and the shutters would be thrown open to dry the glistening walls.

Haunches of the three deer and two huge boar that Sir Jehan had brought down were cooked in this hearth and carved at a sideboard; the smaller fireplace down at the western end of the hall was used primarily for heat. More elaborate dishes were still being borne in from the kitchen—actually an outbuilding connected at this level by a short stone corridor from the hall—by a stream of servants: men, young maids, middle-aged women, most in the livery of Blanchefontaine, some in aprons or voluminous overfrocks. They entered the hall laden with food and drink, and returned to the kitchen with empty platters and flagons. They reminded Hob of columns of ants he watched in his boyhood summers.

At one point a young, dark-haired serving-woman wound her way among the tables, and Hob's thoughts returned with a jolt to Margery. The rapid changes in his circumstances in so short a time, brought home so poignantly, made him feel confused, sorrowful—he hardly knew what. A moment later Hubert's elbow dug into his ribs, and the page's hissed warning returned him to himself, and the necessity of plying basin and towel at the change of courses again. He plunged back into his tasks with a sense of relief.

Dish followed dish: soups, pies, roast meat, boiled meat, fritters; sauces flavored with wine, cloves, cinnamon, onions, ginger, pepper, saffron; smoked herring, salt cod, and loaf upon loaf of white bread and dark. There was less variety if no less quantity at the lower table, but still Hob was amazed at how well the castle ate. Molly had the wealth to feed them well, but she tended toward the simple but hearty, a choice all but dictated by their life on the road.

Every so often Hob would dart up to the table to attend Molly and Nemain, cutting meat, offering ewer and basin in between courses, and holding a towel for them to wipe their hands. Then back to the bench, where crumbs, bones, and mostly empty dishes had begun to accumulate, and where one of the wolfhounds had become an attentive spectator.

MOST OF THE PEOPLE in the lower reaches of the hall were those who lived and worked in the castle, and a few stranded travelers, like Molly and Lady Svajone, but of lesser status. There were two villages not far away, according to Hubert, but they were huddled under the drifts of snow, and no one had come from them to the castle, whether to work or to trade, since the storm began.

Food was piled on the trestle tables, simpler fare than was eaten on the dais, but plentiful. The hum of conversation, the rattle of knives and bowls and wooden mugs, swelled into a muted rumble. Children chased one another under their parents' feet or crawled in the rushes. One or two babies were crying, and two women sat together at a side wall, nursing. Sir Jehan's huge dogs wandered about, foraging for scraps. Above even the wolfhounds' reach, in a deep-set window recess, a white-pawed tabby ignored the turmoil; it dozed with forearms flat and straight before it, one paw turned inward, the picture of peace. The shutters over the window heaved and banged in some sudden gust of wind, and the cat opened its eyes. After a moment they slowly shut again.

As the meal wore on, the din from the lower hall grew less: slowly at first, then more and more, people finished their meals, and withdrew, women with children leaving first, then other castle folk. Tables and benches were knocked down and stacked against the walls as they cleared. A few were left not far from the dais, where some of the newly returned men-at-arms lingered over their ale. Hob could see Jack quietly drinking among Ranulf's squadmates, while Ranulf's little son, fast asleep, dribbled on his father's shoulder, until his mother came to whisk him off to bed.

Below their feet, on the windowless first level, were the storehouses, but above them, two levels up, there was a dorter, subdivided into sleeping alcoves, so that people need not convert the hall to sleeping quarters. Only at the far end of the long room, where the entry guards kept watch by the screen, were cots set up, and curtains hung across recesses, so that the watch off duty might sleep, ready at hand if needed.

A group of the castle's archers had begun one of their games, games that tested the virtue of hand and eye. Halfway down the hall and against the south-side wall, perhaps fifteen or sixteen yards distant from the high table, was a disk of wood, hung from a beam, flat against the plaster of the wall. The disk was a narrow section of trunk hewn from a mountain pine, perhaps two feet in diameter. The archers threw small iron arrows at it by hand; they soaked the target in water every day to soften the wood enough to let the arrowlets stick in it. The outer rings counted for less than the inner, and the pith at dead center counted most of all. Bets were taken and there was a deal of dispute, but all good-natured: no archer would dare an open quarrel in the hall, for fear of arousing the wrath of the sergeants, or worse, of the castellan Sir Balthasar.

SIR JEHAN RETURNED, fresh and clean, in a surcoat of his own murrey, with gold and white embroidery at neck and cuff, blue tunic, white hose; the whole offset by fingers heavy with rings and a pendant of his own fountain symbol wrought in silver. He took his seat beside Lady Isabeau. Food and drink appeared before him, and he beamed at everyone before falling to with a gusto that approached savagery.

When he had somewhat sated himself, though, he began to pick at Molly.

"And this is the charming Demoiselle Nemain, I am to understand?"

"This is the young Queen Nemain," said Molly quietly.

"Ah, yes," said Sir Jehan; and then, with not quite a sneer, not quite a discourtesy: "Queen Nemain."

He tore at the carcass of a roasted pigeon. Before him was a salt cellar. It was silver, and in the shape of a boat with six oars and a sweep rudder, and cunningly made. Sir Jehan reached out and touched it; withdrew his hand; reached out again and moved the cellar along the table a small way, like a child playing at sailing the boat. He fidgeted in his seat; he tapped his fingers against his goblet; he drank.

"Nemain: was that not the name of a terrible goddess?" he asked. "And it means—'frenzy,' is it, in your speech? Surely a large fierce name for such a slender maid?" He nodded toward Nemain; it was not quite a patronizing nod, and his tone was not quite mocking; but near, very near.

"It is one of the three names of the *Mórrígan,* the Great Queen, the Queen of Phantoms," said Molly, now Queen Maeve. Till now Hob had heard only Jack call her "Maeve." She seemed unabashed, as comfortable as if she were relating a tale to Hob by a campfire in the forest clearing. "It is Her guise as the confounder of armies, who causes armed comrades to turn on one another in their terror—"

Here Hob noticed Father Baudoin: he looked at Molly with eyes widened, then narrowed; he leaned back in his chair; surreptitiously he crossed himself.

Molly's voice, ever courteous, began to harden, a faint rasp creeping in, "—and when Nemain has come to be a full woman and has come into her power, we will return to Erin, to the place of our kin, and to those who slew our kin, and then it will be seen if her name lies loose or snug upon her."

Sir Jehan had finished his meat and much of his drink, and he could sit no more. He rose in a swift supple manner, and stood behind his own chair. He ran his hand over the chair back, and then began to pace. He paused by the fire and looked at Molly.

"And you were—a queen, then? Away there in Ireland." Sir Jehan peered intently into the fire for a moment; seemed to lose interest; bent and looked more closely at the smoke curling upward. He straightened and paced away a short distance, then turned and looked suspiciously at the hearth. Hob wondered again at his uneasy movements. "I have been to—to the Irish wars," said Sir Jehan. He gestured toward the giant brindle-furred dogs, now stretched out before the fire. "I had three— three things—of Ireland: wealth, advancement. These dogs."

He moved about again, restless as a stag in autumn. "In Ireland also I have met—hedge kings, sheep-meadow queens. The Irish—each chieftain styles himself a king. . . . Is it thus with you, madam?"

If Molly was offended she gave no sign. She sat at ease as though she were in Osbert's common room, and she laughed so heartily that even Sir Jehan, prowling about tensely, his legs springy and his step soft, his thumb hooked in his belt by his dagger, his eyes darting keenly here and there, must smile in resonance; but it was a smile that came and went, came and went.

"I am a hedge queen now, truly!" she said. "Many's the hedge I've slept beside here in England, and my rule extends to three wagons only. My lands are forfeit"—here her eyes darkened and the deep sweet purr of her voice roughened to an unpleasant snarl—"and my kin scattered, or worse. And it is true, I was not a grand queen like your English queens, but I was a queen in my own right as they are not, and a battle queen, and a chief to my clan. Someday I may return to Erin, and there gather up what kin may yet live, and find those who have shattered our clan"— she paused as if striving for discretion, but only an instant, for she was exhausted from the struggle against the storm, and she had drunk her share of Sir Jehan's wine, and her cheeks were beginning to flush—"and shed blood. Be said by me, I will shed some blood."

At this, Sir Jehan cocked his head to one side and looked at her past his shoulder, as though he struggled to bring her into clearer focus.

"I heard—away there in Ireland—I heard stories—fireside stories, mind you, fireside stories—of battle queens in ancient days; even women who taught war wisdom, and weaponcraft—even the skills of the body, leaping over shields and the like—taught them to warriors," he said, dropping down into his seat again. He dipped a bread sop absently into a dish of frumenty, then put it down untasted on his trencher; he lifted his goblet of wine; he set it down again. "Trapping an enemy between crossed spear points . . ."

A page served him from a bowl: cabbage with gobbets of marrow. Sir Jehan looked at the trencher of cabbage; he reached for the salt cellar; he moved it a hand's breadth to one side on the table. A moment later he moved it back. It was as though life's candle burned so hot in him that he could not bear to be still for long, lest he be scorched. Abruptly he turned back to Molly. "But surely that was long ago—if ever, if ever—and I cannot see you, dear madam, wielding a weapon." His smile flicked on again, and this time it stayed, and he sat grinning like one of his hounds, but with little humor in his eyes.

"Oh, there are a few women yet in Erin who have mastered weaponcraft," said Molly comfortably, settling back in her chair and sighing, all curves and heavy limbs. "And myself among them."

Hob was thinking of Molly atop the wagon, and what Sir Jehan would have said had he seen her, her skirt rucked up above her milky muscular calves, sending her black-fletched arrows humming into the woods; and yet, he thought as he looked at her, at ease and heavily elegant, it was hard to see it in her now.

And because he was looking at her, as was Sir Jehan, he was just able to catch the flurry of movement: Molly's hand blurred toward her waist and the ring-pommel dagger there and whipped the slim knife from its sheath, and in the same motion flung it down the room, as a gardener carelessly flicks a pebble away from the plot he is weeding, seemingly without looking, a spinning metallic flicker that flew along the hall and ended with a *whup!* dead in the pith of the pine target, a third of its blade buried.

There was a sort of iron chord as every knight and most of the soldiers on guard duty tensed, with thumping of heels against the floor, or grasping of hilts, causing a rattle of scabbards; here and there was the whispery rasp-and-chime of long steel sliding out. Sir Jehan and Sir Balthasar were half up from their seats, hands on their own daggers. Yet Molly sat so relaxed and with so pleasant an expression, her empty hand still outstretched toward the target, that there was nowhere for their alarm and anger to go, and Sir Jehan sank back with a muttered curse and a dismissive wave at the guards. Sir Balthasar sat down more slowly, his face dark with suffused blood, and he did not take his eyes from Molly after that. She put her hand down and placidly picked at a stray thread on her gown.

The target was fifteen yards away, and at an angle, and yet the dagger was strongly fixed in the soft center of the pinewood disk, although perforce at a slant.

Sir Jehan had kept his broad smile, although his eyes no longer had any least bit of humor in them, and this, with his wide forehead and triangular face tapering to so sharp and prominent a chin, gave his countenance a singularly wolfish cast; he scanned Molly's features hungrily, as though prepared to spring upon her, and to tear her thoughts from her.

She gazed back at him blandly. He sat back a bit, and cleaned food from his dinner knife by wiping it on one of the pieces of stale bread provided for that purpose. He stuck it deftly into the salt, withdrew it with a small amount of salt on the flat of the blade, and sprinkled it over his cabbage. His movements were ostentatiously sedate, and Hob saw that his hand was quite steady.

"A pretty thing to put in someone's eye, madam," said Sir Jehan in a frosty tone; he tipped his goblet to Molly. Dame Aline put a small hand almost to her eye before she stopped herself and turned the gesture into a smoothing of her wimple.

Lady Svajone regarded Molly with evident admiration, her large gray eyes fixed on Molly's hand, the slight tremor of her own hands stilled, her mouth in a little smile. Vytautas made a gracious gesture of mimed applause and bowed his head to Molly; the two Lietuvan es-quires regarded her with a cool professional appraisal, as did the knights seated about the table.

After that, Molly was treated with respect, although Sir Jehan could bring himself to address her only as "Lady Maeve," and Molly gave no least sign of offense at it because, as she remarked to Jack and Hob later, "I am a queen now only of three wagons and the roads they wend upon, and in any case there is little I may do about it this night. If I can read the fall of crow feather aright, the winds will change direc-tion, somewhere in the sennight to come." The others of his household followed Sir Jehan in this matter of address, but otherwise showed her every courtesy. There was a certain awe and fascination following her dagger cast, and those who were in the hall at the moment told those who were not; the distance of the throw tended to increase by a yard or so with each retelling.

THE REST OF THE MEAL proceeded without incident. At intervals Hob served a fresh course, or offered a fresh ewer of water and towel between courses. But the long day and the long evening were wearing down even Molly's endurance, Nemain was pale and silent, and Hob was near exhaustion. Down at Jack's table, Olivier and Goscelin and three or four others had already left for their sleeping quarters; Ranulf was drinking quietly, his eyes a bit glassy; and even as Hob looked, Roger put his head down on the table and began to snore softly, just au-dible to the pages' bench. Jack himself, with his iron stomach, seemed unaffected, but even he was blinking a great deal, and gazing about him somewhat dreamily.

At last, to Hob's relief, Sir Jehan and his wife rose to take their leave; all stood, and then reseated themselves, but the meal was effectively over, and soon Hob, with Jack close behind, found himself happily stumbling upstairs toward his rest; ahead he could hear Molly and Nemain speaking in Irish, their voices echoing back down the turret stairwell.

Once inside the solar they had been assigned, the door bolted, Molly got them settled for bed. A pair of serving-maids tapped at the door, sent by Lady Isabeau, but Molly sent them away, preferring privacy to service: she did not want such witness to the casual chatter between queens and serving-men, for so she had represented Jack and Hob.

Soon the women had retired to the inner room, candles were snuffed, and Hob and Jack climbed into their cots. Jack spent perhaps five minutes, propped on one elbow, gazing into the dying fire, then abruptly lay down; a couple of deep breaths and he was asleep.

Hob, exhausted but excited as well, his mind racing with new sights and sounds, lay watching the faint firelight play on the ceiling. He turned on his side, then rolled back.

Jack was already snoring. Hob looked around, at the stout oak door to the solar, the walls finished with plaster, the little fireplace with its embers glowing softly. Behind the plaster of the outer wall was the stone of the keep. A shuttered window in this wall, deeply recessed, gave out on the bailey. The window, set with thin plates of horn, opened inward. Outside the horn window, the wooden leaves of the shutter were heaving with the wind against the latch, a muffled thudding. Hob went to the window and put a knee on the deep sill—the wall was three feet thick at this point—and swung the horn window toward him. He climbed up fully into the window recess, leaned out to the shutter latch, and slipped the wooden tongue, holding the shutter open just a bit that he might look out, as he had at the monastery.

But here he was much higher up from the ground. Through the whirl of snow and cloud the waxing moon, a day or two from the full, toiled to illumine the scene: the dark edge of a buttress that sprang out from the wall to Hob's left was rimmed with silver. He could see that the storm was unabated, the snow piling and piling in drifts on roof and parapet. Far below in the bailey, torches shone in niches beside the doors of the stable and other outbuildings. Even in the niches the wind had them fluttering frantically, like so many golden flags.

Hob closed and latched the wooden panels, shut the horn window, climbed down from the sill. He crept into his cot, drawing the bed-clothes up over ear and chin. He thought of the storm, the walls, the gates guarded by armed men, even the stout door to the solar, and he thought happily: *What could harm us here? What could reach us here?*

CHAPTER 15

ORNING AT THE CASTLE. THE
winds had died down toward
daybreak, but soon began re-
building in strength. The dim daylight, the constant
voice of the storm, and the sheer fatigue of the last few
days, left everyone in a not unpleasant lethargic state.
Molly's party slept late, weary to the bone from the
struggle against the previous day's storm, and no one
troubled them except only the little page Hubert. He
appeared with the compliments of Lady Isabeau and
with several serving-men bearing trays with a breakfast
of smoked herring, cheese, toast soaked in wine, so
that they need not leave the solar even to eat.

Molly had them set up a table in the outer room,
and for most of that day they ate, made adjustments
and repairs to clothing, and napped. Jack was sent out
to the wagons for the harps in their leather casings,
and returned dripping melting snow from his struggle

across the bailey. Fragrant oils were brought forth, and the instruments cleaned, and then Molly and Nemain fell to tuning and practicing, for as Molly said, "It's a good refuge that this castle will be to us. If we're ever to make our way to Erin in time to come, and do there what we must, this so-arrogant lord may prove us a fine patron and a protector; and be said by me, we will have need of both." She tested a silver string with her fingernail. "He's after seeing that I have claws, but now, now he must see us fit to grace his table, for hasn't he stopped just this side of calling me an impostor? It's like a skittish new pup he is, and new to the lead, and what's more soothing than a well-played *cláirseach*?"

Hob she dismissed for the afternoon, that he might see some of the castle, with Hubert to guide him, from the dim storerooms on the first level, fragrant with the mingled scents of dried apples and garlic and smoked meats and salted cod, to the dovecotes clinging to the highest level of the keep, overlooking the bailey. Hubert showed him how there was access to the doves from within the keep, and the separate structure that housed the carrier pigeons. They climbed to the rooms, just beneath the roof, where the gutters channeled rainwater into great cisterns: here rainwater was pooled with water hoisted up from the well, and from these cisterns water was sent down through the castle's lead pipes.

Passage from level to level was by winding stone stairs set in turrets embedded in the walls of the keep; the wedge-shaped treads, narrow in the center and wide at the walls, gave Hob trouble till he mastered the trick of them. Many of the things that might interest boys—the forge, the stables, the armory—were outbuildings, down in the bailey, backed up against the curtain walls. The storm was deemed too dangerous for anyone but those who had necessary duties to fulfill to venture outside. There was a real danger that the young and the weak might lose their way in the great yard, blinded by the snowstorm, freezing to death behind a wall of wind-driven white, a few yards from shelter.

But Hubert threw open the shutters in a first-floor passageway.

"There's the bailey," he said, as Hob strained to see through the shifting white veils, "and yon outbuilding is the smithy, and next it is the armory, and—"

Here he broke off to scowl at three children, two boys and a girl, all under six years of age, who had burst around a corner, chasing one another and screaming with laughter. They slowed to an abashed walk when they saw the august Hubert, himself all of eleven years or so, and vanished down a stairway.

Hob and Hubert turned back to the window. Between gusts of snow white as a bride's wimple, the boys could glimpse guide ropes strung from door to door, crisscrossing the bailey, with shielded torches planted in the snow beside each rope line, making lines of fire from outbuilding to keep, and from outbuilding to outbuilding. Very few men ventured to cross the bailey—and they *were* all men, for it was hard physical work to struggle through the drifts, and easy to become lost if one's hand slipped from the rope during a white blast from the storm.

It brought home to Hob, leaning there on the windowsill, how difficult it would be to leave the castle till the storm had abated.

ABOUT MIDAFTERNOON a small page ran up to them and told them that Molly had summoned Hob to attend her in the solar. When he and Hubert arrived, somewhat breathless, at the private rooms, he found Molly, Nemain, and Jack ready to descend to the hall. There was little urgent business for the knights and their ladies during these cold months—no campaigns, no crops, no courts to preside over, only the seasonal holidays, and with a storm like this preventing even hawking and hunting, the castle's high-table folks usually gathered in the hall to amuse themselves. Dinner ran into supper, and Father Baudoin began to include sermons on gluttony and drunkenness in addition to his favorite topics of sloth and lechery.

In the hall, small groups clustered here and there on benches, performing such small tasks as could be done quietly indoors. Men worked on harness; women knit or worked with distaff and spindle; the archers were back at their target, throwing their iron arrowlets. The archers were betting on each throw, and small coins changed hands frequently. There was a constant hum of conversation, and with it the clink of tools, occasional laughter, low cries of triumph or dismay from the archers.

At the high table sat the household knights and the castle's guests, drinking spiced wine, telling stories, plucking small pastries from trays brought round by servants. Hob took his seat on the pages' bench and inhaled happily. A rich scent, compounded of wine, spiced meats, and baked bread, mingled, not unpleasantly, with the unguents and perfumes with which highborn women anointed themselves.

The chevalier Estienne was reciting a long poem in recent circulation, great gouts of which he had committed to memory. Hob found it almost impossible to follow the pure Norman French, his difficulty compounded by the chevalier's Continental accent. Molly seemed to find it perfectly clear, and laughed delightedly several times at what appeared to be humorous passages. Occasionally there was a verse or two of song, embedded in the poem, which the French knight sang in a pleasant flexible tenor. Nemain sat with an enigmatic expression, but Hob knew her well enough to tell that she was paying no attention.

Hubert translated bits here and there, in between his duties, enough to let Hob determine that it was a tale of a young Christian noble, a Saracen slave girl, their love, and their difficulties and adventures, some amusing, before her conversion and their marriage, but Hob found that a great deal of the humor eluded him.

Late in the afternoon Dame Aline proposed a game of chess. Dame Aline, a great enthusiast if an indifferent player, was as pleased to watch others as to play herself; when Lady Isabeau further suggested a tourney, the castellan's wife immediately sent pages for two boards and two sets of chess pieces, had tables set up by the hearth, and divided those who were interested into two groups. The one who remained undefeated from each group would play the other.

Sir Jehan had two fine sets of chessmen, one from the south of Italy, very skillfully carved in elephant ivory, the queens reclining on thrones with three cushions, arched backs, decorated armrests. The other set was French, of deer bone, lacking the skill of the Italian carving but still elaborate. Wooden pieces, much more crude, filled the three or four positions where the originals had broken.

Lots were drawn, and Molly was matched first against Sir Walter, who said little as was his wont; he contemplated the board with his elbow propped on the table and a large hand covering his mouth, as she steadily destroyed his forces.

In the other group's first match, Dame Aline, faced with Sir Estienne, prevailed despite several mistakes midgame; there was some whispered jesting about an excess of Continental chivalry on the French knight's part. Dame Florymonde defeated her handily, and persisted as champion through several rounds, till Sir Tancred overcame her.

Hob had a good view of the games' progress, although he understood little of how it was played. He was kept busy refilling Molly's winecup; Molly as always drank deeply, although there was little apparent effect on her, except perhaps heightened color and a readiness to laughter. One of the giant Irish hounds had come and put its heavy head on her thigh, rolling its eyes upward and sideways to watch her face. She sat and played chess with one hand, while the other toyed with the monster's ears.

Eventually Molly was left with Sir Balthasar as the last opponent on her side; the other team had come down to Sir Jehan and Sir Alain, the brother of Tancred. Molly sat back and took a pastry from an attendant page, and Sir Balthasar set down his wine and came over to the hearthside chess tables.

Dame Aline leaned toward Molly and said, with mock seriousness, "Madam, 'ware that he does not bang upon the table when losing, and so upset the pieces, and so escape the battle."

Hob looked quickly at the dread castellan and saw to his astonishment a meek, almost abashed, grin on the dark hard features, and a rolling of his eyes toward the ceiling. "Aline . . ." he began, and then just shook his head.

Sir Balthasar took his place opposite Molly and picked up the die to roll for first move; the chair creaked beneath his bulk.

"The bane of all chairs," said Dame Aline, with a merry laugh. Sir Balthasar gave her a look of mock ferocity.

"Perhaps a new charge on his shield: a broken chair, *sable,* on a field of *or,*" said Lady Isabeau, sober-faced, with not a quirk of the lips to indicate a jest. Dame Aline began to giggle. A moment later Lady Isabeau added, "Le Chevalier de les Chaises."

But this was too much for Dame Aline, who looked from her husband to Lady Isabeau's expressionless face and back again, and exploded with helpless laughter.

Determinedly Sir Balthasar rolled, producing a five; Molly threw a three. At this time the combatant with the first move chose the color of his pieces: the castellan chose white, and Molly reached for those stained a deep dark brown.

There was a moment or two when there was just the clack of the deer-bone pieces being set in place on the board. Then: "If he is hard on chairs, what must he be upon a mattress?" said Lady Isabeau in a musing tone, with the same sober innocent pondering expression.

This set Dame Aline off again, and finally she managed to gasp, "I have a great deal of sisterly feeling for yon chair," before becoming utterly overcome with merriment.

At this point even staid elderly Dame Florymonde pressed her napkin to her lips; her face grew red and her eyes began to tear, while little snorts and gasps of laughter escaped from behind the cloth.

Sir Balthasar looked to Sir Jehan with a helpless expression. The Sieur de Blanchefontaine said, "Nay, brother, I flee this field of battle; I confess myself a caitiff knight; you must fight yourself free of these ferocious women."

Hob found it difficult to reconcile the ease and good humor of the two women around the two knights, who at other times conveyed such an impression of menace. Sir Balthasar seemed wrought of stone and iron, Sir Jehan of wind-whipped fire. Yet if these men were so evil, would their wives be so calm and gay?

Sir Balthasar opened a blunt and brutal attack; to Hob, who was unfamiliar with the rules, it seemed that a tide of white players poured down the center of the board during the first double handful of moves; then, a short while later, a sort of hunter's net of somber pieces snapped shut on the mareschal's assault, and he was rapidly reduced to staring at the board in dismay.

"She has caught you, husband!" cried Dame Aline, with disloyal glee. Sir Balthasar rose, shaking his head ruefully, and drank wine, first lifting his goblet to Molly in acknowledgment.

There was a brief respite for pastries and spiced wine, the scent of cinnamon tickling Hob's nose; an elaborate jest was told by young Sir Tancred, involving two maids and a blacksmith, enjoyed by all except Father Baudoin; and at last the final conflict was to begin, between Molly and the victor of the other group, Sir Jehan himself.

Sir Jehan took his place more warily than had Sir Balthasar, his gaze rapidly flicking back and forth from the board to Molly's face. They threw, and this time Molly had the better of the toss.

She had first move and her choice of colors; once again she took the darker pieces. She opened with two subtle probes, and Sir Jehan countered as delicately. Moves began to come less and less often; the game became increasingly complex. The slow entanglement of the pieces, the near stasis, and his own ignorance of the game began to tax Hob's attention, and his eye wandered about the room.

A wordless growl from Sir Jehan brought his eyes back to the board. Molly had taken one of Sir Jehan's castles. Sir Jehan moved his hand to the board, moved it back, then darted forth and slid his bishop three squares—at this time the bishop's limit—along a path of diamonds. Immediately Molly captured a knight. Sir Jehan became very still, but his thumb turned the rings on his fingers, a mindless habit. Soon Molly took two more pieces, and Sir Jehan's game collapsed. The Sieur de Blanchefontaine looked at Molly and then at the board, as if in disbelief, but only for a scant few moments, hardly noticeable. He then drew a deep breath and congratulated Molly courteously, and rose somewhat stiffly from his seat. He reseated himself at the main table and drank slowly, lost in thought.

Molly was acknowledged winner of the tourney. The knights seemed surprised, but Hob was not. He had come to the conclusion that Molly could do almost anything. The chevalier Estienne composed a few verses in Norman French in honor of Molly's accomplishment, which Hubert, that critic and veteran of many castle dinners, adjudged barely adequate, detailing his complaints to Hob in a whisper.

SO THE AFTERNOON wore into evening. Members of the company came and went, and gradually began to assemble again for the evening meal. Lady Svajone, absent all day, made her appearance, as always attended by Doctor Vytautas and her two esquires.

They settled her in her usual place, swaddled in a cloak of undyed wool. On the cloak's bosom was a rayed circle, worked in red and yellow thread, and below it a tree, cunningly rendered in brown and green. A repeated pattern of sinuous lines at the tree's base suggested vegetation. Below the tree, echoing the rayed sun above, was the crescent moon, outlined in light and dark blue strands.

On her wrist, all bone and dry loose white skin, was a silver bracelet studded with smaragds, glints of green in the light from fireplace and candle; her hand and arm were so tiny that the bracelet seemed in danger of falling off at any moment. Around her neck, visible whenever the cloak fell open, a string of amber beads glowed against a cotehardie of darkest green.

She seemed somewhat frailer than the day before. She leaned across the table to talk to Molly, who bent to hear; but her voice was so faint that Hob could hear nothing of what was said.

The dinner that night went much as it had the previous night, except that Hob was introduced to the delights of mutton gallimaufry, which had proved uninteresting to the diners at the main table, and which Hubert had managed to secure almost intact for the pages' bench. The dish, composed of mutton and onions, chopped fine and stewed in verjuice and butter and white ginger, provided such a welter of unfamiliar flavors for Hob that he regretted finishing his share, and fell to licking his fingers.

When most of the table had been cleared except for sweetmeats and pastries, and the serious drinking had begun among the knights, Molly offered to provide some music from her native land, a suggestion that found favor with the company, except perhaps for Father Baudoin, and perhaps the castellan—Sir Balthasar's scowl was so habitual that it was no longer a reliable indicator of his mood.

Molly signaled to Jack, who left the lower tables and vanished into the turret stairway. A few moments later he returned with the two harps, one under each arm. He set them down some little distance from the fire, and arranged two small benches near one another.

Molly and Nemain took their seats by the harps. Each took up a *cláirseach,* Molly the larger and Nemain one about two-thirds the size of her grandmother's. The harps were of willow wood, the wood carved with interlaced ribbonwork that terminated in hounds' heads; the brass pegs were strung with gold and silver wire. There was a bit of final adjustment of the tuning, as some strings had expanded from the warmth of the hearth, and then they were ready.

Molly settled her harp on her knees, leaned it upon her right shoulder; Nemain took a moment longer to arrange herself, then nodded to her grandmother. Molly led off and Nemain followed. The women had rings on every finger: Molly's were all of silver, save one that looked to be of iron, on the fourth finger of her right hand. Nemain's were of gold, and the firelight toyed with them prettily as her fingernails struck the gleaming strings.

The two harps rang through the hall; tinkling ripples from each overlapped in a way Hob could never quite follow. The music of each seemed distinct, yet each agreed with the other in some fashion. After the harps had made play for a while, the women began to sing. It was a song Hob had heard them sing many times, in wayside inns, by woodland campfires, and each time more ensorcelling than the last. Nemain had told him it was a song in praise of the moon.

Now he sat and listened in the suddenly hushed hall. Lady Isabeau leaned forward eagerly. Sir Jehan leaned back and turned his head aside and then watched from the sides of his eyes. Even the mareschal was attentive. The pages held off for a bit. One after another, the wolfhounds sank their heads on their front paws; one sighed ostentatiously; they watched the singers, rolling their eyes toward Sir Jehan now and then to reassure themselves that all was as it should be.

Nemain's young voice, clear and high, entered a bit after Molly's, and twined about the elder woman's deep sweet singing, as vines in leaf climb out along a sturdy branch, winding about, adding a light grace to the dark strong tones that bore the strange main melody. The two voices, now diverging, now chiming together, each by turn drawing ahead of the other or lagging behind, conjured an image in Hob's mind, startling in its clarity: the wind piping through ancient stones arranged on a bare hilltop; the moon rising over the trees of the surrounding forest; the scent from the slopes of the hill, covered with rippling purple heather, black in the moonlight; the shadows of the stones reaching, reaching, far down the perfumed hillside.

Whether because of the late hour, or the exalting quality of the music, the two women sat cloaked in beauty: Queen Maeve and young Queen Nemain. Nemain in particular drew Hob's eye: with her face grave in concentration, lit more strongly along one side by the flickering fireplace, she seemed to Hob more as a woman than a child, if only for this moment. Her skin had cleared, and was white as the drifts of snow outside; her hair glowed as ruddy as the cooler embers at the edge of the fire, and when she glanced his way, her eyes caught the fireglow, green as the smaragds in Lady Svajone's bracelet.

The song ended; the music died away. For a moment all that might be heard was the crackle and spit of the flames playing about the logs in the great fireplace. Everyone had been leaning forward, save Sir Jehan and Father Baudoin. Now there was a general sigh and a shifting of position. Only the priest seemed unaffected, sitting well back in his chair and sipping fretfully at his cup. Either the wine within or what he had heard displeased him, for he sat with lips compressed and eyes slitted.

But Sir Jehan seemed genuinely pleased. "Oh well played, delightful, mesdames, delightful." And for once he did not have a mocking edge to his voice, for once he smiled with his eyes as well as his mouth.

Hubert nudged Hob, gave a slight upward incline of his chin toward the high table. Sir Tancred, who looked to be about thirty, sat gazing at Molly with an open admiration that bordered on the ardent, despite the difference in their ages. As they watched, he raised his goblet and offered a salute to skill and beauty. The company joined him in the toast; thereafter through the evening he watched Molly in a fashion that was just this side of impudent.

THE FOUR FILED into the solar; Jack bolted the door behind them. Hob and Jack put down the harps beside the door, and Hob began to put them back in their leather covers. Molly disappeared into the inner room, and Jack went to pull out the bedding from a niche in the wall. He began to set up the cots for Hob and himself with a soldier's practiced movements.

Nemain turned to Hob, who was hunkered down beside the first harp, pulling the drawstrings closed on the cover. He glanced up at her, unaccountably shy: he had never seen her look so poised; he had never seen her dressed so finely; he had never seen this cool, haughty stranger before. He gazed in consternation at the calm blankness of her face for two or three heartbeats, and then, slowly, she pushed her dainty pink tongue out between her lips, and just as slowly crossed her eyes.

Gales of laughter echoed from the plastered walls of the solar. Jack turned from his task, shaking his head and smiling in sympathy, but he had seen nothing and was unsure what the jest might be.

From the inner room came Molly's voice: "It's pleased I am to have such a pair of merry jesters with me, but we'll need the harps away, and yourselves out of yon finery, and some of us are old and stiff, and we perishing with weariness, and must have ourselves some rest." She sounded, as always, anything but old and tired. Still, it was a long time before the two young people could settle to their tasks: just as quiet seemed to be taking hold, a snort or gasp would set off another round of giggles, poorly smothered.

Eventually, everyone was abed; the snow hissed its lullaby, and they settled down to sleep.

* * *

HOB DREAMED OF NEMAIN.

On this night, at peace and fairly safe once more, his prayers said, drifting toward sleep, Jack Brown's snoring bulk between his cot and the door to the corridor, he lay thinking of Margery. He found that he could not quite remember the exact configuration of her face; he could not quite remember how she dressed. He could recall only a general impression, sparked by details of her person: her brown curls, her dark eyes with their heavy lids, the flare of her hip. He tried to see her exactly at the moment that she had paused at his table, or fastened up the sling for the rescued baby, but he could not.

Hob felt a sense of panic that Margery was dying to him a second time. It brought him up partway to a sitting position. After a bit he sank down again. He lay there, disconsolate, watching the faint glow of the fire's embers play across the plastered walls. He closed his eyes, and thought of the inn as it had been, and their short time there. Soon thought grew tangled, and memories of the inn and memories of the priest house came to him in odd combinations, although beneath everything was a sorrow, deep and unchanging, like the drone strings of the symphonia that sang beneath the melody. Then he drifted into dream, and the dream was not of Margery, but of Nemain.

Afterward he could remember little of the dream: he recalled that he was aware of her presence but could not see her clearly. There was only a blurred sense of white and red, and a challenging green gaze, and smooth wet skin beneath his fingertips, and—an echo of the journey through the storm—the warm scent of her unwashed body. There came a burst of pleasure so intense that it jolted him awake, and he lay there dazed and disoriented in the darkness, while a series of diminishing pangs, ineffably sweet, rippled through his flesh.

As he came more fully awake, he became aware that his thighs were soaked: a thick clinging wetness that seemed everywhere. He had been told to expect it, and he knew enough to know what had happened, and that his boyhood was over, and his manhood begun.

He sat up again, and threw off the blanket. He managed to pull on his new shoes and a long overshirt, and, half-asleep, picked his way around Jack's cot, drew the door bolt and the latch, and let himself out into the corridor. In the garderobe, he contrived to dry himself off with handfuls of straw. When he relieved himself he was surprised at the near-painful delight, as urine burned its way along still-sensitive channels.

He went back out into the corridor. A rushlight flickered in a bracket on the wall, the only movement. A quick rinse of his hands at the water basin that Hubert had shown him, the water painfully cold, and then he made his way blearily back down the passage to the solar.

A shutter rattled with the wind at the end of the corridor. As he drew near the solar door, he could hear quiet voices. Sir Balthasar, who as castellan was responsible for the castle's safety, would not station anyone on the walls in such ferocious weather, but the guard-rooms in the towers had a night watch, and the corridors had wakeful guards who walked about in irregular patterns. Two of them were just around the turn of the corridor; Hob could clearly see their shadows thrown on the wall. The conversation, half-heard, seemed to involve the exploits of one of the two guards, a maid named Marie or Cherie, the maid's father and his disapproval, a little-used storeroom where lovers might meet. Hob slipped back into the solar and closed the door as silently as possible. He shot the bolt and climbed back beneath the covers.

As he stretched out beneath the woolen blankets, a faint shiver of pleasure ran between his legs, another ghost of the paroxysm just past; but soon thereafter he felt dark eddies of sleep come washing toward him. Before he succumbed, he had time to think—not in so many words, but vaguely, incoherently—that he had now joined the guard outside with his low-voiced boasts, and Roger with the woman Lucinda so impatient for his return, and mighty Jack himself, who strode forward so eagerly when Molly summoned him to her wagon: joined them in some longed-for guild fellowship—"You men," he could hear Molly saying to him last summer in the clearing, when he had, for all that, still been a boy. "You men."

CHAPTER 16

OB REMEMBERED LITTLE OF the third day and evening that they spent at the castle. He and Jack went with Hubert to hear Mass in the little chapel within the keep. They stood with members of the castle household in the back of the unheated chamber; to the front Hob could just see Sir Walter and Sir Archibald. Father Baudoin said the Mass, and though he was still dour of expression and his shoulders were stiff with tension, his voice sang out the Latin phrases in a clear and even melodious tenor.

The day and evening passed much as had the preceding two days: games with Hubert in the afternoon, riddles and feasting and games in the evening among the adults. It was the feast, and the salt-cod dish that he tasted for the first time, and the corridor in the nighttime, that he recalled in later years.

The folk at the high table were growing comfortable with one another on this third night, and there was laughter and some singing; there was a contest in which a few lines of poetry were recited by one guest, and the next guest had to add a line, and so forth; and amusing anecdotes were told by the better-traveled among the company, notably Sir Estienne, who had fought in Spain, and had been to Rome as well, and had seen the Holy Father.

The dishes followed one after the other, the wine flowed easily, and the pages' bench enjoyed an abundance of cast-off food.

Hubert had collected some spilled salt and put it aside on a trencher; the lads experimented with a pinch in this dish and a pinch in that, whether it was needed or not. In addition, there was a nearly untouched dish of salt-cod mortrews: the fish pounded, mixed with stock and eggs and crumbled bread, and the resulting dumpling poached. Hob ate his share with gusto. The older page, Giles, had brought in some snow to mix with the younger pages' wine, and Hob found the wine cooled with snowmelt just the thing to quench his salt-driven thirst.

This evening passed easily, and even Lady Svajone seemed in better spirits, while the elderly Sir Archibald, having drunk rather more than usual, displayed a hitherto unexpected talent for bawdy riddles, till Dame Florymonde insisted that he stop, although she had laughed as heartily as any at the table. The company retired in a good mood, and Hob, trudging up the turret stair behind Molly and Nemain, found himself quite ready for bed.

He awoke from a troubled sleep. Had there been a rapping at the door, or a voice calling, or was that in a dream? He lay and listened to Jack's snoring. The wind for once had abated; the shutters were motionless. He was still half in the grip of a dream, and the chamber was dark, the fire sunk to barely glowing ash.

He became aware of an uncommon thirst: the wine and the salted dishes at Sir Jehan's table. Salt! Hob had rarely had such free access to it in his short life. He rose and gained the door without incident, but found himself oddly reluctant to draw the bolt. Still, he was parched. He slid the bolt back quietly and stepped out into the corridor. Tonight he could hear no sentries, near or far. He went down to the fountain and drank thirstily from his cupped palm for what seemed a long time.

He turned to go back, and hesitated. The corridor stretched away, silent, flickering in the light of two torches set some distance from one another; shadows pooled in the corners and at the entrance to the turret stairwells. The silence began to seem malevolent, and the corridor looked like a trap. He forced himself to take a step, and another, till he gained the door to the solar. He made himself look up and down the passage. What was wrong? Something was not as it should be: the very air seemed thick and tasteless; the light from the torches had unpleasant orange undertones; the flickering shadows almost made shapes against the walls.

He ducked inside and shot the bolt home. He crawled into his cot. He lay there, surprised and dismayed at the strange atmosphere that ruled this night, and he thought that he would sleep no more before morning. But he was thirteen, and healthy, and in what seemed only a moment or two it was morning, and Jack bustling about, and gray daylight leaking under the bottom of the shutters.

CHAPTER 17

HE NEXT DAY HOB HAD AL-
most forgotten the odd quality of
the night before. He and Hubert
and Giles heard Mass, Father Baudoin's tenor echoing from the stone flags of the chapel floor. Later they
threw a wooden ball back and forth in an unfrequented
corridor on the third level of the keep. After last night's
relative calm, the storm had worsened again, and Hob
could hear the wind howling around the corners of the
great stone building, the snap of ropes worked loose
from the pulleys used to haul freight to the upper levels
of the keep.

Perhaps because of the intrusive din of the gale or
because of the continued gloom of the hallway, the shutters having been made fast against the wind, the three
lads played with less than their usual enthusiasm. The
ball flew back and forth along the corridor, Hob and
Hubert facing the larger Giles. Finally Hubert missed a

catch, and the ball landed and bounced with several loud clacks down along the corridor.

A woman of about forty years came through a nearby doorway, her arms full of bedding, and scolded them for making so much noise as she passed. The pages led the way down a curving stair to an alcove one level down; Giles produced a die and they played at throwing for straws for a while, but this soon palled. The afternoon passed slowly; an oppression hung over the lads' spirits, and Hob, who had delighted in Hubert's company on the previous few days, was relieved when summoned to attend Molly and Nemain.

THE MEAL THAT EVENING went much as others had on the previous evenings, except for an indefinable heaviness to the mood; not quite melancholy, but far from the merry banter of the day before. Dish followed dish, and still conversation languished.

There was a back-billow of smoke from the fire, and at once the hall took on a bluish haze. The fireplace had a flue that ran straight through the keep wall and into two vents, one on each side of a buttress. Servants ran to block the vent on the windward side, leaving the leeward vent open; others opened a shutter on each side of the hall, to clear the air. From the pages' bench, Hob could see slantwise through the open window. Outside, the snow had ceased for the moment, gaps appeared in the wide wall of clouds, and the moon, now full, had just risen above the rim of the curtain wall.

In a moment the hall had cleared of its smoky haze, and the cold air pouring in had become unpleasant. Lady Svajone had recoiled when the shutters were first opened, and a shudder had run through the slight frame. Doctor Vytautas made a gesture to Gintaras; the tall esquire turned and went into the passageway to the kitchen, returning at once with a camlet cloak that they had brought down with them from their quarters. Vytautas and Azuolas wrapped it about her, but she still seemed distressed. She put one frail hand on the table edge, and held tight as though to quench the slight shivering that was just apparent, despite the warmth of the camel's-hair garment.

But now servants hastened to close and fasten the heavy shutters, and within a few breaths the warmth of the fire began to reassert itself. The tiny Lietuvan withdrew her hand from the table and tucked it beneath her cloak. Azuolas tried to interest her in a sugared pastry.

Something had curdled in the atmosphere of the great hall. A further restlessness, a sense of unease, seemed to seep into the air through the walls. The cat, once more in its favored perch in the window recess, began to back up against the shutter, its ears flat and its eyes wide. After a moment even this refuge would not suffice, and it dropped with a small bang onto the table below, leaped to the floor, and scuttled along the wall till it disappeared through an archway near the dais.

The five huge Irish dogs had gathered in a knot near the fireplace, shifting place uneasily from time to time. This caught Sir Jehan's restless eye, and he watched them for a bit, scowling.

"Gruagh!" called Sir Jehan. This was his favorite, the pack's leader, the largest of the five—its name signifying "giant" in Irish. It stood slowly and paced toward him, ears and shoulders drooping and tail tucked beneath its hindquarters. A couple of yards from the table it stopped and sat down suddenly.

"Gruagh!" said the knight again. The dog got up; stood irresolutely for a moment, then bolted back to the hearth, where it huddled again with its fellows. "Damn you," muttered Sir Jehan.

One of the grooms who had bathed the dogs earlier got up from a bench in the lower hall and came up to the giant hound. He put a hand between the braided leather collar and the dog's powerful neck, and tugged, urging it toward the high table. The wolfhound dug in its long legs. Its eyes slitted, its ears went back, and it showed the groom its forest of gleaming teeth.

The man stepped back quickly and looked at Sir Jehan. The knight made a wordless noise of disgust, and gestured to the groom to return to his seat.

Hob saw that an uneasy awkward silence had fallen upon the high table. Lady Svajone pushed listlessly at her pastry; Doctor Vytautas sat grim and preoccupied. The others at the table also showed signs of the increasingly strange atmosphere.

Outside, the wind returned with force, and somewhere in the recesses of the keep a loose shutter was swinging open and closed, each swing producing a muffled boom at irregular intervals: a noise not loud, but one that gnawed at the nerves.

Lady Isabeau's still beauty now looked less like an ivory figurine, and more like an image on a tomb. Only little Dame Aline made attempts at jest for a time, but gradually even her high spirits succumbed to the general air of dull anxiety, and eventually she gave up her attempts at conversation, and sank into a kind of appalled silence.

Sir Jehan's fidgets increased; he made as though to eat more, but hesitated; at last, as though out of patience with something, he threw down his napkin upon the table, took his wife's hand, and made to rise. The other men stood politely and bowed. Sir Jehan and Lady Isabeau said their good-nights and retired through the archway that led past the kitchen.

The meal resumed, but conversation was scant. Soon Lady Svajone's face began to take on a sheen of perspiration, and she moved restlessly. Whether from the woodsmoke or the icy drafts from the window, she was evidently in some discomfort. Vytautas turned to her and took her wrist; the two esquires tensed. A look of deep concern ran among the three men, and they began making preparations to retire. The doctor murmured apologies to the company on the dais. The esquires helped her up, and half-supported her as she tottered from the hall.

Hob just caught the glance that leaped between Nemain and her grandmother: a stony blank stare, whose very lack of expression, between those two who so often smiled on one another, marked it for Hob as some form of warning. A moment later Molly arose, and Nemain after her, close as a shadow. Sweeping her gaze over Jack and Hob, so that those two felt compelled to rise as well, Molly made her excuses to the company and left the hall.

THE MOMENT THEY HAD ENTERED the outer of the two rooms set aside for their use, Molly turned to Nemain.

"It is here, is it not?" she asked her granddaughter.

"It is here," said Nemain.

Molly turned away at once and stamped into the inner room, Nemain and Jack and Hob trailing slowly behind her, as the ocean trails up the strand, following the moon.

Once within the inner room, Molly stood a moment in immobile thought. Then she bade Nemain and Hob to remain, and taking Jack by the arm, drew him back out to the entrance room, and closed the door behind them.

Hob turned in puzzlement to Nemain. "What is here?"

Nemain said, "The bane of Osbert's Inn." Then she added, unhelpfully, "We're just after feeling it, in the hall."

"In the hall? You felt that they were here? The ones who, who killed Marg— The folk at the inn?"

"Aye," she said, but distractedly: she was looking at the door to the outer room, where Molly's and Jack's voices could be heard, but indistinctly.

Hob was stunned. It was as though the castle had been turned inside out. The stout walls that rose about them, the locks, the armed men, changed from haven to snare, and the more tightly sealed the fortress was, the tighter they were caught.

The door opened, and the two adults entered. Molly looked grim, and Jack subdued. Jack closed the door firmly behind them. The clack as the latch engaged sounded like a poacher's bent-branch snare snapping tight.

CHAPTER 18

OLLY WAS PACING THE FLOOR before the fire. Nemain sat on a stool beside the fire, watching her grandmother. They were comparing their thoughts and perceptions, picking at the mystery, but again it was all in English.

Jack Brown and Hob were seated on a bench against the wall. Ever since Molly had spoken to the dark man, something was different about him. Hob tried to watch him without being seen to be watching. What was it? The normally stoic Jack now presented a serious, even a worried, countenance. This was not surprising, given their extraordinary circumstances, but beneath the concern was a furtive air foreign to Jack, openhanded Jack, kindhearted placid Jack. It was almost an air of guilt; and here and there beneath that, far down, glints of a hard glee.

Jack turned sideways and stretched his length on

the bench, and put a brawny arm across his eyes, as though settling for sleep. It was hard to tell if he was beginning to doze, or yet listening to the discussion. Hob looked away. His eyes roamed idly around the room, but he followed the women's debate keenly.

Jack Brown had bolted the outer door to the rooms before coming into the inner room, and closed the inner door as well, another barrier against eavesdroppers. Jack had also reached up and twitched the door cloth across on its rod, so that the door was covered. The door cloth, a tapestry depicting a hunting scene, was there to forestall drafts, but had the additional virtue of muffling what was said within. Now Hob found himself seated opposite the door, contemplating the weaver's art.

In the tapestry a stylized array of knights and foresters rode in a wood, carrying boar-spears: hunting spears with a crossbar that prevented an impaled boar, mad with rage, from forcing its way along the shaft to kill its tormentor. To one side a boar was depicted backed against a tree, encircled by alaunts, the powerful dogs used to hunt boar and bear. At its feet a dog lay dead.

"It may be the moon that is calling to it, and the moon waxing these past nights," said Molly, "or it may be that someone has entered the castle and we not knowing of it. I felt it, I felt it! There in the hall, this night, this hour! As I have not felt it these nights past. Yet I cannot tell where it is; no more can I tell who it might be." She came to the door; she flicked irritably at the edge of the tapestry, then turned and stalked slowly back past the fire. "But be said by me, we should not trust this wolfish lord."

Nemain watched her closely.

"Oh aye, 'twas there tonight," the girl said slowly. "I felt it there, *seanmháthair,* and yet I cannot think it is Sir Jehan."

Molly halted and looked down at her. "That foxy jackeen! 'I have been to the Irish wars.' And him looking at us from the sides of his eyes the while." And after a moment: " 'A hedge queen,' Himself says! This back-of-the-beyond Norman lordling!" Hob realized that she was far more angry at Sir Jehan's gibes than she had appeared the other night. "These Normans! These new men, with their new-wrought titles!"

She resumed her pacing, walking up and down the small room, her arms hugging herself beneath her heavy breasts, her lips pursed, frowning at the floor as though she might find the answer in the random designs the strewn rushes made there. Her passage raised a piquant scent: to the fragrance of the rushes themselves, bruised beneath her feet, was added that of the dried fennel, red mint, cowslips, that were sprinkled in amid the long rustling stems. Hob found it enjoyable even at this tense moment, one of the pleasures of castle life that had not been found in Father Athelstan's austere household.

It was doubtful that Molly noticed the spiced air: she was deep in her own thoughts. "His own dogs would not come nigh him!" she said viciously. And then, almost muttering: "It must be Himself, it must be."

"Never, never. I cannot feel it in him. 'Twas the high table that the dogs would not come nigh."

"Yet 'tis here, you yourself have said it! And why else should not the dogs come nigh the high table?"

"Others sat or served at the high table as well as Himself, *seanmháthair,* and one of them may be . . . I feel it to be here as well . . ." said Nemain, and stopped. And a moment later: "But 'tis not male."

"Not male!"

"I am not to be moved from that belief," said Nemain.

A draft from some chink or crevice set the tapestry rippling. That, and the firelight's flicker over the hanging, drew Hob's eyes again. The figures seemed to move against the forest background. Hob came to his feet, his eyes fixed on the boar at bay, the dogs living and dead.

"Mistress!"

"Hob, what is—"

"Mistress, did Lady Svajone not pass by the inn without stopping?"

Molly and Nemain were staring at him as he stood: his stance was rigid, his voice strained, his mouth drawn down.

"And did she not tell us . . . that, that they parted from the masons at the ford; they came here. They came straightway here. She *told* us this."

"Yes, child, but—"

"Yet she knew!"

That he would interrupt Molly not once but twice was a mark of his distraction. He gazed fixedly at the tapestry, where the shivering fabric made knight and forester, horse and dog, seem to move. The merest mocking semblance of life.

"You told her that the dogs were slain, but naught of the manner of their slaying. Yet she knew! If even those terrible dogs could be slain, she said, *their bellies slashed open like fishes.* As though she'd seen! But Mistress, she said she was past the inn and away and gone long before. And all who were within the inn are dead. *Who is it would know how the dogs were killed?*"

For a moment they both just looked at him, a blue gaze, a green gaze, and then Molly put a hand over her eyes. After a moment she drew it down her face, with a motion as of one who, stepping indoors from a rainstorm, wipes the blinding water from her eyes.

She turned to Nemain. "Have I not chosen well?"

Nemain said gravely, "You have chosen well, *seanmháthair,* and I am pleased with your choice."

Molly turned back. "Blind! Hob, *a rún,* you have seen it, and all our art blind as a mole. Cobwebs, cobwebs! Yet the instant you're after saying it . . ." She tilted her head and spat onto the hearth, a curiously ritualistic action. "The thinnest twig may serve to break a cobweb." She turned and looked away to the corner of the room, her head raised as though to see someone on the level above. "I feel her now, I feel her now! Nemain, it is she, is it not?"

"I believe it's truth he's spoken, *seanmháthair*. It seems so, so . . . Well, now I can see it, I can feel her, now that Hob—and I said 'twas not male! But how did we come to be so blind?" said Nemain.

"She's after hiding from us, and someone else, someone with a mort of power, spreading the cloak under which she's lying concealed. Spinning the cobweb. Someone I did not suspect at all, and who else might that be? Not those two golden guard dogs of hers! I wonder what other accomplishments our outlander doctor may boast. Can he cast such a glamour over that thing, that we could not perceive her, nor perceive the glamour itself?"

Hob had gone back to the tapestry, and to his thoughts, hunting along his own trail; now he spoke up. "If Lady Svajone was there, Mistress, and her wagon is now out in the courtyard, then, then—"

"Then what, lad?"

"Then even now she must have the thing that killed the dogs chained up in that wagon!"

Abruptly Jack got up and passed behind the tapestry and went into the other room, closing the door again behind him very softly.

Nemain looked down; she moved the toe of one slipper in a small meaningless pattern, easing the rushes aside to expose a patch of fine-grained planking. There was a brief silence, and then Molly said gently, "Hob, Lady Svajone—she *is* the thing that killed the dogs."

"Oh, it, no, she couldn't, she—she's just *little,* and she's old, and sickly, and . . ." His voice trailed away.

"She is a shapeshifter," said Molly, "and when she has put on her Beast form, she will be neither little nor will she be sickly."

Nemain had been silent, standing with a blind eye and her mind cast back over what the old woman had done, had said. Now she spoke up: "They are horrid liars entirely: all that trembling and keening when

we came here, clinging to you, *seanmháthair,* and she with a great showing of fear, and saying just that bit too much, about the dogs. And didn't
the doctor speak to her at that moment, in her tongue, and doesn't it
seem that he is fretting about her well-being, and feeling of her wrist and
saying how she must be calm, and she's just after hearing him say this
and we see her flying into your arms. But that was a warning he spoke in
their tongue, in those soothing tones, as though he was comforting her,
that was, and she hearing it knew to beware her speech, and turn our
thoughts elsewhere, and so she's flying into your arms, that we might not
notice her indiscretion."

Molly gave a great gusty sigh. "So it is, and fool us they did, and
it's we who must set it right."

She drew Hob to her, and put a proprietary arm around his shoulder, and looked at Nemain. She spoke in a somewhat distracted fashion.

"He has an eye in his head, and a sharp ear as well, and the cunning to use them." Here she pushed Hob a little distance away and
looked at him and thumped him lightly on the back, as though he were a
horse she contemplated buying. "He is already on his way to be tall, and
will grow strong; and he was not behindhand, on the wagon roof, that
day we fought the forest bandits."

Nemain said again, "You have chosen well, *seanmháthair.*"

Molly turned Hob loose, and sighed again. "*Arragh,* let me think."

Molly sat on the side of the bed, her elbows on her thighs and her
hands hanging down between her knees. Her head was down as if she
studied the rushes at her feet. After a while she spoke to Hob again, but
in a low voice, distant, as though she were thinking hard of something
else all the while.

"These Beasts . . . the Northmen were after using them in Erin;
not always, but now and then, here and there; any road, 'tis long since.
Every Norther king had some in his household; berserkers they called
them, the bear-shirt men. Some people said it was bare-shirt, that they'd

fight all naked, like the British men and my forefathers, so long ago; and some said they wore shirts made from bearskins; but my great-grand-father saw them in battles, and they were not men in bear shirts. They were men, and then they were bears."

She shook her head. "Hard to kill as they were, some of them died, and weren't they men again once death had a grip on them, and they with not a stitch on their bodies. I have myself seen those who turn to wolves, and to . . . other Beasts. Poor Eadmund, the prentice at the inn, maundering of a fox while he was dying—it may be that this outlander witch takes a fox's form when she is at her killing. 'Twould be of a great size, that fox, to deal with ten dogs, and they Osbert's famous killers at that, like so many kittens. These shapeshifters, they grow in power, they grow in size, the more years that they are at it, killing and eating of the flesh of men: and she is old, old."

Hob felt that perhaps this was an evil dream, and he asleep. The castle's defenses—the murderesses, the spiked pit, the high thick walls—all had proved useless to protect them against an enemy who entered in disguise. The castle had welcomed in this demon, cloaked in the form of a frail old woman. In an instant the walls, the gates, the watchtowers, had changed from stronghold to prison.

He looked about him. Outside, the wind howled through the but-tresses; and the snow, the snow that kept them captive here more effi-ciently than locks, the snow that rode on the wind, rattled and pattered against the breathing shutters.

"Oh, Mistress!" Hob cried; he found that he was panting, as though he had been running up a hill. "Then we are, we are trapped in this castle! With, with that *thing*!"

Molly's head came up.

"Nay," she said. "It is trapped in this castle with me."

* * *

Molly sat for a long time, regarding the blank stone of the wall across the room as though it were the tapestry Hob had scrutinized, as though the future were woven there.

Finally she turned to Nemain. "I'm after saying that I asked Mother Babd for safety, and it's you that thought me praying for revenge. Say to me: is it safety we have found?"

"Nay, *seanmháthair.*"

"Then revenge it must be, and it's revenge I'll be having, for Osbert that was a friend to me, and for all those he sheltered under his broad roof; and he not able to save himself, nor protect his own from this demon woman. These Beasts . . . iron will not bite them, not deeply. Flesh must contend with flesh, bone with bone. You have seen Jack with his hammer," Molly said, still in a soft musing voice, as much to herself as to Hob and Nemain. "Jack will be *my* hammer. I have spoken to Jack and he agrees: I will send him against that thing, Beast to Beast, and Jack will be the hammer in my hand."

Finally she stood up and walked from the room. Hob had a glimpse of Jack sitting in the outer room, and then Molly closed the door, the hunt tapestry settling back into place. Hob looked at Nemain in astonishment.

"She will let Jack be a Beast again, and put him at the Fox, as hounds are put at a boar," said the girl.

Hob was struggling: the world tilted beneath his feet; all the air seemed to have departed the room. "Jack will be a Beast?" he said. And after a moment: "Again, you said, again?"

Nemain took his hand. "Hob, *a chuisle*—"

"Again, you said!"

"—when Jack was bitten, away there in the deserts—"

"She said he, he had fevers, that was—fevers, she said."

"More than fevers, more than fevers. Some short while after he's recovering from his wounds, the curse being passed to him, it's working in his blood, and he shifting into a Beast. Sure 'twas rare enough at first, but then more and more, and the while he's being a Beast, he, he . . . And then to awake, as it were, the next day, and him finding that in the night he, that he . . . Any road, he began his wanderings. And hearing of Herself and her skills, he sought her out at Ely Fair, on the Feast of St. Audrey, and Herself penned up the Beast within him, and he returned to the Jack that you know."

"What manner of Beast is this, for Jesus's sweet sake?"

"No one knows, not even Herself. It is like a man, but very big, very strong, and misshapen, and hairy like a beast . . . we call it the Beast, for want of knowing what it is, and it being a kind of beast. There were many such in the old days, but they were bears, or wolves. . . . This is some Southron Beast, that they must have in Outremer, or thereabouts. . . ."

A short while later the door opened, and Molly and Jack came back in. They had plainly been outside to the wagons, for a sparse layer of snow still melted on their shoulders; a hint of the cold still clung to their garments. Jack was carrying a small locked chest. Nemain went and shot the bolt to the outer door, and everyone gathered in the inner room.

Against one wall stood a narrow table with a ewer of water. Nemain swept the ewer from the table and put it over in a corner out of the way. Jack set the small chest down with a thump on this table, and Molly immediately produced a key to unlock the lid. There was a sense of controlled haste to their actions that was apparent even to Hob, still somewhat bewildered at this strange turn his life had taken.

Molly undid the fastenings at her cuffs and rolled her sleeves back to the elbows up over her strong smooth forearms, and Nemain did as well, exposing delicate wrists and forearms notably slim and pale. Molly's hands moved with eye-baffling swiftness among the various vessels and jars, mostly pottery but some, including a fair-sized two-handled flagon, of silver. She had a small cask of the *uisce beatha*;

from this she poured a measure into the silver flagon and a modest amount into a little silver cup, which she drank off immediately, sighing heavily afterward. Nemain already had busied herself with mortar and pestle, mixing and grinding herbs and peppercorns and other substances Hob could not so easily identify. As soon as she had finished milling each ingredient, she would pour the resultant powder into a small dish, wipe the mortar out with a clean cloth, and begin again. Her grandmother chose from among these saucers of powder, here pinching a small amount into the flagon, and there emptying the entire dish into it.

Hob could just hear Molly singing at her work. A moment later he realized that she was not singing, she was chanting in a low voice into the mouth of the pot. She poured in another measure of the fiery drink, sang something more—a little louder, loud enough for Hob to realize that it was in Irish. Molly spat three times into the flagon; her ring-pommel dagger appeared in her hand, and she cut her left thumb, deeply enough to start a little stream of her blood, which she held over the mouth of the vessel. A last dash of the *uisce beatha*, a last muttered phrase, and she clapped the lid on the flagon.

Molly wiped the blood from her thumb with a cloth, holding it there a moment to stanch the flow. Then she poured herself a second drink from the cask, and drank it off without ceremony. She poured a half measure of the *uisce beatha* into the little silver cup, looked around vaguely, and got the ewer of water from the corner. She mixed this into the cup, and offered it to Nemain, who drank it gravely, her eyes big above the rim of the cup. When Nemain had finished, coughing only a little, Molly poured and mixed again, and handed the cup to Hob.

Molly had given it to Hob before, usually when he had been ill; but that was rarely. He knew enough not to gulp it. As he drank, he remembered it, that complex taste: something that was wet, yet burned like fire; something that was not sweet, but that left an impression of sweetness.

When he had finished he was aware of a welcome warmth in his stomach, a growing ease in his limbs.

Molly rinsed the cup, added two fingersful of a mottled powder, and poured a small amount from the silver flagon into it. She stirred the mixture and handed it to Jack, who drank it all without stopping. He coughed a little, and drew the back of his hand across his mouth. Molly took back the cup and rinsed it again.

She turned and contemplated Hob. After a moment she said, partly to herself, "Nay, I cannot leave you here: I have some need of you, and any road, you will not be safer anywhere in this castle tonight than you will between me and Jack."

Molly patted Nemain on the shoulder and pointed to the trunk. Then she turned to Hob.

"Hob, *a chuisle,* you must carry this flagon. You must have it ready when I ask you for it, nor must you spill from it at all."

Meanwhile Jack had thrown off his clothes; for a moment he stood naked in the center of the room, a man so powerfully built that he seemed shorter than he was. Nemain was digging in the trunk; soon she produced a cloak of coarse russet and threw it to Jack. He caught it and tossed it around his shoulders; somberly he began to tie the strings that fastened it at the neck. Molly started to store vessels away in the chest.

There was a hideous cry from somewhere in the castle, and then the sound of many voices shouting, crashes, shrieks, the deep-throated baying of Sir Jehan's giant Irish hounds.

Molly looked up from her work. "She's just after beginning, and ourselves not a moment too soon," she said. She looked around her, at Jack in his cloak, Hob with the flagon, Nemain throwing another cloak about her own thin shoulders; she looked around her as one looks who is leaving on a journey, making sure that nothing has been left behind.

Then she took the veil from her head and unpinned her hair; it tumbled down her back in a silver flood. Nemain did the same, shaking her head a little to free her red mane; ripples ran down its length, glinting in the firelight.

Molly turned and strode through the two rooms, pulled the bolt on the outer door, and led them out into the corridor, where already the uproar seemed to have doubled: a bestial snarling, mingled with the shouts of men to their comrades, and the dreadful outcries of the dying.

CHAPTER 19

UT THE CORRIDOR ITSELF WAS empty. From above came calls of alarm, queries and responses, as the castle's folk tried to determine what disaster was afoot. Now there was the braying of an alarm-horn from below, which ceased with a sudden whine, as though the hornblower had been struck down; and then the clatter of men's feet upon the stairways. A moment's pause, and Molly led them swiftly to the hanging that veiled the entrance to the musicians' gallery. Without hesitation she swept it aside and stepped into the gallery, the others crowding in after her.

Hob was saying a rapid *Paternoster* under his breath. He came up to the rail beside Nemain. He peered through the spaces in the wooden screen, and found that the whole of the great hall was visible to him except the portion of wall beneath the gallery. It was a moment before he would agree with himself to accept that what he saw was real. When he did, he put the flagon straight down and crossed himself, then picked it up again.

At the lower end of the hall, crowding against the entrance from the stairs, seeking to escape down into the snows of the bailey, was a crowd of terrified women, children, and unarmed men. At the hall's front, about the dais, were a score of men-at-arms, and about the table on the dais lay several dead knights, including the aged Sir Archibald and the French knight Sir Estienne, who now would never see Scotland. By the hearth was a great mound of bloody gray fur: the giant hounds of Ireland, dead in a heap. Half-dressed, with a naked sword in his hand, Sir Jehan stood just inside the archway, staring about him in disbelief.

And by the high table crouched the Fox. As Hob stared in horrified fascination down through the screen, the Fox reared up on its hind legs and took a few paces forward, walking like a human being.

Hob's breathing became ragged. The Fox was just that, a monstrous fox: five hundredweight or more of tense power, quick as an arrow, straight as a javelin, bright as a new-polished sword-blade, and female as Eve; Hob could see immediately that it was a vixen. Tall and deadly and graceful: the Goddess of Foxes.

Even as he watched, it dropped back to all fours and leaped over the high table as though it were a tussock of grass, landing amid the men-at-arms, who hacked at it with no visible success.

It leaped in great bounds; it turned about, almost in its own tracks; it dashed here, and swerved there, and always killing, killing. Through Hob's frozen terror a thought came faintly to him: it was gamboling, it was playing at slaughter. It ran past men and with tilted head drew a fang across their middles. Men screamed and cursed; they held their hands over their bellies, that their entrails might not escape through the gaping rents; they lay to right and to left, dead and dying. The men swung mace and sword, hacked, stabbed: their steel would not bite. Their blows went awry. The creature was too fast, too agile, too strong, and its flesh seemed to resist the metal itself. Every so often a blow would land, and the Fox would recoil, but little damage was done.

The Fox sprang from place to place, blithe as a new lamb, and each leap left a mortally wounded man behind. Now and again it would pause to survey its accomplishments, and then the crimson tongue would loll out over serried white teeth, and Hob felt that it was laughing. The skin on top of the long nose wrinkled up in a snarl, the amber eyes closed partway: a gloating expression, an expression of blood-crazed glee.

Sir Jehan shook himself into action. He vaulted with an athlete's grace to the tabletop and down again upon the other side, and without pause swung a great blow at the Fox's neck. But the monster shied away and the blade whistled past. The Fox swirled about Sir Jehan like a red cape twirled by a dancer and appeared at his right hand; the knight, off balance, swung backhand at the Fox and grazed its shoulder. This wound seemed to have no more result than the earlier ones: the Beast staggered but recovered; it did not seem to bleed; in a moment it seemed as though it had not been touched.

Sir Jehan attacked again and again at a furious pace, and the Fox, mischievous as a puppy, avoided each cut or thrust by a hairbreadth, but did not attack the knight. The Sieur de Blanchefontaine had in his hand a heavy Scottish sword with the typical drooping quillons, and between the weight of the weapon and the sheer violence of his assault, as well as the horror of what he faced, he had begun to tire in the space of a dozen breaths. His face was set in a kind of lofty grimace, but his breath came in whistling sobs.

The Fox reared up on its hind legs again; Hob had a sense that it was playing with Sir Jehan, the cruel game that cats play with mice. Hob would remember in later years that lean swift warlord, in desperate struggle, forced backward by the beautiful red flame of the Fox, the Fox that paced forward on its slim black hind paws, weaving like a huge snake, leering down upon the tall lord, the rustle of fabric, the shuffle and stamp of boots amid the rushes, the silver wheel made in midair by the flickering sword, the white hand and wrist that wielded it, the still whiter ridges of teeth that suddenly bent as a willow bends in a breeze to the river ripples, slow-seeming, lazy almost: but all Sir Jehan's speed could not match it. There was a champing clack, and elegant jaws neatly took half the knight's hand; a moment later the scream, the clang of the dropped sword.

Molly made to turn away and descend to the hall, but at that moment, from an entrance into the hall set beneath the gallery, came a squad of archers, seven or eight of them, bows strung. They clattered in; they spread out; they set their feet and nocked arrows: all this within a couple of heartbeats. The next moment they launched a volley of shafts straight at the Fox. It leaped to one side just as the snap and hum of the bowstrings came to Hob's ears, and most of the arrows went wide. Of the three that struck, two seemed to glance off the red flanks with no apparent effect, and one plunged directly into the Fox's shoulder. The creature stumbled for a pace, but the arrow drooped in the wound; loosened; then fell to the floor. In the next instant the Fox charged the group, and the archers broke and ran headlong for the archway beneath the balcony. They disappeared from Hob's sight. The Fox dashed after them, and almost immediately they heard the scream of the hindmost archer as he was pulled down from behind.

Sir Jehan staggered back against a jamb of the fireplace. Slowly his legs gave way, and he slid to the floor. He was a seasoned knight, and his good hand was wrapping a leather thong about his right wrist to stanch the flow of blood from his ruined hand even while his face was slack with horror. Grievous wounds he had seen and even endured before, but none had been inflicted by a kind of demon in the flesh, and here in his own castle at that.

Molly began to curse in Irish. Then: "Now must we be hunting her through these long halls, and it's far better it would be for us to surprise her than for she to surprise us."

Molly turned and went back out into the corridor. The horrid sounds of the Fox's slaughter were dimming. She looked up and down the corridor a moment. She said something low and rapid to Nemain in Irish; her granddaughter ran back toward the solar, partway down the hall.

She turned to Jack. "It's better we'll fare on the morrow, do we have a shield against the Church over our heads, and Sir Jehan is the man to provide it." Jack just nodded slightly. An austere expression had settled over his features.

Nemain came running back with a large leather pouch slung over her shoulder, and Molly stepped through heavy hangings into the spiral stairwell that led to the hall below.

MOLLY KNELT BESIDE Sir Jehan where he lay propped against the wall with a bundled cloak behind his neck. He had bitten into his lower lip to keep from crying out. Nemain stood by them, delving into her leather pouch, handing linen bandage or jar of unguent to her grandmother as required. Molly deftly spread salves, wound white linen strips, administered sips from a small earthenware bottle to Sir Jehan, and all the while murmured urgently to the lord of Blanchefontaine. Sir Jehan endured all with the stoicism of the professional warrior, but on his features was a look of horror that would not fade.

Molly wiped blood and the remnants of her potion from the knight's mouth with a cloth, and then fashioned a sling around his neck to steady the mangled hand, still speaking softly and swiftly, bent almost to his ear. Sir Jehan's face had a sheen, the mist of agony, and sweat beaded on his forehead. Yet he attended to Molly's words, and gradually some hope came to mingle with the horror in his expression. He contemplated what was left of his sword hand, and listened; at one point he cast a startled glance at Jack. At last he tore his gaze away from the ruin of his hand and peered up into Molly's face. His expression changed: a growing tinge of awe, even a little fear.

His free hand clenched and twisted the fabric of his own surcoat as Molly worked on him. Yet when he spoke his voice was strong and clear, and although Hob had not been able to make out Molly's tense mutter, the knight's reply was plain.

"Do you but deliver us, madam," he said, "and you will find me a firm fr—" Here he gasped; his habitual restless movements had caused pain to shoot through his hand. "—firm friend, for as long as I draw—as long as God grants me breath."

Molly sat back and surveyed her handiwork. Then she put her hand lightly on the bandage covering Sir Jehan's dreadful wound, closed her eyes, and muttered, *"Alt fri alt ocus féith fri féith."* Joint to joint and sinew to sinew. Then she stood up.

There was a rattling and clanking from the other end of the hall as Sir Balthasar strode in with a small cloud of men-at-arms at his back. The castellan had donned a mail hauberk, steel gauntlets, and vam-braces, but no helm. His size, his grim visage framed in the chain-mail coif, his powerful stride, made him seem the very figure of some ancient war god. But Hob had seen the Fox, and no longer had faith in the prow-ess of men, even men like the fearsome castellan.

Sir Balthasar knelt swiftly beside the Sieur de Blanchefontaine. The links of his mail rustled as he went to one knee and gingerly ex-amined the bandaged hand, where only the tips of the thumb and two remaining fingers protruded.

Whether from pain or relief from pain, or perhaps from some in-gredient in Molly's potion, the focus of Sir Jehan's eyes began to wander, and he spoke in a thick, dreamy voice:

"Balthasar, my lion, my lion! You cannot prevail against it." The sweat poured down his cheeks. "Not even you—not even you! It is terrible past all belief!"

Sir Balthasar stood. "I cannot do nothing," he said. He looked around at the wreckage and the dogs' corpses, at dead Sir Archibald lying almost at his feet. "I will perish or no; all is in God's hands."

"Nay," said Molly; she faced the castellan. "I have need of you elsewhere." Although she was a tall woman, Sir Balthasar was big among men, and taller than she. Yet her gaze was so intense, the prominent blue eyes so imperious, her carriage so erect, that he seemed somewhat diminished before her.

"It's yourself we must rely upon to bring all to safety," she said. "Gather everyone that may be found, and bring them here, and barricade yourself within. Arrest any of those outlanders you come upon; but in no wise attempt to engage with that fiend. If it comes, retreat; flee if you must. I will destroy it! But you must do all else."

Sir Balthasar's face darkened even more than its usual ruddy hue; he drew breath to protest; he looked into Molly's face. What he saw there Hob could not tell, but the castellan's own expression altered. After a moment: "My lady," he said, and bowed.

Molly looked from Sir Jehan to Sir Balthasar and said, "I will save all in this castle who yet live, but afterward you must be my safety against that priest, and his superiors, and their wrath. Swear to me your protection."

At once Sir Jehan croaked through gritted teeth, "You have my protection," and when Sir Balthasar hesitated a moment, he made as if to sit up, and said, this time in the clear ringing voice of the Sieur de Blanchefontaine, "Swear to her safety."

Over the mareschal's hauberk was his belt, a badge of his knighthood, and now he gripped this near the golden buckle and nodded. "By Sieur Jesus, by my belt and spurs, myself between you and all priests."

He bowed to Molly and Sir Jehan, then he turned and detailed a squad to barricade the hall, another to search the south side of the castle to bring folk down to the hall, or to arrest the Lietuvan grooms, while he himself would lead the party searching the northern staircases. He warned his men to retreat at first sign of the Fox. At his barked dismissal, the squads set off at a half-trot in different directions.

After a very short while, folk began to trickle slowly into the hall, sent there by Sir Balthasar's soldiers. Lady Isabeau arrived with a flock of her attendant ladies and flew to her husband's side. She knelt beside him, cradling his shoulders, her tears falling on his face.

Jack was beginning to move restlessly, rolling his shoulders to and fro. Molly glanced at him, gathered up her flock silently, gave over the care of Sir Jehan to his wife, and strode toward the turret stair. She looked back at Jack and the two youngsters. "Away on!"

CHAPTER 20

OLLY LED THEM WITH WHAT might be called cautious haste, looking narrowly into each shadowed corner, searching solar and storeroom. They had chosen a stairway on the south side of the castle and, having tested each door on the first level up from the hall and found nothing but a frightened servant girl, they went up. As they ascended, they began to hear the clash of arms, the harsh voices of men in conflict. They pushed through the heavy draperies at the next level, and came upon Sir Balthasar's first squad. The men-at-arms had found their Lietuvan almost immediately, and he had turned at bay.

There was an oriel here in the curtain wall, an outward swelling that enabled a lateral view, with arrow slits on three sides so that archers stationed within could defend the wall. Several men could stand side to side in the little circular room thus created. In the entrance to this room stood Azuolas, sword in hand. He was in a strong position, and he was a formidable swordsman. One of the castle guards was down—Hob could not tell if he was dead—and three were badly wounded, a few feet down the corridor. Trails of red showed that they had been dragged back from the oriel doorway by their comrades. A half-dozen others stood back, panting. Azuolas could not escape, but no one wished to come within his reach.

A clatter in the stairwell, and here came Sir Balthasar, the second squad at his back. To his plate gauntlets, the knight had added a small hand targe, strapped to the back of his left wrist. His sword was still in its sheath. He strode down the corridor, matter-of-fact as a man hurrying to supper, but his face was purple with anger. In the whites of his eyes were broken veins. Without slowing or breaking stride he drew his heavy dagger with his right hand as he came and flipped it in midair, catching it so that the point was up, the massive iron pommel at the bottom of his fist.

"You fucking, you fucking outlander swine! You'd break hospitality? You'd break our hospitality?" He was cursing, steadily but low; his voice was like stones being rolled over by a heavy wagon. "You'll never die by steel, you pigshit knave: I'll hang you this night! Hang you by your own guts—by Our Lady!—hang you from the fucking rafters!"

Sir Balthasar was approaching the embattled Lietuvan at a fast walk. Azuolas could not understand what was said, but the castellan's intent could be heard in the tone of his voice; could be read in his face and the slant of his great body. Azuolas, unimpressed, impassive, watched the knight's approach. He reset his feet, made ready for the onslaught.

As the castellan strode up, Azuolas made a swift clever pass at him. Sir Balthasar stopped it on his little targe, and with a quick rolling motion of his wrist clamped the sword-blade with his armored left hand. Azuolas immediately sought to withdraw it, but Sir Balthasar held it fast. The blade screeched against the plates covering his palm and thumb, but only a few inches were drawn back before the knight's fierce grip stopped it, and by then Sir Balthasar was through the opening and closing with the Lietuvan, pushing the shorter man back.

Sir Balthasar's right hand swept up with the dagger and smashed the pommel down on Azuolas's forehead. The Lietuvan fell down, dazed and bloody, and the knight wrenched the sword from his grasp.

"Jesus and Mary!" The castellan angrily threw the sword a little way down the corridor. "Take him down to the hall; hang him with those fucking grooms."

Men crowded in and seized the esquire by the arms, and dragged him away, his feet trailing the floor.

THE FOX HAD GONE UPWARD. Beyond that they could tell nothing, for it moved quickly, and the castle, though only a modest stronghold, was yet a large building, added to over the decades, with many passageways and half-hidden stairways, and rooms opening onto smaller rooms, and these opening onto still-smaller rooms. Molly and Nemain tracked the monster by sound, and by some sense that Hob could only guess at: the two women paused every so often and turned about, listening and looking, and consulted in murmurs, while Hob held the heavy flagon, fearing to set it down even for a moment, lest it be needed suddenly. During these halts Jack looked about him, his face drawn and his manner distant, and Hob avoided his eyes, because Jack seemed so very different from the old, the genial Jack Brown.

Confused sounds came to them, always in another part of the great structure: muffled shouts and screams, snarling, the clang of weapons. Then there would be silence for a brief time, and then a shriek, abruptly cut short. Sometimes these sounds came from ahead, sometimes behind; to one hand or another; always above them. Molly proceeded at a steady pace: she had announced before they began that she did not want the Fox to discover them first and ambush them before she might unleash Jack, and so they must not let haste make them careless.

Molly led the way, followed by Jack and Nemain. Hob she assigned to watch behind them, and he looked frequently over his shoulder; occasionally he turned about, walking backward for a pace or two, as he had in the courtyard of Osbert's Inn, after his glimpse of the mastiff's fangs through the moonlit grille. The memory flickered before him for a moment. Were he able to laugh in this terrible present, he thought, he would laugh at his past self: he had felt himself to be in danger then, but he had not even tasted danger that night. This slow patrol through the deserted castle corridors—*this* was peril. This was immersion in nightmare. He shifted the flagon into the crook of his left arm and held it there a moment, awkwardly, while he crossed himself, then hurried a few steps to catch up with Jack and Nemain.

Jack moved down the corridors with a light and powerful tread, his limp much reduced. He began, every eight or nine paces, to shake his head, a short sharp rapid movement, as a dog shakes its head to shed water, or a man to clear his vision. Finally he reached up beneath his cloak and pulled the leather-bag amulet out, and began to draw it up over his head. Nemain turned quickly and put her hand over his: delicate-boned, narrow, pale, it barely covered half of Jack's scarred and heavy-knuckled fist, now closed upon the amulet. Yet he released the bag and let it fall back against his chest. Nemain took his hand in hers, as though he were the child and she the adult, and so they proceeded, side by side, down the passage: one more strange sight on this strangest of nights.

After a while of this tense promenade, another memory came to Hob: Molly saying, "You men." And then the thought: *This will be revenge for Margery.* And between the one and the other, he straightened up, and he was almost unafraid.

There came a burst of high-pitched screaming, echoing down one of the spiral stairwells. Molly went quickly to the archway that led to the steps. She peered upward a moment, then muttered, "She is at her mischief, and 'tis somewhere up these stairs." And turning to the others: "Away on!"

At the top of the winding turret stair there was a heavy hanging, there to foil the drafts from the upper passageway, which was a sort of unheated gallery, with narrow unglazed arrow-slit windows, open to the air. Molly swept this curtain aside and led them through the doorless archway; they found themselves at one end of the gallery corridor that ran along the south side of the keep on this high level.

Here there was a torch on either side of the stone arch; the four stood in a pool of wavering yellow light. If there had been torches lit anywhere down the length of the gallery, they had gone out; certainly now there was only a near-black tunnel, pierced by narrow shafts of bright moonshine from the open window slits. The window slits were cut in a cross shape, both for piety and to allow an archer to traverse his shots, and the bars of moonlight fell against the inner wall in crosses of pearly light, receding and diminishing down the gallery.

But the corridor's other end, away at the southeast corner of the castle keep, was also illuminated: there another pair of torches showed them the body of a woman, supine, her arms flung wide and her clothes bloodied, and by her another body, a child—no, it was also a woman, but small. Above them crouched the Fox, its muzzle dripping dark gore.

CHAPTER 21

HE SHOCK OF IT FROZE MOL-
ly's party in place for a moment,
and in that moment the Fox be-
came aware of them, and with a rippling movement
surged up and past the bodies, ears and eyes straining toward them, all eager attention. The cold airs
and breezes that played along the gallery brought
their scent to the Fox, and it halted suddenly, ears up
straight and slightly forward, one graceful black foreleg bent up in midstep. Its nose lifted slightly, and it
sampled the air. It cocked its head to one side. Plainly
there was something about Molly, or her people, that
troubled it.

Then its lips writhed back from long ranks of
white, white teeth. The Fox was like a fox in form:
deadly but elegantly, almost delicately, deadly. Yet it
was so huge that it struck Hob, through his rekindled
fear, that this must be what a vole might feel when fac-

ing a real fox. It was looking from one to another of them, and Hob could feel its amber eyes fix on him a moment, and a wave of sick terror began in his belly and washed up through his chest; yet he stood his ground beside Molly and kept the flagon steady and level. "You men," she had said; he held to that.

In the next instant Nemain twitched the cloak from Jack's body, and Molly deftly snatched the cord with the leather bag from Jack's neck. Molly and Nemain now cried out in unison: a long rhythmic phrase in Irish, the two voices in high-and-low harmony, piercing, urgent.

Jack started at the sound; he sprang forward a yard, as though a whip had been laid across his shoulders, and stopped. Then he began to walk down the corridor toward the Fox. In the torchlight Hob could see the muscles rippling in Jack's broad and naked back; yet before the five hundred pounds of the Fox, he no longer seemed large and power-ful. In a moment the darkness swallowed him; two heartbeats later he reemerged, gleaming palely as he passed through a shaft of moonlight. Still the Fox made no move toward them, and Jack sank into the next band of shadow.

He passed through the next strip of moonlight. Hob thought that perhaps Jack was not so small in comparison to the Fox as first he had feared; certainly Jack was broad enough of shoulder. The silent man passed into shadow again; and now the Fox put down its paw and took one pace forward, and a low snarl came to Hob's ears, rasping, vicious: Hob felt an involuntary shiver that centered itself between his shoulder blades. He realized that he was baring his own teeth, in some faint echo of the Fox's dagger-mouthed threat.

Jack reappeared, and Hob was alarmed to see that Jack was hav-ing some difficulty in walking: certainly he was shuffling more, and he seemed bent forward, but his figure had not diminished with distance, and indeed seemed if anything broader than usual.

In its pool of torchlight down at the end of the corridor, the Fox put its ears flat back and crouched, its lips retracting still farther from those glinting fangs.

Hob squinted as Jack passed again into shadow. The next time he emerged he seemed to trip; he pitched forward, arms outstretched, falling through the band of gray light that stretched from the window slit across the floor to the inner wall, and disappearing into the gloom beyond.

When again he came out into the light Hob gasped. Jack's form had darkened with a thick pelt of black fur, and increased tremendously. Across his back the fur had a silvery sheen, and his skull seemed misshapen: it rose to a bony crest, so that it seemed he wore a casque helmet beneath the coarse black hairs. His legs had become bowed and short and immensely thick; his long arms were as burly as a strong man's thighs, with huge wrists and swollen elbow joints and powerful forearms; and he moved on all fours, his hands balled into fists, the knuckles pounding along the floor, serving as feet. His speed increased, and then he was bounding down the hallway in a rapid rocking charge, flicking in and out of the shafts of moonlight. From his throat came a bellowing roar that Hob could feel in the planks beneath the soles of his feet, and if the snarl of the Fox had made Hob shiver, the roar of this new Beast destroyed all thought, and left Hob unable to move while it persisted.

The speed of the Beast's charge was astonishing, given its bulk. It was like the white king bull: much of its mass was muscle, which carries itself. The broad stiff back rocked from side to side, and the Beast flew down the hallway. The Fox sank into a crouch, and then leaped, forward and to the side, so that the Beast went partway past it. The Fox flashed in from the side, fangs glinting, but the whirl of the Beast as it changed direction took its side away from the jaws; they whipped by, and tore a small slit along the bulge of the Beast's shoulder.

Roaring, snarling, the combatants spun about one another, probing for an avenue of attack, feinting, striking, leaping back. The floorboards shuddered; the impact of the giant beasts as they struck heavily against the corridor walls, maneuvering frantically in the narrow space, could be felt down at Hob's end of the gallery. To Hob came the odor of wild things: musk, salt—the pungent scent of two great animals in extreme exertion.

The Fox went up on two legs as it had in the hall, seeking to strike down at the back of the Beast's neck, but the thing that had been Jack stood up itself, jaws wide and lips retracted from its huge teeth, its paws slapping and grabbing at the Fox's head, seeking a handhold, seeking to hold the Fox still that it might bite. For a moment Hob thought that the struggle looked like a battle of snakes: the Fox's head weaving from side to side, the Beast's arms—for it was so manlike that Hob must think in terms of arms and legs—held high, seeking to seize the Fox's head or throat. Whenever a hand sought to close upon its throat, the Fox snapped at it and drove it back.

The Beast dropped down again to three limbs; its right arm flashed up and it struck the Fox such a tremendous blow in the belly that the giant canid was driven back several feet along the polished wooden floor.

The Fox slid backward, scrabbling at the floorboards for traction, and its back leg struck the two bodies lying there. The corpses were dashed back against the wall, fetching up with a thump. It was as though they had no more substance than the straw dolls that little girls had played with in Hob's old village; he had a sudden sense of the bodily weight, the appalling power, of the two beings who strove there at the corridor's end.

The Fox bunched its hindquarters under it and leaped at its foe. Its back paws ripped deep scratches in the planks of the floor, splinters spraying behind it. Its head turned to one side as it ran past the Beast, the long, long canines catching the torchlight for an instant. But the Beast was as brute-quick as the Fox, and turned just enough to avoid being disemboweled, and the Fox succeeded only in ripping a long score along the ribs, that began to drip carmine at once.

Even as it turned to avoid the slashing fangs, the Beast threw a curving fist at its tormentor; the Fox was thrown again against the wall, and was as quickly up on its feet again, and again hurled itself at the thing that had been Jack. There followed a whirl of chaos that Hob could barely grasp, his eye running so far ahead of his comprehension of what he saw, his mind numbed with the deafening roars, pierced by the malevolent snarls of the Fox, a sound of distilled bestial hatred.

The constriction of the corridor forced the antagonists into surges toward and away from Molly's group. Hob and Nemain moved back as far as they were able. Only Molly stood immobile, as the mayhem advanced and retreated like the tides.

Suddenly the Fox broke free and ran toward Molly's end of the corridor; Hob's heart seemed to freeze as it bore down on them, huge and implacable. But it only sought a space to spin about, set itself, and charge with blinding speed at the manlike Beast. It raced a few paces, gathered itself, and sprang on that which had been Jack.

The Beast threw up a great arm, punching the doglike chest, checking the Fox's leap in midair, and the gleaming teeth clacked shut on emptiness. A moment later, so quickly that Hob could not see the movement, one huge hand closed about the blood-drenched muzzle, and the other about its foreleg. Hob could hear small bones in the leg breaking under the pressure of that monstrous hand, a sound like a bunch of twigs crackling in a campfire.

There was a yelping shriek, and the Fox sought frantically to back away with its three good legs, but the Beast had it fast, by leg and snout, and it could neither bite nor flee. The power in all toothed killers is in closing the jaws; to open them requires no great strength and the muscles that do so are small. The grip of that black-furred leathery hand was easily sufficient to muzzle the Fox and then, slowly, to bend its head upward, exposing the bib of white fur on its chest. All the while the Beast backed the Fox up against the stone of the corridor's outside wall, and all the while the Fox's claws were rasping and slipping on the wide planking as it sought to resist.

What had been Jack now dipped its head, hampered somewhat by the stiff muscularity of its short neck, and drove at the Fox's under-throat. The Beast's mouth opened in a parody of a human yawn; indeed its yellow teeth, though huge, seemed much like those of a man, except for the four great fangs, inches long, two above and two below, that now clenched themselves in the Fox's throat, and locked tight.

There followed a period of near-stasis, a strangled wheezing from the Fox; then a frantic scrabbling and clawing; but the Beast was inexo-rable. Blood poured from the Fox's torn throat, and the clamp of the Beast's jaws cut off breath; slowly the Fox's life drained away. Its fore-limbs straightened and stretched out before it, quivered, and went still. The Beast released its hold, and the body of the Fox slid to the floor.

The Beast, on all fours, contemplated its fallen enemy with tilted head. After a moment it reached out a huge hand—it looked to Hob as though the thing wore black leather gloves, with hair on the back—and prodded the Fox. There was no movement. The Beast sat back on its haunches, turned its head to one side, and slapped itself on the breast a few times with alternating hands, not very hard, producing a series of hollow popping sounds. Then it rocked forward, seized one of the Fox's forelimbs by the paw, and prepared to bite into the shoulder, but something about the Fox repelled it. It dropped the lifeless paw—Hob could hear the claws rattle as they hit the floor—and, to Hob's horror, turned its attention to the dead women lying where they had been flung against the wall.

The Beast was pawing at the corpses, plainly preparing to eat of them, and Molly was stirring beside Hob, reaching for the flagon that

Hob held, to reassert control over Jack the Beast, when they heard a sharp hiss of indrawn breath behind them.

Framed in the doorway, holding aside the heavy tapestry, stood Doctor Vytautas, gazing in anguish at the dead Fox. In a moment or two, rage had replaced mourning, and he stepped through into the corridor, letting the thick cloth fall to behind him. He began to stalk toward their little group.

Vytautas had lost his fussy gait. Now he paced forward like a cat mousing, surefooted and ominous. Hob watched him, aghast. How could he ever have thought this man kindly; how could he have thought him weak? The once-benevolent eyes were half-hidden beneath lowering brows, ridges of muscle bracketed a down-turned cruel mouth, and his tall frame seemed to be filled with a sinewy power beneath the fine robe. His attention was all for the Beast at the end of the corridor, and he passed Hob as though the lad were not there.

Vytautas spoke, his voice a harsh grumble, his brow dark as a thundercloud, his upraised hand twisted into a complex clawlike symbol. Hob could not understand a word, but the voice seemed to echo from the walls and each echo seemed further to dim the torchlight. The macabre droning set up a throbbing in Hob's bones, and a sickening weakness seeped through his flesh.

Hob felt he had to do something: the Lietuvan was chanting them to their deaths. He put the flagon down against the wall; as he straightened the corridor seemed to whirl about him, and then steady again. He shook his head to clear it, with limited success.

Hob was a few paces behind Vytautas and a pace to the side, and now he drew his belt knife and stepped forward, intending to plant it in the middle of the wizard's back: anything to stop that hideous travesty of prayer.

But his first step wobbled and he could not take a second and he seemed unable to feel where his fingers were on the hilt. The knife slipped from his hand to plunge itself into the wooden floor, where it stuck, upright and vibrating softly.

And now the corridor rang with sound, the reverberations overlapping, the air pulsing with a ghastly energy. Down the hall the Beast that was Jack had halted, uncertain. Through watering eyes Hob saw that Nemain had doubled over; she held with one hand to the lip of the deep-set window.

Only Molly seemed unaffected. Suddenly her bell-deep voice rang out in Irish, something repeated thrice, and she stepped briskly to Vytautas's side and slapped him across the mouth.

At once his drone ceased. He stood with that one hand stretched out toward Jack, and his mouth open, but his voice had failed, locked within him. He struggled to make a sound, his face empurpling, his eyes bulging, but only a thin croak came from his throat. Molly stepped back away from him.

Hob, released from the incantation's fell power, dropped to hands and knees, his stomach heaving, his ears filled with a sound as of a rushing stream. His tear-blurred vision was narrowed to the wide planks between his hands, and the thin stream of drool that came from his mouth, and the butt of his knife hilt, still shivering in the wood. After a moment that seemed to last forever, his vision expanded, sounds resumed, and he became aware that the floorboards beneath his palms were jumping to a slow rhythm. He raised his head. The Beast had renewed its advance toward Vytautas, its heavy limbs making the planks of the floor tremble with each step.

It began to gallop along, and again gave voice to that blaring bass outcry, and Hob felt his bones turn to water, although surely, he thought, surely, Jack would not harm his own, no matter how deeply he had been submerged in the Beast. He snatched up the flagon again and pressed himself against the inner wall; the lid rattled on the flagon and he clapped his palm on it to keep it secure.

Vytautas plainly could not even turn his head. He stood immobile as the statue of a prophet, while his doom roared down upon him. At the last moment he rolled his eyes toward Molly, a frantic glance, in which hatred and despair mingled in equal parts. His lips trembled, his teeth shone through his beard in a bright grin. Hob felt that Vytautas strove to curse Molly; but her spell held, and all the sinister doctor could manage was a thin throttled whine.

The Beast came bounding down the corridor, flashing in and out of the bars of moonlight, its speed and size and roar enough to paralyze any man, even without Molly's binding cantrip. It was upon them in two breaths. Its last galloping leap ended with a looping overhand blow from the giant fist, and Vytautas crumpled, hammered down like a sheep in a shambles.

There was the briefest of pauses, and then the Beast seized the corpse by its head and arm and bent swiftly toward the doctor's neck. The huge canines tore out Vytautas's throat in one appalling wrench. Hob turned hastily away, but still, still, he could hear the grunts, the obscure moist smacking sounds, a grinding of tooth upon bone, rapid gulps, snarling.

Molly came slowly toward the Beast, where it crouched over the broken husk of the Lietuvan. She began singing, with something of the rhythm of a chant but more douce and delicate, and yet not quite full song. In her right hand was the amulet pouch on its leather thong. As she passed Hob she reached out toward him for the widemouthed flagon; he uncovered it and gave it to her. She took it by one handle, holding it in her left hand. He swung about, much against his will, to see what would come.

He saw the Beast that was Jack look up from its awful business. Hob's eyes skittered away from the thing on the floor. He watched as Molly drew nearer. The Beast reached down. There was a terrible wet rending noise, and it brandished aloft the long bone from one of Vytautas's thighs, meat and gristle still adhering to the knobby terminus. The Beast came forward a pace or so on three limbs, the left fist knuckle-down on the blood-soaked planks. It glared at Molly and raised the thighbone; from the broad hairless chest came a bass rumble so menacing that, dazed as he was, Hob must take a quick step backward. The Beast smote the floor once, twice, four times with the scarlet-stained baton, the floorboards thundering like a war drum, and all the while the red eyes staring into Molly's face. Speech could not have been plainer: *See what blows I will give you, if you come nigh.*

Yet Molly's song, so pleasant, did not falter, nor was there the merest quiver in her deep sweet contralto, though she had halted her advance for a moment when the first blows were struck. Now she moved forward singing, as one sings a lullaby to a tiny-fisted newborn, and she came up to the Beast that was Jack, and she dropped the loop of thong about the short neck where it met the huge back, and she dipped her right hand in the flagon and smeared a bit of the liquid on the fearsome bloodstained jaws. The thing's tongue came out and licked it up, and Molly, still singing, held the flagon to the Beast's lips, and Jack the Beast drank, gulping noisily, and then sank back against the wall beneath a deep narrow window recess where the moonlight slanted in through the arrow slits, and thrust bowed short legs of astounding girth out before him, and sighed.

Molly knelt quickly beside Jack the Beast, gathered a handful of fabric from her skirt and began to wipe the brutal face. In between her ministrations she gave him more sips from the flagon. The torches nearest them sputtered, casting a fitful light on Jack, making shadows move across his face, making his features hard to discern clearly.

Hob blinked. Already Jack's face had assumed subtly different proportions, and—did he seem smaller as well? Hob decided that he did; then thought he did not. All at once he was sure that the great body was smaller, and less hirsute.

Jack lost substance, but slowly, slowly. Hob remembered lying awake in the wagon, watching the moon move through the topmost branches in the forest, a motion just perceptible every so many breaths: at just such a speed did Jack become smaller, become more Jack.

His head lolled back again and rolled weakly against the stone wall. Pale naked skin shone here and there through the pelt upon his shoulders; the black leathery breast began to lighten and soften. Jack made a visible attempt to focus his eyes. His head rolled to the side again and again, as though there was no strength in his neck. But he kept turning back to Molly's face, looking at her as though trying to read a sign, an uncertain but growing comprehension glimmering in his eye, like a new-lit candlewick that sputters and flickers before the wax that nourishes it begins to melt, and the flame begins to steady.

Sooner than Hob would have expected, Jack Brown appeared completely human—his powerful frame, bleeding here and there from cuts and bites inflicted by the Fox, seemed almost boyish against Hob's memory of what he had been as a Beast—but his features were still slack. And now he gazed with desperate attention at Molly's face, and did not look away again, and at last his eyes sharpened, and awareness came into his features, like a drowsy man suddenly coming fully awake, or a drunken man suddenly sobering, and he knew her.

"Maygh," said the dark man. Maeve.

"*Mo mhíle stór,*" she said, stroking the hair back from his forehead, her face very close to his face, her eyes smiling into his eyes, as she called him "my thousand treasures" in the language she used for her inmost thoughts.

CHAPTER 22

LONG THE CORRIDOR A KIND
of numb peace reigned for perhaps a dozen heartbeats. Four
lived; four were dead. At the far end, the corpses of the
women were hidden by the bulk of the dead Fox; at this
end, the body of Vytautas lay in ruin just beyond Jack
and his three attendants.

Molly stroked Jack's face a short while. She
roused herself with an effort and said to Hob, "Run and
fetch some men—we'll be needing to carry him down;
then go tell Sir Balthasar that we have triumphed."
Hob turned, stiff as an old man, and went through the
curtain to the turret stair, looking at Vytautas as little
as possible.

But in the event he had not descended more than
a level and a half before he met Sir Balthasar with a
squad of men, one of them Roger, on the hunt for any

of the Lietuvans who might remain. Hob led them back to the bloody corridor.

The soldiers bunched in a little knot just inside the curtain, transfixed at first by the huge russet carcass of the Fox blocking the far end of the corridor. Then: "Precious Christ!" cried Sir Balthasar, looking down at what had been Doctor Vytautas. "Has he been torn by demons?"

"He sought to do that to you and yours. Let him be," said Molly. "The dead to the soil, the living to the loaf: my man here needs aid, and he cannot walk to his bed."

Sir Balthasar knelt by Jack a moment, then gave orders that the curtain should be torn down and fastened to pikestaffs to make a litter for the wounded man. While this was being done he walked cautiously down the corridor with a few others of the squad to the wreck of the giant canid. The bodies of the two women were discovered, to cries of dismay. Sir Balthasar told off another detail, and the two corpses were quickly and carefully borne off by four soldiers.

Sir Balthasar stood a moment contemplating the Fox. Its half-open eyes held a sheen from reflected torchlight; fangs still gleamed from under the partially retracted lips. But the limbs held stiffly out to the side, the utter immobility, spoke only of death. After a moment the knight turned away, motioned his remaining soldiers back.

Sir Balthasar returned along the corridor to where the litter was almost ready. Molly stood up from her ministrations. The grim knight stood looking down at her a moment, then sank to one knee, took her right hand, and kissed it gravely. He stood up and stepped back, and at once Roger came forward and did the same, and then all the men present, one by one. Molly accepted all this calmly.

Behind her the four bearers had finished their improvised field litter. A man-at-arms reached to take Jack's arm, to move him onto the curtain preparatory to lifting, but Jack tensed and turned swiftly toward the man. Jack's face was turned away from Hob but something in it made the soldier shrink back. Nemain put a soothing hand to the side of Jack's neck, and he subsided; Molly came up and coaxed the dark man to slide onto the litter himself.

Just as the four bearers were about to stoop and lift Jack, a settling or exhalation from the far end of the corridor brought everyone whipping around, palms slapping against hilts. "God's wounds!" said Sir Balthasar.

The Fox was no longer there: in its place was a short and slender young woman, naked and broken-bodied. Nemain stayed with Jack, but Molly and Hob and the men of the castle went up to the corpse and gathered in a silent ring, looking down. Despite the splintered bone protruding here and there, the terrible gashes that Jack the Beast had inflicted, Hob recognized the strong nose, the tilted gray eyes, of Lady Svajone. But this was a woman of perhaps twenty, with long fine white-butter-blond hair and the suave skin of youth, and even now possessed of an eerie beauty.

"She was young for a time each night, or each night that she killed," said Molly. "It is a way they have, and they live long, long. Herself wandering the land over with these three men as her husbands, and this body one more strand of her mastery over them. That itself is another form of sorcery, and not the youngest in the world."

Hob tried to speak, but at first could accomplish only a croak. He swallowed and tried again. "Will she stay this way now, Mistress?"

Molly made a dusting-off gesture with her hands. "When the sun rises, she'll be an old woman again, and a dead old woman at that, and soon thereafter 'twill be the usual road of the flesh."

"We will burn them all before that, and throw their ashes into the river," said the mareschal savagely.

*   *   *

IN SHORT ORDER they had conveyed Jack back down to Molly's quarters and settled him in the great bed in the inner chamber, Molly and Nemain bustling to and fro. Jack was already half-asleep; he lay very still on his back.

Hob looked down at him: despite his burly limbs, Jack seemed somehow frail, for the first time since Hob had known him. His skin held an underlying pallor that Hob had not seen before. He lay on a pillow with a pattern of chevrons, but there was a linen head sheet, a white cloth draped over the pillow, and he was almost as pale as the linen.

Sir Balthasar and his four litter-bearers stood about awkwardly, filling the room, looking at Jack. One of the men-at-arms, after a private assessment of Jack's chances, asked, "Shall I run now for the priest, my lord?"

"No priest!" said Molly sharply.

The soldier looked dubiously at Jack. "But, my la—"

At that Sir Balthasar turned and fixed his basilisk glare on the wretched man. The castellan spoke in a quiet poisonous tone. "No summoning of priests, and no carrying of tales." He swept his glance around the four men-at-arms, and they nodded almost as one.

"There will be guards and runners outside your door, madam," he said to Molly. "Summon me if you need aught, be it day or night." He bowed, and left with his retinue, and Molly was not troubled by priests thereafter.

THERE FOLLOWED A PERIOD of administering various potions to the barely conscious Jack, Molly feeding him with a spoon. She bound up those wounds that the Fox had inflicted and rubbed embrocation into Jack's powerful limbs, while Nemain wiped his brow with a wet cloth redolent of the *uisce beatha*. After a while she sent Nemain to sit with Hob while she continued to work on her lover.

At last Molly turned from Jack's bedside. She stretched, her hands to her lower back. She rubbed her eyes, looked around wearily. Hob and Nemain were sitting side by side on a bench, exhausted, slumped back against the wall. She considered the two young ones briefly.

"One more thing," she said to them. "You must take Sir Jehan a draft I shall give you; it's in pain that he'll wake tonight, and this will provide some succor."

She went into the other room and busied herself at the chest. Presently she returned with a small earthenware crock, with a little stopper wrapped in thin leather to tighten the seal. She handed it to Nemain.

"Go down to the hall by the stairwell just down this corridor," she said, "cross the hall, and ask for directions. Sir Jehan's solar is the other side of the hall and up, but I know no more than that. Ask of those you meet in the hall where to find Sir Jehan. Leave it for him; say he is to take a mouthful when the pain becomes too dire. Hob, go with her. I would take it myself, but I may not leave Jack's side tonight, and I fear to trust it to these pages."

Nemain stood and took her cloak from its peg, threw it about her thin shoulders, and concealed the pot in some pocket within the cloak. Hob opened the door and they ventured into the corridor. Three guards and two lean youths Hob took to be runners straightened as they came out and greeted the two youngsters with respect that contained no trace of mockery: the whole castle had heard by now of their deliverance at the hands of Molly's little clan.

The castle was filled with a diffuse low hum: there was a great deal to do to set right the chaos the Fox had wrought, and everyone was too frightened to sleep, and everyone wanted to speak of what had transpired there, and how they had felt. There was a good deal of praying, and some cursing. Hob and Nemain could hear snatches down the corridor and drifting up the stairwell from the hall.

They descended the turret stairwell and emerged beneath the

musicians' gallery. Immediately before them a dozen or so bodies hung lifeless, swinging gently. Hob and Nemain gingerly made their way around the dangling feet and into the hall. Ranulf and a couple of squads of men-at-arms stood looking grimly up at their handiwork.

Castle servants were already changing the blood-drenched rushes, sweeping them into piles. Boys were strewing new rushes as each section of flooring was exposed. Against the north wall bodies lay under cloths.

Hob turned and looked up at the line of Lietuvan grooms, swinging from stout ropes that were fastened to the gallery above. A little bit away from their feet a table lay on its side where it had been kicked from under the condemned men's feet. The grooms' faces were horrible: swollen, purplish-brown, with protruding tongues. Hob could recognize Azuolas among them only because of his clothing and his golden mane.

As he watched, Ranulf gave orders. The table on which the grooms had stood was righted and moved under the swaying bodies. One of the men-at-arms ran up the turret stair, reappeared behind the musicians' screen. He reached an arm out through the carving and cut the ropes one by one, and the bodies crashed down onto the table. They were seized by arm and leg, carried to an open window, heaved out into the snow of the bailey for later disposal.

"Hob," said Nemain, tugging at his arm. He turned and they went out and, after asking here and there, were directed to a stairwell that led up to Sir Jehan's solar. Hob thought that they would have some difficulty with the three soldiers lounging outside Sir Jehan's door, but the hard-handed scarred men greeted them with something between affection and respect, with a tinge of fear. One went in and returned directly with Lady Isabeau herself. She took Molly's potion from Nemain with a hand that trembled slightly, but her face was as impassive as ever. She kissed Nemain and thanked her, and the two young people set off back to Molly's solar.

It was at this point that they took the wrong stairwell; they descended one long flight of sharply winding stairs, and found themselves not in the passage between the kitchen and the great hall, but rather a dim back hallway. On the outer wall were shuttered openings into a hen coop: the two could hear the rustling and clucking within, and there was a basket filled with straw and a few eggs set at the base of the wall.

Nemain indicated the floor, which was of fitted stone flags. "We're after coming all the way to the bottom," she said, showing off a bit for Hob, she with her greater experience of castles. "Up there, except inside the walls, they're using plank-and-beam entirely."

"But how do we return?" Hob asked.

They looked this way and that. Down the hall was another turret stair. After a moment, they decided that this was the base of their original stairwell, and began to climb. A few steps up from the hen-coop hallway, a tapestry closed off the stairway, so placed to ward off drafts from one level to another. Hob held this aside and Nemain led the way up.

But the stairwell did not have an opening onto the floor at the level of the great hall. They wound up and up, each with a hand against the chill curving stone wall for balance. Here and there a stone set in the wall had a part that projected outward in a rectangular block; in this block a cup-shaped hollow had been carved. The hollow was filled with oil in which was set a wick; this provided a dim flickering light. The low wedge-shaped treads required concentration to avoid a misstep.

Hob became aware that he had been hearing something other than the general background noise of a still-awake castle. Something more urgent: a scuffling, thuds, muted cursing. The strange echoes in the twisting space made it difficult to tell if the sounds came from above or below them.

Here was another tapestry at a landing. Nemain hesitated suddenly, but Hob stepped past her, swept the cloth aside, and strode through. They were in a passage within the outer wall of the keep; the floor was of dressed stone. The passage was lit by torches in iron brackets, and here, by torchlight, was the last battle of this long night being fought in front of them.

Gintaras and one of the castle's men-at-arms circled one another like fighting dogs, broadswords in hand. The soldier's white-on-murrey livery showed two or three slashes; he was bleeding lightly. Gintaras was unscathed.

Past them Hob could see another man-at-arms, sitting in a dark and widening pool, with his back propped against the corridor wall, his staring eyes as blind as the lead-ball orbs in the dagger, Gintaras's bird-head dagger, that sprouted from his middle: merry Olivier, come at last to silence.

Gintaras and the castle guard stamped and shuffled, advanced and retreated, their blades flickering between them as they sought an opening. Their shadows shivered on the far wall in the wavering torchlight; their breath came in harsh gasps. As they watched, the soldier hacked at Gintaras's neck. Gintaras's blade clashed against his opponent's, slid with a screech along the metal, and by some trick Gintaras had the man-at-arm's sword trapped in the angle between the Lietuvan's quillon and his blade.

In the next moment the esquire had whipped his blade back and stabbed forward again, shoving his point in at the crease between belly and leg, a hand's breadth from the guard's groin.

The man gave a soft grunt and stumbled back, blood pulsing from the wound, coursing eagerly down his leg. At once Gintaras stepped back. The Lietuvan fended off a cut aimed at his side, but did not attack.

He waited quietly, watching, maintaining a loose defensive stance. After two short passes at Gintaras, easily parried, the soldier began to stagger. The leg of his hose was soaked and he left ruddy footprints as he moved. His sword arm drooped; Gintaras moved in on him but he collapsed, dying, before the Lietuvan could strike again.

All this had taken perhaps thirty heartbeats, while Hob and Nemain stood transfixed. Suddenly Hob awoke to their danger.

He snatched at where his belt knife should have been. An empty scabbard. A glancing vision came to him, the knife embedded in the floorboard, quivering. He spun about and pushed Nemain back, urging her toward the turret stairs: perhaps the Lietuvan had not seen them.

"He comes," said Nemain in a low voice, looking past him. Hob turned. Gintaras was walking toward them, stiff-legged, head lowered, eyes fixed on their faces.

Hob glanced frantically from side to side of the corridor: no door, no escape, no weapon. His mind, jumping about, came up with only a yearning memory of Jack, the old Jack, and his crow-beaked war hammer, a waste of time and no help at all and Gintaras a pace nearer.

Hob reached blindly behind him till he felt Nemain's cloak. Without taking his eyes from the Lietuvan, he turned his head a bit and hissed over his shoulder: "Run!" He gave Nemain a little shove backward toward the stair.

Hob trotted two steps to the side, crouched, and sprang up the flank of the wall. He caught hold of a sconce and, hanging by one hand, wrested the torch from its bracket. He dropped lightly to the floor and ran with the courage of his despair toward the esquire, swinging the blazing torch high and down again like a comet toward that blond head. Gintaras, his face set in a mask of rage and grief, contemptuously flicked his sword up and out in a circular darting motion, and the torch sped down the corridor, showering sparks on the stone.

Hob slid to a stop and staggered back from the blade's menace.

Off-balance and breathless, he watched with sick dismay as Gintaras advanced, swinging up his sword again. Time slowed. The blade halted like one of the hawks high in the air by Monastery Mount, folding its wings to fall on a field mouse; Gintaras's weight began to come onto his leading foot; Hob's bane began its downward plunge.

It was at that moment when he realized that he was doomed, that as Molly would say *his bread was baked,* it was at that moment that there was a scuttling at his back, a frenzied clutching at his arm, and here with her narrow face white as a cleaned skull, her flying hair red as spilled blood, her glittering eyes green and cold as an old serpent's, came Nemain with a small antler-hilted dagger in her bony hand, leaning sideways to stab around Hob with reptile speed, her long slim pallid forearm ruling a straight line to Gintaras's heart.

The handsome esquire stopped as though he had run into the castle wall; the sword flew from his grasp, to skid along the floor with a ringing clatter. Nemain ripped the dagger out, and Gintaras dropped to his knees before Hob as though to say the *Angelus,* and then, after a little pause, went over backward in an ungainly sprawl of limbs. He gave a deep, liquid, rasping sigh, and then he moved no more.

Hob stood rooted, his breathing fast and heavy, as his life once more unrolled before him, a road that again led into the distant haze of the future. Nemain straightened, releasing his arm, and stepped daintily past Hob to the recumbent corpse. She bent swiftly and, seizing a hank of the long blond mane, calmly wiped her dagger-blade on it once, twice; the steel, scarce as long as Hob's young hand, left red streaks on the gold. Then she stood up and with a flirt of reflected light the dagger was concealed again beneath her cloak. "Away on," she said to him, for all the world like Molly, and paced away down the corridor.

Hob gave one glance at the wreck of Lady Svajone's faithful guard, and followed that slim form down the passageway, past poor Olivier and his comrade, past the torch guttering out on the stone where it had fallen. Hob did not hurry to reach her side, though, as once he might have done.

". . . AND SHE WIPED IT on his hair!" said Hob, alone with Molly in the outer room. They had left Nemain to watch over Jack while the silent man slept the sleep of exhaustion.

But Molly was complacent. "The lynx is growing into her paws," was all that she said.

CHAPTER 23

OR THREE WEEKS JACK LAY pale and nearly immobile, so weak he must be fed on broth, and dosed with Molly's remedies; some of these latter were to prevent him from slipping into the Beast state again. Molly and Nemain took turns on watch, with Hob assisting one or the other as need dictated. Molly would allow no one else to nurse Jack. Food was brought to the solar, but no one except Sir Balthasar came within, and he only to assure himself that they lacked for nothing. So they three watched long hours over Jack, and talked in low tones of this and that, and Molly sipped from her little ceramic jugs, and spooned strange decoctions into Jack's mouth, and dried him when he burst into a sweat in the middle of the night.

In the first few days Molly barely slept; she was wholly occupied in tending to both Jack and Sir Jehan. There were other wounded, casualties of the battles with the Lietuvan grooms, or with one or the other of the two esquires. These injuries were treated with the usual rough-hewn care of a working castle, but only Sir Jehan had been bitten by the Fox and lived. Molly spent long hours talking with him, and brewing things for him to drink, and eventually he had a little leather bag like Jack's, and like Jack he wore it about his neck always, save for bathing.

The Sieur de Blanchefontaine was incapable of affairs for nearly a month—indeed, he burned with fever for at least two weeks—and Sir Balthasar as castellan and mareschal was effectively in charge of the military functioning of the castle, while Lady Isabeau commanded the domestic functions, as always.

There were at least two men-at-arms who had been killed by Doctor Vytautas before he encountered Molly: according to their comrades, "by a touch of his hand." Sir Balthasar was for burning the two bodies, along with all of the Fox's casualties, almost precipitating a mutiny among the castle folk, who demanded Christian burials. Only when Molly assured him it was unnecessary did he relent.

Sir Balthasar had become a staunch friend to Molly. He was as devoted to her now as he had been suspicious of her before. This transformation had taken place over Fox Night, as it was known thenceforth among the castle's people, and although his ferocious demeanor did not change, if Molly required anything, he would see that she obtained it, and he would tolerate no criticism of her.

There was little enough of that: everyone by now had heard of the slaughter at Osbert's Inn, and how nearly it had happened to every soul in the castle, and that Queen Maeve and her powerful retainer had somehow destroyed the Fox. Sir Jehan and Sir Balthasar, and Lady Isabeau, knew the truth of what had happened, but the rest of the folk were content that they had been saved, and the few whispers of witchcraft, and whispers that Jack was some sort of familiar, came to little, and Molly's kind and open disposition erased what uneasiness remained.

Only Father Baudoin, after his initial fright had worn off, began to suffer from fear that Molly's abilities came from some pact with Satan or one of his demons, and that by remaining silent he was condoning this, and so sinning himself, as well as betraying his flock.

Sir Balthasar heard murmurs of this, and undertook to fulfill his own vow of "myself between you and all priests." He accosted the young cleric one brisk March morning, up on the wall-walk where Father Baudoin was accustomed to tell his beads. The priest would pace up and down while praying, muffled to the ears against the constant wind that swept from the treetops to vault the parapets, the wind that made the wall-walk sentries curse and stamp their feet and blow on their reddened knuckles.

The keep backed up flush with the eastern curtain wall, and a strengthened door high in the stronghold's side opened onto the wall-walk that ran the circuit of the curtain walls; this allowed a quick sally from high in the keep to flood the walls with defenders. The eastern wall-walk, with its view down the sheer drop into the little river valley that ran along behind the castle and rendered it impregnable from the east, was Father Baudoin's particular place to walk and tell his beads each morning, fair weather or foul, his overbright eyes downcast, his thin dry lips moving silently. His lean figure—even swathed in a heavy cloak he presented a narrow silhouette—was a familiar sight to all: the bent head, the tense pacing to and fro, the carved wooden beads moving one by one through his gloved fingers.

A castle is like a small village: the inhabitants provide one another's entertainment, and gossip is a kind of local currency. One day, down in the kitchen perfumed with bread, a man-at-arms was telling of the meeting that he and his mates, standing sentry duty on the wall, had witnessed between Sir Balthasar and Father Baudoin.

This occurred one morning perhaps a week or two after the Lietuvans' ashes had been pitched, without any ceremony save some prayers to ward off evil, into the snow-swollen Derwent, the river that rushed along far below that eastern wall. The wall sentries noted that as Father Baudoin was at his devotions, Sir Balthasar stepped from the keep and approached the priest.

After a moment's conversation, the knight was seen to lay a heavy leather-gloved hand on Father Baudoin's shoulder. He contrived to turn the priest toward the parapet; he pointed to the drop into the river beneath; he smiled into the young priest's face.

The sentry's tale had earned him a seat by the kitchen fire, a slice of the hashed-fish pie called narrois, a bumper of ale, and a rapt audience of a dozen cooks, serving men and women, and men-at-arms. At this juncture in the story, a soldier said, "I seen him go into a rage when he heard what Father was sayin', about them two queens and all. Was I to find meself alone up there with the mareschal, and he angry at me? I'd have me arse back in the keep inside two breaths."

"Nay, one," said another.

"Inside one, then."

Roger was leaning against the wall with an arm around his Lucinda. He said, to general nods and grunts of agreement, "Bad as he is when he's dour, he's worse when merry. Yon smile would frighten a fucking bear."

The sentry had taken the opportunity afforded by this commentary to sample the narrois pie; now he resumed his tale, somewhat hampered by the necessity to chew. He had seen the priest and the knight gazing through a crenel down at the plunging side of the coomb, the trees clinging precariously to the near-vertical slope, the rock-girt little river foaming far below. The gloved hand slid off the priest's shoulder toward his neck. Father Baudoin turned a startled face to the knight as Sir Balthasar spoke, gesturing with his free hand as though pointing out sights of interest, and always smiling, smiling. Shortly thereafter Sir Balthasar clapped the young priest on the back, and returned to the keep.

The sentry reported that Father Baudoin remained awhile, lost in thought, or perhaps prayer, although the beads dangled forgotten from his hands. After a time he also returned to the keep.

"I would that I had seen that," said a cook.

Roger said, laughing, "I can all but see it now." His laughter gradually quieted; he looked into the fire; his face became still. He said, very low, perhaps to Lucinda, perhaps not: "I would that I could tell Olivier of it."

The sentry was retelling the story again. The details became more vivid; this time the priest kept dropping his beads on the wall-walk after Sir Balthasar had spoken with him, nearly slipping into the bailey below when he bent to pick them up.

"Frighten a fucking bear," Roger said again.

NOW WITH THEIR TROUBLES receding into the past, and their immediate future assured, safe in Blanchefontaine under Sir Jehan's protection, life should have been pleasant. It was at this time, though, that Hob became haunted.

Others had been visited in this way, women, children, even hardened men-at-arms. "That-un seeks to return," was how it was told, the castle folk unwilling to name the Fox further, unable to shake the fear of that night. Father Baudoin spoke to some, and prayed over them, and anointed them; but he himself had been shaken, and his fiery nature burned low. Some recovered under his care; those that did not sought out Molly.

Molly dealt with each in turn, and ministered to them, and her cures did not fail, and slowly the troubles abated among the castle dwellers. Molly was especially concerned for Nemain and for Hob, who had both witnessed horror at first hand, and who, young and vulnerable, might yet feel some lingering effect of Vytautas's spell.

Nemain, that steely girl, had passed through that terrible night and emerged as yellow-hot steel emerged from Thierry's cold-water tempering barrel: hard but flexible, chilly, strong—a warrior queen-in-waiting. She was untouched by the daylight nightmares. After a week had passed, Molly had come to think that Hob might escape unscathed as well.

But within the fortnight, sleep began to be a torment: no sooner had he closed his eyes than he was back in the corridor with Gintaras's sword poised above his head, or watching the Beast reach down toward Vytautas's thigh, or seeing the dead and dying men sprawled in the Fox's wake. Often he found himself following Nemain down the corridor past the dead Olivier, and just as he came abreast the soldier would give a low and sinister snicker, and Hob would sit up in his bed, his hair drenched in sweat.

The haunting followed him into the daylight. In the great kitchen, as Hob stood by the hearth gazing into the broad fire, chewing on a greasy chop that a cook had given him—for the whole castle spoiled him and Nemain outrageously—a dropped ladle landed with an iron clang on the flags of the floor. At once he was looking at the dying Gintaras, on his knees with his heart's blood spreading in a broad stain across his stomach, the corridor echoing with the sound of his sword sliding to a halt, steel on stone. Hob stepped back with a loud panicked cry, and the blond head resolved once again into yellow flame, and the cooks stood frozen, looking at him in shock.

Hob began to lose weight; dark semicircles appeared beneath his eyes, and he sat listlessly. Jack he avoided, as though afraid of him.

At last Molly noticed, and on a bright chilly day, as the winter wound its way toward spring, took him up to the wall-walk by the southern tower, where they were alone with the brisk wind and the clouds scudding rapidly across the blue expanse.

Molly leaned her shoulder against a merlon. She produced a little clay jug from beneath the fluttering edges of her cloak, pulled the

carved-wood stopper with its leather wrapping, and took a swallow. She
gave it to Hob and he sipped, and then choked a little: it was like liquid
fire. He sipped a second time, gave it back. Molly drank again, and looking out through the crenel across the countryside, said in an unremarkable voice, "There is something that oppresses you, *a rún,* and I would
have you tell me of it."

"I, uh . . ." He cleared his throat. Still Molly looked out over the
sea of barc trees in the forest below, as though looking for a fairy ship to
sail the treetops toward her. The drink began to spread warmth through
his belly.

He spoke again. "I have terrible dreams, Mistress, of, of the . . . the
things that happened. And sometimes I see things, for a moment, that
are not there."

She nodded, still looking toward the horizon. "I thought as much:
it was a terrible time, and these things leave their mark, as a bear leaves
claw marks on the trees. I will come to you tonight, and give you something to ease this dolor; nor will you be troubled again."

"Thank you, Mistress." He smiled, for he knew she was capable
of much, and he believed her capable of still more that he did not know.
And even as he smiled, the smile began to fade, and a shadow came once
again across his features. "But, Mistress, it's Jack as well: if, if Jack . . ."

She put the stopper back into the bottle with a little squeaking
thump; the bottle vanished beneath her cloak. "What then of Jack, lad?"

He did not meet her eyes; he stared at the brooch that secured her
cloak. This was a pin-backed silver disk. On its face was a ring of three
cats, their bodies formed of complex interlaced ribbons that yet suggested the swell of the musculature, the articulation of the joints, of the
powerful limbs. Each cat was depicted with staring eyes and ears back;
each gripped the tail of the next in its fangs. The brooch caught the sun
and flashed amid the green wool folds of Molly's cloak.

Hob looked away abruptly. He felt that he had seen his fill of powerful limbs and gripping fangs. He gazed out over the parapet; he spoke in a low voice, asking as one asks news of kin gone off to war: hesitant but determined. "If Jack is one of them, one of those, those . . . does that mean that again, that Jack will . . . will need to eat . . ."

"No, he will not. I needed him to change, but 'twas only the once. You *know* Jack. Jack is Jack, and will stay Jack from here to forever, and I'll see to that." She turned away, and then suddenly she was back and clasping his shoulders. He caught the perfume of strong drink on her breath.

"How can you know what it was for him?" She shook him lightly; she spoke in a low fierce voice. "He's told me things. . . . The wind bringing him a thousand scents, and the creak of a twig beneath the linnet's foot! And then the strength, the strength of it! Like being ten men at once! What's to come, and what was, just dropping away. To live like an animal, that way they have: no thought for anything, the *hereness* of it all, the *nowness,* the day burning like a bonfire! The terrible hunger for human blood and meat, and the terrible joy of eating!"

A lock of her hair fell forward in a silver curve over one eye as she shook him. He looked at her, his own eyes troubled, the corners of his mouth turned down.

"Ah, Hob, *a chuisle . . .*" She ran her hand along his jaw, where new down was coming in; she folded him in her arms and held him. A strong wind moved in the tops of the sea of trees stretching away, down there below the castle wall: a hushed roaring, a desolate sound.

After a while, in his new voice that cracked and wobbled between high and low, he asked, "But, Mistress, where did . . . all the rest of him come from? And of the, the Fox? Where did it go?"

She pushed him away a little and looked at him. "They are creatures of blood and dream," she said gravely, and then would say no more, but fell to hugging him gently, and gently stroking his hair, until finally he grew calm beneath her touch.

* * *

THAT NIGHT, AS HE LAY ABED dreading sleep, Molly came in and sat on the side of his cot. She produced another bottle, even smaller than the one she'd had that afternoon. She pulled the stopper and said to Hob, "Drink without ceasing, till all is done."

Hob put the cool ceramic neck to his lips and drank steadily. It was by no means as strong as the sip she had given him on the wind-swept parapet, and it had a faint taste of berries. He finished it easily, and she took the bottle away and pushed him tenderly back to his pillow. She placed her big warm hand, strong and soft, no longer chapped after weeks indoors, on his forehead. She stroked back over his brow a few times, and then let her hand lie still.

She began to hum, almost under her breath. He could barely hear her voice, that sweet deep woman's voice, now almost a whisper. He thought to hear words in it, although not any that he recognized; and then again he decided that there were no words. He drifted along on the lake of her voice, his eyes closed, his brow gently warmed beneath her hand. The lake on which he sailed rose and fell in wavelets; he drifted far out over the darkening waters, and presently he came to a shore where the little lapping waves broke on gravel, and he slid up on the pebbly land, and opened his eyes, and it was day, and he lay alone in his bed.

Molly was gone, and from that day, so was his haunting, and his fear of Jack. Hob could feel that the trouble in his heart was gone the very moment he opened his eyes; he felt rested and strong. He swung his legs over and reached down for his shoes, thinking about searching out some food from the cooks.

ONCE HOB HAD BEEN RELEASED from the recurring nightmare of Fox Night, he found that, as his fear subsided, his curiosity increased.

One afternoon, Molly in the inner room with the door closed, tending to Jack, he sat on a bench in the outer room, watching Nemain sort through clothing in her chest; occasionally he was called upon to hold up two garments side by side while she stood a few paces off, looking from one to the other.

He asked at one point, as he stood there with overgowns of different colors, cramoisy in one hand and perse in the other, "Why is Jack so sick? Is it from being a Beast? Was he weak like this at St. Audrey's Fair, when Herself met him?"

"Nay," she said, "it's from stopping being a Beast that he is sick. He was not weak at Ely, but every day he was less a man, and more a Beast; changing more and more often: he was disappearing into the Beast, and 'twas harder to hide it from other folk." Her eyes darkened; she said very low, "He may have killed now and then, driven by that hunger they have."

"May have killed? And eaten . . . ?"

She looked away from him. "Must—must have killed; and they having killed, they eat."

"And at the Ely Fair . . ."

"Herself knew at once, when she met him, and touched him, what it was with him. She brought him back to himself then, as she has brought him back now: with her singing, and the amulet, and the drink."

"The singing brought him back as well?" said Hob. "I thought it was the drink; or it might be the drink and the amulet, working together. The singing as well?"

She took the cramoisy gown from his hand and folded it, and then held the perse up against herself, looking down at it.

"Sure, the singing, that was a song of power, and didn't it let Herself approach the Beast; there was little Jack left in that Beast, I'm thinking, and that little far down." Nemain looked away, a little somber. "And there's another thing, that they're not knowing as we are, when they are in that way, in that animal way, and they're not always remembering who is their own, and who is not. When Herself drew nigh, she could bind it with the amulet, and then ply it with the drink to start the change back; but did she falter in that song, it's we who'd been destroyed, all of us, and Jack all unknowing what he'd done till he awoke to himself."

"And what did Herself sing over that drink, that it had such power?" asked Hob.

"I have not learned it yet myself; that will come to me when I'm ready."

"And will I learn it?"

"You will not, nor any man; it is not something for men to know," Nemain said, but she said it kindly.

"But Vytautas cast spells and glamours," Hob objected.

"This drink, this singing, is that which Herself had from the Great Queen; whatever that smiling spalpeen may have used, it was not this drink, nor this singing," said Nemain, getting angry all over again at the thought of the Lietuvan doctor, so that Hob thought it prudent to praise the perse gown, and the way the blue-gray color chimed with the green of her eyes, and so to slide away from the subject of Lietuvan sorcery.

CHAPTER 24

UT ON A NIGHT SOON AFTER, attending Molly while she sat at Jack's bedside, most of the castle asleep and the wind moaning around the corners of the keep, he pestered Molly with questions about Jack and his strange affliction.

"What sort of Beast is it that Jack becomes, Mistress? It is not a bear, nor a fox, nor a wolf . . ."

Molly sat by a low table with a basket of carded wool from the castle stores, a distaff and spindle and, next to a small jug of the *uisce beatha*, a fired-clay mug from which she sipped from time to time. All women, from high to low, spun thread when time presented an opportunity; it soothed the hands, it freed the mind, and fine thread was always welcome. Molly was deft at it, as she was at so many things, even when she took strong drink.

"It is a Beast as the Fox was a Beast; 'tis some sort

of shapeshifter, but Jack's after bringing it back from pilgrimage to the Holy Land, and 'tis some Southron Beast. I have never seen the like, not before, not since, but it can be dealt with as are other shapeshifters. It is my thought that there are those who can shift their shape, but what shape they choose, or that chooses them, may be different from land to land. Some become wolves, what we call a *coinríocht,* a werewolf; some become bears, and so on."

"Like the berserkers, Mistress? You said the Northmen kings used them; how could they control them?"

Molly took a deep draft of the mug, then picked up her spindle.

"It is my thought that those cruel Norther sea-kings used them as another of their weapons, with the priests of Odin to control them, though they are a weapon that can turn in the hand: sometimes they fall to killing friend as well as foe, and I believe they were not well trusted."

Molly attached a leader thread to the spindle, a stick with a wooden disk attached to the bottom for weight, then attached the leader to a bit of wool that she teased from the roving, the batch of unspun wool. She took another sip from the mug, and then rolled the spindle along the swell of her thigh, imparting a spin to the leader thread. Then she held the spindle up, the spin reversing as the weight hung free, imparting a spin to the carded wool, hooking the fibers into a thin strong thread.

"Or else the sickness was in among them, and it being brought on by the fury of battle. There are those that can control it somewhat, but mostly when it comes on them, it comes, and there's nothing they can do: they must have their blood, their meat. It's more often at night, and more often in moonlight, but by no means always. One skilled in the Art can control them, to some extent, someone like Vytautas."

"Or like yourself, Mistress?"

She did not say anything for a moment; she concentrated on drafting out another piece of wool from the batch of roving, her dexterous fingers moving speedily, albeit with care. At last: "Like myself. And that is not to be spoken of outside this family."

A bit later Molly sent him to the stone basin to draw a pitcher of water. While the chill water was burbling from the wall, Hob suddenly thought back on her words: he heard her again saying "this family." He considered this as he waited for the vessel to fill. In a little while he began to hum softly to himself.

BACK IN THE SOLAR, Hob sat again to listen. The pitcher of water stood beside Jack's bedside; the fire crackled, so hot that one side of Hob's face was uncomfortable and he kept shifting to ease it. The firelight played about Molly's face; her hands, strong and deft, flashed in and out of shadow as she spun the whirling spindle and teased wool from the batch. After a while she spoke again.

"I think that Lady Svajone could control herself while in the monastery: she was just after killing and eating before they stopped there. That poor monk. Brother . . . Brother . . . Athanasius, Brother Athanasius. And further, I think she was of no mind to have any doings with us, or rather I think Vytautas would have advised against us, against Nemain and myself. He cast a glamour on us the moment he sat down at that table, that we would not perceive her for what she was, nor he for a wizard. Nor I nor Nemain expecting it, not in the midst of the monastery; and we sitting there like lambs, all unawares. Once it has taken hold, well, isn't all our judgment flawed from that very moment on. But still, caution would have advised him not to trifle with us."

She paused; the wool had separated from the thread. She cursed in Irish, softly; then she pulled up a bit more wool from the batch in the basket, reattached it to the line on the spindle, resumed spinning. Hob watched, partly entranced from the repetitive motion.

"He would have been wary: he would have regarded the monastery as a kind of trap, and all those warrior monks, and we with them."

"But, Mistress, the castle is also a kind of trap, and all those knights and men-at-arms, and you with them."

"Aye, but by then she was desperate, and the storm growing—they could not leave in that, even they would die of the snow and the cold—and the hunger growing in her, and the moon strong. She had to change, and they had to hope for the best."

The spindle whirled, sank; she twirled it again against the curve of her thigh; then let it hang again. Thread built up in a coil about the spindle. The fire spat, crackled; golden ash fled up the flue.

"Here is how I'm seeing it: they passed the inn, wanting to be away from us, and crossed the Dawlish, and headed south, and the bandits did not encounter them. Then they found the way sealed, where the land had slid down from the mountain, and she being able to wait no longer, she slew the masons. She would have sworn blood oaths against harming her Lietuvan grooms and servants, they being her countrymen, and her needing them in any case; and of course that vile doctor and those two blond lapdogs were the three of them her paramours."

"All three, Mistress?" To Hob's dismay, his treasonous new voice broke into a squeak on the second word. He still had enough of Father Athelstan's influence left in him to be genuinely shocked. "But how could you tell?"

"I could tell, I could tell. Once you broke Vytautas's hold upon my vision, I could tell, by the memory of the way they moved around her. And I could smell them all on her corpse; I could smell her on Vytautas and the others, dead though they were."

"Smell!" blurted Hob, staring.

"Can a crow smell a corpse half a league away? You would be surprised at the senses the Crow Mother grants me, when She wills it."

Hob gave a kind of mental shrug, exhausted by wonder piled upon wonder. There was no question of doubting Molly. He was silent, and after a bit she resumed.

"Now she is sated for the moment, feeding on the masons in the woods, away there by that great slide, but her time is waxing, it will be days before it wanes, and she comes back to the inn. Osbert's Inn has a kind of fame. It is isolated, the villagers retire in the evening, there is human meat confined in a kind of pen, and she and her people can be away again before morning. Also there is Osbert's storehouse. That was a great riddle to me, that some Beast or berserker had slain all within, and yet would be human enough and cunning enough to seek gold for its purse, for they are ever confused and helpless when they change back: their minds are still somewhat the same as a Beast's for a while, and an animal does not understand treasure."

She put the spindle on her lap for a moment, keeping her place on the tongue of roving she had teased out. She took up her mug and drank off a couple of swallows; put it down; wiped at her eyes, which had begun to tear a bit as the strong drink made its influence felt. She picked up the spindle again.

"But it was Vytautas who directed the looting of Osbert's gold. Think you: they must travel and travel through strange lands, and gold buys many favors, and they far from their holdings, and having no way to enrich themselves, save that Vytautas and her pets follow in her wake, like scavenger birds, and despoil the slain. So they maintained themselves."

Hob sat and listened, enthralled. The night hour, the chill late-winter wind outside, Molly's quiet voice, gave the chamber a sheen of enchantment. Even the mug, made of brown iron-rich fired clay, decorated with rampant lions that the potter, adding a touch of copper to the clay, had rendered in green, even this humble mug seemed to glow in the firelight; and Molly's tumble of gray hair seemed wrought of iron and silver in the gleam of the flames.

"It was her cry we were hearing that day at Osbert's Inn, and she ranging the nearby woods. When they're seeing us make the rounds of the walls, they're quick to withdraw into the forest for a few days, fearing to engage us. The night after we left, and ourselves camping by that little ford over the Dawlish, she struck, and killed all within the inn, like a stoat in a rabbit warren.

"The next day they were away south again, and they took the second path to Dickon's Ford, for I think they were aware of us at all times, and where we were, and Vytautas seeking always to avoid us. He was a man of power, and when she was in her human guise, I could detect nothing of her nature, nor yet of his, and all because of the glamour he had cast upon Nemain and myself in the monastery. But he knew me, and Nemain, knew us for women of power, and he feared us, and mayhap he sensed the Beast in Jack, although I had thrust it down, far down."

She paused and put her spindle in her lap again. She picked up the mug, but paused with it halfway to her lips, looking into the fire with blind eyes, retracing the position of the two caravans, hers and Lady Svajone's.

"So they're passing us in the forest, and we returning with poor dying Sawal, and it's then that Nemain and I were feeling that something was in the west, or *should be* in the west, but could never sense nor see them for the blindfold of moonlight and spellcraft that Vytautas had bound about our eyes. They forded the Dawlish and set off east on the castle path, and we yet at the inn, discovering her handiwork."

She finished the mug; exhaled heavily; put the mug down with a thump. Immediately she poured some more of the *uisce beatha*.

"Mistress, I could not move when the doctor had cast his spell, but you spoke and you slapped him, and you silenced him. And he could not break your spell when you slapped him, nor say a word. How comes that, Mistress?"

"I was ready for him, as I was not at the monastery. And mind, it's the men are stronger than the women when iron or stone must be lifted and carried, but it's the women who are stronger in spellcraft: so the world is arranged."

The fire settled, the smaller branches transformed into ash and ember; two large logs were still licked about with flame. A cold draft skittered along the floor, and Hob shifted a bit closer to the fireplace. Another thought occurred to him.

"Mistress, why did you not throw your dagger at the Fox, as you did in the hall? Surely you could have hit its eye?"

She laughed. "You remind me of Nemain, when she was younger, questions upon questions. Nay, you remind me of myself, one who must know everything. It's a way to gain power, that asking, and not the worst thing in the world. In the hall I must convince Sir Jehan that I was all that I claimed, and not some traveling beguiler, as he was coming to believe. The dagger cast, the chess, the harping, all those were to this end, to preserve our sanctuary here, and besides, he was after offending me, and myself thinking it time to bring him up short."

She sighed. "But to throw steel at a Beast . . . they're hardly noticing it, betimes: iron will not bite, it does not do them great harm. They are best destroyed as animals destroy each other, living body to living body, as those Templar destriers trampled Jack's assailant Beast.

"There is another reason, as well: before even we left the solar, I was after beginning Jack's change, and casting him at the Fox by spell and instruction. When we encountered the thing, away there in the upper gallery, Jack's course was set, and having cast him at the Fox, I had yet to bring him under control again afterward, and back to himself, works of power. To work power with a bloody hand is to chance failing in the spell, and that would have been death to us all. And besides, I swore that Jack would be my weapon, and it is peril to go back on words like that, words of high purpose: it is itself like working power with a bloody hand."

Jack began to twitch and mutter in his sleep, as one does who has an evil dream. Molly lowered her voice.

"It may be that he can hear us, in some wise." She put a hand on Jack's brow, *tsk*ed, dipped a cloth in the cold water of the pitcher. She wrung it out onto the rushes at her feet, then draped it over Jack's brow.

"It is not a thing to do lightly," she said in a murmur. "I hated to ask it of him, but I saw no other road to safety. Or to revenge. He agreed. Part of them always longs for it, surely, and I did not want to offer it to him, and blow on the embers once more. But he knew as well that he must change back again, and at once, and again go through the pain of purging the fever from him, and part of him did not want to live through that again. But he agreed, he agreed because I asked it of him, brave lad, and I love him for it."

She poked at the fire until it revived somewhat, and then sat looking into the flames, distant, abstracted. Hob thought it unmannerly to intrude upon her reflections. He began to gaze into the fire instead; in any event, he did not lack for things to contemplate.

CHAPTER 25

OB ENTERED THE CASTLE IN
snow and left in sunlight; entered the castle a boy and left
nearly a man. The months they spent there, as Molly
coaxed Jack and Sir Jehan back to health, saw Hob
shoot up, tall and awkward, with outsize hands and
feet. His voice broke and wavered, and finally sank to
a bass, interspersed with the occasional embarrassing
squeak. But that was much later, toward the summer. It
was in the spring that he grew up.

AS SOON AS JACK was able to leave his sickbed, he
expressed a desire to stand without help. He tottered
about the room, collapsed back into the bed. The next
day he walked about for a while, and then sat for the
rest of the afternoon, and was asleep by dusk. The day

thereafter he walked the corridors, and the next day went down and out into the bailey.

A cool spring rain clattered down on the slate tiles of the stable roofs. Jack stood just outside the keep, and looked about at the wide world, and breathed deeply, as if the homely smells of the bailey's damp earth, horse dung, woodsmoke, were nourishment itself, and the rattle and gurgle of rain, the ringing of iron hammers on steel from old Thierry's forge, were the music of Molly's harp. Then he turned and made his way upstairs and slept through the night.

Jack had always had a formidable constitution, and Hob suspected that some residue of the Beast in Jack's blood lent him a measure of further vitality. He remembered Molly saying, ". . . and they live long, long." Within a sennight Jack Brown was helping old Thierry in his smithy, which was also the castle's armory. At first Jack performed light chores for Thierry, pausing frequently to rest. Another fortnight brought Jack to full participation at the forge, and Thierry was pleased at the help.

Even when not hammering at the anvil, or thrusting bars of iron into the forge, Jack would spend hours picking up and moving lumps and bars of raw iron, or handfuls of horseshoes, from place to place at the forge. Hob thought it strange and purposeless; Thierry, whose joints now barely troubled him at all, thanks to Molly, looked on with an uncomprehending but benign gaze.

One day when rain roared on the smithy roof, Jack brought Hob into the forge with him, the chill spring air from the open doorway thwarted by the heat from the forge, the dark smithy glowing with firelight, sparks showering from the prentices' hammers as they struck down upon the anvil, the glowing fragments bouncing on the floor and winking out in the shadowy corners.

Without explanation, Jack handed Hob a short bar of iron. The weight sank immediately toward the ground, but Hob gripped it the tighter and managed not to drop it.

Jack gestured for Hob to give it back. The lad did so, wondering. Then Jack gave it to him again, and Hob recognized it for a sort of game, although to what purpose he could not see. This went on for a while, then Jack picked up a sledge and turned again to the forge.

The next day Hob's arms were sore, and he applied to Molly for some salve, "For Jack kept handing me these bars of iron, and then taking them back, I know not why, and now I ache from wrist to backbone."

"It's a way Jack has: it's getting his strength back he is, and giving you your own as well. Jack was by way of being a master of strength, even before"—she lowered her voice abruptly—"he met that Beast"—and in more normal tones—"and it's a mort of power that you can gain from him."

A FORTNIGHT OR SO LATER, Hob's muscles began to grow, and while he was becoming gangly with increased height, his limbs began, though slowly, to thicken. A few more weeks, and he began to help hammer at the forge, and he discovered calluses on his palms from handling tools and iron and steel. He ate well each night, for Sir Jehan stinted them nothing, and Hob and Nemain were honored and even pampered by all the castle's folk.

One night, Molly called Hob over, looked at his wrists and ankles, turned his hands over to inspect his palms. "Coming into your growth, you are: 'tis time you knew weapons. I've asked Sir Balthasar to set you at learning Norman swordcraft, he being the grandest killer of the North Country, or so I am to hear."

The fire was burning merrily now, and the firelight shone in Molly's silver hair, making ruddy highlights reminiscent of Nemain's. She had a ceramic crock of the *uisce beatha* by her side, and her eyes had a glassy sheen.

"He will show you those arts that he knows, and afterward, when we have left this castle, I will show you those arts that he does not know. One day you will be even more dangerous than Sir Balthasar."

A twig popped in the fireplace and drew her gaze to the flames. She suddenly sat very still, looking into the blaze as though there were something there, far down in the fire.

She turned back to him, and looked at him with the same glistening, empty eyes. She was drunk, or she was fey; perhaps both.

"Be said by me, one day kerns will call you Robert the Englishman, and you dwelling in Erin the while, and an adopted man of the O'Cearbhalls, and a high man at that, and you will walk the fields of battle all unscathed. Foemen will step away to the right hand and the left, fearing to engage you, the dread champion in Erin. I tell you that men will be boasting, not that they prevailed against you, but only that they had a passage at arms with English Robert, and lived to walk the earth afterward."

She came to herself a little, and used her shawl to dab at her brow and upper lip, and drank again; and that was all he heard from her that night.

HOB PRACTICED WITH THE SQUIRES in an exercise yard formed from a part of the bailey and defined by an internal wall, only two stories high, that ran from the keep to one of the northern watchtowers. They grunted and strove with wooden weapons, wrestled and ran, covered in sweat and dust.

Whether it was Molly's healing power, or his own resilience, when Hob now looked back on Fox Night, it was to draw from the memory strength rather than weakness: what mortal foeman would he ever face that would be as terrible? He threw himself into learning combat with such zeal that often Ranulf or whoever else was instructor that day would have to pull him back, like an overeager hound. Hob felt in some obscure way that he must prepare himself, to make himself worthy to be in Molly's troupe, and worthy, as well, to be Nemain's companion. He remembered that slim pale hand and its dagger and the thrust that had saved his life, and his ferocity at practice soon caught him up to the older youths, and indeed dismayed them somewhat; indeed they began to fear him a little.

"See there; there she is again!" Giles had paused, panting, and tipped his head toward the wall. Hob and the pages Bernard and Drogo all turned, looked upward.

Along the top of this internal boundary wall ran a walkway. On this a woman stood watching them. The sun was behind her; all he could see was the graceful outline of bosom and hip as the wind blew her garments and unbound hair streaming out to one side. The sun was so bright behind her, it made her a woman cut from darkness.

As soon as she saw them looking up at her, she turned, albeit without haste, and moved off toward the keep. As she turned away, the sunlight caught her face and lit her wind-tossed locks to red flame.

It was Nemain.

SIR BALTHASAR SUMMONED HOB one day from his practice with the squires and pages of the castle. Hob came away, wondering if he was in some kind of trouble. The knight led him by circuitous ways to a small cloister, another of the secret spaces in Blanchefontaine.

Sir Balthasar turned and faced Hob, and handed him a wooden dagger. The knight stepped back a pace, his arms at his sides, and said, "Come kill me."

"Sir?"

Hob stood still a moment, uncertain, and then, realizing what was required of him, sprang at the knight, swinging the dagger in a rapid arc toward Sir Balthasar's abdomen.

Sir Balthasar made play with his open hands and a nimble foot, and Hob found himself on his back in the soil of the little yard, the dagger a yard away and his wrist aching.

The knight looked at him without anger, but without sympathy either. He picked up the dagger, hauled Hob to his feet, and slapped the dagger-hilt back into the lad's palm.

"Again, but move slowly, and watch what I do."

This time the castellan showed him how his wrist had been seized and his dagger hand forced open and his ankle kicked from under him. "You will need to put on some meat before this will be of use to you, but you should learn what to do now, even before you have the strength to do it."

He handed Hob the wooden dagger for the third time.

"Again."

Hob came in again, but with his free hand held above his dagger hand, guarding it. Sir Balthasar did a quick shuffle, and Hob still landed in the dirt, but the knight contemplated him for a long moment, plainly surprised at Hob's improvisation. Then he set Hob on his feet, and gave him back the dagger.

"Again."

AT FIRST THE BUDS on the trees, seen from the wall-walks of Blanchefontaine, seemed like a green spray on the ocean of black and gray and brown twigs that stretched away from the castle walls. Hob and Giles and Hubert, up on the wall, flew kites in the early spring breezes. As the leaves broadened, the verdant mass grew dense; the ground could no longer be seen for the sea of forest that stretched away from the castle to north and south and to the west, till it broke upon the flanks of hills blue in the distance. To the east the land fell away to the Derwent far below, but there, too, spring surged to life.

Molly began to speak of taking the road again.

*   *   *

SIR JEHAN WAS of one highborn family and his wife of another, and their influence reached down to London. He was able to explain the loss of so many knights at his castle with artful tales of more than one battle with Gold-Beard's bandits, and an encounter with a rogue bear, and for the French chevalier, a horse that tripped and bore Sir Estienne with it over one of the precipitous drops in that steep hill country. Stern warnings from Sir Balthasar, as well as loyalty to Molly among the castle's common folk, who realized what they had escaped, kept the tale from spreading among the country folk, except in the form of occluded fireside tales. In time, as the years rolled over the Pennines, all that was left was one of those skipping rhymes that older children teach to younger ones, generation unto generation, a few incomprehensible verses, each of which ended:

Blanchefontaine,
Fox's bane

CHAPTER 26

LUE SHADOW DRENCHED THE bailey. The sun had breached the horizon a little while ago, but it had yet to clear the eastern wall. The green-scented early summer air was still cool in the dim dawn. The bustle of preparation about Molly's wagons, the murmurs of the crowd gathered to bid fare-well to their saviors, the *ching* of the knights' spurs and the creaking of saddle leather as the escort mounted up, echoed from the curtain walls. Behind it all was a faint splashing: in the center of the bailey gleamed the imported marble of the eponymous white fountain. The snow that had covered it had thawed; the ice that had blocked it had melted. The spring that fed it was once more free to spout in four streams into the air, collect in a shallow pool, and run off in a stone channel past the stables, widening briefly into watering troughs before exiting through a grille under the east wall, to fall in a spray toward the Derwent.

Molly was embraced by Lady Isabeau and Dame Aline, kissed on both cheeks. Jack and Nemain were already on their wagon seats; Hob stood at Milo's head, holding his lead rope. The ox had grown stout in the last few months, and seemed by no means eager to take the road: it kept tossing its head, trying to reclaim the lead rope from Hob, and looking back sadly at the stables, with their excellent mangers.

A last word with Sir Balthasar, who bent to kiss Molly's hand, and with Sir Jehan, who kissed her on both cheeks, and then Molly swung up to her seat on the second wagon. Jack was in the lead this day, and now he gathered up the mare's reins and clicked his tongue to start her moving.

The sun touched the crenellated rim of the east wall, streaming through the crenels, blocked by the merlons: for a long moment golden rays shot above their heads to throw the silhouette of the ramparts against the western wall, playing on the gatehouse towers.

The advance guard clopped into the gatehouse tunnel, along with Jack's wagon. The inner doors were closed; the outer doors were opened. The first contingent clattered out of the castle, thundered across the bridge, and pulled up some way up the road, to wait for the next batch to pass through the gatehouse. When all were across the moat, the caravan re-formed in the road, and began to move off through the forest that surrounded Blanchefontaine.

They swung along, through oakwood rich in wood sorrel and wood anemone; this gave way to ash forest with its ground cover of bluebells, and primrose whose leaves Molly used in some of her wound-healing salves, and wild garlic. Red squirrels scampered through the branches; the air was alive with birdsong, blackbirds and mistle thrush predominating; and over all was the scent of fresh breezes, green life, sun-warmed earth: forest delights after so many days cooped up indoors.

After a while Jack leaped down from the wagon seat and stretched; he threw the reins over the mare's head and walked ahead, using the reins as a lead. As Hob trudged forward, he kept his eyes on Jack, walking in front. For a time Jack walked along with his gaze on the ground in front of his feet, but after a while his pace picked up; he looked about; he breathed deep of the clear air. He straightened, and despite the slight limp left him from his crushed ankle on that day, so long ago, when his Fate came bounding out at him from a seething cloud of sand, he began to fall into a marching rhythm, and now for just a moment Hob could see him as a younger man, as the soldier he had been, trudging stolidly down the long and dusty road to Jerusalem.

At a pass where the road began its descent to the eastern coast and the roads to Durham and York, the escort halted, the knights backing their mounts to the side of the road and saluting as Molly and her troupe passed them. Hob looked back a few times, and the knights remained motionless, till they had dwindled to specks, a courtesy: watching over them as long as possible.

ALL THE REST OF THAT DAY they wound down out of the hills at the familiar plodding pace, dropping down toward the moorlands, the wind from the fells rising to meet them. Jack was up on the wagon seat again, he and Molly and Nemain working the brakes, and Hob trying to keep Milo from wandering onto the downslopes at the side of the path. Blocks of worn diabase formed giant steps down which cold gray streams poured, foaming into white at each successive level. Cool mist hung over the downrushing water, and drifted over them whenever the wind shifted their way, wetting Hob's garments, forming a sheen on Milo's hide.

Molly had elected to keep her original configuration of animals, rather than accept the offers of horses and gold and an escort and such that Sir Jehan had wanted to press on them. She had seen some signs—in the flight of crows, in the movement of dark rain-heavy clouds—that she had interpreted as guidance from her patron Babd, telling her that she must remain as inconspicuous as possible for a bit longer. Nemain teased her about this, pointing out that Molly was noticed wherever she went, but Molly was adamant.

"And at any road, we'll be back in Blanchefontaine this fall, when the weather begins to turn, for Sir Jehan must have care just as Jack must have care, lest he find himself howling at the moon, and changing to a Fox, and what then? Mayhap being burnt alive by the Church."

"Does he know his peril, Mistress?" Hob asked.

"Aye, he is well aware of this—and that being one other reason for him to be our staunch ally, and like to be a great help when we return to Erin. And you, young man," she said to Hob, "he has said he will make a rider of you, and help you win belt and spurs: for Sir Balthasar's after telling him he sees something in you that he sees in few others, and that a fine knight in the Norman style might be made of yourself. And if so, so much the better for yourself, and for ourselves and our hope to return to Erin."

For now Hob was content with the sun on his face and the road before him, and the wheels rumbling along, bearing the little troupe into an uncertain but promising future.

MOLLY CHOSE A SPOT on the slope of a hill crowned with a copse of trees; a common sight in Britain, where wooded hills served as sacred groves for sacrifices, before the coming of Christ. They pitched camp just below the trees. Jack busied himself clearing a place for a campfire, and gathering wood for it.

A stream ran down out of the grove to the meadow below. Where it passed the camp, though, it was choked with rushes and soggy leaves from last fall. There was no way to bring the wagons into the wood. Molly sent Hob with a bucket to follow the stream up the hill, into the trees, to obtain cleaner water from the source.

Somewhat to his surprise, Nemain trailed after him. Up and up they made their way, in the dim aisles between the trees, through fern and violet, following the lively gurgle of the brook as it rushed downhill past them. A last push through vines and wood anemone and herb Paris, and they came upon a little clearing where the space between trees was somewhat greater.

There a spring welled up into a natural rock basin of no great size. The water in the basin was clear as air, and Hob could see the several sources of the spring as disturbances in the water, bubbling up through the smooth gray stones on the bottom. The irregular bowl was constantly spilling from the lower, downhill side of its lip, silver sheets splashing out and away down the hillside in the stream they had followed here. It was as beautiful in its rough way as the formal white-marble fountain of which Sir Jehan was so proud.

Nemain knelt beside the spring and drank from her cupped palm. Hob watched her, the curve of her back as she bent over the water, and it came to him that she had gained some weight during the spring, and her face was a little fuller; it was softer and prettier than it had been; and her skin had long since cleared. There was a curving width to the once-narrow hips, no longer much like a boy's, and a slight but distinct swell to her bosom.

Nemain stood and retreated a pace or two, wiping her lips on her sleeve. She leaned back against a tree, and the dappled light fell across her. This time Hob was not behindhand: he set the bucket down with a muffled bump, took two strides toward her, and put a hand on the curve of her hip. She looked up at him, that look he had seen before, enigmatic, challenging. Green eyes, green eyes! He raised his hands and placed them gently to either side of her face, as someone had taught him once, so long ago, and kissed her full on the mouth.

She threw her arms about his neck, and kissed him back with an ardor that surprised him. "Hob," she said, and gripped his shoulders. She hesitated a moment, distracted by the new musculature beneath her hands.

"Hob—Robert, Herself was in the right," she said. "She's just after seeing you in the priest house, and she tells me, 'That's your man-to-be,' and you a wee boy, so that I laughed."

"Herself said—" Hob began, dazed, happy.

"But after a time I was no longer laughing, and I knew it also, that you should be my man, and I not needing yarrow under my pillow come Midsummer Eve, that I might have a dream of my future consort."

She kissed him again, with a kind of ferocity, and the mention of yarrow that had put him in mind of last summer's camp slipped away, his arms full of her warm body and her face so close to his, so that what he remembered was not the yarrow but the glade where he drew water for that other camp, and how her green gaze reminded him of that deep fern-shaded pool, and how her hair was like the tumble of wild roses down the water's bank in that glade, and how her face was the white of lilies.

"Nemain," he said simply, and then found that he could say no more; then he thought that there was no more that he need say.

"And next year," she said, "it's you and I, Robert, will be clasping hands over a stream, and swearing to one another, and then you will be my consort for aye." And after the next kiss she slipped from his arms, and said, "Are you ever going to fill us that bucket?"

She walked away laughing, with some of the mockery that he knew so well from Nemain the little girl, but she turned and looked at him over her shoulder, and it was not a little girl's look; and she was no longer the scrambling child he remembered: she moved as a lynx moves, with a dangerous grace.

She was away and down the hill before he could rouse himself to dip the bucket into the rock basin. He set off down the hill, the weight of the water unnoticed, because of either his new strength or the exalted singing of his blood. He came out from the shelter of the trees in time to see her climb into the small wagon, and he stopped.

He stood there for a long time. He could just barely make her out through the open window as she moved about within, busy, perhaps, preparing one of Molly's mysterious remedies. He took a fine deep breath. He had the sense that the ground had shifted underneath his feet, and that he saw his life from a new vantage point: it was like looking down on the hawks by Monastery Mount, instead of up at them.

Later, when he was a man of property and power in Ireland, and a queen's consort as well, Hob could still recall unaltered this moment, this fragment of life in which his time-to-come stood forth and revealed itself to him.

The world seemed to widen, rippling outward from where he stood, and the air to take on a luster, so that the sunlight playing in among the clouds of leaves bore a brilliant clarity he had never before encountered. The wind twirled the leaves on their stems; the alternating surfaces, green above and silver beneath, twinkled before him. Within all this woodland glory was set the wagon like a jewel box, and within the wagon Nemain, that jewel, moved back and forth across the window. And this was all his.

He thought that he almost remembered this scene, and all this beauty, from another time, or from another campsite, or from a dream: her bare forearm as she reached for the wagon's high shelves, that quick gleam of white skin; and her hair swinging forward to hide her features as she bent to her work, that flicker of something red.

Glossary of Irish Terms

a chuisle   pulse, heartbeat
("O pulse")

a rún   love, dear
("secret treasure")

Mavourneen   my sweetheart
(mo mhuirnín)

mo chroí   my heart

mo mhíle stór   my thousand treasures

seanmháthair   grandmother
(literally: "old mother")

stór mo chroí   treasure of my heart

uisce beatha   whiskey
("water of life")

ACKNOWLEDGMENTS

I would like to thank my editor, Emily Bestler, for her enthusiasm for this book, and for her intelligence and good cheer. I am grateful to my agent, the excellent George Hiltzik, a man who gets things done. My gratitude also to dear friends Patricia and Michael Sovern for their support of this project, and, always, the pleasure of their company. My thanks to Susan Holt, for her unfailing advocacy and encouragement; to Polly Pen, Susan Blommaert, and Craig Every for their kind and helpful comments; to Juosef Natangas Tysliava for help with the pronunciation of Lithuanian names; and, for her sharp eye and shrewd advice and heartening words, to the First Reader and Fairy Bride, Theresa Adinolfi Nicholas.

About the Author

Douglas Nicholas is an award-winning poet whose work has appeared in numerous publications, among them *Atlanta Review, Southern Poetry Review, Sonora Review, Circumference, A Different Drummer,* and *Cumberland Review,* as well as *South Coast Poetry Journal,* where he won a prize in that publication's Fifth Annual Poetry Contest. Other awards include Honorable Mention in the Robinson Jeffers Tor House Foundation 2003 Prize for Poetry Awards, second place in the 2002 Allen Ginsberg Poetry Awards from PCCC, International Merit Award in *Atlanta Review*'s Poetry 2002 competition, finalist in the 1996 Emily Dickinson Award in Poetry competition, honorable mention in the 1992 Scottish International Open Poetry Competition, first prize in the journal *Lake Effect*'s Sixth Annual Poetry Contest, first prize in poetry in the 1990 Roberts Writing Awards, and finalist in the Roberts short fiction division. He was also recipient of an award in the 1990 International Poetry Contest sponsored by the Arvon Foundation in Lancashire, England, and a Cecil B. Hackney Literary Award for poetry from Birmingham-Southern College. He is the author of *Iron Rose,* a collection of poems inspired by and set in New York City; *The Old Language,* reflections on the company of animals; *The Rescue Artist,* poems about his wife and their long marriage; and *In the Long-Cold Forges of the Earth,* a wide-ranging collection of poems. He lives in the Hudson Valley with his wife, Theresa, and their Yorkshire terrier, Tristan.